THE BURYING PLACE

By Brian Freeman and available from Headline

Immoral
Stripped
Stalked
The Watcher
The Burying Place

Write to Brian Freeman at brian@bfreemanbooks.com
or join the mailing list at www.bfreemanbooks.com

Find Brian on Facebook by clicking the link on his web site.

THE BURYING PLACE

Brian Freeman

headline

First published in 2009 by
HEADLINE PUBLISHING GROUP

First published in paperback in 2010 by
HEADLINE PUBLISHING GROUP

1

Cataloguing in Publication Data is available from the British Library

ISBN 978 0 7553 4877 0 (A-format)
ISBN 978 0 7553 7027 6 (B-format)

Typeset in Sabon by Palimpsest Book Production Limited, Grangemouth, Stirlingshire

Printed and bound in Great Britain by
Clays Ltd, St Ives plc

Headline's policy is to use papers that are natural, renewable and recyclable
products and made from wood grown in sustainable forests. The logging
and manufacturing processes are expected to conform to the
environmental regulations of the country of origin.

HEADLINE PUBLISHING GROUP
An Hachette UK Company
338 Euston Road
London NW1 3BH

www.headline.co.uk
www.hachette.co.uk

For Marcia

'O, are you come, Iago? you have done well,
That men must lay their murders on your neck.'

Othello

Prologue

Kasey Kennedy drove through a rain of dead leaves.

With each gust of wind, paper bullets swarmed out of the fog and slapped against her windshield, rat-a-tat-tat. Kasey flinched as they struck. She clutched the steering wheel and peered into the mist, but her headlights illuminated barely twenty feet of wet pavement. When she clicked on her high beams, it was worse, like shining a light into a mirror and having it bounce back in her eyes. The world was nothing but a sheet of gauze wrapped around her car. No street lights. No signs. No yellow lines on the highway. Nothing to guide her. She was blind and lost.

'Where the hell are we?' Kasey worried aloud.

She knew she wasn't where she needed to be. Highway 43 zigzagged left and right as it cut through the farmlands north of Duluth, Minnesota, and somewhere she had made a wrong turn. Then, trying to correct her error, she had turned several times more. All she had accomplished was to lose her sense of direction entirely. She couldn't be far from home, but a mile felt like a hundred miles in the fog.

Her eyes flicked to the rear-view mirror, where she caught a glimpse of her own nervous face. Her shock-red curls draped limply on her forehead, moistened by sweat and rain. Her blue eyes were wide and glassy with tears. Her freckled cheekbones were flushed, the way a little girl gets when she's guilty and afraid. She tried to muster a smile, but she couldn't pretend. She had made a terrible mistake. She had wandered off the face of the earth and had no idea how to get back. Her cell phone was at home. She didn't own a GPS navigator. The only thing that made her feel better was the gun on the seat beside her.

These days, women who lived in the north farmlands slept, ate, and took showers with a gun nearby.

Kasey carried a gun every day, but she'd never had to unholster it on the job. She worked for the Duluth Police, but she wasn't the kind of cop who dealt with drug dealers or armed robberies. Jonathan Stride and Maggie Bei, who led the Detective Bureau that handled the city's major crimes, probably didn't know who she was. She busted kids for breaking windows; she cooled down the hotheads at the bars in Lakeside; she checked out reports of cars parked in the woods and usually found teenagers making out. That was her beat.

Cops weren't supposed to get scared, but Kasey was terrified. It had been days since she'd had a good night's sleep. She was running on adrenaline and caffeine. Her shredded nerves had been on edge throughout the two-hour drive, and now her anxiety spiraled out of control, leaving her dizzy with confusion and panic.

She glanced in the mirror again. 'What do I do?'

The spitting drizzle outside grew heavier. Some of the fallen leaves began to stick to the glass, where they resembled disembodied handprints with outstretched fingers trying to get inside. The swirling threads of fog played tricks on her mind. She saw deer leaping across the narrow road and silhouettes of young children frozen in front of her. The hallucinations became so real that when she saw a car dead ahead, she swung the wheel hard to veer out of the way and pushed the accelerator to give her old Cutlass a burst of speed.

It was another mistake.

A mistake that would change everything.

The asphalt road vanished under her tires and became dirt. Tree branches grasped out from the shoulders and scraped her doors. The car lurched into uneven ruts, making the chassis shiver. She wasn't on a highway anymore, but on a trail leading deeper into the forest.

Kasey stopped. Rain leaked on to the windshield. She put her bony fingers over the lower half of her face, and her breathing was ragged and loud. She closed her eyes and prayed that the fog would lift, but when she opened them again, she was still marooned in a cloud. She knew she couldn't stay here. She had to figure out where she was and find her way home.

Kasey switched off the engine, shut down her headlights, and opened the driver's door. The bitter November air blew into the car with a thick scent of pine. She climbed out and eased the door shut behind her with a quiet click. Her boots landed in mud. Evergreen trees swayed like drunks above her. She pushed past the trees into the dark, and as her eyes adjusted to the night, she found herself on the edge of the stripped ruins of a corn field that hadn't been plowed in years. Short, knobby stalks pushed out of the dirt. It looked like a desolate moonscape.

People told her how much they loved fall in Minnesota, but Kasey hated it. She knew that the long death of winter was coming. The trees were already shrugging off their leaves and becoming frozen skeletons. This would be Kasey's fourth winter in Minnesota, and she was glad that they would be gone before it was over. She couldn't wait to escape with her husband and child to the desert of Nevada, baking in the heat, closing her eyes against the bright sunshine.

But that was far away. This was here and now.

Kasey realized what she'd done. In her panic, she had turned off the highway into the unpaved driveway of a Duluth farm home. She could make out its peaked roof and dark windows, and when she wrinkled her nose, she smelled a remnant of fireplace smoke. Beside the house, she saw the foundation of a steel tower, and as the fog ebbed and flowed, she glimpsed the soaring triple wings of a windmill overhead, turning with slow grace. She retraced her steps quickly. She couldn't afford to stray far from her car.

Kasey clambered inside her Cutlass and cursed when her key ring slipped through her fingers. She banged her head on the steering wheel as she hunched over to hunt for the keys on the floor of the car.

Then something thumped. Pounded. Right next to her.

Kasey reared up and screamed. Like a garish painted scarecrow, a woman's face popped into her line of sight. They were no more than six inches apart. Kasey saw frenzied green eyes, raven hair pasted in wet, messy strands across her face, and two hands pressed in supplication against the window. The woman's slim neck was ringed with what looked like a red necklace, but was really a deep and violent abrasion, dripping pearls of blood.

'Help me, oh Lord, help me!'

Kasey froze. The woman hammered her fists on the glass. She wore a flannel nightgown, one sleeve ripped off, jagged tears in the chest flapping over her exposed left breast.

'Let me in! Please!'

The woman didn't wait. She flung open the rear door of the Cutlass and piled into the back seat. Kasey smelled her fear and the sick odor of urine and feces where she had soiled herself. The woman dug her nails into Kasey's shoulders and shook her like a doll.

'Drive! Go! Don't you understand? *He's coming for us.*'

Kasey grabbed her gun off the passenger seat and wheeled around to confront her. 'What's going on? Who are you?'

The woman shrank into the back seat and cowered with her hands in front of her face. 'Oh, my God, you're *with* him? You're part of this? Please, please, for God's sake. I'm a mother too. Don't kill me, just let me go.' She kicked open the rear door to escape, and Kasey leaped halfway over the seat and grabbed her arm to stop her.

'I'm a cop!' Kasey shouted. 'Stay right there.'

The woman hesitated. Reality penetrated her consciousness slowly, as if she didn't dare believe it. She became aware of Kasey's uniform. Saw her badge. 'You're with the police?'

'Yes. Now what happened to you?'

'Oh, thank God!' the woman cried in relief. 'You have to get us out of here. There's no time. He'll kill us all. *Hurry.*'

Kasey reached for the ignition but realized that her keys were still lost on the floor of the car. She bent over and pushed her trembling hands blindly around the mat. As her fingers closed on the key chain, she heard a panicked scream behind her.

'It's too late! Oh my God, *he's here!*'

Kasey's head snapped up. Her hand flicked to the head-lights, and when the two beams split the night, she saw the black outline of a man ten feet in front of the car. He had no face, like a headless monster, and Kasey realized he wore a ski mask pulled down over his skull.

'*Kill him!*'

Kasey lifted the gun, but the man outside the car ducked to his knees and rolled away. She snatched up her keys and fired the engine, and the Cutlass motor roared to life. She shoved the gear into reverse and pressed the accelerator to the floor, and the car shot backward, swerving. Before Kasey could control it, the Cutlass veered into the long grass and collided with the trunk of one of the trees bordering the driveway. Pine needles and branches sprinkled over the windows. The impact knocked her gun out of her hand, and it disappeared between the seat cushion and the right-side door.

'Shit, I dropped the gun.'

'Oh, my God!' the woman screamed.

Kasey jumped across the seat for the gun, but she wasn't fast enough. When she looked up, he was outside the car window. The man's black eyes gleamed at her, and for a split second the two of them stared at each other through the glass. She thought he was smiling. He reached for the door handle.

Behind her, the woman dissolved into panic. Her cry was like an animal's howl, and she reacted the way an animal would, by trying to flee. The woman flung open the rear door and bolted into the night, running in bare feet toward the deeper woods beyond the farm, swallowed up by the fog. The man outside the window abandoned the car and followed her. In an instant, he was invisible too. Kasey was alone.

She wanted nothing more than to drive away. Escape to safety. Pretend that nothing had happened here. She wanted to return to the highway and block out the last five minutes from her brain and criss-cross the empty roads until she found her way home. But she couldn't let this woman and her pursuer run off into the woods. She had to go after them.

Kasey located her gun wedged inside the door frame and locked both doors behind her as she scrambled out of the Cutlass. Outside the car, she froze with indecision. She squeezed her right hand against her forehead and took several loud, open-mouthed breaths to hold back her terror. Her body was soaked with sweat. She listened and heard a scream not far away and tried to pinpoint the direction of the voice.

Her mind said again: *Escape. Run.*

Kasey had no choice but to ignore what her instincts told her. She ran from the car, her heart in her mouth, her stomach churning with acid and fear. On both sides, the pines loomed like fat soldiers. She slashed through the branches, trying to see what was ahead of her, but the fog left her sightless. She found herself in an open patch of wet grass and ran faster, and then the grass ended in a thick stand of paper birches. She stopped and listened again, trying to hear sounds above her own breathing. Somewhere ahead she heard the noise of branches cracking and heavy footfalls in the woods. Kasey followed.

She pushed through sharp brambles that ripped at her sleeves. The trees were matted and close together here, like passengers at a crowded train station. She held her gun high, pointed at the sky. Her feet tripped her up as she fought her way forward, stumbling on bulging tree roots and indentations in the soil. Her wet red hair sagged over her eyes. In some part of her soul, she realized she was crying, but she shoved aside her emotions. She hadn't come this far for nothing. Her heart hardened, becoming cold and furious.

As she ran, she heard a wet, roaring noise far below her. She realized what it was, but not before the ground beneath her became air. Her momentum carried her off the edge of a steep slope, where she tumbled shoulder over shoulder through mud and trees. The contents of her pockets spilled across the slope; her badge was ripped from her shirt; one boot fell away and left her right foot bare. She fell twenty feet, thirty feet, forty feet, and finally landed heavily on the soggy earth at the bottom of the hill. She tried to clear her head. Nothing felt broken. She got up slowly and realized with relief that she still had her gun clutched in her hand.

Water cascaded through the narrows. She recognized where she was now, at the edge of the Lester River where it ran southward toward Lake Superior. She knew this area from her beat, knew that a highway bridge crossed the river barely fifty yards away, knew that a single turn of the wheel would lead her back to Highway 43. Of all the horrors of this night, she had gotten lost only ten minutes from her home.

Another scream rose above the noise of the river from the opposite shore. Kasey stumbled on to the marshy rye grass at the bank, and the water flooded to her ankles. She could make out the black water; the fog was thinning. The river was barely twenty feet from shore to shore, but she forgot that the narrows also meant the water here was stronger and faster. She waded in with a shudder, and the impact slammed her body and knocked her off her feet. The hurtling current whipped her downstream before her feet clawed for purchase on the slippery rocks of the river bed. She fought to the opposite bank and dug her fingers into the eroded clay soil above her. With a silent groan, she pulled herself out of the river and on to the soft grass.

She still hung on to her gun. She was drenched and freezing. Shivers wracked her body.

She ducked under the arms of a huge spruce and crept through fallen branches that snapped under her feet. Just ahead of her was a low, square building of white cinder block, an abandoned dairy she passed on her beat every week. From the other side of the stone building she heard a strangled cry. With both hands, Kasey pointed the way with her gun and followed their trail behind the rear wall of the dairy. The stonework was cracked, the white paint peeling. The windows were shattered and covered over with chicken wire. She passed a rusting propane tank.

Carefully, she eased around the corner to the open field of grass behind the building.

They were there. Both of them. Wet to the bone. The man tightened a metal wire around the woman's neck, biting into the bloody line he had made there earlier. She struggled, but faintly, her limbs twitching. When the man saw Kasey, he jerked the woman's body in front of him as a shield. All that was visible was one of his dark eyes, shining brightly.

Kasey extended her gun. Her cold, tired arms trembled. 'Let her go.'

They faced each other across twenty feet of mist and darkness.

Kasey knew she barely had a shot. She focused on what she could see of his body. Half of his head. The meat of his shoulder. His right leg. He was taller than the woman in his grasp, but his knees were bent as he crouched behind her.

'Let her go now,' Kasey repeated. 'Run if you want.'

'Drop the gun, and I'll let her go.'

'I'm going to take the shot.'

'And risk killing her? Not a chance.'

Kasey took a step closer. The man backed up, dragging the woman with him, her feet scraping the ground. 'I already told you. Run.'

The noose strangled the woman, choking off her air. Her near-dead eyes bulged.

Kasey sighted down the barrel of her gun. She planted her feet in the sodden soil. She exhaled slowly and felt a serene calm wash over her freezing skin. Her finger eased on to the trigger.

Behind the mask, the man taunted her. 'You won't do it,' he said.

Kasey took the shot.

PART ONE

PANIC ATTACK

One

Jonathan Stride watched the knife fall to the floor.

It was a simple thing, the knife falling. His hand laid it on the counter wrong; it slipped off, blade pointed down. But in the past month, nothing had been simple for Stride. His eyes followed the downward path of the knife and just like that, he was falling, too.

He was no longer in the cabin where he had gone to recover from his injuries. He was over Superior Bay, hurtling through one hundred and twenty feet of air to the hard water below. He felt the speeding rush of his body as it became a missile; he endured the helplessness and fear of those three long seconds; he suffered the excruciating pain of impact, his bones breaking, the water choking off his oxygen, the lights around him extinguishing to blackness and cold. Everything he had tried to forget, he remembered.

Stride's eyes sprang open. He stood in the cabin's small kitchen with his palms flat on the granite counter. He felt on his neck for his pulse; his heart was racing. He wondered how long he had been gone this time. The knife stood straight up, its point jabbed into the wooden floor, but it wasn't vibrating like a tuning fork. He had been standing there frozen, caught up in the flashback, for a minute or more.

He grabbed the back of a chair to keep his knees from buckling. He sat down and propped his chin on his clenched fists. Gradually, the longer he sat, the more the memory retreated. His breathing slowed down. He studied the cabin and let his eyes linger on the furnishings to remind himself that he was far away from the bridge. The brown tweed sofa. The deer head trophy with its antlers and staring eyes on the wall. The 1920s photo of grimy workers in the iron mines. The oak door to the master bedroom, where Serena slept, unaware that he was awake for the tenth night in a row.

Stride pushed his hand back through his messy shock of black-and-gray hair. He got up, retrieved the knife from the floor, and opened the refrigerator to grab a half-full bottle of water. He shook a few Advil tablets into his hand and washed them down with a long swallow from the bottle. When he closed the refrigerator door, he caught sight of his face reflected in the black oven and didn't like what he saw. The skin on his craggy face was pale. His dark eyes were tired.

He favored his left leg as he walked into the great room. The fall from the bridge had broken his leg and left him in a cast for six weeks, and although he was walking on his own again, the lingering pain was a daily reminder that he wasn't fully healed. He drove into the nearby town of Grand Rapids for physical therapy four times a week. He used breathing exercises to restore full capacity to his lungs, which had collapsed as he hit the water. He was getting better, but slowly. What he hadn't admitted to Serena was that, as his physical injuries healed, his mental health had been deteriorating.

Two months ago, as he climbed into his Ford Expedition, he had dropped his keys. Out of nowhere, the sight and sound of the keys hitting the ground had triggered a storm of memories from his fall. The panic attack was debilitating, like a fire sucking the oxygen out of a room. He'd told himself that it was a one-time occurrence, but then it had happened again several days later. And then again.

Stride decided to get out of town in the last month before he returned to his job as Lieutenant in the Duluth Police. He and Serena had escaped to a getaway cabin outside the city to fish, hike, and make love. But they had done almost none of those things. Instead, he had tunneled deeper inside himself, pulling away from his job, his life, and even from Serena. Now he was supposed to go back to the Detective Bureau in another week, and he wasn't sure he was in any shape to do so.

Stride saw the red light flashing on his BlackBerry. A new email had arrived. He slid the phone out of its holster and saw a message from his Duluth partner, Maggie Bei. The subject line read: **Number Four.**

Stride stiffened with unease, because he knew what Maggie meant. When he opened the message, he saw a brief note: **Get your ass back here soon, boss. We've got a body near the Lester River.**

In the past month, three women had disappeared from their homes in the rural farmlands north of Duluth. Despite a massive search, no trace of them had been found, but the evidence suggested they had each suffered a violent assault. Now the assailant had struck a fourth time and left behind a body.

Stride was frustrated that one of the most disturbing strings of crimes in the city in recent years had been laid at Maggie's feet while he struggled with his injuries in the woods more than an hour away. He trusted her instincts as an investigator, but they both preferred working as a team. Without him, she felt adrift. He felt the same way without her.

Maybe he should go back early. Tomorrow.

Or maybe not at all.

He didn't text her back. He never got the chance. Before he could key in a message, he saw headlights cut through the room. He looked out the front window and saw an Itasca

County Sheriff's vehicle parking in the damp ground near his Expedition. As he watched, the lights disappeared, and a woman in uniform climbed out and walked up to their front door.

He knew her. In her uniform, she could have passed for a beat cop, but Denise Sheridan was the Deputy Sheriff for Itasca County. She was as close as Stride had to a counterpart in the sprawling, sparsely populated countryside northwest of Duluth. He opened the door. It was a freezing night, and the wind scattered oak leaves on the hardwood floor as he waited.

'Hello, Stride,' Denise said, marching past him into the great space of the cabin without an invitation.

'Hello, Denise.'

She smelled of sweat and smoke. The knees of her trousers were wet, and her boots tracked mud across the floor. Denise did a quick survey of the cabin as he shut the door.

'What are you doing out here?' she asked, chewing on the stump of a fingernail. 'It took me twenty minutes to find you on these back roads.'

'Recovering,' he said.

'Yeah, I heard about your fall. Nice to see you're not dead.'

Denise didn't waste time on sympathy. For as long as he'd known her, she had been a no-nonsense cop, full of rough edges and discipline. She had recently turned forty, and her face had the spider's web of wrinkles at her eyes and lips to prove it. She was tall, only a couple of inches shorter than Stride, who reached six feet one in his bare feet. She wasn't heavy, but her muscular arms and legs stretched out the fabric of her uniform. Her brunette hair fell to the middle of her neck, and she kept it parted in the middle and shoved back behind her ears. She wasn't wearing make-up. Dark crescents sagged under both eyes.

'It's three in the morning,' Stride said.

Denise shrugged, as if the time didn't need any explanation or apology. 'Maggie told me where you were hiding.'

'Did she send you here to hijack me back to Duluth?' he replied. 'The guy struck on another farm tonight. He left a body this time.'

'I heard. No, it's not about that.'

'Then what?'

'It's a different case. I need your help.'

'I'm on leave, remember?' Stride said.

'I remember. I also remember we were partners once upon a time. I wouldn't ask if it wasn't important.'

That was true. Denise had started her police career in Duluth fifteen years earlier. She and Stride had spent four years working together after Stride was chosen to lead the Detective Bureau. Then Denise married her high school boyfriend and moved back home to Grand Rapids. The next cop Stride had hired to work at his side was Maggie Bei.

'Don't keep me in suspense,' Stride said. 'What's the case?'

'Look, get dressed, will you? There's no time.'

'If you want my help, you can tell me what the hell is going on,' Stride retorted.

Denise folded her arms in impatience. She cocked her head and frowned. 'A child is missing. A baby. Snatched right out of her room tonight, according to the father. I need you to take over the investigation.'

When Stride slipped inside his bedroom, he saw that Serena Dial was already half-dressed. She buttoned a burgundy flannel shirt over her bra and pushed a brush several times through her long black hair. She sat on the end of the bed and began to squeeze her long legs into a pair of jeans.

'What's up?' she asked.

'Denise Sheridan wants to pull me into one of her cases. Missing kid.'

'Why can't the locals handle it?'

'I don't know. We haven't gotten that far.'

Serena stood up, zipped up her jeans, and left the flannel shirt untucked. 'Couldn't sleep again?' she asked him.

'No.'

She stepped into leather boots and hooked dangling ruby earrings in both ears. Even though it was the middle of the night, in the middle of the northern Minnesota woods, Serena wasn't casual about her looks. She had spent most of her life in Las Vegas, and two years in Duluth hadn't softened her touch of glamour.

He shrugged a charcoal turtleneck over his chest and tucked it into his jeans. He rubbed his chin and decided to push an electric razor quickly around his face. When he was done, he retrieved a wool sport coat from the closet and squeezed into it.

Serena came up to Stride and kissed him on the cheek. In her heels, she was as tall as he was. 'This is a mistake,' she murmured.

'What?'

'You. Working. You need more time.'

'I didn't tell her I was in. I just said I'd listen.'

'Sure,' Serena said. Her voice was cool.

He opened the door and waited for Serena to go ahead of him into the living room, where Serena and Denise shook hands. He could see Denise sizing Serena up with suspicion. Most cops in the northland knew Serena because of her relationship with Stride, but that didn't give her a free pass with the local police. To them, she was a big city detective treading on small town turf.

'Maggie tells me you used to be a Vegas cop,' Denise said.

'I spent ten years in the Metro Police,' Serena replied with a cynical smile. She could read the hostility in Denise's face. 'Homicides, mostly,' she added.

Denise shoved her hands in her pockets, and her gun bulged from the holster in her belt. 'Good for you.'

'If I'm in, Serena's in,' Stride told her. 'I want her on the case with me.'

'My boys won't like it,' Denise replied sourly.

'I don't care. Do what you have to do. Serena's worked more abductions than either of us. She's in.'

Denise scowled but didn't protest. 'Fine. Whatever. Look, let's be quick about this. The clock is ticking. There's a surgeon named Marcus Glenn who lives out on Pokegama Lake. Rich doctor, big house. He called nine one one about two hours ago to report that his eleven-month-old daughter was gone. A couple uniforms reported to the scene, did a search of the house and found no trace of the girl, and called me.'

'The cops searched the scene?' Stride said unhappily.

'Yeah, I know, they probably screwed up the forensics. We don't get many cases like this, and these guys are twenty-three year olds working the graveyard shift.'

'Did they find anything?'

Denise shook her head. 'No. There was nothing disturbed in the house, nothing taken, no sign of forced entry at the doors or windows. Everything was locked and intact. The girl just vanished.'

'Does Marcus Glenn live alone?' Stride asked.

'No, he's married,' Denise snapped with surprising venom. 'His wife was in the Cities last night. They only have the one child.'

'So what happened?'

'Marcus says the baby was sleeping in her bedroom by seven o'clock. He checked on her and went to bed around ten. He got up about one, and she was gone. The baby was there, and then she wasn't. Or so he says.'

'Did the cops look for a ransom note?'

'They did, and they didn't find one. Marcus checked his email, too. Nothing. He's well-known around Grand Rapids, though. People know he has money.'

'What's the girl's name?' Serena interjected.

Denise softened and smiled for the first time. 'Callie.'

'Have you gathered all of her physical information? Photograph, weight, hair color, identifying features?'

'Yes, I've already got the BCA doing a statewide notice to the crime alert network. They're sending a team up here to run the scene in the morning.'

'Do you have her picture?' Serena asked.

Denise reached into the shirt pocket of her uniform. 'This is Callie.'

Serena held the picture in her hand, and Stride looked at it over her shoulder. Callie Glenn sat on a quilted blanket and looked at them with happy blue eyes from under a fluffy mop of blonde hair. Two white teeth peeked out from her smile. She was dressed in a white T-shirt and a pair of pink sweatpants, and she clutched one of her bare feet awkwardly in a pudgy hand.

'Sweet little girl,' Serena said. 'Is she walking?'

'She can walk a few steps if she's holding on to something.'

'What about climbing?'

'She hasn't climbed out of her crib yet, but even if she could, the window was closed and so was the bedroom door. She didn't wander off.'

'No offense, Denise,' Stride told her, 'but what does this have to do with us?'

'I'd like you to run the investigation.'

'Yes, but why give up the case?' Stride asked.

Denise snorted. 'Marcus raised a stink. He wanted me to call the Attorney General, the FBI, hell, he probably expected me to call the Governor. He wants me to give the case to the feds.'

'That's what parents always want,' Serena said.

'Yeah, but most parents don't have the clout in the north-land that Marcus Glenn does. If I'm going to put someone else in charge, I'd rather it be someone I know and trust, and that's you, Stride. Anyway, not that I would ever say so to the bastard's face, but the fact is, I don't really have the resources or experience on my team to handle something like this. This is about the kid, not about my ego.'

'What are you leaving out?' Serena asked Denise.

'What do you mean?'

'I mean, you obviously know Marcus Glenn. There's something personal going on here.'

Denise took back the photograph of Callie Glenn from Serena and held it tenderly between her fingers. 'OK, there's a conflict, too. I can't take the lead on this one. It hits too close to home.'

'What's the conflict?' Serena asked.

'Callie is my niece,' Denise replied. 'Marcus Glenn is married to my sister.'

TWO

Stride and Serena followed Denise through the dirt roads to Highway 2, which was the main artery connecting the lakeside city of Duluth with its closest inland neighbor to the northwest, Grand Rapids. The two towns were less than ninety minutes apart in good weather. At three in the morning, the highway was deserted, and the dense fog that had dogged the area for most of the night had dissipated as a dry front pushed southward from Canada. At high speed, it took them ten minutes to reach the heart of downtown Grand Rapids.

They passed the giant superstructure of the UPM mill, which served as the economic engine of the region, chewing up trees and pulping them into paper products. The other backbone of the town was tourism. In a state pockmarked with lakes, Grand Rapids played host to thousands of tourists who came to fish in the warmer weather or ski and snowmobile during the harsh winters. November was an in-between month, however, when the summer lake dwellers had gone home and the winter sports season was still a few weeks away.

Stride sailed through the green lights. Serena sat beside him, and he felt the tension simmering between them.

'So you want to tell me what's going on, Jonny?' she asked.

'With what?'

'With you.'

Stride kept his eyes on the road, but his hands tightened on the wheel. 'Nothing.'

'Nothing? You're not sleeping, we're not having sex, and you're constantly on edge.'

'I'm impatient,' Stride said. 'I'm going stir-crazy doing nothing. This case is exactly what I need.'

'Is that all it is?'

'That's all,' he insisted. 'I'm fine.'

Stride wasn't fooling her, but she let it go. He regretted his stubborn denials, because that wasn't what he wanted to say. He wanted to tell her about the panic attacks. He wanted to admit that he was scared of feeling dead, without any ambition or desire. But he hid behind the lie that nothing was wrong.

Ahead of them, Denise turned her Jeep left off the highway and crossed the bridge on Sugar Lake Road. Stride followed. Almost immediately, they found themselves away from the developed land. They drove for another mile and then turned left again on to County Road 76, which tracked the northeastern border of Pokegama Lake. Stride passed dirt roads carved into the forest which led to expensive homes bordering the water. It was a desolate area.

'This isn't good,' he said. 'It would be easy for someone to come and go here without being seen.'

They turned left on Chisholm Trail and headed toward the lake. The road stretched for half a mile and curved sharply in front of a sprawling white fence. Through a gap in the fence, he saw a circular driveway where five police vehicles were parked with their light bars flashing. Cones of white light waved like lasers as uniformed men hunted in the woods and grass.

'Oh, son of a bitch,' he muttered.

He parked, and they joined Denise Sheridan at the entrance

23

to the driveway. Stride jerked a thumb at the cops on the property.

'What the hell are these guys doing?' Stride barked. 'You've got them trampling the crime scene.'

Denise folded her arms over her chest in annoyance. 'We're trying to find a missing baby. Look, Stride, the BCA techs will be here in the morning, but I made the call to run my people around the grounds now. It's a long shot to think that someone dumped her in the woods, but I'm not about to miss that chance, OK? The county attorney may have my ass when we try to prosecute whoever did this, but right now, I'm more concerned with anything that might help us find Callie.'

Serena interjected. 'Have you interviewed the neighbors along the road?'

'We woke them all up, and we're working our way up and down the lake. So far, nobody saw any vehicles here after ten o'clock or spotted any boats on the water. It was a perfect night to make a snatch and not be seen. Assuming that's what happened.'

'What does that mean?' Stride asked.

'Nothing. This is your show now, not mine. Just tell me where my guys can help.'

'We need to set up a command center over at your office,' Stride told her. 'We'll need to coordinate media queries, answer the tip line, feed leads for follow-up, coordinate with the FBI, NCMEC, the Wetterling Foundation, etc. This is going to take a lot of manpower.'

'I can get people from the neighboring counties. We'll get plenty of support.'

Stride studied the nearby homes, which were ablaze with light. 'You realize this is going to be a media circus, right?'

'Hey, I was here when the damn ruby slippers got stolen from the Judy Garland Museum,' Denise said. 'That was a circus.'

'We need to talk to Marcus Glenn,' Serena added.

'Fine. Talk to him.'

'You should be there too.'

'No way,' Denise snapped. 'He won't want me there, and I don't want to be there. We can talk after you're done.'

'You don't like Marcus, do you?' Serena asked.

Denise shrugged. 'He's my brother-in-law. What does that tell you?'

Marcus Glenn was a surgeon and, in Stride's mind, that said it all.

He wasn't yet forty years old, which meant he had the arrogance of his own accomplishments but hadn't aged enough to confront his imperfections. He wore a frown of impatience and irritation as he paced the sunroom of his estate. He was extremely tall, and his long legs were lean and muscled. He had jet-black hair, cut extremely short, and thick eyebrows. His face was angular, hard-edged and taut, without the sag of a double chin. He wore a burgundy golf shirt with a logo from the Bellagio Hotel in Las Vegas, pleated gray slacks, and black dress shoes. He had large hands, in which he gracefully moved two cat's eye marbles above and below his knuckles like a magician. Behind him, a glass wall of windows framed him against the black night and the back lawn that led to the lake.

'Dr Glenn,' Stride said, extending his hand. 'My name is Jonathan Stride. This is Serena Dial.'

Glenn declined to shake hands and instead slid his hands and the two marbles into the pockets of his slacks. 'Yes, I know who you are. Denise called me. I'm sure you're both qualified and capable, but I have to tell you I would be more comfortable if this investigation were being led by the FBI.'

'I understand how you feel,' Stride replied. 'Obviously, we'll be coordinating our efforts with the resources of federal law enforcement wherever it can help us.'

Glenn cut him off. 'Yes, yes, coordination, consultation, I'm sure you all send wonderful memos to each other. I'm talking about expertise. My patients don't come to me because I'm capable. They come to me because I'm the best. I want the *best*.'

'I know exactly what you're saying, Dr Glenn,' Stride told him. 'The truth is that we're the best people to handle this situation, not the federal authorities. You want investigators who know the terrain and have relationships throughout the state law enforcement community. The FBI would have to fly in special agents who are unfamiliar with the area, the people, the police, the media, the nonprofit resources, everything we need to find Callie and bring her home safely. These first few hours are very important. We're here, we're good, and we want to help.'

Glenn rubbed the toe of his dress shoe on one of the marble tiles on the sunroom floor. 'Yes, all right. I apologize for my attitude, detectives. I do appreciate your help. It's been a long night.'

'Of course,' Stride said.

He and Serena took seats next to each other on a leather sofa on the wall facing the house. Glenn sat and crossed his legs in an armchair by the windows. He drummed his fingers on his knee.

Serena picked up a framed photograph from an end table beside the sofa. The picture showed an attractive woman in her early thirties, with flowing blonde hair and an athletic build. Her blue eyes stared beyond the camera, caught in a reflective moment. When Stride studied her features, he could see a resemblance to Denise Sheridan, but God had played favorites between the sisters. Denise had a face you could look at and then put out of your mind. Her younger sister was memorably gorgeous.

'Is this your wife?' Serena asked.

Glenn nodded absently. 'Yes, that's Valerie.'

'She's beautiful.'

'Thank you,' he replied.

Stride thought that was what you said if someone complimented your choice of wine, or your choice of décor. He looked around at the sunroom and realized that Glenn collected beautiful things. Eastern European crystal. French wines. Brandenburg photographs. A trophy wife. Those were the perks of his profession.

'Where is your wife?' Serena asked. 'Does she know that Callie has disappeared?'

'Yes, of course, I called her immediately. She was staying overnight in the Cities because of the fog, but I'm having a driver bring her home. She'll be here shortly.'

'I'd like to clarify some personal information, Dr Glenn,' Stride said.

'Such as?'

'Can you tell us about your job?'

'I'm an orthopedic surgeon specializing in knee repair and replacement,' Glenn replied. 'I do surgeries three days a week at St Mary's in Duluth. Mondays, Wednesdays, and Fridays. Naturally I'm cancelling today's appointments.'

'Were you home all day Thursday?'

'I was.'

Serena smiled at Glenn. 'You have a lovely home.'

'Translation: am I rich? Yes. Between my income and my investments, I make well over two million dollars a year and have done so for nearly a decade. I've lived in Grand Rapids most of my life, so this would be no surprise to anyone in town who's aware of who I am, which is pretty much everyone. Please don't feel the need to sugar-coat your questions, detectives. If you want to know something, ask.'

'Why don't you tell us what happened this evening?' Stride said.

'I wish there was more to tell. I put Callie down for the night after dinner. I was in my study for the rest of the evening reading medical journals. At ten o'clock, I checked on her and then went to bed myself. When I got up at one in the morning and went to her bedroom, she was gone.'

'Were you sleeping between ten and one?' Serena asked.

'I was asleep by ten thirty, so whoever took her must have done so after that. I didn't hear anything.'

'Do you have a security system?' Stride asked.

'Of course, but I don't activate it when I'm home.'

'Who has keys to the house?'

'Valerie and I do.' Glenn's stoic calm fractured for a moment. 'Oh, and Migdalia has a key, too.'

'Migdalia?'

'Migdalia Vega. She's our babysitter.'

'Where can we find her?' Stride asked.

'She lives behind the old cemetery in Sago. She's a reliable girl. I can vouch for her character.'

'We'll still need to talk to her.' Stride added, 'The police officers who searched the house didn't find any signs of forced entry. Do you have any idea how someone was able to get inside?'

'I don't, I'm sorry.'

'Has anyone contacted you to say that they have Callie?' Serena asked.

'No.'

'Sometimes parents don't like to admit it when they hear from a kidnapper,' Serena told him. 'A ransom note may tell you not to inform the police, or a caller may threaten a hostage's life if you involve the authorities. Even in those situations, it's far safer if you *do* tell us.'

'I understand, but there has been no contact of any kind.'

'With your permission, we'll put a tap on your phone in case you do receive calls,' Stride said.

Glenn hesitated. 'Is that necessary?'

'Given your financial situation, we have to consider kidnapping a real possibility,' Stride told him. 'Perhaps even a probability. In those cases, you'll generally receive some kind of demand for ransom. A phone trace is essential.'

'Yes, I suppose so. I'm thinking of privacy considerations for my patients. There are confidentiality issues. I'll have to find a way to deal with it, but that's my problem.'

'We'll have the trace installed in a matter of hours,' Stride said. 'Speaking of your patients, have there been any issues that could have left a patient or a family member holding a grudge?'

Glenn's mouth turned upward in an ironic smile. 'You mean, did I kill someone on the operating table? No.'

'Accidents and misunderstandings do happen.'

'True enough, but I'm very good at what I do. I've never been sued, which is something of a miracle in my profession.'

Stride nodded. 'Have you received any threats? Or has your wife?'

'No.'

'Have you ever felt you were being followed? Or have you noticed strangers watching you at home or at work?'

'No, nothing like that. However, there's a mobile home park on the lake, and we do get some unsavory types staying there. I have a large boat, and no doubt many of them have seen me, Valerie, and Callie on the water.'

Stride nodded but didn't reply. He had seen it before – rich victims pointing a finger down the class ladder. Grand Rapids, like Duluth and other northern Minnesota towns, suffered from an uncomfortable gap between rich and poor. There were wealthy professionals and transplants from Minneapolis who could afford seven-figure lake homes. On the other end of the spectrum was a much larger community of mill workers, waitresses, road crews, and farmers who struggled with the spiking prices for food, gas, and healthcare.

'How old is Callie?' Serena asked.

'Ten and a half months. She was a New Year's baby, born shortly after midnight.'

'Here in Grand Rapids?'

'No, at St Mary's in Duluth. I wanted Valerie to give birth at my own hospital.'

'What kind of baby is Callie?' Serena asked. 'How does she act with strangers?'

'Callie has always been a mellow girl,' Glenn replied. 'She'll behave for just about anyone who smiles at her. In this circumstance, I guess that's unfortunate.'

'Callie is your only child, is that right?'

'Yes.'

'How long have you and Valerie been married?'

'Eight years,' Glenn replied.

'Having a baby can turn your life upside down,' Serena said. 'Has it caused any problems for the two of you?'

Glenn stared at her in stony silence. 'No.'

'How about your wife? Some women struggle with depression after having a child.'

'Not Valerie. She was overjoyed. She'd been trying to conceive for years.'

'I'll want to talk to your wife as soon as she's home,' Serena told him.

'I understand.' Glenn stood up from the chair and again shoved his hands in his pockets. 'Please keep me posted on the investigation, detectives.'

Serena nodded. 'Either Lieutenant Stride or I will be in touch every few hours to give you a status report on the investigation, and you can reach us on our cell phones whenever you need us.'

'Thank you. How long will you need to have police officers tramping around my house?'

'I'm afraid it will be several more hours,' Stride said. 'We'll have a forensics team here from the Bureau of Criminal Apprehension in St Paul at daylight. They'll do an exhaustive search of the property inside and out.'

'Hasn't that already been done?'

'These are experts in handling crime scenes,' Stride explained. 'They'll be looking for trace evidence from any strangers who might have been in Callie's room. Or other evidence to suggest how an intruder came and went.'

Stride didn't mention what else they would be looking for. In the crib. On the walls. In the sinks. Under the carpet.

Blood.

Three

Stride found Denise Sheridan alone by the shore of Pokegama Lake on the southern edge of the Glenn property. The white two-story estate shone brightly on the slope behind them, thanks to the lights that glowed in every room of the house. The vast backyard was scattered with birch trees and a deep layer of dead leaves.

Denise smoked a cigarette. When she saw Stride approaching her down the hill, she took a last drag and flicked it into the water

'Sorry,' she said. 'I don't need a lecture right now, OK? About crime scenes or death sticks.'

Stride wanted a cigarette himself, but he didn't say so. He stood silently next to Denise with his hands in his pockets. Out on the lake, he saw the shore of a small island lined with cedars. The water was choppy and white-capped, agitated by the cold breeze. He noted that the dock for the Glenn boats had already been pulled from the water for the season. Any intruder who approached the house from the lake would have found it difficult to land in the shallows.

'So how are you, Denise?' Stride asked.

She shrugged. 'Me? Life goes on.'

'I meant to send you a card last year when you had the baby. That makes four, doesn't it?'

'Yeah, I pop them out like a big furry rabbit,' Denise cracked.

'How old are they?' Stride asked.

'Ten, seven, five, and eighteen months. I thought I was done after number three, but Tom had other ideas. It's not like we ever have sex anymore, but he managed to hit the bullseye the one time I got drunk.' She extracted the cigarette pack from her shirt pocket and lit another. Tilting her head up, she blew smoke into the air. 'Not that I want to send any of them back. Although, God, there are days.'

'Managing two jobs and four kids?' Stride told her. 'I'm not sure how the two of you do it.'

'Neither am I.' Denise glanced behind her at the spread of the Glenn home. 'Sometimes it pisses me off. I go fishing on Pokeg, and I see all these fucking mansions on the shore. Lawyers, doctors, CEOs, rich wives who winter in Scottsdale. And I'm sitting there worried about the gas mileage on my truck.'

'Sorry,' Stride said.

'Yeah, look at me, the green-eyed monster.' Denise threw away her second cigarette rather than smoking it. 'I suppose this is the wrong time to say so, but you look like shit, Stride.'

'Thanks.'

'It's none of my business, except I just handed you a big case. Was I wrong to get you involved?'

'I'm fine,' he said. It was the same lie he'd told to Serena.

'Did you have an audience with King Marcus?' Denise asked. 'I'll bet he wouldn't shake hands with you.'

'You're right. What's that about?'

'It's a surgeon thing. He doesn't want to risk injuring his hands. I think he's germophobic, too.'

'Tell me what you know about him,' Stride said.

'Marcus? There are guys who are studs in high school, quarter-back of the football team, and then twenty years later they're fat slobs working in a gas station. Well, Marcus is still the stud.'

'Have you known him a long time?'

'Sure, he grew up in this area. He was a couple years behind me and Tom in school. He's rich now, but he didn't come from money. His parents owned a farm near Sago. I knew his dad. He was a son of a bitch; nothing Marcus did was ever good enough. Pretty ironic. Marcus was this tall, athletic kid, took the Grand Rapids hockey team to the state championship twice. I mean, you do that around here, and you are a *star*. But not at home.'

'I'm surprised he stayed around the area,' Stride said.

'Yeah, well, Marcus is a Minnesota boy. Went to the U of M and did several years at Mayo before coming home. I think he likes being the big fish in a small pond up here. Being this hotshot surgeon. All the girls coming after him.'

Stride wondered how much Denise's opinion had to do with Marcus and how much it had to do with her sister, marrying him and living in their estate on the lake. 'Valerie's stunning,' he said. 'I saw a photograph.'

Denise kicked at the dirt. 'Oh, yeah. Valerie got the good genes.'

'That's not what I meant.'

'It doesn't matter. You're not telling me anything I haven't dealt with my whole life. I won't say it doesn't get old hearing how gorgeous my baby sister is all the time. And yes, you don't have to say it, I'm envious. Who wouldn't be?'

'How did she hook up with Marcus Glenn?'

Denise laughed sourly. 'Valerie never wanted anything *but* Marcus Glenn. She had a crush on him back when she was ten years old and he was a teenager on the hockey team. She had guys drooling after her throughout high school and college, but she'd made up her mind that Marcus was the only one she wanted. When he came back to Grand Rapids, she was the hostess at the country club, and that's when he noticed her. It took her another couple years to land him, but my sister is nothing if not determined.'

'You make it sound mercenary.'

'Hey, if you're beautiful, money is your birthright. That's life. I don't think Valerie went after Marcus because he had money. That was just an expectation. She was always going to have the lakeside mansion. Me, I've got the shack by the river, the mortgage, all the crap called real life.'

Stride let the silence stretch out between them. Then he said softly, 'Denise, her child is missing. Maybe you should cut her some slack.'

'I know. You're right. Look, I try not to let it eat me up, but sometimes it does, OK? You wanted the whole truth. I'd like to tell you I'm a bigger person, but Valerie's always been the golden child, and I've been jealous of her my whole life. Hell, I'm sitting at home with four kids, and now all I'm going to hear is, poor Valerie. Does that make me petty? OK, I'm petty.'

'What's this really about, Denise?' Stride asked. 'I don't think it's just sibling rivalry.'

'I'm sorry,' she said, wiping her eyes. 'I'm scared for Callie. And yeah, I'm angry, too. I warned Valerie that something like this might happen, and she didn't listen to me.'

'Something like what?' he asked.

'I told her not to leave Callie alone with Marcus,' Denise said.

'Ah.'

Stride wasn't surprised. Denise's body language had been eloquent since she showed up at the cabin. He had simply been waiting for her to say it out loud: *this wasn't a kidnapping.*

'I can't prove it,' she went on. 'I know that instincts are crap compared to evidence, but this is what my gut tells me.'

'Instincts count for a lot with me,' Stride said. 'Fill me in.'

Denise crouched down and dipped her hand in the lake and rubbed her wet fingers together. She got up and wiped her hand on her sleeve. 'He's arrogant, and I know being arrogant isn't a crime. But it's not just that.'

'Then what?'

'I know him,' Denise said. 'Valerie and Marcus have been married for eight years. She figured out pretty quickly that winning the prize isn't as exciting as going after it.'

'Meaning what?'

'Meaning Marcus is exactly what you see. A cold prick. He doesn't love anything or anyone except himself.'

'He's a bad husband,' Stride said. 'That's still not a crime.'

'Maybe so, but Marcus never wanted kids. He was clear about that with Valerie before they got married. No kids. He wanted money, work, travel, all the perks, and nothing to tie him down.'

'Why did Valerie agree to marry him if that's not what she wanted?'

'Oh, please. Valerie wanted Marcus Glenn, and that's all she was thinking about. She convinced herself she didn't want kids. She figured having Marcus was enough. She sobered up real fast about that.'

'So what changed?'

Denise's face darkened. 'About five years ago, Valerie swallowed down half a bottle of aspirin. It was a close call. We nearly lost her.'

'What prompted it?' Stride asked.

'If you ask me, she was so lonely she couldn't handle it anymore. That's when she told Marcus she wanted a baby.'

'What did he say?'

'Your wife's in the hospital promising to kill herself if she doesn't get a child? He said yes.'

'So maybe Marcus changed his mind about kids,' Stride said.

'No, nothing changed. Valerie didn't get pregnant for almost three years. I was worried she was going to go over the edge again. But Marcus? He didn't care. He could barely contain his annoyance when Valerie finally got pregnant. After Callie was born, he hardly touched that girl. It was like she was an unwanted house guest who was messing up his perfect life.'

'He could have divorced Valerie.'

'Yeah, and how much of his fortune would that cost him?'

Stride shook his head. 'You're not giving me anything, Denise. This is all smoke and no fire.'

'I know. All I'm saying is that you need to take a cold, hard look at Marcus Glenn. I'm a cop and a mother, and I'm telling you, there was something not right about his relationship with his daughter. It chilled me whenever I saw them together, because there was *nothing*. No love. No interest. No passion. Valerie closed her eyes to it. Now here we are.'

'Do you honestly think Glenn could have harmed his own child?' Stride asked. 'Is that what you're saying?'

'I think he's capable of anything. I think this whole thing doesn't add up. Someone breaks into the house without leaving a trace, takes the baby, and then vanishes? Come on. It makes no sense.'

'Children get abducted all the time,' he told her.

'Of course they do. But they get grabbed off the street, not whisked out of their lakeside mansions in the middle of the night. Look, I can't prove it, and it's not my case anyway. I'm just telling you what I think in my heart of hearts. OK?'

'I understand.'

'There's one other thing,' Denise added. 'Marcus said he was alone tonight, right? Just him and Callie?'

'That's right.'

'Well, if that's true, it would be the first time ever. Valerie took care of her. The babysitter took care of her. Not Marcus. No way. Don't you find it a little odd that Marcus is alone with the baby for one night, and she disappears?'

Four

Maggie Bei parked her yellow Avalanche on the outskirts of the crime scene near the Lester River. She could see the abandoned cinder block dairy illuminated under the light poles erected by her team, and she watched her evidence technicians pawing through the grass surrounding the building and in the woods on the other side of the rapids. The crew from the medical examiner's office had a more gruesome task. Two of them, in white scrubs, attended to the dead body in the field.

The fourth victim.

Maggie steeled herself to join them. For years, she had built up an immunity to the grisly discoveries of her job, but the assaults in the previous month, one after another, had tested her objectivity. She knew she could have been any one of these women. It was too easy to imagine herself on the ground, lifeless and humiliated.

Fingernails tapped on the passenger window of her truck, interrupting her thoughts. Maggie saw the round, cherubic face of Max Guppo, who waved at her and pulled open the door. She held up her hand, stopping him in his tracks.

'Freeze! What did you have for dinner?'

Guppo thought back. 'Chili con carne.'

'Shit, what are you trying to do to me? Don't you dare get in this truck.'

'I take Beano now,' Guppo protested. 'The commercials all say, "Take Beano before, there'll be no gas."'

'Beano never met your digestive tract,' Maggie told him. 'Stay where you are, I'm getting out.'

Maggie hopped down from her truck. She cursed as her square-heeled boots landed in the wet dirt and splashed mud on to her jeans. She slammed the door and bent over with her hands on her knees and sneezed. She sniffled, yanked a tissue from her pocket, and blew her nose loudly.

'You got a cold?' Guppo asked, coming around the front of the Avalanche.

'Yeah. Just what I need. I'm hopped up on vitamin C.'

Guppo pointed at the tiny diamond stud in Maggie's nose. 'Doesn't that hurt when you sneeze?'

'I shot it halfway across the room once.'

'So why not take it out?'

'Because I like how it looks.' Maggie whiffed the air as Guppo came closer. 'Did you think I wouldn't smell that?'

'Sorry.'

'Chili con carne,' Maggie told him. 'Unbelievable.'

The two of them headed across the Strand Avenue bridge over the river. They were an odd couple. Max Guppo was in his mid-fifties and had led crime scene investigations for the Detective Bureau for as long as Maggie could remember. He was only four inches taller than Maggie, who barely made it to five feet tall in her boots, and he waddled through life with cannon-sized thighs and an oversized snow tire permanently anchored around his waist. He had worn the same three suits – brown, brown, and blue – on any given day for the past decade. Maggie, by contrast, was a diminutive Chinese cop who snagged Hollister fashions off the racks for teenage girls. The closer she got to forty years old, the more she dressed as if she were twenty-five.

As they neared the dirt road that led to the white dairy building, Maggie pointed her thumb and forefinger like a pistol at Kasey Kennedy, who sat in the rear of a patrol car twenty yards away. 'How's the kid?' she asked Guppo.

'She's shaken up.'

Maggie nodded. Kasey had the door of the squad car open and sat with a blanket wrapped around her shoulders. She wore a baggy blue sweatshirt and ripped jeans. She stared into space with eyes that were nervous and shell-shocked.

'Wow, check out that red hair,' Maggie said. 'Is that natural?'

'Beats me,' Guppo replied, smoothing down the strands of his comb-over.

'No way that's natural,' she continued. 'Did Kasey give you a statement?'

'Yeah. She thinks you're going to fire her.'

'I'll calm her down,' Maggie said. 'Have you pieced together how this all happened?'

Guppo nodded. He led Maggie along the shore by the river. The water tumbled frantically over the rocks in the narrows and then calmed as the valley widened below the highway bridge. Maggie tested the ground with her boot. It was soft.

'The three of them came across the river here,' Guppo said, pointing to the spot where the current was fastest. Twenty feet separated them from the opposite bank that led sharply uphill to the dead woman's farmhouse. 'The victim, the perp, and then our girl Kasey.'

'They came down that hill?' Maggie asked.

'Yeah. Kasey took a header.' He dug in his pocket. 'Here's her badge. We found it in the weeds on the other side.'

'Then what?'

Guppo led Maggie up a shallow slope under the evergreen trees, around the rear wall of the cinder block dairy, and into the small grassy field behind it. Twenty feet away, the medical examiner's team was zipping the woman's body into a black vinyl bag.

'Hold on a minute, guys,' Maggie called. She turned back to Guppo. 'Kasey confronted them here?'

'Right. The perp held the vic with a garrote around her neck. Kasey took a shot. Pretty ballsy move, if you ask me. It was foggy, and she didn't have a good angle on the killer.'

'She missed?' Maggie asked.

'Yeah, but the perp got the message, dropped the vic, and ran. Kasey says she took one more shot and missed again. He sprinted toward the highway and disappeared. We're still trying to figure out where he parked his car, in case he left anything behind. Kasey tried to revive the victim, but she was already gone. Two minutes earlier, and she would have been the big hero.'

Maggie shoved her hands in her pockets and marched over to the dead woman in the wet grass. 'What's her name?'

'Susan Krauss.'

'Married?'

'Divorced. She's got a teenage son in Florida with his dad.'

'What did she do for a living?'

'She was a personal trainer at the Y.'

'Have we found anything that ties her to the other victims?'

'Not yet.'

Maggie pushed her black bangs out of her eyes and stared at the body of Susan Krauss. She looked violated, the way murder victims do, probed by the technicians in white, stripped of dignity by the men who hunted through the grass around her as if she weren't even there. Her skin leached of color. Her hair wet and messy. Her clothes ripped, exposing most of her private parts. Her neck, slashed open and practically severed by the wire that had killed her.

'OK,' Maggie said quietly, nodding to the medical techs. 'You can take her.'

Susan Krauss. Number four.

The first was Elisa Reed in mid-October. Single, never married, twenty-three years old, a first-year teacher. She'd lived with her parents on a farm three miles north of here. Elisa vanished on a Tuesday night while her parents were vacationing in San Francisco. They'd called her that night, but she didn't answer, and when they hadn't reached her by Thursday, they decided to call the police. There was no evidence of Elisa in her bedroom, other than traces of blood on the sheets and a smashed alarm clock on the floor.

Two weeks later, on Halloween night, Trisha Grange disappeared, becoming the second victim. Thirty-five years old, married seven years, mother of two. Her husband Troy had taken their oldest daughter to a Halloween party, leaving Trisha at home with the baby. When he returned at ten o'clock, the baby was sleeping, but Trisha was gone. They'd found no blood this time, but they found Trisha's shoe in the field behind their farmhouse and strands of her blonde hair caught in the screen door that led outside. She'd lived seven miles northeast of Susan Krauss.

The third victim had disappeared only six days ago. Another farm, barely a mile away. Barbara Berquist was a widow in her early fifties who didn't show up to her job at the Duluth Library. That was enough to trigger suspicion, given the two earlier disappearances, and Maggie and her team had checked out the farm without waiting forty-eight hours to see if Barbara showed up somewhere else, alive and well. They'd found blood again. Lots of it. But no body.

'What did you find inside the house?' Maggie asked.

'We think the perp came in through a basement window with a broken lock. It looks like Susan Krauss was awake and in her bathroom when this guy made his move. That's probably what bought her a few more minutes. There's blood and evidence of a struggle near the doorway. Looks like she got away from him and bolted outside.'

'OK, keep at it. Inside and out. This guy's plan got screwed up this time, so maybe he made a mistake during the chase.' She added, 'I better go talk to the redhead.'

'Hang on,' Guppo replied.

He peered over her shoulder at the whitewashed stone wall of the dairy. He crouched down with a heavy breath, studying the ground where Susan Krauss now lay in her body bag, and then his eyes traveled up to a high section of the dairy wall.

'Anyone got a step stool?' he called.

One of the evidence technicians produced a stool from the trunk of his car, and Guppo opened it next to the wall. He climbed up the two steps, and Maggie winced, hearing the metal joints groan under Guppo's weight.

'Shine a light up here, OK?'

Maggie obliged, illuminating a peeling section of white paint in front of his face. Guppo slid a magnifying glass out from his pants pocket and squinted through it. When he climbed down, his face was flushed, and he was smiling.

'Spatter,' he said.

'From the victim?' Maggie asked.

'Based on the angle and location? I don't think so. I think Kasey winged a piece of our killer after all.'

Kasey Kennedy looked young, which was a reminder to Maggie that she wasn't so young herself anymore. Kasey was twenty-six and had served on the force for three years. Maggie recalled seeing her in City Hall, but that was only because Kasey and her neon-red hair were hard to miss. They had never met. Kasey's features were plain, but she had fresh, freckled skin and a body that was skinny and toned, and the overall result was attractive. She was an odd combination of girlish and intense. Her blue eyes looked lost. Her left knee bounced up and down nervously, and her fingernails were cotton-candy pink. She looked like a naïve kid in need of rescue, and yet this kid had nearly chased down a killer on her own in the middle of the fog. Maggie couldn't accuse her of lacking courage.

'Here,' she said, handing Kasey the badge that Guppo's team had found near the river.

'Oh, you found it. Thanks.'

'How are you doing, Kasey?' Maggie asked.

The young cop hung her head and squeezed her thumbs into the pockets of her jeans. 'I'm sorry, Sergeant. I screwed everything up.'

'Call me Maggie. And you didn't screw up.'

Maggie told her about the blood trace that Guppo had found on the dairy wall. 'The best case is, we get a hit in the DNA database and we ID this guy. Even if he's not in the database, we can tie him directly to the murder scene when we do nail him. Thanks to you.'

'Except the real best case would have been for me to kill the bastard, right?' Kasey said. 'I let him get away.' Her voice had a lilting pitch that could have come from the mouth of a teenager. It sounded strange to hear her talking about killing someone. She should have been gossiping about boys and sharing make-up advice.

'Don't second-guess yourself,' Maggie told her. 'It took guts to do what you did. You could have been the one to wind up dead here. You know that, right? You took a hell of a risk.'

'I know.'

'Why didn't you call for backup?'

Kasey rolled her eyes. 'No cell phone.'

'Now that was stupid.'

'Yeah, I was charging the battery in my bathroom, and I forgot to grab it before I left. I had to drive home to call nine one one, and then I came right back here.'

'Do you live nearby?'

44

Kasey nodded. 'I'm just a couple miles away, but I could have been on the moon tonight. I had no idea where I was.'

Maggie leaned on the open door of the squad car. 'So how'd you wind up in the middle of this mess?'

'I got lost,' Kasey told her. 'I drove up to Hibbing after work to hang out with a girlfriend, and I got a late start coming home. I ran smack into the fog and made a wrong turn.'

'What can you tell me about the killer? You're the only one who's seen him.'

'I wish I could tell you more. I never saw his face. He was tall.'

'Tall as in how tall?'

'Over six feet, definitely. Not heavy. He was in good shape. He had dark eyes, too. Deep brown, almost black.'

'Caucasian?'

'Yes.'

'What about the mask?' Maggie pointed two fingers at her eyes. 'One eyehole across both eyes or two separate holes?'

'Just one hole for both eyes. There was no hole for the mouth.'

'So you could see the bridge of his nose, too?'

'I guess so.'

'Did you notice any other distinguishing features? Moles, freckles, scars, that sort of thing? Did you see any hair coming down from his forehead?'

'I'm sorry, it happened too fast. I didn't notice anything.'

'Would you recognize him without the mask if you saw him again?'

Kasey shook her head. 'I don't think so.'

'What else?' Maggie asked.

'That's all I saw.'

'What was he like?'

'I don't understand.'

'How did he behave? Was he scared? We need to get inside this guy's head.'

Kasey scrunched her pale lips together. Her chest swelled as she took a deep breath. 'He wasn't scared,' she said.

'No?'

'No, he was aggressive. Confident. When I looked at him through the car window, it was like he was smiling at me. Then later, by the dairy, he laughed. He didn't think I would shoot. He was sure of himself.'

'He spoke to you?' Maggie asked.

'Yeah, he did.'

'What did he say?'

'He said he would let the woman go if I dropped the gun. And he taunted me, you know, that I wouldn't shoot because I might hit her.'

'Describe his voice,' Maggie said.

'Uh, it was cocky. Arrogant.'

'Did he have any kind of accent? Was there anything distinguishing about his speech pattern?'

'No. Nothing like that.'

'Would you recognize his voice if you heard it again?'

'I might,' Kasey told her. 'Yeah, I think I probably would.'

'That's excellent.' Maggie squeezed the young cop's shoulder. She could see Kasey's eyes blinking shut. 'Listen, why don't you go home now? Get some sleep.'

Maggie turned away, but Kasey grabbed her forearm. 'Sergeant? There's something else. I want to get in on this case.'

'What do you mean?'

'I want to help on the investigation.'

'I appreciate the offer, but this isn't your beat,' Maggie replied.

'I know that, but this guy murdered that woman right in front of my eyes.'

Maggie crouched down. Kasey stared back at her with fierce blue eyes. The cop's wet red hair was a curly mess on her head. She was definitely young. Way too young. Maggie had worked with cops like Kasey for years; they were full of enthusiasm, but they made immature mistakes. You had to take the bad with the good.

'Are you married, Kasey?' she asked.

'Yes.'

'What's your husband like?'

Kasey smiled. 'Oh, Bruce is a big bear of a guy. Looks like a blond lumberjack.'

'What does he do?'

'Right now? He's not working. We moved here when Bruce got a job in Two Harbors, but he got laid off. So mostly he does conspiracy research. That's his hobby.'

'What, like aliens shot down the space shuttle?'

'It's mostly who shot JFK,' Kasey said. 'Bruce is like a cousin of a cousin of a cousin of a cousin. He takes it personally.'

'Do you have kids?' Maggie asked.

Kasey nodded and held up one finger. 'Jack.'

'Jack Kennedy?'

'It was Bruce's idea.'

'Well, good for you. You've got a family. Don't let what happened here tonight get in the way.'

'What do you mean?'

'I mean, let it go. You stumbled into the middle of something horrible, and you did your best to stop it. Go back to your life, and let us take it the rest of the way.'

'I really want to help,' Kasey insisted. 'Whatever it is, even if it's gopher shit, I want to be part of the investigation.'

Maggie stood up and wiped her nose with the back of her hand. A cough rattled in her throat. 'Look, I've got to meet with Troy Grange tomorrow. He's the husband of the second victim, and he's a friend of mine. I need to talk to him about what happened here. Why don't you come with me?'

'Really? Yes, absolutely. Thank you.'

'It won't be easy, Kasey. Before tonight, we didn't know

what this son of a bitch was up to, but now we have a body. No matter what we tell him, Troy Grange is going to realize that his wife is probably dead. There's nothing harder than that.'

'I understand. I really appreciate it.'

Maggie patted Kasey's knee. 'Go home, go to sleep.'

'I will.'

'One last question.'

'What is it?' Kasey asked.

'How do you get your hair that color? What do you use?'

'It's natural.'

'I'll be damned,' Maggie said.

Five

Serena Dial walked down Chisholm Trail from the highway toward the Glenn estate on Friday afternoon. The street was unnaturally dark. Light didn't easily penetrate the wooded lots of the lake homes, and the fall sky was a bed of charcoal. She smelled snow in the cold air and heard the honking of geese overhead flying southward. The dead street around her spoke to the waning season. Carved jack-o-lanterns grew moldy and soft on porch railings. The trees were mostly bare.

She imagined the same street at midnight the previous day. In the fog. In the dark. Stride was right; someone could have come and gone easily without being noticed and without leaving a trail.

Assuming someone had been there at all.

So far, there was no conclusive evidence to prove or disprove that an intruder had entered the Glenn house. The forensics team from the Bureau of Criminal Apprehension in St Paul had arrived at five in the morning and spent seven hours at the scene, without much to show for their efforts. It would be weeks before they sifted through the fingerprints on the doors and windows. They had bagged traces of wet soil on the upstairs carpet, but those could be ascribed to the boots of the policemen who had responded to the 911 call. The front and backyards were similarly a mess of footprints from the first wave of searchers at the scene.

Callie's disappearance had broken on the morning news shows, competing with reports of the latest murder in the farmlands north of Duluth. Serena and Stride had spoken live to a gaggle of reporters. By now, most people in Minnesota had seen the photograph of the missing baby girl with blonde curls and a toothy smile. Stride had spent most of the morning mobilizing the statewide alert system, and Serena had overseen the network of interviews with neighbors on the roads surrounding Marcus Glenn's home and along the fifty miles of populated shoreline on Pokegama Lake. The result of all that effort was little or nothing to help their investigation. No witnesses. No credible sightings. No reports of vehicles coming or going that could focus their search.

Callie Glenn was there, and then she wasn't. The magician had waved his black sheet and made her vanish. As the clock ticked, each hour increased the risk that they would never find her.

Serena knew what Denise Sheridan believed. Marcus Glenn had killed his own child, either accidentally or deliberately, and then hidden the body to cover up his actions. There was no evidence to suggest that he had done so, but there was also no evidence to suggest he *hadn't*, and in these cases that omission was damning. The finger of suspicion always pointed first at the parents when a child vanished. Serena knew the rumor of guilt had begun to spread around town like a virus. She could hear it in the questions of the reporters, asking about Marcus Glenn, quizzing her about his background and personality, hinting about his capacity for murder. The cold, aloof surgeon was a perfect target.

Serena didn't discount the possibility that Glenn was guilty, but she found herself doubting Denise's instincts about him. For one thing, she had already pegged Denise Sheridan as hopelessly biased by her own relationship with her sister and her husband. She might be a good cop, but she despised Marcus Glenn so much that she would believe anything bad about him. For Serena, Glenn's frigid demeanor actually made him seem innocent. She had dealt with parents guilty of heinous crimes during her time in Las Vegas, and they were always the best actors, the ones who pleaded on television for the return of their children and wept in the arms of their spouses. Glenn wasn't exaggerating his grief or putting on a show for them. If anything, he had invited their scrutiny by showing his true colors.

And yet. And yet. The intruder theory didn't make sense either. There were too many holes in this case.

Serena made her way down the curving driveway that led to the Glenn front door. Several members of the Grand Rapids Police were on hand to guard the scene and keep reporters and spectators away from the house. They nodded politely at her, but she could sense their uneasiness. She understood. As of this morning, she was a detective on the payroll, but she was still a stranger, an outsider. They all knew Stride because of his years in northern Minnesota, and the police here didn't have any problem accepting his authority. But not Serena. It didn't matter that she had dealt with street crime and violence for a decade in Las Vegas on a level that no one here would see in their lifetimes. She was different, and that made her suspect.

It was easier for her in Duluth. Duluth was a larger city, and there was something about its icy remoteness that made people welcome strangers who had the courage to live there. Out here in Grand Rapids, she was in a small town. If you lived here, you were a known quantity, regardless of whether you were a saint or a sinner. If you didn't, you had to prove yourself.

Serena studied the country-style house. It was low and wide, with three gables over the second-story rooms and white, freshly painted wood siding. A triple garage was on her left, and she saw the windows of an upstairs apartment above the garage doors. The chambered windows of the first-floor dining room faced the yard, but most of the house was built to take advantage of the lake view in the rear. Marcus Glenn, in the master bedroom, wouldn't have seen what was happening in front of his house at night.

If the kidnapping was the work of an intruder, Serena was convinced that he came from the street, by car. Arriving by boat was too risky, with too many variables: launching a boat at night, navigating the waters without lights, keeping a baby quiet in an area where sound would travel easily across the lake, and landing without a dock. There were too many ways a plan could go wrong. No, the straightforward strategy was to park in the driveway under the cover of trees and go into the house from there.

But how to get into the house without a key? The locks on all of the doors looked unmolested. The windows were solid and tight.

Serena let herself in the front door and stood under the glamorous crystal of the chandelier in the glossy oak foyer. After the chill outside, the house was warm. The ivory carpet on the stairs directly in front of her led to the second floor of the house. She followed the stairs to the second story and looked up and down the long hallway at the series of closed white doors. There were at least eight of them, leading to different rooms. Four bedrooms, two bathrooms, a walk-in closet, and an upstairs laundry. None of the doors gave any clue to its contents. How would an outsider have found the nursery? And how would a kidnapper know whether Callie Glenn still slept in the master bedroom with her parents? That was a big risk.

Serena turned left down the hallway. Callie's nursery was the third door on the right. She opened the door, expecting the bedroom to be empty, but instead she saw Valerie Glenn in her daughter's room. A bay window on the far wall looked out on the lake, and Valerie sat on its polished ledge, her knees pulled up to her chest. She leaned forward with her head buried in her arms; her blonde hair tumbled over her legs. For a long minute, she didn't realize that she was no longer alone. Serena noticed the empty crib in the middle of the carpet. The childish wallpaper showed fairytale cartoons of princesses and frogs. Toys were scattered on the floor.

'Mrs Glenn?' Serena said softly.

When Valerie didn't react, Serena said her name again. This time, Callie's mother jerked up in surprise. 'Oh. Serena. I'm sorry.'

'I didn't mean to disturb you,' she said.

'Is there news?'

Serena shook her head, and the brief glimmer of hope in Valerie's eyes faded. Valerie rested her back against the window frame and turned her head to watch the gray waters of the lake at the end of the lawn. Her face was in profile. Even in grief, with strands of blonde hair mussed across her cheek and tear stains on her face, Valerie Glenn looked perfect and attractive. Her skin had a tan glow, despite the gloom of November. Everything about her was in proportion. Her legs were taut but not muscular, her frame trim but not skinny. She wore tan slacks and a long-sleeved black fleece top. It was a look that said: I'm not trying to be beautiful, really I'm not, but I can't help it.

Serena sat down opposite her on the window ledge. Valerie brushed her hair from her face and offered a weak smile.

'What can you tell me?' she asked.

'I can tell you that a massive search is going on for Callie across the entire state,' Serena assured her. 'Her photo is everywhere. The police, FBI, media, business owners, everyone will help us. Tips are already coming in.'

'What do you think they want?' Valerie asked. 'Is it money? If we pay, will they give her back to me?'

'I don't know enough about what happened to give you any answers,' Serena said. 'But I promise you that our first priority will always be Callie's safety.'

'I heard someone on the news say that rich foreigners sometimes pay to have babies stolen for them. God, I hope it's not something like that. You don't think you could be a target in a place like Grand Rapids.'

'It doesn't do any good to speculate. You'll drive yourself crazy.'

Valerie nodded. 'I know. I need to let you do your job. Honestly, Serena, I'm pleased to have a woman on the case. All these men clomping around the house – to them, it's just another crime.'

'We all want to get Callie back,' Serena said.

'Yes, but you know what I'm going through. A man can't really understand. Do you have children yourself?'

'No.'

Valerie looked momentarily disappointed. 'Oh. I'm sorry. Please forgive me, I shouldn't be asking you questions like that. It just helps me to know who you are.'

'That's all right.'

'For the longest time, I thought I didn't want kids. But then my mom died, and thirty started looking big down the road. Suddenly, it was all I could think about.' She stared at the empty crib and rubbed away a tear that escaped from her eye. 'It took me three years to get pregnant. I had given up hope.'

Serena chose her words carefully. 'How did Marcus feel about having kids?'

'He had doubts. I had to convince him.' Her face darkened, and she looked away. 'I know what people are saying. About Marcus.'

'You shouldn't listen to anything they say on the news.'

'It's ridiculous. Mean. Marcus would never, never, never hurt Callie.' Her fists clenched. 'He loves her.'

'Of course.'

'Do people know how hurtful they are?' she asked.

'All I can tell you is to close your ears to the gossip. Focus on getting Callie back.'

'I suppose next they'll be saying I was involved,' Valerie said.

'No one thinks that. You were out of town.'

'But you checked, didn't you, Serena? You called the hotel. You made sure I was there.'

'Yes, we did,' Serena admitted. She added, 'Why were you in the city?'

'I had a nonprofit board meeting in Minneapolis. It went late. I wanted to drive back, but Marcus said the fog was getting bad. So I got a room.'

'He encouraged you not to come home?'

'Yes, he said he didn't want me out on the roads.' Valerie read Serena's face and said, 'See, you think that's suspicious when it's nothing. No one trusts anyone anymore. I guess we all hate to face the horror of finding out that people aren't who they pretend to be.'

'I do need to ask you some personal questions,' Serena said.

Valerie winced, almost as if expecting a physical blow. 'Yes, go ahead.'

'If a stranger did this, they knew things about you and Marcus and Callie and your lives. The crime was carefully planned. Whoever did this was able to get into your house, find Callie, and leave quickly and quietly, as if they knew where she slept.'

'So you want to know how this person knew all these things.'

'Exactly.'

'You don't think it was a stranger, do you?'

'I don't know. It's possible that someone has been watching

55

you and gathering information about your life. But that's not easy to do in a small town without being noticed. It's also possible that someone who knows you gave up information to the wrong person without being aware of it.'

'Well, I think if someone had been watching our house, I'd know it. You're right about small towns. Nothing gets past anyone around here. I also think that if a stranger had been asking questions about us, we'd have heard about it.'

'And there's been nothing like that?'

'No.'

'Forgive me, Valerie, but I need to know. What's your marriage like? Are there any problems?'

Valerie stared at the ceiling. 'Is this really necessary?'

'It is. I wish it weren't.'

Valerie twisted the square-cut diamond ring on her finger. She studied Serena with the eye of a woman admiring another woman. 'You're beautiful, Serena. You know what it's like.'

'What do you mean?'

'A beautiful woman can't have any substance. People look at me, and they think, trophy wife. Come on, that was your first reaction, wasn't it? Marcus didn't marry me, he hired me to dress up the place.'

'I don't think that,' Serena told her.

'Well, that was the general consensus in town,' Valerie said. 'I was twenty-five when we got married. I'm not a fool. I know I'm attractive, and when you're a man like Marcus, you don't settle for anything less. Are there days when I feel more like a portrait on the wall than a living, breathing human being? Yes. Sure. But the truth is much more complicated than people think. I love him. He loves me.'

Serena thought she was trying to convince herself that it was true. 'You've been married for eight years?'

'Yes.'

'Have there been any affairs?'

'I don't see what that has to do with Callie,' Valerie said.

'Probably nothing, but I don't know what's relevant and what's not until I know everything.'

'You have an ugly job, Serena. I guess I see why Denise didn't want to do this.' She added, 'I feel pretty worthless compared to my sister. Four kids and the kind of job she has. Talk about strong. I'm fragile compared to her. Of course, she has Tom to help her, and he's a gem.'

'You didn't answer my question.'

'No, I didn't, did I? All right, yes, there have been other women. Flings. Men look at these things differently. When you're a wife, you have to decide if it matters or not, and I just decided that it didn't. At least until Callie came along.'

'Were there any relationships that were more than a fling?' Serena asked. 'Someone who wasn't just a one-night stand?'

Valerie's lower lip trembled. 'Yes. Last year.'

'Who was it?'

'I don't know. Someone at the hospital. I made a point of not knowing who.'

'How did you find out about it?'

Valerie sighed. 'How hard do you think it is? How many times do you have to smell the same perfume on his clothes and in your bed? How many hang-ups do there have to be on your phone?'

'I'm sorry.'

'When Callie was born, I made him end it,' Valerie said. 'I didn't want any details. I just wanted it over.'

'And he stopped seeing her?'

'Yes, he did.'

'Are you sure?'

'No, but if he's being deceitful, he's much better at it now than he used to be. And honestly, I don't think Marcus would bother hiding it.'

'Do you think this woman was in your house?' Serena asked.

57

'I'm pretty sure she was, yes.'

'Could she have a key?'

Valerie shrugged, as if the weight on her shoulders had grown impossible to bear. 'I have no idea. As far as I know, Marcus, Migdalia, and I are the only ones who have keys.'

'Migdalia is your babysitter?' Serena asked.

'Yes.'

'Tell me about her.'

Valerie rolled her eyes. 'Let's just say she wouldn't have been my first choice. I don't mean to sound like a snob, because that's not me, but Migdalia is coarse. She swears. She doesn't dress well. Oh, she's lovely with Callie, don't get me wrong. But she's not exactly Mary Poppins.'

'Why hire her?'

'Micki lives in Sago, where Marcus grew up. Her mother is sick, her father is out of the picture. Marcus wanted to help her.'

'Is that all?' Serena asked quietly.

'You mean, is he sleeping with her? He says no. Believe me, I asked.'

Serena heard the resignation in Valerie's voice and tried to imagine an eight-year marriage of loneliness and suspicion. Nothing surprised her any more. Lives that looked pretty and perfect on the outside were often as fragile as glass.

She got up from the window box. 'I'll let you know as soon as we have any new information.'

Valerie took Serena's hands. Her fingers were slim and warm. Serena could feel the woman reaching out to her, as if for a lifeline. 'You have to find her, Serena. I need my baby home with me. If you don't have children, I'm not sure you can understand how desperate I feel.'

Serena squeezed Valerie's hands in reassurance. She knew that Valerie, like Stride, had gone off a bridge, with nothing and no one to keep her from falling. She'd seen too many parents like her grasping for a fragment of hope, and she wished she could give Valerie a promise: *I'll bring Callie back to you.*

But she couldn't. She could only make that promise in her own head.

'I do understand,' she said.

Six

Stride found the Sago Cemetery on a dirt road off Highway 2, twenty miles southeast of Grand Rapids. There was no town, just an occasional dented mailbox marking the trail to an old farm tucked away among the trees and fields. He parked on the shoulder and got out of his truck. A hundred or so gravestones climbed a gentle slope from the road, some in the open grass, some shadowed by towering pines. The thick trunks of sixty-foot evergreens groaned as the wind blew. A white flagpole sat beside the cemetery sign, and the metal brackets on the flag rope banged rhythmically against the pole, creating a lonely clatter.

Stride didn't see another living soul in any direction. Not that he felt particularly alive himself right now. He couldn't remember a time when he had felt so disconnected from who he was. He wanted to care about something, but he didn't seem to care about anything at all. Each panic attack left him more and more remote, until he felt as if he were standing at the rim of a desert canyon and his life was a mile away, on the opposite edge.

With his hands shoved in his pockets, Stride strolled among the graves. He read the names on the headstones and brass markers built into the turf: Tolan, Niemi, Sorenson, Davis.

Halfway up the slope, he found twin gray monuments for Edward and Lavinia Glenn, parents of Marcus Glenn, who had died two years apart more than a decade earlier. He had a difficult time imagining Marcus Glenn, who was so particular about the finer things in life, growing up in these remote, lower-class farmlands.

'You're the cop, aren't you?'

Stride looked up and saw a girl about nineteen years old standing near the edge of the cemetery land, where the dormant grass ended at the trees. She held a rake in her hand and stood next to a hillock of dried leaves.

'Are you Migdalia Vega?' he asked.

'Call me Micki,' she said, scraping the ground and gathering leaves into the pile. 'You find Callie yet?'

'No.'

'I hope you find her soon. She's a beautiful girl.'

Stride approached her. Micki Vega looked like a girl who hadn't outgrown her baby fat. Her wide hips were packed solidly into beige corduroys. She had a round face, with a tiny mole above her upper lip, and golden skin. Her black hair was tied into a ponytail. She wore a red sweatshirt, which didn't hide the pooch that bulged over the belt of her pants.

'Are you the caretaker for the cemetery?' he asked.

Micki shrugged. 'I cut the lawn, rake the leaves, throw out the flowers when they die. That sort of thing.'

'Do you live around here?'

She gestured over her right shoulder, where he saw a cluster of mobile homes and a few dated pickup trucks hidden behind the trees. 'Me and my mama, we live there.'

'You work for the Glenns too, is that right?'

'Yeah, they call me when they need someone to look after Callie for a few hours. They're busy people. I work a lot of jobs, because Mama has lung disease, and she has to stay home.'

'I'm sorry.'

'Yeah, well, that's how it is. My dad skipped out a couple years ago. Mama has her lung thing from smoking. Somebody's got to make the dough.'

'How did you meet Marcus Glenn?' Stride asked.

Micki pointed down the slope. 'You saw the stones. Dr Glenn visits his family every month. I met him here a couple years ago, and he knew I did babysitting and stuff. I really needed the money, so when Callie was born, he said I could help. That was real nice. If it was up to his wife, she wouldn't have let me in the house.'

'Oh?'

'Oh yeah, I heard her talking. She didn't want me around her baby.'

'Why not?'

'I'm Hispanic, and I live in a trailer. You think a woman like her is going to trust a girl like me? But she saw how good I was with Callie. We didn't have any problems after that. She still looks down her pretty little nose at me, but she knows Callie likes me. That's all that matters to Mrs Glenn. That baby is everything to her.'

'What about Dr Glenn? Does he feel the same way?'

Micki's eyes narrowed with suspicion. 'I know what you want me to say. You want me to say that Dr Glenn did something to Callie. Well, that's bullshit. The TV people, they have it all wrong. Dr Glenn does more to help people around here than just about anybody else in the world. If you knew him like I did, you'd know he would never do anything to hurt another person, let alone his baby girl.'

Stride realized that Migdalia Vega was the first person he had met who had bothered to defend Marcus Glenn. 'You like him, don't you?'

'Damn right I do. This thing with his daughter, it's terrible, but he had nothing to do with it.'

'So do you have any idea what happened to Callie?'

Micki shook her head. 'Somebody took her. Probably somebody trying to shake down Dr Glenn. When you have money, everybody wants a piece of you.'

'But you have no idea who it could be?'

'If I did, don't you think I'd tell you? It could be anybody.'

'We're trying to figure out how somebody got into the house,' Stride told her. He added, 'You have a key, don't you?'

'Sure I do.' She folded her arms over her chest in anger. 'What, you think I had something to do with this? Is that what Mrs Glenn said? Because I would never do anything to hurt Callie. Never.'

'I didn't say you would. I was just wondering if anyone could have stolen your key.'

'No way.' Micki dug in the tight pocket of her pants and pulled out a bulging set of keys. 'The houses where I babysit, the keys are all right here. I always have them with me. I never set them down anywhere except when I go to sleep at night.'

'I have to look at all the possibilities, Micki. I'm not saying you would intentionally do something wrong, but it's easy to make a mistake. Maybe you told somebody what a nice house the Glenns have or how much money Marcus Glenn makes. Maybe a girlfriend said something to a boyfriend. Things happen.'

'I already said no,' Micki insisted. 'You think I have time to hang out in bars and drink margaritas and tell stories? You think I can park my pussy in somebody's bed when I'm working every day of the week? I already learned my lesson about boyfriends. They're happy to stick it between your legs, but they don't want to be there to watch you brush your teeth in the morning. So I'm doing this for me and my mama, and that's it.'

'OK,' Stride told her. 'I understand. If you remember talking to someone, even if it was totally innocent, I want you to call me. It's very important. This is about getting Callie back home safely.'

'I know that, but I can't tell you what happened. I didn't hear anything, OK?'

Micki's eyes darted to her feet. She knew what she'd said. So did Stride. The truth hung between them like laundry on a clothes line.

'When was the last time you babysat for Callie?' he asked.

'Last weekend, I think.'

'You think?'

'Yeah, Saturday, I guess. Dr Glenn and his wife were in Duluth for some kind of charity thing.'

'That was the last time?' Stride repeated. His voice was hard.

'I guess.'

Micki attacked the wet leaves on the grass again. Some of the leaves stuck to her tennis shoes.

'Does Dr Glenn call you to look after Callie when his wife isn't around?'

'Sometimes.'

'Mrs Glenn was in Minneapolis yesterday, right?' he asked her.

'Yeah, I heard that.'

'So did he call you yesterday?'

Micki shook her head. 'No.'

'You weren't there?'

'No.'

'So where were you last night?'

'Here,' she said. 'I was home.'

'Alone?'

'Just me and my mama. You can ask her.'

Stride waited. Micki still didn't look at him.

'What kind of car do you drive, Micki?' he asked.

'A white Ford pickup.'

'One of the neighbors saw your truck at the Glenns' yesterday,' he lied.

64

'They must have had the wrong day. I wasn't there.'

I didn't hear anything, OK?

'I think you were,' Stride told her. 'You were in the house last night when Callie disappeared. I think you better tell me what the hell happened.'

Seven

'All right,' Micki admitted. 'I was there. Big fucking deal. I don't know what happened.'

'Marcus Glenn lied to us,' Stride snapped. 'He said he was alone in the house.'

'It's not what you think. This isn't about Callie, and it wasn't Dr Glenn's idea. I begged him not to get me involved. The last thing I needed was cops all over me, OK?'

'Why?'

Micki's round face flushed with anger. 'Why the hell do you think? I'm illegal. So's my mama. I knew what would happen if I stuck around. Cops asking me questions. Reporters taking my picture. You don't think someone would hook on to the fact that I don't belong here? You don't think that would make the papers? Next thing you know we'd be on a plane to Mexico.'

'I don't care about your immigration status,' Stride told her.

'Yeah, until you don't need me any more.' Micki threw down the rake.

'Why did Marcus Glenn lie for you?'

'Because he's a good man! He's not like the papers say. He's helped me ever since I met him.'

'Are you sleeping with him?' Stride asked. 'Were you with him in his bedroom last night?'

Micki stormed toward the pile of leaves and kicked her way through it, scattering them across the grass. Her chest swelled with fast, angry breaths. She jabbed a finger at Stride. 'That's what you think, huh? He helps me because I fuck him? Well, fuck you, cop, you can go to hell.'

'Micki, we can do this right here, or we can do this in a cell in Grand Rapids,' Stride told her. 'Got it? Now answer my question.'

'The answer is no! You think a man like Marcus Glenn needs a girl like me? If he said the word, you can bet I'd straddle him and give him the ride of his life, because I owe him. But he'd never do that.'

'I don't believe you. You were there in his bedroom, weren't you? You're trying to protect him.'

'I was not with him! I was in the apartment over the garage watching television. I fell asleep. That's it. I didn't see him until he came into my room and told me about Callie.' Micki's eyes widened, and she stomped toward Stride. 'You son of a bitch, that's what you wanted, isn't it? You wanted to know if Dr Glenn was alone. I'm telling you, he didn't do anything!'

'Start at the beginning. Tell me everything.'

'You see? Never trust a cop. I'm not saying a fucking thing.'

'You're not helping yourself, Micki,' Stride said. 'When did you go over to the Glenn house?'

Micki shrugged. 'Yesterday afternoon.'

'Did Dr Glenn call you?'

'Yeah, he said his wife had to go to the Cities and could I come over and watch Callie. So I said yes.'

'When was this?'

'About two o'clock. I stayed with Callie all afternoon, gave her dinner, and I put her to bed around seven. Dr Glenn had work to do, so he asked if I'd stick around through the evening and check on Callie again before I left.'

'Where did you spend the evening?'

'They have a pool table in the basement. I played pool and listened to music on the stereo.'

'Did you see or hear anything during the evening? Did anyone come or go in the house? Were there any phone calls?'

'No, there was nobody but me and Dr Glenn as far as I know. The phone rang a couple times, but he must have picked up the calls in his office.'

'Then what?'

'Around ten o'clock, Dr Glenn came downstairs and said his wife was stuck in the Cities because of the fog. He asked me if I'd spend the night in the garage apartment in case Callie needed anything. I do that every now and then. It's no big deal. I wasn't too crazy about being on the roads, so I stayed.'

'How did Dr Glenn seem?'

Micki shook her head. 'He was fine. Nothing was wrong. Callie was sleeping.'

'What time did you go into the garage apartment?'

'I don't know, about ten fifteen, I guess.'

'That apartment overlooks the front of the house, right?' Stride asked.

'Yeah, there are a couple windows toward the street. I didn't see anything. Not headlights, nothing. I didn't hear anything, either.'

'Did you leave the room at all?'

'No. The apartment has its own bathroom. I got in there, took a shower, climbed into bed, watched TV. I fell asleep with the TV on.'

'What time did you fall asleep?'

'I started watching The Simpsons at ten thirty. I didn't see the end of it. Next thing I knew, it was one in the morning, and Dr Glenn was knocking on the bedroom door.'

'What did he want?'

'He wanted to see if Callie was with me, but she wasn't.'

'Exactly what did he tell you?' Stride asked.

'He said Callie was gone, and he was going to call the police. That's when I started freaking out.'

'How did Dr Glenn look?'

'I don't know. He was upset. I mean, he wasn't crying or shouting, but that's not how he is. He's calm, he's in control. It doesn't mean he wasn't scared. He was trying to figure out what could have happened, and me, I was going crazy. That's when he told me to leave. I told him I didn't know anything, so it's not like I could help anybody.'

'Did you hear or see *anything at all* between ten thirty and one in the morning?'

'Nothing,' Micki insisted. 'I was out cold.'

Stride shook his head in frustration. He knew that somewhere in that two-and-a-half hour span, one of two things had happened. Either someone came into the house and took Callie, or Marcus Glenn made his daughter disappear. But even with another witness in the house as the crime was taking place, they were right back where they had started. Without answers.

He left Micki and returned down the slope of the cemetery, past the collection of headstones. He stopped at the graves of Marcus Glenn's mother and father and thought about the surgeon making a pilgrimage here to the cemetery, returning to his roots. There were several other stones nearby carved with the name Glenn. The heart of the family was buried here through multiple generations – cousins, aunts, uncles, grandparents. He wondered if Marcus planned to be buried here too, or whether he would choose higher ground.

Stride thought he knew the answer. You don't go backward, even to join the dead. Marcus Glenn already lived a world away on the shore of Pokegama Lake. Beautiful wife. Beautiful house. Beautiful daughter.

The perfect family. Minus one.

'Where are you, Callie?' Stride asked aloud.

He listened for an answer, but all he heard was the ringing music of the flagpole rope.

Eight

He wondered again: did they do the right thing?

Now that it was over, he'd hoped that his doubts would leave him. He stared at the child's bed and told himself: the only way to right a wrong is to take matters into your own hands. They'd done what needed to be done. It was the only thing that could be done. They were on the side of the angels.

All he wanted to do was forget. Put away the memory. Forgive the mistake. It seemed like a small thing to ask after the horrors of the past year. But no. He couldn't escape. When he tried to sleep, he cried in the darkness instead. When he finally closed his eyes, he was back in the woods.

He chose the burying place among the sheltering arms of the evergreens.

Cold wind roared in his ears. He tramped through low, woody brush, his footsteps crackling on the litter of fallen limbs and dried pine cones, until he reached a gap in the forest where he could dig. From where he stood, he stared through a web of spiny trunks and across the dirt road to the silhouettes of gravestones on the far slope. The trees quivered and whispered, as if they were afraid of him.

He stopped and waited to make sure he was alone. Night

enveloped the cemetery like a blanket pulled over a child's head. There were no stars, no view of heaven above the crowns of trees and the angry clouds. Nothing dwelt in this place except animals and the dead souls. He didn't even believe that God was here with him tonight. God had spent the past year traveling elsewhere.

The animals stayed hidden in the darkness, but he felt their eyes watching him. His flashlight lit up their black droppings on the forest floor. He was afraid of marauders that could smell decaying flesh buried in the ground and scavenge on it. The thought appalled him. That was why he needed to dig deep.

His spade cut through the soft bed of pine needles into the spongy earth. He levered the handle down with a heavy breath and turned over a shovelful of coffee-black soil. Then another and another, making a tinny noise of metal scraping against loose rock with each thrust. He worked quickly, wanting to be done with this gruesome task. The mouth he opened up in the ground grew deeper and wider. Loose grains of dirt spilled down the pyramid of ripped turf and back into the hole, which was almost ready to swallow up the linen-wrapped bundle at his feet. Swallow it down and consume it.

He continued to carve out the grave. When he was done, he dropped the shovel and sat down with his back against a thick tree trunk. His sweat made him cold. His nose ran, partly because of the night air and partly because of the grief breaking inside him. He was at the point of no return, and he wondered if he could really do it. Lay the child in the ground, cover it up, and leave it behind.

At least he had brought the child here, where the family ghosts could commune. Surely the dead souls would welcome a baby into their midst. Maybe, finally, God would come back and do what He had failed to do for so long. Watch over. Protect.

He couldn't put it off any longer. Even at this late hour, on a lonely road, someone might drive by and wonder about his car parked on the shoulder. Take down a license plate. Call the police. A teenager from one of the nearby farms might see his light and decide to explore. There was no reason for anyone to search here after he was gone, as long as he came and went undetected.

He picked up the child wrapped in clean cloth. It was practically weightless. He got down on his knees, balanced his elbows on the wet edge of the hole, and leaned down to lay the bundle carefully on the floor of the grave. Then he pushed himself up and wiped his face. He retrieved the shovel, took a wad of earth, and tipped it back into the pit. When the dirt hit the fresh white linen, his mouth twitched with dismay. He shoveled faster, covering up the body until only a postage stamp of white sheet remained, barely visible in the darkness. With the next scattering of soil, that was gone, too. His breathing came easier. He scraped all of the uncovered turf back into place, and then he began gathering handfuls of yellowed pine needles and scattering them over the circle of disturbed ground.

When he shone his light down, the forest floor again looked pristine, as if no one had been there. There was no evidence of a grave. It was as if the child had never existed at all. He should have left it like that, but he knew there had to be some marking. Some memorial. He dug into his pocket and found a crumpled paper toy and decided he would leave it behind. With the solemnity of a father placing flowers at a headstone, he laid it down among the twigs and dirt.

It was done.

He picked up his shovel and retreated through the woods to his car. He saw fog gathering in the valleys and hanging over the road like a cloud. With his lights off, he disappeared into the mist.

73

Nine

Stride returned from the cemetery late on Friday afternoon and parked outside the Itasca County Courthouse in Grand Rapids, where the Sheriff's Department was housed. The three-story building took up an entire city block and included space for most of the county offices. He and Serena were lucky to have a top-floor office not much bigger than a closet that served as the war room for the investigation.

He passed the granite veterans' memorial and under the snapping US flag on his way to the building entrance, but before he went inside, his stomach growled. He realized he hadn't eaten anything but a chocolate donut since dinner the previous night, and he was running low on caffeine to keep himself awake. On the other side of 4th Street, he spotted a Burger King restaurant, and he crossed the street to grab a late, greasy lunch.

In the parking lot, he passed a rusting Ford Taurus. A wafer-thin woman sat in the driver's seat and wolfed down a double Whopper and an oversized pop. Their eyes met, and she spat a bite of her sandwich into a paper bag and hurriedly rolled down her window to wave at him.

'Hey!'

Stride stopped. The woman spilled out of her car, trailing

the smell of fried food, and jutted out her hand. He shook it and wiped ketchup from his fingers.

'It's Lieutenant Stride, right? I'm Blair Rowe with the *Grand Rapids Herald*.'

He groaned. 'No interviews, Blair. If I had something new, I'd tell you. I've got ten minutes to eat and then I need to get back inside.'

'Ten minutes is great. Perfect. Off the record, just background. Please?'

The last thing Stride wanted was to eat lunch with a reporter, but this was one case where more media exposure was a good thing. He needed Callie to stay on the front page until someone came through with a solid lead. 'Ten minutes,' he said.

'Great, fabulous. Go get lunch, and I'll meet you at a table inside. I really appreciate it, Lieutenant.'

Stride ordered a chicken sandwich, skipped the fries, and added a Diet Coke. By the time he got his tray of food, he saw Blair Rowe at a window table, waving both arms to get his attention. She'd already consumed most of her hamburger and was shoving three fries into her mouth at a time.

'How do you stay so thin?' he asked.

'Adrenaline,' she replied.

Blair never stopped moving. Even as she stuffed food in her mouth, she tapped her fingers on the table and crossed and recrossed her legs as she shifted in her chair. He felt a little motion sick, watching her.

'You're reporting on the Callie case for CNN, right?' he asked her.

'Yes! This is big, big, big. I'm going to be on *Nancy Grace* tonight. They want someone who knows the area. For once in my life, it pays to be in nowhere-ville, Minnesota.'

'Congratulations.'

She ran right over the irony in his voice. 'Thanks! This is a hell of a break for me. I mean, you know, it's a terrible thing, but I can't tell you how cool it is to be part of a national news story. My mom is TIVOing every broadcast. Normally, Grand Rapids in the off season is *slow*. If a clown throws up at some kid's birthday party, that's news here in November.'

Blair's thick black glasses slipped down the bridge of her nose. She pushed them up with her index finger.

'Have you been at the newspaper for long?' he asked.

'Two years,' she replied, sucking pop through her straw. 'I'd love to get to the Cities, but the dailies are shedding jobs left and right. It sucks to be a journalist right now. Who knows, maybe I can make the jump to TV. I never really thought about being on-air talent, but it's fun when the red light goes on.'

Stride didn't reply. Blair's intense personality felt like machine-gun fire, and he doubted how well it translated to the intimate medium of television. He also didn't think she had the coiffed, blown-dry, perfectly sculpted look of an on-air reporter. Her brown hair was stringy, and he could tell from the thickness of her glasses that she was almost blind without them. The glasses magnified her dark eyes and made them look larger than life. Her face was narrow, with a nose like a bumpy ski slope and a pointed chin. He saw a couple of pimples she was hiding with make-up, and her white teeth needed straightening. She wasn't really ready for her close-up.

Blair finished her hamburger and licked her fingertips. She glanced furtively around the half-empty restaurant and leaned forward. 'So you know the question everybody's asking,' she whispered. 'Did Marcus Glenn do it?'

'No comment,' he said.

'Oh, come *on*, Lieutenant. We can help each other out. I know Grand Rapids inside and out. My dad's worked on the floor of the UPM mill his whole life, and my mom teaches seventh grade English. This is my town.'

'So?'

'So there aren't many secrets around here. Heck, why do

we need turn signals? Everybody knows where everybody else is going. You think I haven't heard rumors about Marcus Glenn for years?'

'What rumors?' Stride asked.

Blair grinned. She pushed her glasses up her nose again. 'You first.'

'This isn't a game, Blair. We're trying to find a little girl.'

'I know, but we both have our jobs to do. Mine is to stick my nose into everyone else's business.'

Stride took two bites of his chicken sandwich and decided he wasn't hungry anymore. He pushed his tray away. 'I have to go.'

'OK, OK,' Blair interrupted, grabbing his arm. 'I'll show you mine, and you show me yours. The word on the social circuit is that Marcus and Valerie Glenn's marriage is shaky. Really shaky. Did you know she sees a shrink?'

'How do you know that?'

'I keep telling you, it's a small town. Doctor-patient confidentiality isn't worth much when people have two eyes in their head. They see who goes in which doors in town, you know?'

Stride was silent.

'She's already had at least one nervous breakdown,' Blair continued. 'Everybody knows why. Marcus has a parade of other women. He flies off for weekends in Vegas, and you can guess what he does down there. It's a screwed-up family living in that house.'

Stride shrugged. 'Show me a family that isn't.'

'Yeah. Point taken. Everybody's got secrets. But I have a nose for what smells bad. Have you been to the hospital in Duluth where Marcus practices?'

'My partner is going there tomorrow.'

'I was there this morning,' Blair said with a smug smile. 'Hardly anyone will talk about him. They're scared.'

'Why?'

Blair tilted her bag of fries to drain the last crumbs and salt into her mouth. 'I love fries. Does anyone not love fries?'

'What are the hospital people afraid of?' Stride repeated.

'If Marcus doesn't like you, you're fired,' Blair told him. 'No one would go on the record about him. But you know how somebody does something bad, and his neighbors and friends all say, no way, not him, couldn't be. Well, no one at the hospital was rushing to tell me that Marcus was innocent. What they *did* say was that they were surprised he and Valerie ever had a baby at all.'

'That doesn't mean anything.'

'I hear you, Lieutenant. You have to play it close to the vest. Just answer me this. Can you rule out the possibility that Marcus Glenn murdered his daughter?'

'As far as I'm concerned, Callie is alive, and I'm going to find her,' Stride said. 'The best thing you can do is keep her face on the news, so someone sees her.'

Blair chewed on the end of her straw. Underneath the table, her knee bounced, rocking the table so hard that Stride's pop sloshed over the side. 'Oh, I will, but if there are skeletons in Glenn's closet, I'm going to find them.'

'Just don't withhold evidence from us,' Stride snapped.

'Withhold it? Are you kidding? You'll see it on CNN.'

Stride reached out under the table, took hold of Blair's knee in an iron grip, and held her leg steady. 'Blair, you're new to the game. I know that the TV news shows don't set a good example because they turn every crime into a whodunit. But you're dealing with real people's lives here.'

'I'm not stupid,' she said.

'I don't think you are.'

'But I'm impatient, and I don't like to wait for the police to throw me crumbs.'

Stride stood up from the table. 'Do you have kids, Blair?'

'Yeah, I've got a little boy. My mom looks after him when I'm at work. So what?'

'Then try to put yourself in Valerie Glenn's shoes for a minute.'

'Hey, I'm with you. I am. I hope you find her daughter. I'm just not convinced you ever will.'

Stride turned to leave.

'Lieutenant?' Blair called.

'What is it?'

'I know about the babysitter.'

'Good for you,' Stride said.

'You want to hear my theory?'

He scowled at her. 'What is it?'

Blair scouted the restaurant again and then stood on tiptoes and put her lips next to Stride's ear. 'I think Marcus Glenn and Micki Vega committed this crime together.'

Ten

Serena drove from Grand Rapids to Duluth on Saturday morning. The sky was slate gray with wavy clouds like smoke trails, and ice crystals of snow whipped across her windshield. She passed boggy fields where skeletons of trees jutted out of the standing water. The northern woods were no longer brick red or flaming orange as they had been in September, but dirty shades of rust and brown. Every few miles, she drove across black rivers and sped through block-long towns, with nothing but an old brick liquor store or a shabby five-room motel to attract a few tourist dollars. Most of the time, she was alone on the road.

As she drove, she thought about Stride. She'd stood at the foot of the bed this morning and watched him while he slept. Wherever he was, it was a million miles away from her. He'd been walking away, retreating, escaping, for weeks, until they were strangers again. They'd drifted apart as easily as they had come together. What made her angry was that she had let it happen without fighting back. She'd watched him go rather than confront the hurt she felt. If that was what he wanted, if that was how it was going to be, then she would protect herself and pretend she had known it would happen this way all along.

Maybe she had. Maybe they'd both been kidding themselves.

There had always been fault lines, little hairline cracks that seemed like nothing until the weight of pressure and time burst them open. She knew it happened that way, and there was no one to blame. Things are fine until suddenly, unexpectedly, they are not fine at all anymore, and both of you know it, and neither one of you wants to admit it.

Her phone rang. It was him. The man she loved.

'You didn't wake me up this morning,' he told her.

Serena wiped her eyes and squelched the anguish she felt when she heard his voice. 'I'm sorry. You haven't slept much lately, and I thought you could use the rest.'

'You're right. Thanks.' He added, 'You sound strange. Is everything OK?'

'Sure,' she said.

It was easier to lie. It was safer to pretend. Things are fine, Jonny, but we both know they're not. She heard him hesitate, as if he might push her for the truth, but she knew he wouldn't do that.

'What's the latest on the search?' he asked.

He was a colleague talking to a colleague. Serena heard a noise in her head, and she thought it was a fault line, a crack, a fracture, splintering apart and growing wide.

'We've gone through the guest lists from motels around Grand Rapids,' she reported to him in a flat voice. 'We're still doing follow-up, but there aren't any red flags. The Highway Patrol has been hitting gas stations with Callie's photo. We've got leads, but nothing hot.'

'What about cameras on the roads in and out of town?'

'We found a couple ATM cameras that face toward 169 and Highway 2. Between the fog and the video quality, there's not much to see. I sent them to the BCA to see if they could do a digital enhancement.'

'I think we need to drag Pokegama Lake,' Stride said.

Serena pulled her Mustang on to the shoulder of the highway.

She switched off the motor and listened to the silence. 'That'll kill Valerie Glenn.'

'I'm hoping we *don't* find anything, but if we wait too much longer, we'll lose the lake to ice.'

'Give it a few more days.'

'Yeah, OK, but I'm not feeling good about this.' He added, 'If it was an abduction for money, we'd have heard from the kidnappers by now.'

'I know.'

'I keep coming back to Marcus Glenn,' Stride told her. 'I don't want the reporters getting wind of it, but I think we should ask him to take a polygraph. He's already lied to us about Micki Vega. Who knows what else he's hiding?'

'He'll lawyer up and stop talking,' Serena said.

'That tells us something.'

'I don't know. I don't like Glenn either, but I'm not sure I see him as violent or depraved.'

'See what you can find out at the hospital,' Stride said.

'I will.'

When there was nothing left to say, the dead air between them stretched out and grew awkward. Serena stared across the highway at a wasted barn, its roof open to the elements in jagged holes where the beams had collapsed. Blackbirds flew from inside. The grass grew long and wavy around the bowing walls.

'Hey, Jonny?' she murmured.

'Yes?'

'We're not so good, are we?'

She couldn't believe she had said it aloud. That was all it took to quit pretending. Now they were on dangerous ground.

Stride waited a long time, and then he said, 'It's me.'

'No, it's not just you,' she told him.

Two hours later, Serena walked along Superior Street in downtown Duluth with a nurse from St Mary's Hospital named Ellen Warner. At Lake Avenue, the two of them crossed the street and found a bench protected from the wind. It was too cold to be outside comfortably, but Ellen had insisted that they talk where there was no risk of being overheard. Few people at St Mary's were anxious to talk about Marcus Glenn.

Ellen opened a white takeaway bag and pulled out a hot dog from the Coney Island restaurant up the street. She unwrapped the foil and took a large bite. A drop of mustard stuck to her lips.

'I appreciate your meeting me,' Serena told her.

'Well, keep it under wraps, OK?' Ellen said, wiping her mouth. 'Dr Glenn is prickly. If a nurse gets on his bad side, she's gone.'

Ellen was dressed in purple scrubs with a jean jacket over the top. Her sneakers were neon white. She was in her early fifties with short silver hair and a squat, heavy physique.

'How long have you worked with him?' Serena asked.

'Must be almost ten years,' she replied. 'I have to tell you, he's good. Make that great. The man's ego wouldn't fit in a football stadium, but he's a wizard in the OR. Good with patients, too. You wouldn't think it, because he's a titanic pain in the ass to everyone else. But he can switch it on with patients, and they love him. I've never understood people who can compartmentalize their lives like that, but with Dr Glenn, you have to overlook his personality and respect his talent.'

'Do you know his wife, Valerie?'

'Enough to say hello. She comes in every now and then.'

Ellen finished her hot dog, crumpled the wrapper, and put it back in the bag. She reached into the hip pocket of her scrubs and removed a pack of cigarettes. She lit one and noticed the surprise on Serena's face. 'It's the stress. I know it's stupid, but that doesn't stop me.'

'What's the relationship like between Dr Glenn and his wife?' Serena asked.

'Strained,' Ellen said.

'How so? Do they fight?'

'No fights, at least not at the hospital. They're distant. She tries to get inside his head, but he doesn't want anyone else in there.'

'Do you know their daughter Callie?'

'Sure, Mrs Glenn brings her in sometimes. Cute girl.'

'What's Dr Glenn like as a father?'

Ellen blew out a cloud of smoke and regarded Serena coolly. 'You mean, would he do something to Callie? No, I don't believe that. If Marcus Glenn is one thing in this world, he's a doctor. He'd never harm another human being.'

'That's not what I asked.'

'Well, that's what everyone's saying. Would I call him a loving, doting father? No. He's not going to get down on the floor and play games or make baby talk with a stupid grin on his face. That's not who he is. But a monster? I don't think so. Although you'd probably find people in the hospital who disagree with me.'

'Is there anyone who hates him enough to want to harm him? Or his family?'

Ellen's brow furrowed. 'That's a difficult question. A lot of people dislike him because he's a perfectionist. He has no patience for mistakes. But would someone hurt him by taking his daughter? That's hard to imagine.'

'You said nurses have been fired because of him.'

'Yes, that's true.'

'Is there anyone who would hold a grudge?'

Ellen shrugged. 'Most were reassigned elsewhere. A couple wanted to get out of nursing anyway. It chews people up.'

'What about the personal side?' Serena asked. 'I've heard rumors about Glenn having affairs with women on the hospital staff.'

Ellen cocked her head and stubbed out her cigarette on the concrete of the bench. She brushed ash on to the pavement. 'Yes, Marcus has a weakness for pretty young things. In his defense, nurses join the staff, and they see a tall, rich, handsome surgeon, and they make a play for him. It's not like he's going to leave Valerie for any of them.'

'Maybe someone thought he would.'

'Hey, you fool around with a married man, you take your chances. Don't look to me for sympathy if you get hurt.'

'I heard there was one affair that was more serious,' Serena said.

Ellen glanced at her watch. 'I should be getting back. I've already said too much.'

'Come on, Ellen. Who was it? Do you know the woman?'

'Oh, yeah. Everyone knows Regan.'

'Regan?'

'Regan Conrad. She's a nurse. I never saw them together, but I heard people talking about the affair. It was hot and heavy for a while, although you wouldn't believe it to look at her.'

'Why?'

'Well, Regan is no Valerie. Hell, she's almost anorexic, lots of tattoos, boy breasts, lip ring. All I can figure is she must be dynamite in bed.'

'Are they still seeing each other?'

'No, I heard that Marcus wised up and dumped her earlier this year. I think he figured out she's crazy.'

'Crazy?' Serena asked.

'Volatile,' Ellen said. 'She's a good nurse, but man, she can go off on you. And she plays dirty, too. A few years ago, she had a run-in with a young lab tech. Not long after, they found hundreds of hardcore porn images on the guy's computer, so they fired him. And hello, who was Regan sleeping with at the time? Some geek in IT.'

'She sounds like someone who carries a grudge.'

'Oh, yeah, but if you're thinking she had something to do with Callie's disappearance, you can forget that. She didn't do it.'

'How do you know?'

'She worked the graveyard shift on Thursday night. So did I. I remember seeing her in the cafeteria, because she got into a shouting match with the cook over a hair she said she found in her pasta.'

Serena didn't care if Regan had an alibi. 'How do I find her?' she asked. 'Does she work in the orthopedics area with you and Marcus Glenn?'

Ellen shook her head. 'Regan is an obstetrics nurse in the maternity ward. She works with mothers and babies.'

Eleven

Maggie Bei ripped open the latest letter from the lawyer at the adoption agency in Minneapolis. She unfolded it and read it carefully, then tore the letter into pieces. The paper scraps fluttered to the floor around her. She pushed her black bangs out of her eyes and slapped the dinette table with her palm.

'Fuck it,' she announced.

She stomped into the kitchen and swung open the doors of the liquor cabinet. She extracted a half-empty bottle of Brazilian cachaça, then grabbed a lime from a basket near the refrigerator. After slicing the lime and squeezing it into a lowball glass, she added sugar and ice and filled the rest of the glass with Brazilian rum. Out of deference to the remnants of her head cold, she also dropped in a couple tablets of vitamin C and watched them fizz. She swirled the concoction around, drank it down in two swallows, and made another.

'That's better,' she said.

Maggie carried her drink into the living room of her condominium. She lived on the upper floor of condo units built over the Sheraton Hotel in downtown Duluth, with a view toward Lake Superior. There were still unpacked boxes scattered around the apartment. She had moved in a month earlier, and since then, most of her time had been taken up with the murder investigation in the north farmlands. She'd barely had time to do anything in her new place except sleep.

Maggie sipped her caipirinha and stared at the lake. She knew she shouldn't be drinking, but she didn't care. It was Saturday afternoon, and she needed to pick up Kasey Kennedy in a few hours. The two of them were going to visit Troy Grange, whose wife Trisha had disappeared on Halloween night more than two weeks earlier. She could sugar-coat it however she wanted, but after the discovery of the fourth victim, Troy knew the truth. He was now a single father to two young girls.

The intercom near her front door buzzed. Maggie put down her glass and walked over and pushed the button. 'Yes?'

'You've got a visitor downstairs,' the lobby guard told her. 'Her name's Serena Dial.'

'Tell her you need to do a strip-search.'

Maggie heard an expletive in the background.

'She's coming up,' the guard said, laughing.

'Thanks.'

Maggie retrieved her drink and waited. Two minutes later, she heard a knock on the door.

'Hey, stranger,' she told Serena.

'Hey, yourself.'

Serena nodded her head in approval as she cast an eye around the apartment. 'Very nice. I love the place.'

'One day I'll actually move in,' Maggie said, nodding at the boxes. She swirled the ice in her drink. 'You want something? I can do non-alcoholic beverages under duress.'

'No thanks.'

Maggie slumped sideways into an oversized chair and dangled her feet over the cushion. 'Have a seat. Talk to me. The diet's working; you look great.'

'The last five pounds are the hardest,' Serena said. She took a seat on the sofa opposite Maggie and leaned forward with her elbows on her knees. 'You look good, too.'

'Yeah? How do you think I'd look with red hair?' Maggie asked.

'Red? You?'

'There's this cop named Kasey Kennedy with this amazing red hair. Makes me want to try it. I'm bored with black.' She added, 'I hear you're back on the job.'

Serena nodded. 'I'm official.'

'Good for you. Are you in town because of Callie Glenn?'

'Yeah, I was asking questions over at St Mary's,' Serena told her. 'Tonight I'm seeing a nurse who lives on the north side of Duluth. She was having an affair with Marcus Glenn.'

'The media has been hitting the doc pretty hard,' Maggie said. 'Do you think he was involved?'

'We haven't crossed him off the list.'

'How's Stride?' Maggie asked. 'Is he still coming back next week?'

'I guess.'

Maggie raised an eyebrow. 'You guess?'

'Something's wrong, but he won't talk about it,' Serena said.

'I'm sorry.'

Serena took a long time to reply. 'Yeah, it's the old story with us. Two stubborn people with baggage.'

'He loves you,' Maggie said.

'I know, but if he won't let me in, what the hell am I there for? I'm getting tired of being alone even when we're together.'

Maggie didn't say anything. This wasn't a conversation she particularly wanted to have with Serena. They both knew the score. Maggie had made her one and only play for Stride in the months after his wife died, but to him, she was still the young kid he had hired as his partner. Not a lover. Then Serena – who wasn't much older than Maggie – had arrived in town, and Stride fell for her hard. Maggie liked Serena as a friend and a cop, but they still tiptoed around their mutual feelings for Stride, trying not to let the competition come between them.

She couldn't help the occasional stabs of jealousy that Stride had turned to Serena, not her.

'What do you think I should do?' Serena asked.

'I wish I could tell you.'

'I know I'm not a saint in this. I should push him, but I'm too busy wrapping barbed wire around myself.' She got up impatiently. 'I want a drink.'

'No, you don't.'

'I'm not going to, but I want one. I hate that.' She shook her head and changed the subject. 'What about you? How are you?'

'If I'm thinking about dyeing my hair red, what does that tell you?' Maggie asked.

'I heard you got DNA on the bastard who's been snatching these women.'

'We do, but we don't have results back. Either way, we still have to catch him, and I don't think he's done yet.'

'What about the adoption agencies?' Serena asked. 'Are you any closer to finding a kid?'

Maggie clucked her tongue in frustration. 'I always thought this was the good old USA, where money can buy you anything. Apparently not a baby, however.'

'Give it time.'

'Yeah, time. I don't have time for a kid, so I don't know why I'm trying.' Maggie raised her glass in a toast. 'We're really having a Thelma and Louise kind of day, aren't we?'

'Totally.'

Maggie finished her drink and climbed out of the chair. Outside the window, the sky grew blacker as dusk approached. Serena came and stood next to her, and they watched the lights come on around the harbor below them. An ore boat muscled through the canal underneath the city's steel lift bridge. Beyond the bridge was the strip of land called the Point, where Stride and Serena lived.

'This nurse you're seeing, where exactly on the north side does she live?' Maggie asked. 'Is it in the city or in the farmlands?'

'Up in the farmlands. Lismore Road near McQuade.' Serena added, 'And no, you don't have to remind me.'

Maggie nodded, but she reminded her anyway. 'That's not a very safe place to be these days.'

Twelve

'You're telling me that Trisha is dead,' Troy Grange said.

Maggie winced. Troy didn't waste time with pretty ways to share bad news. 'We don't know that for sure,' she told him. 'I don't think we can automatically assume the worst. One woman is dead. That's all we know for certain.'

'Liar,' Troy snapped.

He wasn't being hostile, just honest. Maggie knew he was right, but she couldn't say so. She couldn't say that to any victim's spouse and certainly not to a friend.

Troy Grange was the senior Health and Safety Manager at the Duluth Port. They had worked together for five years on immigrant smuggling, outbreaks of communicable disease, and crimes in the harbor ranging from arson to rape. Through it all, she had never known Troy to hide behind his lawyers or his budget. Anything that went wrong in the port was on his watch. He was solid.

Troy ran his hands over his bald head. He was forty years old, not tall, but built like a circus strongman. His face was big: lumpy nose, broad chin, and puffy cheekbones like a squirrel with a mouthful of acorns. He wore a form-fitting red undershirt and baggy black sweatpants.

'You know what I keep thinking about?' he said. 'I used to

work on the ore boats, but Trisha made me give it up. She said it was too dangerous, and she didn't want to be left alone with the kids. And now I lose her from inside our own house.'

'I'm so sorry, Mr Grange,' Kasey Kennedy murmured.

Kasey sat on the opposite end of the sofa from Maggie, her knees pressed together. She looked uncomfortable, her eyes darting between Maggie and Troy. Maggie felt bad about bringing Kasey into the middle of this scene, but she wanted Kasey to understand that investigative work wasn't glamorous. Too often, it was filled with suffering.

'You saw him, didn't you?' Troy asked Kasey. 'You saw this bastard?'

'Not his face, but yes.'

Troy got up from his chair and folded his arms over his barrel chest. The floor timbers shivered as he paced in front of the fireplace.

'Tell me what you think,' he said. 'You saw what he did to this other woman. Is he just a fucking murderer? Is there any way my wife could be alive?'

'I don't know what to tell you, Mr Grange,' Kasey stuttered. 'I sure hope she's alive.'

Maggie wanted to say: *If Trisha's alive, she's better off dead.* But she didn't.

'How are the girls, Troy?' Maggie asked.

He sat down again and wiped his nose on his bare, thick forearm. 'I took them to visit Trisha's parents in Chicago on Friday, and I left Emma there. I've got to go back to work on Monday, and I can't take care of a baby right now. Plus, it will be good for her parents to have something else to focus on.'

'What about Debbie?'

'Debbie doesn't understand what's going on.' He twisted his silver wedding ring around his finger and added, 'I shouldn't have gone to that goddamn Halloween party. Not with that other woman disappearing in October.'

'You had no way of knowing,' Maggie told him. 'We didn't know we were dealing with a pattern crime.'

'Yeah, but security's what I do. I knew there was a risk. Hell, I upgraded our security system three days after I heard about that woman going missing. A lot of good that did us.'

'Don't blame yourself.'

Troy shrugged. 'I do.'

'We're going to be blanketing the north highways with cops every night,' Maggie said. 'If this guy tries again, we'll get him.'

'That's a lot of ground to cover,' he said, shaking his head. 'I don't want to sound skeptical, but you're going to be spread pretty thin across a few hundred square miles.'

'We've got extra manpower. Volunteers. Nobody's sleeping, Troy.'

'I know. I appreciate it.' He looked at Kasey. 'Will you be out there too?'

'Um, yeah, I'm sure I will,' Kasey murmured.

'You be careful.'

Kasey nodded and stared at her hands.

'Daddy?'

All three of them looked up. Debbie Grange, six years old, stood in the doorway of the living room. She wore polka-dot pajamas and carried a stuffed Pooh bear under her arm. Troy Grange sprang up immediately.

'What is it, sweetheart?'

'I want Mommy to tuck me in,' Debbie murmured.

Maggie felt her heart breaking. She saw Kasey look away and bite her lip. Troy wrapped his bear arms around his little girl.

'I'll tuck you in, baby,' he said.

'I want Mommy to tuck me in,' the girl repeated.

'Oh, honey, I know, but Mommy's not here. Remember? She had to go away.'

Fat tears dripped down the girl's face. 'Where is she?'

'I told you, sweetheart, she had to take a trip, OK? I'll tuck you in. I'll stay right there with you.'

'*No*. I want *Mommy*.'

Troy cradled his daughter as the girl cried into his shoulder. He sang to her under his breath, and Maggie found she could barely watch. She gestured to Kasey, and they both stood up. Maggie met Troy's eyes and pointed at the front door. He nodded.

'Thanks for everything,' he called to her softly. 'You too, Kasey. Please keep me posted.'

They left without saying anything more. Outside, on the front porch, Kasey leaned heavily against the railing and looked sick. 'God,' she said.

'Yeah, this is the worst part of the job,' Maggie told her.

'Do you ever get used to it?'

'Nope. I hope I never do.'

Both women climbed inside Maggie's yellow Avalanche. Maggie normally drove fast, even at night, and she punched the truck to seventy-five miles an hour on the highway. Beside her, Kasey clutched the handhold on the door. The headlights lit up the dark stretch of road through the lonely farmlands.

'Do you still want to work on the investigation?' Maggie asked.

Kasey leaned her cheek against the cold glass and stared at the fields whipping by outside the window. 'I don't know. I don't even know if I want to be a cop anymore.'

Maggie glanced sideways at Kasey's face. 'You had a rough experience that night,' she told her. 'Some people never get over it. Even tough cops.'

As she said it, Maggie thought about Stride. He was a tough cop, but she knew that he took all of his stress and grief and sucked it inside himself, where very little of it ever escaped. She remembered how lonely he had been in the months after his wife died, when his wound was greatest. She had tried to fight her way inside to rescue him, but he had pushed her away, just as he was doing to Serena now. She wondered if he knew how to ask for help.

'I keep thinking about that woman's eyes,' Kasey said.

'You can't change what happened. It's over.'

'Yeah, but I feel so guilty.'

'You have to put it behind you.'

'That's the thing. I just want to get out. I want to forget all about it.' She turned and stared at Maggie. 'Do you think I'm wrong if I quit? Would you feel like I was running away?'

'That's not my call, Kasey,' Maggie said.

'I don't know what to do,' Kasey told her. 'I can't get that guy out of my head, you know? I feel like he's haunting me. Like he's still out there.'

Under the night sky, he was barely visible, just a silhouette marching quickly through the field in the north farmlands.

He kept his hands in the pockets of his fleece jacket. His breath became a warm cloud in front of his face. He splashed through ice-glazed puddles in the indentations where tractors ploughed the spring soil, and the noise made by his boots was like glass breaking. Needles of frost made the brown grass brittle. His nose picked up the animal smell of cattle from the barn across the highway.

The field ended in a nest of trees. He slipped between the shaggy branches and tracked wet footprints across the driveway as he approached the house. It was a modest two-story farm home that showed signs of neglect. The wood siding needed fresh paint. On the sidewalk that led to the front door, two squares of concrete had buckled and cracked. Dead flowers wilted over the sides of clay pots on either side of the detached garage.

He studied the house carefully, but he knew she was gone now. Every window was black.

He made his way to the rear of the house. On the back wall, he saw three steel half-moons buried in the earth at intervals along the foundation. They were open and shallow, about two feet in depth, protecting windows that led to the basement. He stepped down inside one of the window wells and drove the toe of his boot into the glass. It shattered in shards that spilled inside to the floor below. He kicked several more times, knocking away the remaining fragments, then squatted down and squeezed his legs and torso through the tight hole. Letting go, he dropped to the concrete floor.

He slid a Maglite from his pocket and cast a narrow beam around the space. The air was cold and musty. He ducked to avoid pipes overhead and picked his way through the glass to the stairs that led to the main level of the house. The old steps squealed like mice. He took them slowly. At the door, he waited and listened, then pushed the door open and found himself in the unlit kitchen. Dirty plates were stacked in the sink. Half a pot of coffee grew cold on the counter. The butcher block table hadn't been wiped down, and he saw remnants of mashed carrots and banana strewn in front of a rickety high chair. He whiffed the air and smelled fried fish.

He moved from the dinette to the family room, which was crowded with garage sale furniture scattered over the small square of worn beige carpet. A brown tweed sofa faced the television. The coffee table in front of the sofa overflowed with magazines and dog-eared paperback books. He spotted three photo frames on top of the television, and he illuminated each of them with the beam of his flashlight. One photo showed an older couple on a desert highway; the other two showed a young man and woman. The man in the photos was burly, with blond hair and a mustache that overflowed his upper lip.

The woman had dazzling red hair.

Hello, Kasey.

He remembered her vividly as she'd looked in the field behind the dairy. Her body like a wet cat. Her eyes big and desperate. Her arms trembling and her hands looking small clapped around the big gun. He'd never dreamed she would fire. The wound in his shoulder still burned where her bullet had grazed him.

'You're a bad girl,' he said aloud. *And bad girls need to be punished*.

He scouted the ground level and then took the steps to the second floor. The first room in the hallway was an office with a computer desk and filing cabinets. A pale light glowed inside from a video loop repeated endlessly on the computer monitor. It was a screen saver of the Zapruder film showing the Kennedy assassination. As he watched, Kennedy took a fatal bullet in the head over and over.

Well, isn't that sick. Then he smiled at his own joke. *Takes one to know one*.

He rifled through the cabinets and desk drawers, pulling out months-old bank and credit card statements and cell phone bills. People never threw anything away. He flipped through a copy of the Duluth newspaper from the previous January and a February issue of *Sports Illustrated*. The swimsuit edition. He dug deeper, extracting file folders with tax information, which he paged through one by one. Toward the bottom of the desk drawer, he found a photograph of Kasey in a bathrobe holding her newborn son, his naked skin red and wrinkled. *You look tired, darling*.

But her eyes were the same. Blue. Fierce. He slipped the photograph in his pocket.

The next room was the bathroom. Kasey used bar soap that smelled like lavender. He spied threads of her red hair in the bathtub, which he picked up and twirled around his gloved finger. He imagined her stepping out of the porcelain tub, toweling her body dry, and studying her reflection. The tiny room would be humid and fragrant with her scent. When he opened her medicine cabinet, he found vitamin bottles containing fish oil and St John's Wort and prescriptions in her name for Xanax and Ambien.

Don't you sleep, Kasey? Poor baby.

He closed the cabinet and stared at his own face in Kasey's mirror. He kept his hair in a severe black crew cut. A gold earring hugged the lobe of his left ear. His right cheek was scarred and cratered from the acne he had suffered as a teenager. Looking at himself, he watched his dark, dead eyes come to life, like a doll turned on by a switch. He grinned and picked up an open tube of lipstick and scrawled a message for her on the glass. Two words to tell her who she was.

I want you to know I was here. I want you to know it's not over.

He found her bedroom at the end of the hall. The linens on the queen-sized bed were rumpled and unmade. Her closet door was ajar. He opened it and explored the contents, touching her blouses, running his fingers along the satin sleeves. On a hanger, he found a lace nightgown, which he removed and held at arm's length. It would fall barely past her thighs. The cups of the bra were sheer. He took the nightgown and draped it over the bed, as if she were lying there.

Looking down, he felt the familiar rage bubbling up like lava. For him, desire was rage. But it was different this time, because Kasey was different. She wasn't like all the others. He thought about waiting for her in the darkness and taking her now, but he willed himself to be patient. He wanted her to *know*. To feel him coming. To realize there was nothing she could do to keep him away.

As he turned for the doorway, he heard three muffled electronic beeps. He reached into his shirt pocket and extracted the small electronic receiver. The red light on the front of the black box was flashing.

He cursed silently.

Someone was at the school. Someone had tripped the sensors he had installed on the perimeter of the ruins. He couldn't have anyone discovering the burying place. Not now. Not yet.

Not before he was done with Kasey.

He ran into the hallway. By his mental calculations, he needed two minutes to sprint across the dark field to his van and another ten minutes to speed through the empty highways to Buckthorn.

He wondered: who's there? Who's going inside?

Was it the police?

He didn't have time to think. He hurried to the top of the stairs, and then he froze.

Headlights swept across the downstairs rooms. A key scraped in the front door lock. Someone was coming inside the house. He was trapped.

Thirteen

Kasey let herself inside and closed the door behind her. The house was dark and unusually cold. Through the front window, she watched the tail lights of Maggie's truck disappear toward the highway. She kicked off her boots and padded in her black athletic socks through the landmine of toys in the family room. She poured herself a cup of cold coffee in the kitchen, but when she tasted it, she poured it out in the sink.

'Bruce?' she called.

There was no answer. She was alone. She dug in her back pocket for her cell phone and dialed his number. The call went straight into voicemail.

'It's me,' she said in her nervous, child-like voice. 'I figured you'd be back by now. Is everything OK? Call me as soon as you can.'

Kasey hung up. She untucked and unbuttoned the shirt of her uniform, letting it hang open. A draft snickered from under the basement door, making her shiver. It was the kind of house where all the windows and doors leaked cold air. She couldn't really complain, because the rent was dirt cheap. A farm widow had died here five years earlier, and the woman's family rented out the property now to cover their expenses. They didn't put much money into the place, but they didn't ask for a lot of money in return. She and Bruce had lived here since they moved to Duluth.

Her eyes kept blinking shut. She wanted to wait for Bruce to get back, but she couldn't think about anything but sleep. She had slept badly all year, and even a couple hours felt like bliss when she could get it. She frowned, seeing the dirty dishes in the sink, but decided they could wait until morning.

Kasey dragged herself upstairs. Her foot landed on a wet spot in the carpet, and she cursed as the water soaked through the fabric of her sock. She reached down and peeled it off, leaving one foot bare. She squeezed the damp sock like a stress ball as she wandered down the hallway into her bedroom. She tossed the sock into their dirty clothes basket and stripped off her shirt and undershirt, leaving herself in a sports bra and her uniform slacks. She began to unbuckle her gun belt, then stopped in surprise when she noticed her sexy nightgown stretched across their bed.

'Bruce?' she called again.

She waited and listened. There was no sound, but even in the silence, something felt wrong. She fingered the lace fringe of the nightgown and frowned. With a quick glance, she noticed that her closet door was wide open, which wasn't how she'd left it. Little hairs stood up on the back of her neck.

She poked her face into the hallway and studied the succession of doors. The office. The bathroom. The nursery. Something shiny attracted her eyes. In the crack of the bathroom doorway, she spotted a silver cylinder on the linoleum by the toilet. It was her Walgreens lipstick.

That was wrong, too. She'd left it on the sink.

Her skin rippled with a wave of fear. She nestled the butt of her gun in her palm and yanked it out of the holster. She crept toward the bathroom and nudged open the door with her toe. The tiny room was empty, but when she reached around and turned on the light, her eyes fixed on the blood-red message scrawled on the mirror.

BAD GIRL.

Kasey stumbled backward, and her bare foot landed in another damp spot on the carpet. She understood now. He had been up here, him and his wet shoes, leaving tracks.

'Where are you?' she screamed, like an animal that puffs its fur to appear larger than it is. 'I know you're here! This time I won't miss. This time I'll blow your goddamned head off!'

She pushed her toe in an arc across the carpet and found another wet footprint. And another. The trail led her toward the nursery.

Kasey pointed her gun at the door. Inside, she heard a noise now, like a deck of cards being shuffled. It was the sound of the wind slapping the vertical blinds together through an open window. She squatted down to peer under the door. Cold air roared through the crack and made her face cold. She put her eye to the carpet but didn't see anyone standing in the room.

Not waiting, she cocked her knee and kicked her heel into the door, connecting near the flimsy metal knob. The door flew round and banged into the wall, and Kasey stepped into the doorway and blocked the door with her shoulder as it bounced back. She surveyed the room. The crib, undisturbed. The pirate wallpaper. The baby monitor on top of the white dresser. The closet door, closed.

She eyed the window, which was open. The blinds danced and flapped crazily against each other as the night air swirled through the room. She made her way to the window frame, but with each step, she watched the closet door, in case the knob began to turn. At the window, she pushed the blinds aside and squinted at the darkness outside. She gauged the distance below her. It was a long way down, and the ground was hard.

The height was too far to jump, she realized, but by then it was too late.

She caught the movement out of the corner of her eye. The

closet door flew open. He was inside, tall, masked, dressed in black, the same way he had been two nights earlier. She turned to aim her gun, but he leaped across the narrow bedroom before she could bring her arm around. His momentum drove her into the window frame. His hand locked around her wrist and jammed her knuckles into the glass, which shattered and made stinging cuts across her skin. Instinctively, her fist uncurled, and her gun dropped away, tumbling past the window ledge to the ground below.

He backhanded her chin with his forearm. Her head snapped back, colliding hard with the wall. The impact rattled her teeth. Before she could clear her head, she was airborne; he lifted her bodily off the carpet and hurled her toward the opposite wall. Her feet hit the ground first, and she pitched forward into the closet. Her cheekbone struck the wooden floor.

Dazed and bleeding, she twisted on to her back. She expected him to throw himself on her, but instead, he watched her, frozen. His eyes were bright behind the mask. The intimacy of his expression made her sick. She suddenly felt exposed, as if he could see all her secrets, see past her clothes, see what she cared about and fantasized about. He knew exactly who she was, and it terrified her.

Then the moment passed, and he ran.

Kasey got dizzily to her feet. Distantly, she heard the thumping of his footfalls on the stairs, getting further away. She felt the pressure in the house change as the front door was ripped open.

He was gone. Everything fell silent again, except for the twisting of the blinds.

Kasey realized that she couldn't run away from him. He wouldn't let her. That was her last thought before she passed out.

Fourteen

As Serena hunted for Regan Conrad's home on Lismore Road, a black van approached from behind at extreme speed. One headlight was broken, but its single remaining beam grew blinding in her mirror like a searchlight. As the van careened past her Mustang in the adjacent lane, a rush of air pushed her toward the shoulder. The van continued east into the no-man's-land of farm towns like Stewart and Buckthorn, leaving her alone on the two-lane highway.

She slowed to a crawl at McQuade Road and scouted the numbers posted on the mailboxes on the opposite side of the rural road. Half a mile later, she spotted the address for Regan Conrad and turned into the nurse's long driveway. The houses in the countryside were built far back from the road, with several hundred yards of fields and trees separating neighbors. When she reached the house, she was surprised to find the kind of luxury country home that local professionals like doctors or lawyers afforded. Not nurses. A swimming pool, now closed for the season, sat amid a sprawling expanse of brown lawn. A multi-level redwood deck was built off the side of the house, with access from dual sets of French doors.

The living-room window was brightly lit with a broad bay window, but she didn't see anyone inside. She parked beyond the house, where the driveway ended, and got out. As she walked to the front door, she spotted two cars parked in front of the garage. One was a black Hummer. The other was a 1980s-era Ford Escort.

Serena rang the bell and waited nearly a minute before Regan Conrad opened the door a few inches and studied her suspiciously. From inside, Serena heard the bluesy strains of a soul singer on the stereo.

'May I help you?'

'Ms Conrad? My name is Serena Dial. I'm an investigator working for the Itasca County Sheriff's office on the disappearance of Marcus Glenn's daughter.'

Regan's mouth twisted into a frown. Her lipstick was so dark that her lips looked purple. 'What does that have to do with me?'

'I'd like to ask you some questions.'

'Why? Do you think I swooped in and stole the baby and I'm hiding her here in my house?'

'I don't know,' Serena said. 'Did you?'

Regan didn't answer, but a ghost of a smile flitted across her ivory face. She invited Serena inside with a flick of her hand. She led the way to the living room on her right, where the bay window overlooked the yard.

'I'll be back in a minute,' Regan told her.

Serena ran her hand along a sofa that had a plush, almost velvet finish. 'This is quite the place,' she said. 'Did you win the lottery?'

Regan stopped in the doorway and folded her arms over her chest. 'It was my break-up box, courtesy of a corporate lawyer from Minneapolis.'

She disappeared.

Serena examined the living room. Regan liked blown glass; there were several multi-colored bowls shaped like flowers. An original oil painting, abstract with thick squiggles of color, hung over the fireplace. From somewhere inside the house, the volume of the music increased. Serena realized there were hidden speakers in the living room. She recognized the singer now; it was Duffy belting out 'Mercy'. Just as the volume went up, she thought she heard something else, like a faint echo from another room. The noise didn't recur, but she wondered if the music was meant to drown it out.

She thought she had heard a baby crying.

Serena was on the verge of investigating when Regan re-appeared in the doorway with a glass of red wine. 'Do you want something to drink?' she asked.

'No.' She added, 'Did I hear a baby?'

'Only if you brought one with you,' Regan replied. 'Come on, we can talk in the library.'

Regan led her out of the living room into the foyer. Walking beside Regan, Serena finally had a chance to study the nurse up close. She wasn't as tall as Serena, and she had a gaunt but attractive face. Her skin was paper white and appeared even paler against the dark make-up on her eyes and mouth. She had a pierced lower lip, four earrings in her left ear, and three in her right. She wore a black tank top that hung straight down, barely swelled by her small breasts, and Serena saw an elaborate serpent tattoo stretching down her forearm to her bony wrist. The head of the snake poked out of Regan's shirt near her neck. Her black hair was short and spiky with strands of blue highlights. Serena guessed that she was about thirty years old.

'Do I look like a biker chick?' Regan asked, catching Serena's eye. 'Or just white trash?'

'More like a goth Kate Moss,' Serena said.

Regan smiled.

'You live out here alone?' Serena asked.

'That's right.'

'I hope you're careful.'

'I sleep with a shotgun by my bed,' Regan told her. 'I know how to use it.'

She led Serena into a small den and used a remote control to replay 'Mercy' on her iPod dock. She mouthed, 'Yeah, yeah, yeah' along with the background vocals on the song, and she did a slithery dance across the carpet and then settled into a leather recliner.

'You like Duffy?' she called over the music.

Serena nodded, but she winced at the volume. Regan pushed a button that muted the sound. The silence was startling.

'Better?'

'Thanks,' Serena said. She eyed the books on the shelves and saw a collection of homeopathic medical reference guides and cookbooks devoted to vegetarian and organic foods. The furnishings in the library, like the rest of the house, were upscale.

'I left most of the rooms the way my dickstick lawyer decorated them,' Regan explained. 'I like the idea that he and his fat wife spent years getting the house just the way she wanted it, and then he had to hand me the keys.'

'That's a pretty nice consolation prize for a busted affair,' Serena said.

'Well, if you're going to play fast and loose with your client's money, be careful who you tell. He liked to whisper secrets in my ear when he was fucking me.' She added, 'If you're a museum piece like Valerie Glenn, men want to make love to you. Me they like to fuck.'

'I heard you and Marcus Glenn were having an affair,' Serena said.

'That's not a secret.'

'I also heard he dumped you.'

'So what if he did?'

'Were you angry?' Serena asked.

'What do you think? I was furious. But I'm not exactly the girl you show off at the country club on Saturday nights.'

'People at the hospital call you unstable,' Serena said.

'Unstable? That's rich. His wife is the one who's unstable. Clinical depression. Meds.'

'Where did you hear that?'

'I told you, men like to tell me secrets. Marcus included.'

'You didn't look surprised to find the police on your doorstep,' Serena said.

'I'm not stupid. Exactly what is it you want to know, Ms Dial?'

'I want to know if Dr Glenn gave you a key to his house.'

Regan shrugged. 'Oh, I understand. No forced entry. No broken windows. Very suspicious. It must have been the crazy, jealous nurse.'

'The key,' Serena repeated.

'Why does it matter? I was nowhere near the Glenn mansion on Thursday night. I was working. Lots of people saw me.'

'So I hear.'

'Then why are you bothering me?' Regan asked.

'You blame Marcus for your break-up. You work with babies. A baby is missing.'

'I spend my *life* with moms and babies,' Regan retorted, jabbing a finger at Serena. 'I'm a nurse. A midwife. A counselor. I *help* women, Ms Dial.'

'Do you have children yourself?'

'I have hundreds. Every baby I've delivered or cared for is in some way mine.'

Serena leaned forward. 'That's an interesting thing to say.'

'Every nurse feels that way.'

'Were you in the ward when Valerie Glenn gave birth?' Serena asked.

'I was in the hospital that night, but I didn't assist.'

'But you were there?'

'I was there. So what?'

'Was that before or after Marcus dumped you?'

Regan's mouth made an angry slash. 'Before.'

'So was it hard for you to watch him and Valerie with their new child?' Serena asked. 'Did you know right then that he was going to give you up?'

'You don't know anything, Ms Dial. The baby didn't make any difference to Marcus.'

'Then why did he dump you?'

'Because a divorce would be too ugly. And expensive.'

'You hate Valerie Glenn, don't you?'

'She's exactly the kind of blonde rich bitch I despise. So what?'

'She convinced Marcus to drop you by the side of the highway like a bag of trash. That must have stung.'

Regan pointed a finger at the doorway. 'We're done talking.'

'You didn't tell me if you had a key to the Glenn house,' Serena said.

Regan stood up. 'OK. I did. But not anymore.'

'Where is it?'

'In a landfill. I didn't need it after Marcus and I split up. Now I'd like you to leave.'

Regan turned her back and stalked out of the library, and Serena followed. In the foyer, she yanked open the front door, and as Serena went past her, Regan grabbed her shoulder. 'Instead of interrogating me, you ought to be looking at the people who were *inside* the house that night, Ms Dial.'

'Meaning what?'

'Meaning you never asked me how I met Marcus. Aren't you curious?'

Serena nodded. 'How?'

'He came to me last year about that girl. The teenager in the trailer near Sago. Migdalia Vega.'

'What about her?'

'Marcus wanted me to help her. Off the books. He didn't want anyone to know.'

'Know what?' Serena asked.

'She was pregnant,' Regan told her. Then she pushed Serena out and slammed the door.

Serena sat in her Mustang in Regan Conrad's driveway. She pressed her cell phone to her ear to hear Jonny's voice through the static. The signal came and went unevenly this far north of the city. He sounded distant.

'Pregnant?' Stride said.

'That's what Regan says.'

'So what happened to Micki's baby?' he asked.

'I don't know. I think we should find out.'

'I'll talk to her,' Stride said. He added, 'Are you coming back here tonight?'

Serena hesitated. 'I thought I'd stay at our place.'

'Oh.'

'It's a two-hour drive at night,' she told him. 'And the deer are running.'

'I know. You're right, that's a good idea.'

'If you really want me to come back there, I will.'

'No, stay at home,' he said. 'I'll see you tomorrow.'

The silence told her that he had hung up.

She thought about calling him back, but she wasn't going to do that. It was easier to be alone. She turned on the Mustang. The radio station played a ballad by Trisha Yearwood. It was something sad, something about loss, with Trisha's voice so smooth that you didn't realize you wanted to cry. She turned it off, because she couldn't deal with the song, and she didn't want it going over and over in her head all night.

As Serena turned around and headed out of the long driveway, she noticed Regan Conrad staring at her from the bay window, with her hands planted fiercely on her hips. She also noticed that one of the two cars that had been parked in front of Regan's garage was gone. The Hummer was still there, but the old Escort had vanished.

Someone had been in the house. While Duffy begged for mercy, someone had used the music as cover to get away.

Fifteen

Nick Garaldo studied the silhouette of the ruined school across the open stretch of dirt and grass. He reached into the side pocket of his backpack and fitted a hands-free voice recorder over his ear. He tapped the switch and spoke softly.

'I'm outside the Buckthorn School. I'm preparing to make my assault.'

Nick emerged from the protection of the tall weeds lining the creek basin and picked his way through a minefield of dirty glass. He dug into his pocket for a handful of red pistachios. One by one, he pried apart the shells and popped the nuts into his mouth. As he chewed them, he sprinkled the shells on the ground. Pistachios were his weakness – he ate three bags a week – and his calling card, too. On every assault in the urban caves, he left a trail of salty red shells behind him. The Duluth Armory. The steam tunnels underneath the University of Minnesota. The abandoned mental hospital in Cambridge. The silos of a shuttered flour mill in the western prairies. He had invaded them all and signed his name with pistachios. It was his little joke for the police and the security firms that tried to catch him.

When he had scouted the old Buckthorn School over the summer, Nick wasn't concerned about access. The ruins were wide open for anyone who was brave or foolish enough to explore inside. But not now. He assumed that someone had been killed or raped at the site, and the liability had finally forced the township to shut up the building against marauders and post *No Trespassing* signs. The popular teen sport of tossing bricks through the glass of the old school was over. The windows were now boarded up, nailed shut with sturdy plywood. Chains and locks looped through the door handles. It wasn't going to be easy to get inside, but for Nick, that was part of the challenge.

He switched on his flashlight. The beam of light speared the bright eyes of a raccoon, which lumbered away into the field. He crunched through brick and rubble into the open lower level that had served as the plant for the school's utilities. Most of the foam ceiling tiles had fallen and decayed, and those that remained were water-stained and furry with mold. Electrical conduits dangled from the ceiling.

'They can lock it up, but they can't keep the kids out entirely,' he recited into his voice recorder. 'You've got cans of Budweiser, Big Mac boxes, and used condoms. God, who would be crazy enough to have sex in this cesspool?' Nick wrinkled his nose. 'There's a nasty smell, too. I think it's coming from upstairs.'

He did a reconnaissance of the stairwell leading up to the main level of the school but, like the windows, the concrete stairwell had now been sealed. He made a complete circle, navigating around fallen stonework and pipes. He never noticed the black box cemented to the stairwell or the red light that flashed once as he crossed through an electronic beam.

Nick retreated to the field behind the school and made his way up the grassy slope at the northwest corner so that he was on the same level as the main floor of the school. He ate more red pistachios and tossed the shells. He followed the wall of the school, stepping over a rusted radiator that lay on its side like a lazy pig. A row of sixteen windows cut through the brick wall. He could reach up and touch them with his hand but, like all the others, the windows were sealed. He turned the next corner, stirring a nest of blackbirds that startled him as they screeched and flew away in a huff of wings and feathers.

From where he was, he was now visible to traffic on Township Road but, so far, he hadn't seen a single car. He pointed a flashlight beam toward the high end of the wall, where five sets of windows stretched in a row to the front of the school. The plywood on two of the windows was loose, thanks to rain dripping from the roof and rotting the wood. The windows were frosted and square, large enough to allow him to squeeze through, but they were set at least twenty feet above the ground.

Nick continued to the front of the school, where a large sinkhole marked a section of the building that had burned down. He hauled himself up on the jagged edge of a low concrete wall. Minding his balance, he grabbed the edge of the roof and pulled himself up far enough to swing his leg on to the tar surface. He completed the climb and found himself on the roof of one of the lower wings of the building, abutting the brick wall where the plywood hung loose from the window.

He ripped off the plywood so easily that he almost fell. Half of the frosted panels on the window had long since been broken in. He leaned through the open space and examined the interior with his flashlight. The beam illuminated steel braces and the backdrop of what had once been a basketball frame. He was breaking into the school auditorium.

'Here we go,' Nick said.

He removed a coil of rope from his backpack and secured it to a steel pipe on the exterior wall of the auditorium, then threw the rest of the rope through the window where it dropped to the floor below. Hanging on to the rope with gloved hands, he pushed himself through the gap, bracing his legs against the inside wall. Inch by inch, he worked his way down the wall until his feet splashed into a puddle of cold water at the floor. He let go.

'I'm inside the ruins,' he said.

With the windows covered over, the interior of the school was darker than the night outside. He listened to the dripping of water and felt it spatter on his face. Somewhere in the great space, he heard a familiar squeal. Rats. He couldn't see them, but he knew they were there, scrabbling through the stagnant water.

Then there was the smell.

Now that he was inside, it was ferocious, like rotting meat in the hot sun, so strong and nauseating that he had to pinch his nose shut with his fingers. He wanted to gag, and even when he breathed open-mouthed, the stench rose up anyway through his nasal passages.

'Something's dead in here,' Nick said.

He waved the beam of his flashlight ahead of him. The floor was a mess of ventilation pipes, wire netting, and steel I-frames. The interior walls had gaping, jagged holes where bricks had caved in like missing teeth. He took fragile steps toward a doorway on the far side of the auditorium. Dark shapes scurried in and out of the puddles and hid inside the pipes as he came closer. He saw red eyes in the tunnel of light.

The doorway led to a narrow hall, where the line of dark, boarded-up windows stretched along the wall. Glass littered the floor. He shivered from the cold and dampness. The smell, as he moved down the hallway, got even worse. So did the gathering of rats.

Nick stopped.

It was impossible to move silently through the debris, and for a moment he was certain he had heard the clatter of someone else's footsteps on the far side of the school. He waited to see if the noise would recur, but a minute passed, and it didn't. He told himself he was letting the place get the best of his imagination. He was alone. No one else would dare to be inside.

When two more minutes of silence passed, he kept going.

He reached a doorway leading to a smaller room, where a broken wall of cinder blocks rose to the ceiling like a honeycomb. His flashlight shone on a row of concrete beams. Green algae bloomed on the floor. In this room, the smell soared, feeding rancid decay into the air. He covered the whole lower half of his face with his gloved hand, but he couldn't extinguish the stink. The rats were bolder here, running back and forth in front of him. Urgent. Excited. Hungry.

Four feet away, where the light made an arc on the floor, he saw them.

Six bare feet.

Nick lifted the flashlight and then dropped it and shouted. The flashlight fell and broke, bathing the room in darkness, but it couldn't erase the awful image from his brain. Three women, naked, were tied to old-fashioned school chairs. Their skin was bloodless and white, where they still had skin. Most of it had been eaten away, exposing muscle, organs, and bone. Rats scampered on the desks and in their laps and across their shoulders and breasts.

'FUCK FUCK FUCK!'

Nick backed up and staggered like a blind man, hands outstretched, colliding with the concrete pillars as he hunted for an escape. His feet tripped on debris, and he fell, cutting his hands and arms on sharp metal. His skin grew slippery with his own blood. He pushed himself up and felt along the wall until it ended, and he spilled into another hallway, tunneling through a house of horrors.

'Help!'

He reached out with his spread fingers, and his hand found the bat-shaped remnants of broken glass in one of the windows.

He hammered his bloody palm on the plywood nailed to the outer wall, but the stiff wood refused to yield to his panicked blows. He wailed for someone to hear him in the lonely land outside.

'*Help! Oh my God, help me!*'

Behind him, out of the darkness, a human hand clapped on his shoulder. Nick screamed and spun. A flashlight dazzled his eyes. He saw the shadow of someone tall and large looming over him like a bear, and he thought for an instant he'd been rescued.

'Oh, thank God,' Nick cried.

His relief was short-lived. A fist as hard and strong as a brick hit his face and snapped his head against the peaks of glass. The light in his eyes went black. Nick tasted pistachios again and realized his mouth was filled with bile. His knees buckled, but as he fell, a powerful forearm locked around his neck, choking him and jerking him off the ground.

His chest roared, bellowing for air.

His legs kicked and flailed.

As he struggled, the cold and the stench slowly disappeared and left him in a vacuum of perfect silence. He floated away from the pain and, eventually, he floated so far that he felt nothing at all. He was somewhere else entirely, listening to water drip like the ticking of seconds on a clock. He was in a cave that he had all to himself. He was exploring.

PART TWO

FRAGILE SOULS

Sixteen

On Sunday morning, the third day after Callie Glenn disappeared, frustration began to seep into the police war room in downtown Grand Rapids. Stride had seen it before. The first forty-eight hours were an adrenaline rush of urgency and determination. The phones rang incessantly. Emails flew back and forth among agencies throughout the state. Leads overwhelmed the system the way a sudden downpour overflows the sewer drains. No one complained because every contact in those precious early hours was an opportunity to break the case open.

Find a baby girl. Bring her home.

By Sunday, however, the lack of progress began to suck oxygen out of the investigation. Everyone knew that time was an enemy, and the enemy was winning. Two hours after a kidnapping, you can draw a small circle on a map and estimate the maximum area in which a missing person is likely to be found. You can set up road blocks. Canvass the region. Ten hours later, the diameter of the circle grows by hundreds of miles, bulging past the resources of the police to enclose and investigate it. Two days later, the universe of hiding places is essentially limitless.

Stride hoped that Callie Glenn was still alive somewhere

within northern Minnesota, but the reality was that she could be anywhere by now.

He pored over hundreds of contact reports, hunting for a needle in a haystack. The tiny office on the third floor of the county headquarters was knee-deep in paper and littered with empty coffee cups and food wrappers. He knew that the dimensions of the search forced them to rely on a simple philosophy: do the right things, and hope they got lucky. If they were going to find Callie, someone had to remember the girl's face. Someone had to see her and make the call, and the police – wherever they were – had to make the right follow-through. He could manage the process, but Stride and the small team inside the Sheriff's Department couldn't have eyes and ears everywhere.

After an hour, he pushed the papers aside and got up and wiped the whiteboard hung on the opposite wall. His instinct was to go back to what really happened on Thursday night. Figure out *why* and *how* Callie disappeared. With a black marker, he drew a line down the center of the board and then wrote OUTSIDE on one half of the board and INSIDE on the other half.

Those were the two possibilities. Someone from outside the house came and stole Callie, or someone inside the house took her away. Underneath the OUTSIDE header, he scribbled several bullet points:

- Stranger or local?
- Had to be Callie or could have been any baby?
- Ransom or other motive?
- Needed to *get to house, get in, get away*
- Alive or dead?
- Where is she now?

Underneath the INSIDE header, he wrote different comments:

- Alive or dead?
- Accident or murder?
- Marcus or Micki? (Both?)
- Where is she now?

Stride stared at what he had written. In the past two days, his team had reconstructed the movements of Marcus and Valerie Glenn – and their baby – over the five days leading up to the disappearance. Members of the Grand Rapids Police and the Itasca County Sheriff's Department had checked every building, house, store, and street in Grand Rapids and Duluth visited by the Glenns during that time, hoping to find a witness who remembered something or someone unusual. The follow-up was continuing, but so far they had no credible evidence of an intruder watching the Glenns or their home.

He wasn't surprised. Grand Rapids was a small town. Even Duluth was small compared to a large urban center like Minneapolis. He doubted that a stranger could identify a target and plan a kidnapping in such a tightly knit region without leaving some kind of trail for them to follow.

So maybe it wasn't a stranger. Maybe it was someone who already knew the Glenns, their baby, and their home. But if that were true, he didn't know how someone local could hope to hide a stolen baby for any length of time without being discovered. How long could you really do that? A week? A month? Sooner or later, someone would expose the secret.

Assuming that Callie was still alive. If not, it was easy to hide a body in the northern woods.

The other question was *why*. Why would an outsider go through such risk and trouble to abduct Callie Glenn? There had been no ransom demands, and Grand Rapids was an unlikely locale in which to scout designer babies or white slaves. Not that Stride could entirely rule it out. Evil had a way of reaching its fingers even into the remote corners of the world.

He turned his attention to the INSIDE half of the board, which in his mind offered a simpler and more plausible explanation of the crime. Either Marcus Glenn or Migdalia Vega had used the time between ten thirty and one o'clock to make Callie disappear. He had a much easier time ascribing possible motives to either of them, and he had evidence in hand that both had been lying, or at the very least hiding important aspects of their relationship.

Stride knew he needed to talk to them again, and he chose to start with Micki. She was the weak link.

He grabbed his leather jacket and took the stairs to the ground floor. His car was parked on the street outside. He headed southeast on Highway 2, where there was no traffic to slow him down. It was Sunday; everyone was in church. As he drove, he finally thought about the one subject he kept trying to push from his mind.

Serena.

Last night he had slept alone. Actually, he had tossed and turned in the empty bed. He had thought of Serena at home in their cottage in Duluth, and the distance between them made him feel as if she were another of the pieces of his life stranded on the far side of the canyon. He could imagine her face, hear her voice, and feel the softness of her skin, and yet for all that, she had become flat. Two-dimensional. Like everything else in his world. He told himself that he was in love with her, but he didn't feel it, because he didn't feel anything.

When his phone rang, he thought it might be Serena, and he wondered what he would say to her. Instead it was Maggie.

'Hey, boss,' she said brightly. 'I miss your face.'

Stride relaxed and smiled. 'Back at you, Mags. What's going on?'

'I have a quick update on the farmlands case. I offered kinky favors to one of the techs down at BCA to bump our blood sample to the top of the list.'

'Good.'

'He's gay, by the way, so I told him you'd pay up, not me. Hope that's OK.'

'Anything for the team,' he told her.

'I thought you'd feel that way. Anyway, I got the results back, and it's bad news. No hits. He's not in the system.'

'Damn.'

'Yeah, nothing ever comes easy.'

'How's Troy Grange doing?' Stride asked. 'You saw him yesterday, right?'

'He's hurting. His oldest girl is a wreck, and he had to leave the baby with his in-laws. I told him not to give up hope, but he knows the score. Trisha's not coming back.'

'Yeah.'

'Speaking of tough guys,' Maggie said, 'how are you?'

'Me? I'm fine.' The same old lie.

'A little bird told me you weren't so good.'

Stride tensed. 'You talked to Serena?'

'Uh huh.'

'It's no big deal,' he said.

'It sounded like a big deal to me. And to her.'

'I don't really want to talk about it, Mags.'

'Yeah, well, that's just too damn bad,' she snapped. 'You think you can blow me off like that? I'm your best friend.'

'I know that, but this isn't easy for me—'

'I don't care if it's easy or hard. What the hell is going on with you?'

Stride closed his eyes and opened them again. The empty highway spilled off the edge of the horizon. 'It's not Serena. It's me. I'm struggling.'

'Give me details.'

He didn't know what to say. 'I wish I could, Mags. I may as well be dead. I don't care about anything. Not a damn thing.'

'I don't like to hear you talking like that,' she said.

'Neither do I.'

Maggie was silent. Stride slowed and turned off the highway as he reached the intersection that led toward the rural town of Sago. A cloud of dirt rose behind his tires and trailed him down the deserted road.

'When are you coming back to Duluth?' she asked.

'I've got a couple meetings at City Hall the day after tomorrow.'

'I want to see you.'

'I appreciate the thought, but there's nothing you can do. This is my problem.'

'Don't be such a hero. Get an early start. I'll make you breakfast.'

'You?' Stride asked.

'Damn right. A couple sausage McMuffins and some of that twisty cinnamon roll kind of stuff.'

Stride laughed. 'OK.'

'I'll see you Tuesday morning.' She added, 'And hey, can I tell you something?'

'Sure.'

'I'm sorry I wasn't with you.'

'What are you talking about?'

He heard her voice catch with emotion, which was unusual for Maggie. 'On the bridge. I'm sorry I wasn't there when you fell. That was the hardest thing for me, not being there when you needed me.'

'There's nothing you could have done,' Stride said.

'Maybe, but I'm still sorry.'

Stride thumped his fist on the aluminum door of Micki Vega's trailer. Curtains were drawn across the windows, but he saw her pickup truck parked in the dirt nearby, and he smelled bacon frying. When no one answered, he pounded again.

'Micki, it's Lieutenant Stride. Open up!'

He heard the rattle of a chain as Micki unlatched the door and peered out. Her dark hair was loose and frizzy. She had bloodshot eyes. She wore flannel pajama bottoms and a pink halter top. Her feet were bare.

'You woke up my mama,' she told him, her voice cross.

'You didn't answer.'

'I thought it was that damn chica from the papers. Blair Rowe. She's been hassling me all weekend. Did you tell her about me?'

'No.'

'Well, she found out anyway. I'm fucked.'

'I need to talk to you, Micki,' Stride said.

'Talk about what?'

'Callie Glenn.'

'I already told you everything I know, which ain't much. Leave me alone, OK?'

'I have more questions. Can I come inside?'

'Hell, no. I don't want you bothering my mama.'

'Then put on some clothes and come out here.'

Micki scowled. 'Whatever.'

He waited for her in the middle of the dirt road. Through the slanted trunks of the birch trees, he could see the slope of the Sago Cemetery fifty yards away. Dots of snow flurries drifted in the air and landed on his skin in cold flecks. It was a quiet morning, with almost no wind. The trees seemed to be holding their breath.

Micki joined him two minutes later. She'd shoved her feet into boots, and she wore a blue down coat. Her black hair spilled messily over the collar. She took bites from a bagel and a crispy piece of bacon.

'So what do you want?' she demanded, her mouth full.

'I know about your baby,' he said.

Micki blanched. She stopped chewing, and a few crumbs

clung to the side of her mouth, which she wiped with her sleeve. Her cheeks flushed with anger. 'Fuck you. That's private.'

'Callie Glenn is missing, and now I find out that you had a baby that no one knows about. Coincidences like that make me suspicious.'

'Who told you?' Micki asked.

'It doesn't matter.'

'Yeah, nothing matters when you're trailer trash, right? Other people get to scream about their privacy. Not me.'

'Where's your baby?' Stride asked.

'I don't have to tell you a thing.'

'Is he inside the trailer?'

Micki jabbed a finger toward the cemetery. 'He's in the ground. Are you happy?'

'I'm sorry,' he said. 'Tell me what happened.'

'What's to tell? I got knocked up. I couldn't afford the pill, and I was dating a guy who thought rubbers were for homos. I learned my lesson. My knees stay shut from now on.'

'Who was the father?' Stride asked.

'Nobody. Some farm kid.'

'I think it was Marcus Glenn,' he said.

'Dr Glenn? Are you crazy? No way. I told you I'm not sleeping with him.'

'So how did he get involved?'

Micki shoved her hands in her coat pockets. 'When I found out I was pregnant, I didn't know what to do. I don't have any insurance. I wanted to get rid of it, but Mama said that was a sin. So I asked Dr Glenn for help.'

'What did he do?'

'He knew I couldn't go to a hospital, so he arranged for a nurse to come here. She was supposed to deliver the baby, too, but I never made it that far.'

'How far along were you when you lost him?'

'Three months,' Micki said. 'It was just one of those things. I didn't do anything wrong.'

'When was this?'

'Last summer. August.'

'So Valerie Glenn was already pregnant when you miscarried?'

'How should I know? I mean, I guess she was, but I didn't know. Dr Glenn never talked about his wife having a baby.'

'What did you do with your child?' Stride asked.

Micki's eyes flashed. 'I buried him.'

'What about the nurse? What was her name?'

'Nurse Regan. She was a scary bitch to look at, but she was nice. Even after I lost the baby, she came back to help me. My head was all screwed up, and she told me it's normal to feel that way.'

'Did you know that she was having an affair with Dr Glenn?' Stride asked.

Micki looked genuinely shocked. 'Dr Glenn and Nurse Regan? No, I didn't know that.'

'Did you ever see them together?'

'Sure, a couple of times, he drove her here to see me. That doesn't mean anything.'

'Has Regan Conrad been in touch with you recently?'

'Me? No. Why would she?'

Stride didn't hear a lie in her voice. 'I'm sorry, Micki, that must have been a terrible experience for you.'

She shrugged. 'I was upset, but God calls the shots, not me.'

'Where did you bury your son?' he asked.

'On the other side of the road,' she said after a long pause. 'It happens a lot around cemeteries, you know. My mama and I hear noises out here at night, and I'll find places where the dirt's been dug up.'

'People bury things in the woods?' Stride asked.

'Yeah. Sure. I keep a collection of things I find out there.

Photos of pets. Silly stuff like rings and corks from wine bottles. I think it makes people feel better to bury something near the cemetery. Like they figure God is nearby. If you dig in the trees, I bet you'd find a lot of bones.'

Seventeen

Serena found Valerie Glenn at her sister's home on Sunday after-noon. Denise Sheridan and her husband lived in downtown Grand Rapids, on a forested lot near the river. It was a small home for a family with four children. Its wood siding was dirty and needed paint, and several of the red roof shingles were missing. A fishing boat sat on a rusted trailer by the side of the house, and the yard was strewn with old toys. Half a dozen mature pines dwarfed the house and blocked it from the street.

Denise answered the door. Her face was pinched and impatient. When she saw Serena, she jerked a thumb down the hallway behind her. 'Valerie and Tom are in the living room. I've got to check on my youngest.' She lowered her voice and added, 'Do you have anything new?'

Serena shook her head.

Denise frowned and went upstairs, where Serena could hear the squeal of children. She found her way to the living room, which was a boxy space, crowded with old furniture. An upright piano was pushed against one wall, with stacks of sheet music piled on the bench. A little boy, no more than five years old, sat on the floor, humming as he pushed a red crayon around an illustration of a cow in a coloring book. The house smelled of burnt toast.

Valerie Glenn sat on the leather sofa, looking luminously out of place. Her clothes, her make-up, her hair, were all perfect. By contrast, the leather where she rested her slim arm was worn, with cuts and punctures bruising the surface. She had a sad, far-away smile as she watched the boy playing on the floor at her feet.

A man sat next to Valerie and held her hand. He was about forty years old, with gray strands lining his brown hair and a neatly trimmed beard. He wasn't heavy, but he had the stocky shoulders and slight beer gut of a typical Grand Rapids outdoorsman. His jeans had a frayed hole in the pocket, and the sleeves of his sweatshirt were rolled up past his elbows.

'Oh, hello, Serena,' Valerie murmured, looking up as she saw her in the doorway. 'Have you met Tom Sheridan?'

'I haven't.'

Tom got up from the sofa. He was a big man, but his handshake was gentle. 'I'm Denise's husband.'

'And who's this?' Serena asked, squatting down in front of the boy on the floor.

'This is Evan,' Tom said. 'Evan, can you say hello?'

The boy didn't look up from his work on the coloring book. 'Hello.'

Serena laughed and straightened up. 'You have a budding artist,' she said.

'I just wish he didn't practice on the bedroom walls,' Tom replied. He sat down again and put a comforting arm around Valerie's shoulder. With a glance at his sister-in-law, he said to Serena, 'I hate to be the bad guy here, but we're getting frustrated.'

'I understand. So are we.'

'How could Callie just vanish into thin air?' Tom asked.

'Believe me, we're doing everything we can to find her,' Serena said.

'I know the drill, Ms Dial. I'm married to the law. I know you can't snap your fingers and get answers for us. But I'd be lying if I didn't tell you how worried and impatient we all are. Every day makes Callie feel further away.'

Valerie glanced at the television in the corner of the room. The sound was low. 'Is there anything you can do about the media?' she asked. 'I know it's free speech and all, but I feel like they're trying to destroy our family. Did you see Blair Rowe last night? She was spreading all these lies about Marcus. Who's going to look for Callie if they think that my husband is a monster?'

'The best advice I can give you is not to watch,' Serena said. 'Even if it's garbage and gossip, it helps having Callie's photo on the news night after night. The more people who see it, the more likely we are to find her.'

'She's right, Valerie,' Denise said, strolling into the living room behind Serena. She moved a stack of children's books from the cushion of a recliner and dropped into the chair with a groan. She chewed a fingernail and contemplated her sister. 'I know Blair Rowe. She's a wet-behind-the-ears brat who thinks this is her big break. Forget about her.'

Tom Sheridan looked at his wife with concern. 'How's Maureen?'

Denise shrugged. 'Fine.'

'Our youngest has Down's syndrome,' Tom explained. 'She doesn't hear well, and she becomes quite agitated if she wakes up from a nap and one of us isn't around.'

'You don't need to share our life story,' Denise snapped.

'It's nothing to be ashamed about,' Tom said.

Denise's eyes shot daggers at her husband. 'Did I say I was ashamed?' She bent over and closed her son's coloring book. 'Evan, can you take this to your room, please? Thank you.'

There was silence among the adults in the room while the boy gathered his crayons and headed upstairs. Denise watched him go, her arms folded over her chest. 'Honestly, Tom, what are you thinking? Talking like that in front of the kids.'

'I'm sorry.'

Denise didn't reply.

'Maureen's condition has been a struggle for us,' Tom continued, with an apologetic smile at Serena. 'As if four kids weren't enough of a challenge to begin with.'

'Oh, for God's sake,' Denise barked. She flew out of the recliner and stomped through the swinging doors that led to the kitchen. The doors flapped madly before slowing down. Serena heard the clatter of pans and the exaggerated noise of cupboard doors opening and closing.

'I'm really sorry about this,' Tom told her. 'Bad day.'

'Don't worry about it.'

Valerie stood up. 'I suppose you'd like to talk to me.'

'Yes, I would.'

She nodded and bent down to hug her brother-in-law. 'Thanks for everything, Tom. Really.'

Tom held on to her hand. 'Call if you need anything at all, OK?'

'I will,' Valerie said. She said to Serena, 'Shall we take a walk?'

Outside Denise's house, Serena and Valerie wandered to the end of the block and on to the middle of the bridge that crossed over the river. Flurries landed in their hair, and the cold raised a flush on their faces. Valerie leaned on the railing and stared at the dark water. She knit her fingers together.

'I owe you an apology,' she said.

'Why is that?'

'The first time I saw you, I told you that you couldn't understand how I felt because you didn't have children. It was a stupid thing to say.'

'Don't worry about it.'

'Well, I felt like an idiot after you left. I'm sorry. I'm the last person who should make another woman feel bad about not having kids. I tried for three years before I got pregnant, and it was the worst kind of hell for me.'

'I'm sure it was.'

'I'd like to tell you that Marcus was a comfort in all of it, but I'm afraid that's not his specialty. It's funny, isn't it? Marcus is in a healing profession, and Tom sells insurance, and which one is a better listener?'

'Denise and Tom look like they're having problems,' Serena said.

Valerie nodded. 'They've been sweethearts since high school, but somewhere along the line, Denise forgot that they were supposed to be in love.'

'What about you and Marcus?' Serena asked.

A sad smile drifted across Valerie's face. 'We've never been the best of couples. I thought having a baby would bring us closer together. Or maybe I wanted a baby to give me the kind of love that my husband couldn't. Not that I blame him – that's just the man he is. But three years of trying and failing? The longer it went on, the more desperate I became.' She gave Serena a sideways glance. 'I don't come across as a desperate woman, do I? Honestly, if Callie hadn't come along, I don't know what I would have done. She saved me.'

'I have an unpleasant question for you,' Serena said.

Valerie turned around and leaned against the railing. She stared at the cold blue sky. 'Those seem to be the only kind of questions you have.'

'I know. I'm sorry.'

'That's all right, go ahead.'

'Do you know a nurse at St Mary's named Regan Conrad?'

Valerie looked down at the water. 'Is that her? Is she the one that Marcus . . . ?'

'Yes.'

'I'm sorry, no, I don't know her. She must not be in orthopedics. I know all of the staff where Marcus works.'

'She works in maternity,' Serena said.

Valerie turned her head sharply. 'Maternity?'

'That's right.'

Valerie cupped her hands over her nose and mouth. She shook her head. 'I knew it. I knew she was there.'

'What do you mean?'

Valerie brought her hands down to her chin, so it looked as if she was praying. 'I went into the hospital on New Year's Eve,' she told Serena. 'There were only a few other women in the ward that night, and one of the babies was in distress, so most of the nursing staff weren't really focused on me. We were waiting for my doctor to get there from a party, and they had me on an epidural. I was drifting in and out a lot of the time. I remember, it must have been right after midnight. There was a lot of noise, people blowing those little horns, shouting about the New Year. I woke up, and I was alone, but I knew she'd been there. I smelled her perfume. It was the same perfume I'd smelled in my bed all those times. Ever since then, I thought it was my imagination, but she must have come to see me.' Valerie shivered.

'Was Marcus with you at the hospital that night?' Serena asked.

'Off and on,' she replied, with a hint of defensiveness. 'I told you, I slept a lot because of the drugs.'

'Of course.'

Valerie shook her head. 'She was there in my room. On that night of all nights. My God, tell me he didn't . . .'

'What?'

'Nothing. It's nothing. Why did you want to know about Regan? Do you think it's possible she could have taken Callie?'

'I honestly don't know. I'm trying to find out everything I can about her. It looks like she was in the hospital on Thursday night when Callie was abducted, but that doesn't necessarily mean she wasn't involved. She had a key to your house, too. She also knows – well, she also knows Migdalia.'

'She knows *Micki*? Oh, Jesus. I knew it. I never trusted her.'

'It doesn't mean that Micki was involved in what happened to Callie,' Serena said. 'But we're looking at both of them.' She added, 'Did you know that Micki lost a baby last year?'

'Micki? I had no idea.'

'Your husband helped her. Regan was the nurse.'

Valerie spun away. She bent so far over the railing that Serena was afraid she would throw herself into the river. 'Marcus did that?'

'Yes.'

'Was it his baby?' she asked, her voice bitter.

'Micki says no.'

Valerie opened her mouth and closed it again. She hugged herself, shivering. 'I'm sorry, what does any of this mean?'

'We're not sure. It may be nothing at all. But I have to tell you, I'm concerned that Marcus has been keeping things from us. He never mentioned his relationship with Regan, and he concealed the fact that Micki was with him on the night Callie disappeared.'

'You think he was involved, don't you?' Valerie asked. 'You think he did something to our daughter.'

'I'm *not* saying that,' Serena told her. 'But we're going to ask him some hard questions, and we want him to take a polygraph.'

'I can't believe this.'

'Valerie, people hide things for all sorts of reasons. Don't leap to conclusions. If we can use a polygraph to prove that Marcus *wasn't* involved, we can shift our focus elsewhere. We can take a closer look at Regan and Micki, too.'

Valerie pushed past Serena on the bridge. 'I have to go.'

'Please, wait.'

'I'm sorry. I can't deal with this right now.'

Serena called after her, but Valerie kept walking, not looking back. She walked with her head down and her hands in her pockets. At the end of the bridge, she began to run, with her long blonde hair flowing messily behind her. She ran until she disappeared behind the pine trees lining the street, where Serena couldn't see her anymore.

Eighteen

At midnight on Sunday, Stride turned off the lights in the war room. Standing in the dark office, he glanced at the streets of Grand Rapids, which were empty under the glow of neon signs and stop lights. The flurries had lasted most of the day and left behind a dusting of snow on the grass. He shrugged on his leather jacket and locked the office door as he left. As he waited for the elevator, he ran both hands through his wavy hair, massaging his scalp. He had a fierce headache and wanted nothing more than a few hours of sleep.

The elevator doors opened, but before he could go inside, he collided with a short, skinny woman barreling through the doors.

'Oh!' Blair Rowe chirped. 'Lieutenant Stride! They told me you were still here.'

He shook his head. 'I'm not here, Blair. This is a recording. Leave a message, and check back with me in the morning.'

She giggled. 'That's funny. You're cute. No, I've got something for you. You *have* to see this.'

'How'd you get up here, Blair?' Stride asked. 'I left shoot-on-sight orders downstairs.'

'Funny again! But don't forget, I went to high school with half the cops in the building.' She held up a circular cookie tin. 'Plus, my mom made peanut butter blossoms. No man can say no to these babies. You want one?'

'No.'

'Oh, lighten up, Lieutenant!' Blair scolded him. 'I'm doing my part. I'm keeping you clued in. This is going to be on Headline News in the morning, but I thought *you* would want to see it first. See? I'm a team player.' She dug into the pocket of her navy blue trench coat and waved a DVD at him.

'What is it?'

'It's hot. You know how they say everything that happens in Vegas, stays in Vegas? Not this time. One of our reporters found a stripper who says she sleeps with Marcus Glenn on his trips to Sin City. She's got some juicy quotes.'

Stride didn't want to be surprised in the morning. 'Yeah, all right. Come with me. Let's put it on.'

They returned to the office halfway down the hall, where Stride turned on the lights and dropped his coat on the back of a chair. Blair tottered on her heels, and her eyes drifted to the stacks of paper littered around the room.

'No spying on anything in here,' he told her. 'Got it?'

'Yeah, OK. Did you see me on the air last night?'

'I did. You better be careful, Blair. You pretty much accused Marcus Glenn of murdering his daughter. You're going to get sued if you keep it up.'

Blair shrugged. 'Oh, I say "alleged" and all those other weasel words. All I do is point out the facts.' She peeled the lid off the cookie tin and pulled out a round peanut butter cookie with a chocolate kiss pressed in the center. She popped the whole thing in her mouth and chewed. 'You sure you don't want one?'

'I'm sure.'

She licked her fingers and studied him through her thick glasses. 'How do I look, by the way? The network paid for my hair and make-up. Pretty smokin', huh?'

Stride realized that Blair did look more polished now. Her hair, which had been dirty and stringy when he first met her, was now cut, swirled, and sprayed into place. Her once-blotchy skin was smooth and pink. 'You're looking good, Blair.'

'Good? That's the best you can do?'

He pointed at the DVD in her hand and then at the television stand in the corner. 'What's on the disk?'

Blair popped the disk into the DVD player on the shelf below the television. 'This is an interview that a Las Vegas reporter did with a black bombshell down there this afternoon. She strips at a club north of downtown. Her name's Lavender-something.'

'Lavender?'

'Yeah.'

Stride chuckled. 'How did this reporter find her?'

'She came to him. She saw the story about Callie on the news.'

As the video rolled, Lavender filled the screen. She had straightened black hair and full, pale pink lips, with white teeth that looked capped. She tapped a long fingernail against her cheek impatiently as the camera man took his time to get focused, scrolling up her long legs and lingering on the surgically enhanced breasts filling her T-shirt.

'*How did you meet Marcus Glenn?*' the reporter asked.

'*He's a regular at the strip club where I work. He's in Vegas three, four times a year.*'

'*What's he like?*'

Lavender's broad lips curled into a smile. '*He's a doctor, baby. Doctors have the whole God thing going on. When they screw you, it's like they're delivering the seed of the Savior, know what I mean?*'

Blair laughed. 'I love that part.'

'*So this was a sexual relationship you had with Marcus Glenn?*'

'Oh, yeah.'

'Did you know he was married?'

'Sure. I like it that way. No strings. They don't come around on one knee with a ring. It's expensive dinners, a few sweaty rides, and then they go home.'

'Was this a . . . paid relationship?'

Lavender's eyes flashed with anger. 'Nobody buys me.'

'Yeah, except for the lobster dinners and the bling,' Blair commented.

'Did Marcus Glenn tell you much about his personal life?'

'Not a lot. Men in Vegas are looking to forget what they've got back home, you understand? But I saw a photo he had of his wife. She was a looker. One time I asked him if his wife wasn't enough for him, if that's why he was with me.'

'What did he say?'

'He said you only use the good china on special occasions.' Lavender's laugh was deep and throaty.

Stride winced, imagining this video on the news, knowing it would drive a knife through Valerie Glenn's heart. He didn't have any sympathy for Marcus Glenn. Stride just hated the collateral damage that always seemed to strike families when they became crime victims. It wasn't enough to lose a daughter. Now Valerie Glenn had to face the hollow reality of her marriage.

'This is the good part,' Blair told him. 'Listen.'

'You know about Marcus Glenn's daughter? That she's missing?'

'Missing. Yeah, that's what he says. I don't believe it.'

'What do you mean?'

'I saw Marcus in the spring. April, I think. He let slip over dinner that his wife had had a baby a few months earlier. So what am I going to say? I told him congratulations.'

'What did he say?'

'He said it was his wife's idea. He said he would have been a hell of a lot happier if the baby had never been born at all.'

'Never been born? He used those words?'

'Yeah, he did. Honestly, for me, that was the end. Next time he was in town, I ducked him. As far as cheating goes, boys will be boys, OK? But any man says that about his own kid, I don't want him in my bed.'

Blair hit the stop button on the machine and ejected the disk. 'That's it. Does that freeze your blood or what? I told you Glenn was a cold character.'

'Are you going to run that?' Stride asked.

'You bet. Tomorrow morning. I tried to get one or both of the Glenns on camera too, but they won't talk.'

'I'd like a copy of the disk,' Stride told her.

'Sure. How about a quote for my story? Or better yet, a live interview?'

'Not yet.'

Blair's face wrinkled in frustration. 'Seems like this source stuff is all one-way, Lieutenant. I'm giving you dirt, you're giving me squat.'

'When I have something, you're first in line,' Stride said.

'Yeah, promises, promises. So what do you think, anyway? Does this change your mind about Marcus Glenn?'

'Off the record?'

'If it has to be.'

Stride stuck a hand in the cookie tin and pulled out a peanut butter blossom, which he ate in two bites, saving the chocolate kiss for last. 'You're right, these are good cookies,' he said. Then he added, 'Off the record, Marcus Glenn has been lying since day one. I'd like to know why. I'd like to know what he's hiding.'

Nineteen

Stride removed his clothes silently in the bedroom of the cabin. He saw the moonlit glow of Serena's bare shoulder above the blanket, but he wasn't sure if she was asleep. When he was naked, he slid under the blanket and lay on his back with his hands laced behind his head. On the night-time drive along Highway 2, he'd struggled to keep his eyes open, but now he was wide awake. He stared at the rounded log beams lining the ceiling. Outside, snow hissed and pricked at the window, and he could hear the wind, which had been calm during the daylight hours, roar back to life.

Beside him, Serena turned over on to her back. The blanket drew down, exposing most of the cream-colored slopes of her breasts. Her black hair fell in loose strands across her face. He could see that her eyes were open. They lay next to each other for long minutes, not speaking. He wanted to talk, but it felt like a momentous effort to say anything at all. Talking about his panic attacks, his depression, his hopelessness, his fear, was impossible. So he said nothing.

Under the blanket, Serena's hand slid closer until their fingers touched. He didn't move his hand away, but he didn't reach over to lace their fingers together, as he usually would. He closed his eyes, pretending to sleep, but after a while, he gave up and opened them again. On Serena's cheek, he thought he saw a wet trail of silver. Tears. He wanted to reach out and comfort her, get inside her head, let her back inside his life. All he could do, though, was lie motionless on the bed. Paralyzed.

Serena turned on her side. She stared at him in the darkness, but they still didn't say a word. She lifted his arm and stretched it out behind her, and then she folded herself into the crook of his neck. Her bare skin bonded with his own body; she was soft and smooth against his muscles. He was conscious of the touch of her nipples, hardened by the cool air. Her left leg draped over his, and the warmth of her mound pressed against his hip. Her face was damp on his shoulder. She laid her arm across his chest and made circles on his breastbone with her thumb, but her warmth and pressure against him felt sterile. His nerve ends were dead. His mind and body drifted apart, as if they were separate and unconnected things.

She kissed his cheek, which was rough with stubble. Her lips traveled along his face in a soft line of kisses, until she reached his ear lobe, which she sucked between her teeth and bit tenderly. Her tongue flicked at his neck. She pressed her body firmly against him; he felt her need, and she was moist between her legs. Her fingernails scraped along his stomach. She flattened her hand there, undulating her fingers like waves. At his ear, her mouth whispered, 'I want you.'

Serena pushed her hand across his middle to the inside of his thigh and alternated between a penetrating massage and feathery caresses. From there, he felt her fingertips glide on to his shaft. Rubbing. Touching. Trying to arouse him. He wanted more than anything to feel his body react, but despite her attentions, he remained unresponsive. She didn't give up, but instead redoubled her energy, her hands alive and busy. She straddled him, her full breasts dangling over his chest. Her hips sank lower over his waist, and she caressed him with her body.

She cupped his face, bent down, and kissed him full on, exploring his mouth with her tongue.

He stroked along the curve of her spine, and his touch felt clumsy. His mouth closed over each of her breasts in turn, and he felt her respond, but he knew it was artificial for both of them. The easy grace of their lovemaking had vanished and left them like strangers, unfamiliar with the other's body. He knew every inch of her skin and the touch she liked and how her toes curled as she came to the edge and spilled over it. It wasn't that he had forgotten. He simply had nothing to give her.

'Serena,' he murmured.

She refused to give up, but her intensity felt forced. Her face grew flushed with frustration and humiliation, as if it were somehow her failure, not his. Eventually, she rolled off him. She faced the other way, toward the window. Her shoulders shook as she cried. He put a hand on her back, but when she didn't react, he pulled it away. He stared at the ceiling for a while longer, and then he turned to face the wall. When he put his head on his arm, he smelled her perfume on his fingers. He closed his eyes, but he didn't sleep.

Maggie arrived early at City Hall on Monday morning. It was dark, and the roads were slick with an inch of snow. The old stone building took forever to heat up after the weekend, and the Detective Bureau felt frosty. She took off her ankle-length burgundy leather coat and replaced it with a wool pullover that Stride had left behind. The baggy sweater reached to the middle of her thighs, and she had to roll up six inches on the sleeves.

Even after three months, it didn't feel like her office. It would always be Stride's. She'd left his photographs on the bureau as a reminder that he was coming back. Standing under the harsh fluorescent light, she picked up each of the frames, which gave her a tour of his life. She saw Stride and Cindy, ten years younger, before the cancer stole her away. Maggie had liked Cindy a lot. Those were the old days, when Maggie was a kid, a Chinese immigrant slowly shedding her starchy upbringing and awakening to a new personality. Cindy had known all about Maggie's crush on Stride, but she had never shown even a glimmer of jealousy. Maggie wondered how Cindy would have felt about her slipping into Stride's bed six months after she died, only to be rejected by a man who didn't want to hurt her.

Maggie picked up the next picture, which was of Stride and Serena in Las Vegas, then just as quickly put it down, rather than stare at the two of them. The last picture on the bureau was of herself. She was on the beach behind Stride's cottage, her sunglasses pushed to the end of her bottle-cap nose, her bowl haircut windblown by the lake, her grin lopsided and sarcastic. She thought it was a terrible picture, but Stride had refused to let her replace it. He had taken it himself.

She sat down and propped her heels on the desk. Guppo had prepared his typically thorough report of the crime scene forensics near the Lester River, and she reread it, looking for details she had previously missed. Some connection among the victims. Some strange motive in the man's actions that night. She read it twice without finding anything, and the words blurred on the page.

'Knock knock,' someone said, startling her.

Maggie looked up. The husky frame of Troy Grange filled her doorway.

'Oh, hi, Troy,' she said.

'Is this a bad time?'

'No, come on in.'

The rest of the Detective Bureau was dark behind him. Troy, like Maggie, was an early riser. He sat in the chair in front of her desk, and the overhead light bounced off his bald head like a sunbeam.

'What's going on?' she asked.

'Well, first, I wanted to thank you for coming to the house on Saturday. You and Kasey both. I really appreciate it.'

'I just wish I had better news for you. I'm sorry.'

'I know. I'm due back at work today, but I'm still in a fog.'

'Take more time,' Maggie suggested. 'The director of the port will understand. I can have the chief call him.'

'It will probably do me good to work again,' he said.

'How's Debbie?' Maggie asked. 'Poor kid, this must be hitting her hard.'

'It's hard now, but it'll be worse later. I hate the idea of her growing up without her mother. I'm a guy. What the hell do I know about raising girls?'

'You'll do fine, Troy,' Maggie told him, smiling. 'But I know it's not what you planned.'

'No, I never signed up to be a single parent, that's for sure.'

'Was there something else you needed?' Maggie asked.

'Yes, but this isn't about Trisha,' Troy said. 'It may be nothing.'

'What is it?'

'I got a call late last night from a secretary in my office. She was pretty upset.'

'What happened?' Maggie asked.

'Well, she's dating a guy named Nick Garaldo. I know him. He's a young kid, twenty-something, a wiry little squirt. He works on one of the tugboats in the harbor. Solid and reliable, from everything I've heard about him.'

'OK.'

'He's missing,' Troy said.

'Oh? For how long?'

'That's the thing. It's just a day. This gal who called me, she talked to him on Saturday morning. They were supposed to meet for coffee at Amazing Grace on Sunday. He never turned up. He doesn't answer his cell phone, and he doesn't answer his landline. She went to his apartment, but nobody answers the door. He also had a five a.m. shift in the harbor this morning, and he's a no-show.'

Maggie frowned. 'It's too early to declare him a missing person.'

'Yeah, I know. I told her I'd report it and see what you can do. She swears this is not like him at all, and his boss says the same thing. He's never missed a shift without calling.'

'Where does he live?'

'He's got an apartment in the Central Hillside area downtown.'

'People pick up and move sometimes,' Maggie said. 'Especially from that area.'

'Sure they do. There's probably nothing to worry about, and he'll turn up tomorrow with a hangover. Or he'll call from South Padre Island or something. But his girlfriend was pretty upset.'

'Of course. What's his address?'

Troy recited the location of Nick's apartment on Fourth Street and Lake. It was one of the tough areas of downtown, a haven for drug dealers.

'I'll have someone check it out,' Maggie told him.

'I appreciate it.'

'In the meantime, if *you* need anything, just call me.'

'I will.'

Troy squeezed out of the chair, and they shook hands. She listened to his heavy footsteps walking away, and she heard the outer door of the Detective Bureau open and close. She was alone again.

Alone with a dead woman near the Lester River and three other women missing and presumed dead.

Alone with the photographs on Stride's bureau.

Twenty

In the morning, they pretended as if nothing had happened between them.

They got up, showered, made coffee, shared their notes on the case, and acted as if the elephant in the room was invisible. On some level, Stride knew it was the worst thing they could possibly do, but that was who they were. They each retreated to their corners and nursed their wounds.

They drove slowly into Grand Rapids because of the snow. The driveway at the Glenn house was white and pristine, and behind the house, the lake was deep blue under the sunshine. Valerie Glenn answered the door. He didn't need to ask if she'd seen the morning news and the Vegas interview with Lavender. Her blue eyes were furious. She led them into the warm sunroom at the back of the house, and she sat in a wicker chair near the windows and stared at the snow-covered lawn leading down to the water.

'It might be better if you weren't here for this,' Serena told her. 'There may be things that Marcus won't tell us with you in the room.'

Valerie laughed humorlessly. 'Do you really think he'll spare my feelings? We're a little late for that.'

Stride had spent less time with Valerie than Serena had,

but even so, he could see the change in her. She was a woman who didn't need make-up to be beautiful, but this morning she hadn't bothered to attend to her face. She wore a loose sweatshirt from the local country club, old jeans, and white athletic socks. He wondered if it was a silent message to her husband: I'm not your trophy today.

Stride saw Marcus Glenn in the doorway of the sunroom. There was no eye contact between him and Valerie as the surgeon sat down on the sofa on the other side of the room. His long legs jutted out like stilts over the end of the cushions.

'Good morning, detectives,' he said. 'I hope this won't take long. I've already had to cancel two surgeries today in order to be here.'

'We have some things we'd like to go over with you,' Stride said.

'Do I need a lawyer?'

'I don't know. Have you done anything that would make you need a lawyer?'

Glenn glanced at his wife. 'A divorce lawyer, perhaps.' He added, 'That's a joke, Valerie.'

Valerie didn't acknowledge him.

'Dr Glenn, there was an interview on television this morning with a woman in Las Vegas who claims to have had a relationship with you,' Stride said. 'Are you acquainted with this woman?'

'Yes.'

'Did you have a sexual relationship with her?' Serena asked.

'I don't see what that has to do with anything.'

'*Answer the question!*' Valerie snapped from the other side of the room.

For the first time, Glenn flinched. 'Yes, all right, I did. Intensely sexual. Is that what you want to hear, Valerie? As long as we're sharing family secrets, maybe you'd like the detectives to know that we haven't had sex since Callie was

151

born. The gates to the magic forest have been kept tightly locked while you manage all of your issues. Well, forgive me for not being satisfied with a celibate lifestyle.'

'You bastard,' Valerie murmured.

'This woman says you told her you wished that your daughter had never been born,' Serena said. 'Is that true? Did you make that statement?'

He shook his head. 'No.'

'So she's lying?' Stride asked.

'She's misremembering. I probably made some comment that my life was easier before Callie was born. Most people feel that way when a child comes into their lives.'

'The reporter specifically asked if you used the words "never been born". She says you did.'

'And as I told you, she's wrong.'

'You never said it?' Stride asked.

'No.'

'Is that how you feel?' Serena interrupted.

'What do you mean?'

'Well, regardless of whether you said it, do you believe you would be happier if Callie had never been born?'

'No. That's ridiculous.'

'Your credibility has taken some hits, doctor,' Stride told him. 'You lied to us about Migdalia Vega. You told us you were alone in the house the night Callie disappeared. We know that's not true. Exactly why didn't you tell us about her?'

'I think you know why. I didn't want Micki to get in trouble. She's an illegal, and she was afraid she'd be deported. Or worse yet, she'd be branded a suspect. She didn't know what happened, so she couldn't add anything to your investigation.'

'Was she with you in your bedroom that night?' Stride asked.

'No, she was in the guest room over the garage on the other side of the hall.'

'You told us you were asleep by ten thirty,' Serena said.

'That's right.'

'So you don't know where Migdalia was or what she was doing during that time until you discovered Callie was missing.'

Marcus hesitated. 'I suppose not, but it's insane to think—'

'Do you think there could be any connection between Callie's disappearance and Migdalia losing her baby last year?' Stride asked, cutting him off.

'What? No, certainly not.'

'Were you the father of her child?'

Marcus leaned back and folded his arms over his chest. 'Absolutely not.'

'Have you ever slept with her?'

'No.'

'What about Regan Conrad?' Serena asked.

Marcus turned his head sharply at the mention of Regan's name. 'Excuse me?'

'You heard me,' Serena said.

'Yes. All right. I had – past tense – a relationship with Regan Conrad.' He turned to Valerie. 'I broke it off. I told you that months ago.'

Valerie didn't reply.

'When did you sever your relationship with Ms Conrad?' Stride asked.

'This winter.'

'After Callie was born?'

'Yes.'

'Why did you choose to end it?'

'My wife knew about my affair,' he said, with another glance at Valerie. 'With Callie born, she wanted it over. I agreed.'

'I was told that you were concerned about Regan Conrad's behavior,' Serena said. 'You told people she was crazy. Crazy in what way?'

'Regan is extreme. She's manipulative. She tries to get you to do what she wants, and she's very good at it. I kept it going longer than I should have because of that.'

'How did she take it when you broke it off?' Stride asked.

'Not well,' Glenn said.

'How so?'

'She hit me in the face and tried to break my fingers. She wanted me to divorce Valerie and marry her. Obviously, those were delusions. Nothing like that was going to happen.'

'Has she ever been in your house?' Serena asked.

He exhaled and looked unhappy. 'Several times.'

'So she knows the layout of your house?'

'I suppose she does.'

'Did you ever give her a key?'

'I may have loaned her a spare key once.'

'Did you get it back?'

'I honestly don't remember,' he replied, hesitating. 'I don't think I did. But this is all academic, detectives. Regan was working the night Callie disappeared. Believe me, I checked.'

'You did?' Stride asked. 'Why?'

'I told you. She's erratic. Violent.'

'Why didn't you tell us about her if you thought she could be involved in kidnapping your daughter?'

'Do I have to explain it? Look at what's happened to my life in the past four days. I've been excoriated in the press and subjected to humiliating questions by you in front of my wife. I was trying to avoid all of this.'

'Did Regan Conrad ever make any threats regarding you, your wife, or your baby?' Serena asked.

'Not explicitly, no.'

'But there were implied threats?'

'She's vengeful and clever. Anything is possible with her. She's even been arrested a few times.'

'Arrested? For what?' Serena asked.

'I don't know. The charges were dropped. She referred to it once in passing.'

'How well did Regan know Micki Vega?' Stride asked.

'They were close,' Glenn said. 'Regan may be unstable, but she's a brilliant nurse. I've seen her with new mothers. She becomes their lifeline. The bond between mother and midwife is exceptionally strong during and after the birth of a child, particularly when there are problems.'

'Problems?'

'Difficult labor. Post-partum depression. Things like that. And obviously, in Micki's case, losing a baby.'

'Could Regan have manipulated Micki into helping her kidnap Callie?'

Glenn thought about it and shook his head. 'I really don't think so. Not Micki. She's too loyal to me. Besides, kidnapping a baby? That's a heinous thing to do. Micki would never be involved in anything like that.'

Stride looked at Serena, who nodded.

'Dr Glenn, let's be very clear about this. Did you in any way harm your baby?'

'No. Absolutely not.'

'Were you in any way involved in her disappearance? Either taking her from the house or helping someone else to do so?'

'No.'

'Do you know what happened to her?'

Marcus stood up. 'No. I can't be any clearer than that. I was not involved in Callie's disappearance in any way whatsoever. You're wasting your time listening to the nonsense spread by Blair Rowe and the rest of the media. I know it makes good television to paint me as some kind of devil, but the fact is, I'm innocent. The best thing you can do is stop harassing me and do your jobs. Find out what happened to her.'

He turned to walk from the sunroom, but Serena interrupted

him. 'We can clear this up once and for all, Dr Glenn. We'd like you to take a polygraph test.'

Marcus looked at her with suspicion. 'A polygraph?'

'Yes.'

'Polygraph tests are notoriously inaccurate and inadmissible in court, isn't that right?'

'The test helps us cross people *off* the list,' Serena explained. 'When you pass, we'll know that we should be focusing our investigation elsewhere. Otherwise, a cloud of suspicion will linger over you, particularly given the omissions in your statements to us.'

Valerie leaned forward. 'I think you should do it, Marcus. We both should. Let them clear us, so they can figure out who really did this.'

'Oh, so you think I'm involved too?' he retorted. He shook his head firmly. 'Sorry. No. I won't do that. Certainly not without consulting an attorney.'

'Marcus,' Valerie gasped.

'I said no. It doesn't mean I had anything to do with this, but innocent people wind up in legal jeopardy all too often. I'm sorry.'

Marcus Glenn shoved his hands in his pockets and stalked from the room.

Twenty-one

Valerie had known Marcus Glenn long before they ever met.

She remembered the big celebration in the high school gymnasium when she was ten years old. Her sister Denise and Denise's boyfriend, Tom, had taken Valerie with them to the city-wide party in honor of Grand Rapids bringing home the high school hockey championship for the second year in a row. Marcus Glenn was the star. The most valuable player. The tall teenager with the black hair and the reluctant smile. Valerie had watched him in his hockey jersey with the kind of crush she had previously reserved for singers on MTV. It didn't matter that Denise made snarky comments to Tom under her breath about Marcus thinking he was king of the world. Right then and there, Valerie remembered staring at him and thinking: I'm going to marry him.

It was only a juvenile fantasy. She never took it seriously, not until a dozen years later, when she was the hostess at the Sugar Lake Lodge restaurant. Marcus Glenn walked in with three other men, and Valerie may as well have been ten years old again when she saw him. He wore a perfectly tailored black suit and a hint of cologne; he was taller than anyone else around him; and he was talking in casual tones about the PGA star who had just won the Phoenix Open, a year after Marcus had done knee surgery on the man.

Marcus Glenn was back home in Grand Rapids. Young, wealthy, unmarried, a surgeon with gifted hands.

She remembered how their eyes had met. How his stare lingered on her face. She knew she was beautiful – plenty of men had gone after her over the years – but it still gave her a thrill to realize that *he* was interested in *her*. Of all the women in Grand Rapids who would have thrown themselves at him and his Lexus, she was the one he wanted.

He asked her out that night. She knew about the rumors: Marcus went from one girl to the next, sleeping with them and moving on. He wasn't ready to settle down. So she was surprised when he didn't invite her to a romantic dinner for two, but instead invited her to accompany him to a cocktail party thrown by members of the hospital board. He bought her a stunning dress. Kept her on his arm the whole night. Kissed her cheek when he dropped her off at her apartment.

They didn't make love until six weeks later, and it was a short, awkward coupling, strangely devoid of passion. That didn't matter to her. What mattered was that he asked her to marry him the next day. It didn't even take her two heartbeats to say yes.

Looking back, she knew how naïve she'd been. It never occurred to her that he had simply added her to his collection like a butterfly, that she was exactly the kind of wife that a successful surgeon needed to show to the world. It was three years before she discovered that he had continued having sex with other women throughout their marriage. By then, they were in their new lake home, and she had a beautiful wardrobe and a new car, and she was on the board of nonprofit organizations in the northland where Marcus made lavish gifts. She had sold her soul, and it was too late to buy it back.

Valerie descended into a loneliness that was so black she couldn't see her way out. She went through her days like a robot. She remembered spilling her soul to Denise and Tom, but Denise – who was pregnant with her third child at the time – had little time or sympathy for a sister who had been blessed with all the breaks in life: money, looks, the successful husband, the big house. That was the beginning, the real intersection where they began to drift apart as siblings. Valerie had never dreamed how empty she could feel with no partner in her life to talk to, with no one outside the sterile mansion who would listen to her.

On one January night five years into their marriage, Marcus arrived home late from the hospital in Duluth. He had grown careless – or maybe he didn't really care at all – about hiding the evidence of his affairs. When he crawled into their bed, he stank of sex. After he fell asleep, Valerie lay awake for nearly three hours, crying soundlessly into her pillow, before she got up and emptied the remnants of a half-full bottle of aspirin into her sweaty palm and swallowed them down.

She had awakened in the hospital. Marcus was there. She realized that, in his way, he loved her and had been frightened of the idea of losing her. She also knew that, if she was going to stay with him, she needed something else in her life that would take the place of an emotionally distant husband. He had been adamant when they got engaged that he had no interest in having a child, but she essentially blackmailed him by telling him the truth. Without a baby, she would try to kill herself again, and she would keep trying until she got it right. So he said yes. She threw away the condoms. And they had their usual sex, bareback now, every Sunday morning.

Valerie never dreamed that three interminable years would pass from that breaking point. She had been tested; he had been tested. The first year had been exciting; the second year had been frustrating; and the third year had tipped her into a depression even deeper than she had known in the early years of her marriage. She knew perfectly well that she was the one who really wanted a baby. Marcus had his same perfunctory sex with her, but he didn't bother to pretend that he was disappointed when her period came back month after month. The loneliness came back along with it. And the emptiness. She craved a closeness with her husband to beat back her desperation, but that was something he could never give her. It wasn't who he was or would ever be.

More and more, she had thought of suicide again. She even swore to herself that the next time she got her period would be the last. She would quit trying. She would just quit. And like a miracle, her next period never came. Instead, nine months later, Callie came. Her beautiful child. Her savior.

Valerie sat on the floor of Callie's room, hugging her knees. She stared at the empty crib and didn't notice the tears on her face. Behind her, through an open window, cold air and wet flakes of snow blew on her neck.

'Valerie.'

She looked up as a shadow stretched across the carpet. It was Marcus.

'Get out,' she told him.

He hesitated, but he didn't leave.

'Are you even disappointed, Marcus?' she asked him, her voice raspy with grief. 'Are you even sad that she's gone?'

'Of course I am.'

He sounded like a man who said what the world expected him to say. She had always known that he didn't love Callie the way she did, but she had never dreamed that he would be just as barren as a father as he was as a husband.

'Tell me you didn't do this,' she whispered.

'Oh, for God's sake, Valerie.'

'*Tell me.*'

'I can't believe I have to convince you. I didn't do this. It's absurd.'

'Is it?'

He took a step closer. 'I may be a bad husband, but that

doesn't make me a bad man, Valerie. You know me, warts and all. Some things I do well, and some things I do badly. But harm Callie? I would never dream of taking her away from you. I know she's your whole life.'

'You could have been my whole life, Marcus. But I guess I don't screw you like your whore in Vegas.'

Marcus sighed loudly. 'We've been down this road before.'

'Yes, we have.'

'You know it's only sex to me. It doesn't change how I feel about you.'

'Oh, get out, Marcus,' Valerie snapped. 'Get away from me.'

'I've *told* you who I am,' he insisted, grabbing hard to the door frame. 'I want things I would never ask you to do. If I could resist them, I would, but I can't. You know that. I can't be a great surgeon and switch off my other needs. It doesn't work that way. But this girl in Vegas was nothing.'

'What about the nurse? Regan Conrad?'

Marcus shook his head. 'I don't know what it was about Regan. That's the truth. But it was still all about sex. And when you told me to break it off, I did.'

'She was there,' Valerie said.

'What?'

'The night Callie was born. She was there, wasn't she? She was at the hospital.'

'I guess she was,' Marcus said, looking uncomfortable.

'You guess? Tell me the truth. You slept with her that night, didn't you? *Tell me!* I was in a hospital bed giving birth to your daughter, and you were *fucking* your little nurse. Right? Don't you dare lie to me about it.'

Marcus rubbed his tired eyes with one hand. With his other hand, he clung to the frame of Callie's crib. 'OK. You're right.'

Valerie pushed herself off the floor. She marched toward the doorway, and Marcus grabbed her arm in a hard grip to stop her. She shoved him furiously away, nearly losing her balance.

She stumbled down the hallway toward the stairs and heard her husband shouting behind her.

'Valerie.'

She ran, not wanting to hear anything else. She flew down the steps to the foyer and wrenched open the front door.

'*Valerie*,' Marcus called again.

She stopped and looked back over her shoulder at him. His face was screwed up with rage and bitterness.

'Don't pretend you're some wounded angel,' he bellowed from the railing above her, his voice dripping with sarcasm. 'You're not exactly *innocent*, are you?'

Valerie stepped into the snow and slammed the door behind her. She saw police cars and media vans on the street at the end of her driveway, and she froze as heads turned in her direction. She reversed course and stomped to the rear of the house, making heavy footfalls in the slush as she headed for the lake. She went all the way to the shore, where a translucent glaze of ice crept a few feet on to the blue water.

She crumpled to her knees and buried her face in her hands. Her jeans grew wet, and the cold worked its way inside her clothes. She hoped no one was behind her, that no one had tried to follow her. She stared at the lake and thought about wading in and allowing her body to grow numb as the frigid water shocked her skin.

You're not exactly innocent, are you?

No. That was true. She wondered if he was guessing or if, somehow, he knew what she had done. But she had given up trying to decide what it really meant to be innocent or guilty. Did God punish every sin, or did He forgive you for the things you did when you were desperate and had nowhere to go?

Her phone vibrated in her pocket.

Valerie yanked the phone out of her pocket and prepared to throw it into the lake. But it wasn't Marcus on the other end, calling to shred her last ounces of self-respect. Whoever was calling had a blocked number.

'Hello,' she said wearily.

'Is this Valerie Glenn?'

She didn't recognize the voice. It was a woman.

'Yes.'

'I know what happened to your daughter,' the woman told her.

Twenty-two

Maggie sat in the chair and stared at herself in the mirror. With the black smock tied around her neck and draped over her body, she looked like a pawn in a giant chess game. Behind her, Sara Wolfe reached round and played with Maggie's bangs with her fingers.

'Are you sure?' Sara asked.

'Yeah, I'm sure. Do it.'

'I just don't want you waking up tomorrow and blaming me.'

'I know what I'm doing,' Maggie said.

'Whatever you say, girl.' Sara worked at the dye with a mortar and pestle. 'Where's Stride, anyway? I haven't seen him in a few weeks. Either he's found someone new, or he's getting shaggy.'

'He's been in a cabin in Grand Rapids for the last month. I'm seeing him tomorrow morning.'

'Oh, now I understand,' Sara replied, winking at Maggie in the mirror.

'What?'

'Nothing, it just makes sense now.'

'This has nothing to do with him,' Maggie told her.

'Right. Sure. Well, tell him to stop by. I'll get out the machete and cut through that tangled forest he calls hair.' She put down the white bowl and primped the highlights in her own sandy blonde hair. 'You know, when my husband's on stage doing a guitar solo, I still get as breathless as a groupie sometimes.'

Maggie eyed her suspiciously. 'Yeah, so?'

'So it's nice when you've known someone a long time and they can still make you go weak in the knees.'

'That's not what this is about.'

Sara nodded. 'I hear you, girl. Message received loud and clear.'

'You're such a bitch.'

'Never say that to someone who stands behind you with a pair of scissors.' Sara wagged her finger at Maggie and picked up the mortar and pestle again.

'You're right. I'm sorry.'

Sara's face grew serious. 'Are you close to nailing the guy who's doing these farmland murders? I have to tell you, all my girlfriends are pretty scared. So am I.'

'We've got patrols blanketing the roads northeast of the city all night long.'

'If I lived on one of those farms, I wouldn't be sleeping,' Sara said. 'I'd be sitting up with the lights on and a big gun in my lap and a couple German shepherds on either side of me.'

'That's not a bad plan,' Maggie told her.

Sara tilted the bowl and showed her the color of the dye. 'How's that? Is that what you want?'

'Redder.'

'If it gets any redder, you'll look like Ronald McDonald.'

'I want it to stop traffic,' Maggie said.

'You're the boss.'

At nine o'clock on Monday evening, Kasey spotted the one headlight trailing behind her patrol car like a watchful eye.

It appeared near the airport and matched her on the remote roads turn for turn. She didn't think anything was wrong until she turned for the fourth time, heading north toward Island Lake, and the same single headlight followed in her wake. When she slowed to draw the vehicle closer, whoever was behind her mimicked her speed. She was being followed.

Kasey drifted to a dead stop, her engine idling, her eyes locked on the rear-view mirror. Giant stretches of black water loomed on both sides of the highway. Her patrol car shuddered as wind hurtled across the open lake, bringing streams of snow. Half a mile behind her, the car with the lone headlight stopped too. They played cat and mouse on opposite ends of the bridge.

She didn't want to give in to paranoia. It might be nothing. It wasn't uncommon for teenage thrill-seekers to shadow police cars. She turned on her light bar, and almost immediately, the headlight winked off. She saw red tail lights as the person behind her did a U-turn and retreated at high speed. In the darkness, she couldn't make out details of the car that had tracked her.

She waited another minute, and when the odd headlight didn't return, she continued to the far side of the lake and followed the highway where it hugged the north shore. On her radio, she listened to chatter among the other cops as they patrolled the farmlands, sweeping back and forth across the zigzagging roads. It was a cold, lonely evening. For the most part, they had the countryside to themselves.

Her cell phone rang. She dug it out of her shirt pocket and saw that her husband was calling.

'Is everything OK?' Bruce asked her.

'Yeah. I'm fine.'

He picked up on the nervousness in her voice. 'Are you sure? You sound freaked.'

'It's nothing,' Kasey told him, glancing in her mirror again.

'I thought somebody was following me. I thought maybe it was him, you know?'

'Jesus. I don't like the idea of you out there alone.'

'I'll be all right. How are things at home? Are you taking precautions?'

'I checked the basement and all the windows,' Bruce said. 'I put a baby monitor down there too, so I could hear if anyone tries to get in.'

'Good. I should be home sometime after midnight.'

'I'll be up,' Bruce told her. He added, 'We can't live like this forever, you know.'

'I know. We're going to get out of here, just like we planned.'

'So let's do it. Now. Pack up and head for Nevada. We can leave tonight.'

Kasey let the silence drag out. 'Not yet.'

'What are we waiting for?'

'If we leave and this guy is still out there, I'll never sleep again,' Kasey said. 'I'll always wonder. It doesn't matter where we go.'

'Do you think he'd follow us?'

'I don't know!' Kasey shouted. She took a deep breath and lowered her voice, reining in her panic. 'I have no idea what he'll do next. He's obsessed with me now, don't you get that?'

'All the more reason to *get away*,' Bruce pressed her.

'Let's talk when I get home. OK? I can't talk about this now.'

'I know. Watch your back.'

Kasey hung up. Her hands were trembling. She chewed her upper lip and peered through the windows. Farmhouses and vacation homes were notched into the forest every quarter-mile or so as she wound through the roads bordering Island Lake. She spent an hour doing a reconnaissance of the gravel roads near the water. Twice she had to brake for deer frozen in the lane, staring at her. The animals were the only things out here that were alive and awake.

She knew that Maggie wanted a mammoth police presence to spook the killer. Let him see cops on every road. Let him know that the risk of another assault was too big to take. If it was a waiting game, though, he was bound to win. There were too many long miles of rural land to watch them all.

Kasey radioed in her position. The dispatcher routed her on a reverse course south and east toward Highway 44. More travels through no-man's-land.

She retraced her path and headed across the open stretch of lake again, where the wind was worst. As she cleared the bridge, she spied a black van parked on the shoulder, its lights and engine off. She didn't think the van had been there as she headed north, but she'd been distracted. As she passed, she studied the driver's window but didn't see anyone inside. There was no steam gathered on the glass.

She pulled on to the side of the road twenty yards ahead of the van. Watching for movement behind her, she opened her door and climbed out next to the patrol car. She unhooked a flashlight from her belt and aimed it at the van's license plate, but the surface of the plate was caked with mud. She couldn't read the numbers. When she shot the beam at the windshield, she realized that the van's windows were smoked. She couldn't see through them.

She didn't like it.

At that moment, inside her patrol car, the radio crackled to life.

'All units in vicinity respond to a nine one one emergency call, felony assault in progress.' The dispatcher gave the address, which was on Highway 12 in the heart of the north farm-lands. Kasey was fifteen minutes away at high speed. *It had to be him.*

She hesitated, studying the black van. Had it been there the whole time? Was it abandoned? She didn't have time to worry about it. She got back in her patrol car, slammed the door, and shot southward along the highway between the dark columns of pines.

Less than a mile later, her eyes flicked to her mirror, drawn to a sudden beam of light like a moth.

'Shit,' she said aloud.

The single headlight was back. Following her.

Kasey had a split second in which to decide whether to join the units responding to the assault call or find out who was in the van behind her. She chose the van. At the next intersection, she spun the patrol car into a hard U-turn. She pushed the accelerator to the floor, and the car leaped forward with a growl. Ahead of her, she heard the squeal of brakes, and the van lurched into an awkward turn in the middle of the highway. Its engine was no match for Kasey's patrol car.

'I've got you,' she whispered, taking one hand off the wheel to unsnap the thumb break on her holster.

She closed the gap quickly, but when she was a quarter-mile behind the van, its lights vanished. She switched on her high beams, but the black stretch of asphalt was empty. The vehicle had disappeared. Too late, she spotted a dirt road winding eastward off the highway toward the lake. She braked hard, but as she turned the wheel over, the rear of her car skidded on the snow piled on the shoulder, and her tires spun. She jammed the accelerator, but the wet slush gave her no traction. Frustrated, she feathered the pedal, and the car inched forward in fits and starts until it cleared the shoulder, where the tires grabbed the road and shrieked as she bolted forward.

The dirt road was barely a crease in the forest on her left. Nearly a dozen mailboxes leaned out toward the highway. When she turned, she realized she was on a private road that dead-ended at the water. There was no way out. The van was trapped somewhere ahead of her, between her car and the lake.

She slowed to a crawl, studying the maze of driveways that split from the main trail toward the lake homes, which were dark squares nestled among the trees. Snow-covered spruce branches dangled over the road, hanging low enough to brush the roof of the car. Gravel scraped under her tires. She drove for a mile until the road ended at a concrete boat launch that sloped downward, disappearing into the dark water.

The van was in the lake.

It floated away from the ramp into the open water like an off-balance toy. Its driver's door was open. As she watched, the vehicle sank lower, water spilling inside. The frame wobbled and dove awkwardly on to its side with a splash. Its tires broke through the surface. The van made a slow circle, spinning lazily from the shore before the heavy engine drove it downward front first. With hissing and ripples, the entire vehicle settled to the muddy bottom.

Kasey withdrew her gun from its holster. She squinted through the windows and did a careful scan of the area around her car before she opened her door and slid out, staying behind it. Her eyes moved from tree to tree, watching for movement. She listened. Dried leaves clapped as the wind blew. Snow sprinkled from the evergreens and made a cold landing on her face. A chorus of crows erupted nearby, and she jumped.

Where was he?

Behind her, something hard and loud rustled in the brush. Kasey spun, lifting her gun. She saw a driveway, overgrown with shooting vines. The silhouette of a large house hugged the beach. She followed the noise and took slow, soundless steps down the driveway. Every few seconds, she glanced nervously behind her. She was scared and blind. The driveway lasted for forty yards, and then she broke into the open grass around the house. Snow covered the steps leading to the door, and there were no footsteps in the blanket of white.

From the other side of the road, back where she had parked her patrol car, Kasey heard another noise. An engine fired. Through the web of trees, she saw headlights and heard tires grinding on the dirt. She ran back along the driveway, but she spilled head first over a tree root breaching like a whale out of the earth. Her gun dropped from her hand and skidded into the brush, and she wasted almost a minute feeling for it with her bare hands. When she finally found it, she ran again, following the driveway to the trail where her car was parked. She stopped and listened, but the sound of the engine was distant. She heard the squeal of its tires as it swung on to the main highway and headed north.

Escaping.

Kasey swore. She went to her patrol car to call for back-up. As she leaned inside, she saw a rectangle of glossy white paper on the seat. She picked it up and turned it over.

'Oh, my God,' Kasey murmured.

She stared at her own face. It was a photograph that Bruce had taken of her and Jack a year ago. She felt the breath leave her chest as if it had been sucked away.

There it was again. The same message he had written on her mirror. Two words scrawled in red marker across the front of the photograph in block letters.

BAD GIRL.

Twenty-three

Valerie Glenn turned off Highway 2 into the empty church parking lot at midnight. She parked her white Mercedes and got out and shoved her hands into the pockets of her suede jacket. Ahead of her, the one-story church was surrounded by tall pines whose branches spread outward like a priest's outstretched arms. She crossed the lawn, her boots stamping down the thin layer of snow. At the front of the church, she sat on the concrete steps, and the cold stone felt icy through her jeans.

I know what happened to your daughter.

The woman on the phone had told her to come alone and keep the call a secret from the police and her husband. Despite everything Serena had told her, Valerie had done exactly as the woman wanted. She was here, miles outside the city, on her own. Waiting.

Deer tracks criss-crossed the snow. Overhead, the moon was a faint glow through the shroud of dark clouds. Twenty minutes passed as she sat on the steps, and she felt the bitter cold numbing her face. No one arrived. She began to think the call had been a hoax and that no one would show up to tell her about Callie. She told herself that she would wait ten more minutes and then go home, but the truth was, she wasn't going to leave. She would stay all night if there was even the slightest chance that it would bring her daughter home.

On the highway, from the southeast, she saw the twin beams of headlights. A black Hummer came around the curve. The heavy vehicle slowed sharply and turned into the church parking lot across from Valerie's Mercedes. She felt her heart rate accelerating and, out of nowhere, anger bubbled up and made her fists clench. She didn't know who was in the Hummer, but whoever it was, she wanted to kill them. If they had taken her daughter, she wanted them to pay.

The door opened. A woman climbed down. She wore a winter coat with a fur hood pulled up over her head, cloaking most of her face. She was thin, with legs like drainpipes. Valerie watched her come closer. She stopped in the snow ten feet away and slipped her hood back from her face. Her skin was white, and she had dark, almost purple make-up.

Valerie erupted. *'Where's my baby?'*

She launched herself off the steps and threw her body across the short distance between them. Her sudden assault took the woman by surprise, and she didn't have time to move before Valerie collided hard with her chest, tumbling both of them to the ground. The woman landed on her back in the snow, and Valerie climbed on top of her, pummeling her torso with her fists and shouting in her face.

'Tell me! Tell me where she is!'

The woman shoved hard with one hand against Valerie's shoulder and dislodged her, but Valerie climbed back and struck her repeatedly until her tears and the cold got the better of her, and she ran out of strength. The woman grabbed Valerie's fists and held them and then pushed her away again as she rolled out from under her. Both women breathed heavily. Valerie lay on her back like a snow angel, watching the sway of the pine branches above her.

'Who the hell are you?' Valerie asked. 'What have you done with Callie?'

The woman staggered to her feet and braced herself against the railing beside the church steps. 'I don't have her.'

'Who are you?' Valerie repeated.

'I'm Regan Conrad.'

It took Valerie a moment to remember the name. She scrambled to her feet and drew back to throw herself on the woman again, but Regan held up her hands to stop her.

'Wait! Hear me out.'

'What is this about? What are you trying to do to me?'

'I didn't think you'd come if I told you it was me.'

'You're right.'

Regan shrugged. 'I know you hate my guts. That's OK. I spent a lot of time fucking your husband. I could tell you I'm sorry, but I wouldn't mean it, and you wouldn't believe me. So I won't waste your time.'

'What do you want?' Valerie asked.

'To talk.'

'About what?'

'Your husband,' Regan said.

'I have nothing to say to you.'

'Then listen to me.' Regan sat down on the steps. She touched her chest gingerly and twisted her neck. 'You pack a punch for a rich bitch. I figured you for the girly type who wouldn't get her hands dirty.'

'You figured wrong.'

'You didn't call the cops like I said. That was smart.'

'I can call them right now if you'd like.'

Regan didn't look concerned. 'Go for it. I'll just tell them what I was going to tell you. I told you not to call the police because I figured you'd want to hear this for yourself. Then you can decide what to do. You're the only one who knows whether you can live with it.'

'What are you talking about?' Valerie asked. 'You told me you knew what happened to Callie.'

'We both know, don't we?'

'No, I don't. Tell me.'

Regan shook her head. 'You're closing your eyes because you don't want to see it. But everyone else knows. That reporter, Blair Rowe, she knows, but she has to dance around it to keep the lawyers happy. The cops know it, but they can't prove it. And you know it, too. You feel it in your gut. Right?'

'No. You're wrong.'

'Maybe you can't say it out loud. I get it. I'll say it for you. I'm a nurse, and I work with mothers, so believe me, I know how awful this is for you. But Callie is gone. Marcus made her go away. Maybe it was an accident and he had to cover it up, but I don't think so, and you don't think so. We both know what kind of man he is. He's cold to the bone.'

Valerie turned her back on Regan. 'I'm leaving.'

Regan let her get halfway back to her Mercedes before she called after her. 'Run away if you want, but don't you want to know why?'

Valerie stopped. She knew she should get in her car and go. She knew she was being manipulated, but she couldn't resist. She had to know what else Regan was going to say. The evil bitch had put her sharp red fingernail squarely on all of Valerie's doubts and fears. She had echoed the voice in Valerie's head that had been whispering like a drumbeat ever since Callie disappeared. The same whisper, over and over.

Marcus.

She turned around. 'Why?'

Regan got off the steps and marched closer. Valerie stared at her, this woman who was barely younger than she was. A woman with no curves and ragged hair and a face marred by purple make-up and ugly piercings. Valerie tried to imagine what it was her husband could have seen in a woman like this, what could have possessed him to bring her into their bed.

It was as if Regan could read her mind.

'It doesn't matter whether you're beautiful,' Regan said. 'That's not what it's about, and you know it.'

'What I know is that you were in my hospital room while I was in labor. What I know is that you slept with my husband while my baby was being born.'

'Doesn't that tell you something?' Regan asked.

'It tells me who you are.'

'It should tell you who Marcus is, too. He never cared about Callie. He never wanted her.'

'You're wrong.'

'You think that whore in Vegas is the only girl he confessed to? He told me the same thing. How he wished you would lose the baby. How he wished she'd never been born. That's the man you're married to, Valerie.'

Valerie yanked her glove off her hand and slapped Regan across the face. The blow raised a spidery welt on the nurse's pale face the color of a strawberry. Regan stumbled backward, but otherwise, she didn't react.

'Don't kill the messenger,' Regan said calmly.

'If you think you're messing with my head, you're wrong.'

But she wasn't wrong. They both knew it. Valerie's face betrayed her. She felt as if a flood were washing away the foundations of her world, and Regan could see her grasping for a lifeline.

'I don't have to tell you why, do I?' Regan asked.

'You're crazy.'

'Come on, Valerie. Isn't it obvious? Don't you know?'

'I don't know a thing,' Valerie snapped. 'I'm not listening to any more of this. Marcus loves Callie.'

Regan laughed. Her teeth were as white as her skin. 'My God, you really don't know. That's hilarious.'

'Go to hell!'

Valerie stormed away, but Regan took two hurried steps and stopped her with a firm hand on her shoulder. 'Wait.'

Regan unzipped her parka and extracted a sealed envelope from an inside pocket. Valerie recognized the logo for St Mary's Hospital on the paper. Regan extended the envelope in her outstretched hand, and when Valerie didn't take it, Regan moved closer and nudged the top of the envelope into the waist of Valerie's jeans.

'I can't believe you didn't know,' she whispered in her ear.

She sidled past Valerie, who stood frozen, listening to the sound of the woman's footsteps. Behind her, Valerie heard the door of the Hummer open and close. She still didn't move. She stood there like an ice sculpture while Regan drove away, leaving her alone in front of the church.

Twenty-four

In the gray light of dawn, Maggie watched Guppo and his team pore over the black van they had dragged from the shallow water of Island Lake. She rubbed her eyes; it had been a long, sleepless night. Behind her, Kasey Kennedy lay across the snug rear seat of the Avalanche. With her eyes closed, the young cop's face was angelic, but once again, she had demonstrated equal parts foolishness and balls.

There was no way around it. Maggie liked Kasey. The young cop's pig-headed intensity reminded her of her own early years on the force. She had the kind of determination that meant you would never quit until you got where you wanted to go. It could also get you killed.

Near the lake, Guppo gestured to her. Maggie slid out of the truck without disturbing Kasey and joined the overweight detective near the boat ramp. The small clearing was crowded with police vehicles and crime scene investigators. Everywhere Maggie went this morning, a dozen heads followed her.

Guppo's stare was focused two inches north of her eyes.

'Quit it,' Maggie told him.

'I can't help it,' he said. 'It's just so . . . so . . .'

'Red.'

'Exactly. Red.'

'I told you I was thinking about it.'

'Yeah, but I never thought you'd actually *do* it,' Guppo replied, laughing. 'And especially so . . . so . . .'

'Red.'

'Yeah. It's red.'

'Are you done?' Maggie asked.

'For now.'

'What's the report?'

'It's his van,' Guppo told her, but she noticed that he was talking to her hair, not her face. 'Despite the water damage, there's blood all over the interior. It's not a pretty sight.'

'Shit,' Maggie said. 'Match it to the missing women, and make sure we don't have any other samples in there. We don't know how long he's been doing this.'

Guppo nodded. 'The Minnesota plates don't match the van. They come from a Volvo sedan. We called the owner. He's a personal injury attorney in St Paul, and he says the car is parked in the garage of his summer home south of Duluth. He only drives the Volvo when he's up here, and he hasn't been in the city since early September. He had no clue the plates were gone.'

'Let's run his house for prints.'

'We're getting the warrant now.'

'What about the van itself?'

'According to the VIN, it was stolen in Colorado Springs six months ago,' Guppo told her.

Maggie arched an eyebrow. 'Colorado? That's interesting.'

'We'll contact the authorities down there today and see what we can find out.'

'See if they have any unsolved murders in the area that match our MO,' Maggie told him. 'And get them our DNA report to run through the state database there.'

'I'm on it.'

'What about the car he stole last night to get away?'

'It's a Cadillac. The owner left it unlocked. People are too damned trusting around here.'

'Any hits?' Maggie asked.

'No, nobody's seen it yet.'

Maggie nodded. 'We're getting closer to this asshole.'

'It feels that way.'

'Any prints inside the van?'

'We're still checking,' Guppo said. 'It doesn't help that the thing went for a swim.'

'You heard that the nine one one call was a fake, right?' Maggie asked. 'He deliberately lured us away.'

'Yeah. You know what that means?'

'It means he was going after the kid. This guy's got a hard-on for Kasey.'

'That could help us,' Guppo said. 'Do you have people watching her house?'

Maggie nodded. 'Yeah, she doesn't like it, but I've got a black-and-white on the other side of the highway.'

'Well, maybe we don't want to scare him away,' Guppo suggested. 'Maybe we ought to be using her as bait.'

Maggie shook her head fiercely. 'No way.'

'I'm just saying—'

'I told you, no. We're not risking that girl's life. She's a cop, a wife, and a mother. I want to scare this guy a hundred miles away from her.'

'Whatever you say,' Guppo told her, but his round face frowned.

'I'm going back to City Hall,' Maggie added. 'I'll take Kasey with me. I want to get a photo of the van out to the media. That may jog some memories.'

'We've still got a few hours left out here,' Guppo said.

'OK, check in when you're back. I have to see Stride this morning out on the Point. I also want to see if we can find anything more on this Nick Garaldo.'

'Is that the young guy who went missing over the weekend?'

'That's him. He still hasn't turned up. It's been two days. I'm going to stop by his apartment and see what I can find.'

Guppo gestured at her bangs. 'You're seeing Stride, huh? You tell him about the hair?'

Maggie shrugged. 'You really think he'll notice?'

Stride drove into Duluth on the northern route that took him through Hermantown and across Miller Hill. As he headed down the sharp slope into the streets of downtown, he could see the harbor and the giant swath of Lake Superior filling the valley. White waves surged against the beach. A gray layer of clouds made the brick city buildings look old, as if time had frozen here in some extreme winter decades ago.

He took the overpass over Interstate 35 and continued through Canal Park to the lift bridge that led to the ribbon of land known as the Point. He followed the road toward his cottage and found that he was having trouble breathing. His chest felt heavy. As he reached his driveway at 33rd Street, he slowed to a stop and inhaled deeply with his mouth open, until his lungs relaxed. He lowered the window and could hear the thunder of lake waves on the beach on the other side of the sand dune. He was home.

He pulled into his driveway, but rather than go inside, he hiked over the dune to the lake, where it was wild and blustery. A seagull hung motionless over the beach, lofted by the gusty currents. The sand was littered with driftwood rubbed smooth by the water. The wispy rye grass quaked, and the pines swayed with casual elegance. He continued down the slope to the long stretch of sandy beach. The surging waves rose out of the lake in long, silent shadows and then fell back in a fury of thunder, surf, and mud. In the calm between waves, he heard the hiss of bubbles breaking and saw thousands of exposed silver flecks skittering down the beach like frightened stars, as if they were running for cover.

Stride couldn't put it off any longer. He climbed back across the dune and up the rear steps of the cottage and let himself inside. Everything was as he had left it, except for the dust on the surfaces and the musty smell of air that had been shut up for weeks. The house had a funereal quiet. The only noise was his footsteps on the uneven floorboards. He went like a visitor from room to room, reacquainting himself with his possessions. When he went into the master bathroom, he detected a trace of the floral soap that Serena used and a lingering hint of her perfume. She had been here, but she was gone now. Just like himself. He stared at his reflection in the mirror, but no one stared back at him.

It happened again. The constriction in his chest. The sensation that his lungs were struggling for air. He held on to the sink as light-headedness washed over him and made him dizzy. A vise tightened around his skull. When he looked in the mirror again, his skin was pasty and damp with sweat. His eyelids were dark hoods over his eyes. He ran water in the sink and splashed it on his face.

He needed something to drink. Slowly, he made his way through the cottage's great space into the kitchen and found a can of Coke in the refrigerator. He opened it and set it on the counter and then reached up to the top shelf of a cabinet for a large glass. He wasn't thinking about what he was doing. His hands were wet. He took the glass between his fingers, but it slipped from his grasp.

It fell.

He fell with it.

Goddamn.

He was high above the water again. His body shot like a bullet from the bridge, knifing toward the harbor. The night air became a searing whistle in his ears. Three seconds, that was all it took. Three seconds to realize he was about to die, three seconds to hammer into the bay. His nerve ends erupted with agony. The hard, cold water became his tomb. His mind drove him into the deep jaws of the bay, over and over, and each time his body rocketed through the air, he wished that the impact would kill him once and for all. He could almost hear the words forming in his chest.

Kill me.

Stride was on the kitchen floor when he awakened. Broken glass surrounded him, some shards as pretty as diamonds, some large and deadly like arrowheads. Crimson trails oozed from the cuts on his arms. His shirt was dyed with stains from the blood that dripped down his cheek and neck, where the eruption of glass had sprayed his face. He spread his hands wide and watched the smears as if the blood were coming from a stranger's body. The cuts didn't sting. His leg, the leg he had broken in the fall, didn't throb. He was numb.

On the floor, he saw a pointed shard with edges as sharp as a razor. So sharp they could slice through tissue like a surgeon's knife. He picked it up and rubbed it between his fingers. The glass glinted in the light. He squeezed his fist and saw the veins in his wrist bulge like twin lengths of rope. If only the fragments had cut him there, opening him up like a fountain. If only he hadn't awakened at all. He didn't want to live like this.

Twenty-five

'Where did you go last night, Valerie?' Serena asked.

They sat in front of the fireplace in the lobby of the Sawmill Inn in Grand Rapids. Valerie wore a conservative gray suit, with her blonde hair pinned up. She stared at the fire with an uncomfortable expression and refused to meet Serena's eyes.

'Go? What do you mean?'

'Don't play dumb. Do you think we're not watching your house? You left last night at eleven thirty, and you got back shortly before one in the morning.'

Valerie rubbed her fingers along the smooth oak on the arm of the sofa. 'Oh, that. I couldn't sleep. I went for a drive.'

'Where?'

'Around town. I do that sometimes. I'll sit in a park by the river at night. I like to be by myself when I'm sad.'

Serena put a hand on Valerie's shoulder. 'It doesn't help when you lie to me.'

'I'm not lying.'

Valerie glanced at the hotel door. Serena had stopped her as she emerged from a breakfast meeting in the hotel's restaurant. Valerie's friends lingered, watching them. 'I've been part of this prayer group for almost five years,' she added, changing the subject. 'Are you a religious person, Serena?'

'No.'

'I try to be.'

Serena said nothing.

'One of the older women asked me if I had sinned,' Valerie continued. 'She thinks I'm being punished.'

'That's a load of crap,' Serena said.

'Who knows? Maybe she's right. Then again, when you're a sixty-six-year-old virgin, it's easy to be pious. It's a little harder for the rest of us.'

Serena sipped coffee from a styrofoam cup. 'Were you meeting someone?'

'I'm sorry?'

'Last night.'

'I told you, I went for a drive.'

Serena shook her head. 'I understand that you don't want to tell me, but when the mother of a missing child starts lying to me, I wonder why.'

'Why are you so sure I'm lying?' Valerie asked.

'Because your lower lip is trembling, your smile is fake, you keep changing the subject, and you won't look at me. Is that enough?'

Valerie didn't say anything.

'Was it about Callie?' Serena asked. 'Did they tell you not to talk to the police? I realize you're scared, but if a kidnapper made contact with you, you have to tell me. I need to know.'

'It wasn't that.'

'Then what was it?'

'It was just someone playing head games with me.'

'Who?'

'Regan Conrad.'

Serena leaned closer, her voice low. 'What did she want?'

'She said she knew what happened to Callie, but that was a lie.'

'Did she tell you not to talk to the police?'

Valerie nodded.

'What exactly did she say?'

'It doesn't matter. She didn't know anything.'

'Tell me what she said, Valerie. Why did she want to see you? What did she say about Callie?'

'I don't want to play her game,' Valerie replied. 'If I tell you, I'm giving her what she wants.'

'I'm going to talk to her anyway. You know that. I don't care if you think she was lying. If she told you she knows what happened to Callie, she's a suspect.'

'She was just trying to get under my skin. She wanted me to believe Marcus was involved in Callie's disappearance. This is about her getting revenge on the two of us. That's all.'

'Did she have new information?' Serena asked.

'No.'

'Then why did she think Marcus was involved?'

A flush rose on Valerie's face. 'She said – she said he told her things. About him not wanting me to have a baby. Like he told that stripper in Vegas. I don't believe her. I think she made it up to torture me.'

'What else?'

'That was all.'

Serena could see Valerie covering up the rest of the story the way a mother covers a baby. She was protecting a secret. 'You're holding out on me, Valerie,' she said.

Valerie stood up and smoothed her skirt. 'There wasn't anything else. She didn't know what happened to Callie.'

'I can't find your daughter if you keep things from me. Even the things you don't want to face.'

'I'm sorry. I don't have anything more to tell you.'

Valerie walked away. Serena watched her leave the hotel with the elegant march of a woman who was at ease in high heels. Two of the women from the prayer group waited by the door, but Valerie didn't acknowledge them. When Serena went outside herself, she saw Valerie climbing into her Mercedes in the parking lot. Their eyes met. In that instant, Serena saw through Valerie's shell and felt the other woman reaching out to her for help, as if she were apologizing for having a secret that was too awful to share. Then the moment passed, and Valerie drove off on to Pokegama Road.

Serena wondered what sin Valerie thought she was being punished for. How could any sin be worth the life of a child?

Valerie didn't go home. She didn't want to see Marcus or run the gauntlet of police and media. Instead, she drove to her sister's house by the river and parked outside. Denise was gone; she always left early. Tom's car was in the driveway. The kids were already in school, except for the youngest, and Valerie knew that Tom dropped Maureen at day care on his way to work.

She sat in the car with the engine running and reached over and opened the glove compartment. The envelope that Regan Conrad had given her was inside. She took it out and turned it over gently in her hands, feeling the slight bulge of the paper sealed under the flap. All she had to do was rip the envelope open.

I don't have to tell you why, do I?

Valerie shook her head. She wouldn't let her mind be poisoned by Regan Conrad, and she wouldn't let Serena be poisoned either. Whatever it was, she didn't want to know. She slid the envelope back into the glove compartment and closed it.

'Valerie.'

She looked up at a knock on the window and the muffled sound of a voice. Tom Sheridan stood outside the car with

Maureen in his arms. He wore a heavy coat over a brown business suit.

'Hi,' she said, unlocking the door.

Tom climbed inside. He warmed a hand at the hot air vent and didn't say anything. Maureen was bundled up in a fleece blanket, with a pink cap on her head. Valerie reached out and ran a finger along the girl's soft cheek and was rewarded with a giggle.

'Hello, sweetheart,' she said.

Valerie couldn't help it. Seeing Maureen made the pain of losing Callie even worse. Despite Maureen's disability, there was a resemblance between the faces of the two girls. Denise's daughter had Callie's eyes and an echo of her smile.

'How are you, Val?' Tom asked.

'I'm OK,' she murmured, not taking her eyes off Maureen. 'Do you want to come inside?'

'I can't. I just needed to get away from the circus for a couple of minutes.'

Tom nodded and stared at his lap. Valerie held out her hand and let Maureen grab her fingers. Their breath made steam on the car windows.

'Is there anything I can do to help?' he asked.

'No. I wish there was.'

'I can't think about anything else,' he said.

'I know. I appreciate it.'

'Are you sure you don't want to come inside with me?'

'No. I shouldn't have come here. I'm sorry.'

'Don't be.' He added, 'I was going to call you this morning, but this is easier in person.'

Valerie tensed. 'What?'

'That reporter Blair Rowe came by my office last night.'

'What did she want?'

Tom hesitated. 'It's a problem.'

'What is it?'

'Someone gave her some information. I begged her not to go ahead with it, but she's going to put it on the news tonight.'

'Oh, my God.' Valerie closed her eyes. 'What is it this time? Is it something new about Marcus?'

Tom shook his head. 'No. I'm really sorry, Val. This one's not about Marcus.'

Twenty-six

Maggie grabbed two bags of fast food breakfast and a foam drink caddy that held coffee and orange juice. With her hands full, she navigated the steps of Stride's cottage in her heels. Her sunglasses – which were mostly for show, because the sun wasn't shining – slipped to the end of her nose. Red hair swished in front of her eyes. She reached Stride's front door and kicked with the toe of her boot.

'Hey, it's me,' she shouted.

No one came to the door. Maggie put down the tray of drinks and dug in her pocket for her keys. Stride's key had a purple tab on her chain. She maneuvered her body between the screen door and the oak front door and undid both locks. With her shoulder, she shoved the door open and spilled inside.

'You around? I've got McMuffins and a couple breakfast burritos.' Maggie listened for the noise of the shower, but the cottage was quiet. 'Hello?'

Maggie deposited the food on the dining-room table. She unwrapped a straw and stuck it into the lid of one of the cups of orange juice. Her cheeks dimpled as she sucked on the drink. She strolled around the island separating the dining room from the kitchen, in order to retrieve plates for the table.

That was when she saw him.

'Oh my God.'

Maggie dropped her drink. The lid popped, and orange juice splashed on the floor. She sank to her knees. Stride sat with his back against the cabinets. Sharp glass fragments surrounded him like popcorn. There was blood on his face and on his hands. His eyes were open, but he stared through her as if she were invisible.

'Are you OK?'

He didn't reply.

Maggie crawled to him, dodging the crumbles of glass. She took his hands and wiped away some of the blood on her shirt. She held his face and lifted his chin, and his eyes slowly focused on her. They were no more than six inches apart.

'Stay there,' she said, holding his shoulders as he tried to move.

She pulled a towel from the oven handle, soaked it in water under the sink, and washed the blood from his face. She did the same with his arms. When she was finished, she saw that he had no serious injuries, just surface cuts that had bled profusely. The cool water began to bring him back to life.

'Damn, I'm sorry,' he murmured. 'I'll be fine.'

Maggie stroked his hair. One of the cuts on his cheek began to bleed, and she used the damp towel on his face again.

'Can you stand up?' she asked.

He nodded.

'Take it slow,' she said.

With an arm around him, she helped him to his feet. He swayed as he stood upright and grabbed the counter for balance. She led him through the great space to the bathroom, where he held on to the sink with both hands. He bowed his head, and his hair fell across his face. She yanked the shower curtain back and turned on the water. She grabbed another towel, put it under the water, and carefully dabbed at the remaining blood on his skin. When she switched on the faucet, pink liquid swirled in the wash basin.

She helped him off with his bloody shirt. His bare chest was damp with sweat. 'Take a shower, OK?' she said. 'That'll help.'

He ran his hand through his hair. A few pieces of glass sprinkled to the floor.

'I'll clean up,' she said.

Maggie left him in the bathroom. She returned to the kitchen and grabbed a broom from the utility closet and swept up the glass. With a fistful of paper towels, she swabbed the blood and orange juice from the floor. Everything went in the trash. She went into Stride's bedroom and found a pair of boxer shorts in his bureau. She opened the bathroom door and saw his shadow behind the shower curtain. His hands were propped on the shower wall. She grabbed his dirty clothes under her arm and left the boxers on the towel rack, then picked up the remaining pieces of glass with her fingers.

When she was done, she sat on the floor in the great space, with her back against Stride's red leather chair and her arms wrapped around her knees. Her heart raced. She swallowed hard and stared at her feet and held back her own breakdown.

'I'm really sorry.'

Maggie looked up. Stride was in the doorway leading to the bathroom. He wore the boxers and nothing else. Drops of water clung to his body, and his dark hair was wet. She rubbed her eyes and looked down at her feet again without saying anything. He padded across the carpet and slid down beside her. Their shoulders touched, and his skin was warm. He put his big arm around her and pulled her into him.

'Thank you,' he said.

She lost it. She cried into his shoulder, hating herself for letting him see her as weak and vulnerable. That wasn't who she was. She wiped her face and pulled away from him. 'You scared the shit out of me.'

'I know.'

'What happened to you? Talk to me.'

'I dropped a glass,' he said.

'Did you have a stroke? A heart attack? Should I get an ambulance over here?'

'No, it's nothing like that.'

'Then what is it?'

He hesitated. 'I don't think I can talk about it.'

She twisted her body to stare at him. Their faces were inches apart again. Her voice caught in her throat as she scolded him. 'I don't care. Talk to me.'

'Mags,' he murmured.

'I'm serious. You are not going to lock me out.'

He steepled his hands and laid his chin against his fingers. He closed his eyes. 'It's been happening for the last couple months,' he whispered.

'What?'

'Panic attacks. Flashbacks.'

'Flashbacks of what?' Maggie asked. Then she understood. 'The fall.'

He nodded. 'I drop something, anything, and it's like I'm back there. It isn't just a memory. I'm *there*. And it's not getting better, it's getting worse. It's driving me crazy.'

Maggie exhaled with a loud sigh. 'Have you talked to anyone?'

He shook his head. 'No.'

'You need help,' she snapped. 'Since when do you have to be Superman? Oh wait, who am I talking to? You can't lean on anyone. You always have to be strong.' She stopped and mentally cursed herself. She leaned into him and rested her forehead on his cheek. 'I'm sorry.'

'You're right,' he said.

'Is it just the flashbacks?' she asked. 'Or is there more?'

'There's more,' he admitted. 'I'm dead inside. I don't care about anything or anyone. When I was sitting in the kitchen, I wished I was dead. I mean, I really thought about—'

He stopped talking.

'Now you're scaring me,' she said.

'I wasn't going to do anything, but I thought about it.'

Maggie took his hand in hers. Their eyes met, and for the first time in their relationship, she felt as if the differences between them had melted away. There was no span of years separating them. No division of boss and partner. No history of one-sided emotions she had tried to suppress. They were on a level playing field, one man, one woman.

'You're not nuts, you know. It's normal.'

'Normal? Please.'

'If it was anyone else, you'd see it immediately. You just can't look in the mirror.'

'What are you talking about?'

'PTSD. Post-traumatic stress disorder. For God's sake, wake up, will you? Three months ago, you nearly died. You think your body can heal and that's the end of it? You've been digging a hole for yourself because you won't face it.'

He stared at the ceiling. 'It doesn't make sense, Mags. I've been through worse shit in my life than this. Even when I lost Cindy, I still hung on to myself.'

'I was there,' she reminded him. 'You've blocked out how bad it was.'

She didn't add that she had tried to come inside with him then and share his grief and help him through it, and he had shut her out.

'I think it's worse to feel nothing,' he said. 'I'm somewhere else. Gone.'

Maggie caressed his neck with the back of her fingers. 'You're not alone.'

'I know. Thanks.'

'It's not a sin to need help.'

'Maybe, but I'm used to dealing with things on my own,' he said.

'No, you don't deal with them at all, you stubborn ass.'

His face softened. He laughed. 'I've missed you.'

'Me, too. Don't go running away again, OK?'

'Deal.'

It felt normal to continue to caress him, and she did. She saw what looked like an invitation in his eyes, and she brought her fingertips along the line of his chin and then across his lips.

'You haven't said a word, you know,' she said.

'About what?'

'About me.'

He blinked, not understanding. He stared at her until he finally saw her. Really saw her. She watched herself get inside his head. She had been standing on the outside for so long that it felt disorienting to have him look at her that way.

'Oh, my God,' he said with a smile. 'Look at your hair.'

He reached over and pushed away the bangs that fell over her eyes, and the intimacy of the gesture took her breath away.

She smiled back. Just with her lips. Teasing.

'Like it?'

He didn't have to answer. His expression said everything. She didn't know if it was gratitude or desire, but she didn't care. His hands slid around the back of her neck and pulled her toward him. Her chin tilted upward. Their breath was warm on each other's faces. Their lips moved closer, as if drawn by gravity, and came softly together. He kissed her; she kissed him back. When he pulled away, she thought in the recess of her brain, *so that's that*. It was over, a moment where they had danced at the edge of a dangerous line and then come to their senses, exactly as they needed to do.

But it wasn't over. The first kiss ended, and with the fragile ice breaking underneath them, they began again. Their need was ferocious and immediate. Before she knew it, the dangerous line was so far behind them that she couldn't see it any more.

A voice sang in her head – *mistake, mistake, mistake* – but she shut the door firmly, and the voice grew faint and unimportant. They didn't think about what they were doing; they just did it. She helped him undress her, and she peeled away the silk boxers around his waist, and when they were both naked, he pressed her downward into the carpet. He loomed over her, and his arms scooped under her shoulder blades. She rose upward to meet him, clutching his face. In the next instant, as her legs spread and tightened around his back, he filled her with a single, wanton thrust.

Mistake, the voice said again.

She didn't listen. She didn't care any more. She drowned out the voice by telling him how much she wanted him. She told him to make love to her. She held on to him so tightly that her fingernails drove into his skin. She couldn't be too close, couldn't have a square inch of her body not touching him. He responded with the same intensity, making love to her with the same urgent abandon.

Somewhere, drifting outside herself, she wondered if there was a voice in his head, too, whispering that this was wrong. If so, he didn't listen either. They simply clung to each other and leaped from the bridge together, and for a time she was convinced they could fly. Even if they couldn't, it made no difference, because the water was so far below that she couldn't see it coming closer.

Twenty-seven

Serena found Regan Conrad sitting alone in the hospital cafeteria. The nurse picked at a green salad and drank from a plastic bottle of Aquafina. She wore lilac scrubs. When Serena sat down opposite her, Regan glanced at the other tables to see who was within earshot.

'I guess you talked to Valerie,' Regan said with a small smile.

Serena leaned across the table. 'This isn't a joke. You're lucky I'm not arresting you.'

'It wouldn't be the first time,' Regan said, chewing on her salad. 'But I suppose you know that by now, don't you?'

Serena did. She had done her homework.

'When you were nineteen, you were picked up for breaking and entering in Two Harbors,' she said.

Regan shrugged. 'I was sitting in my boyfriend's car. I didn't know what he was doing.'

'I read the police reports,' Serena told her. 'He said it was your idea. He said you egged him on. The house belonged to a man you'd been sleeping with.'

She stabbed a grape tomato with her fork and pulled it between her teeth. 'Men will say anything. You know that.'

'When you were twenty-four, you left threatening messages for a girl you blamed for stealing your boyfriend,' Serena continued.

'She did steal him. Little bitch.'

'The girl found her cat beheaded in her backyard,' Serena said.

'It wasn't me,' Regan replied, 'although I'm not much of a cat person.'

'Someone put a pipe bomb under her car, too. The police were convinced you were involved.'

'I had an alibi. They never charged me.'

'They thought you got someone else to do your dirty work.'

'I must be really persuasive,' Regan said.

'You had an alibi when Callie Glenn disappeared, too,' Serena told her.

'Oh, I get it. There's no way I could have done it myself, so that must mean I had someone else do it for me. Are there any other crimes I couldn't have committed that you'd like to talk to me about?'

'You told Valerie Glenn you *know* what happened to Callie.'

'Sure I do. So do you. It was Marcus.'

'Do you have any evidence that he was involved?'

'Marcus is smart. I don't think he's likely to leave any evidence behind.'

'Why did you contact Valerie?' Serena asked.

'I thought she deserved to know the truth.'

'The truth? What exactly did you tell her?'

Regan shrugged. 'Just that Marcus said the same things to me that he said to that girl in Vegas. He wished Callie had never been born.'

'That's all?'

'If there was anything else, I'm sure Valerie would have told you.'

'Don't be cute,' Serena said. 'Why didn't you want her calling the police?'

'I didn't think she wanted *you* to know the kind of person Marcus is. Wives have to make difficult choices about what they can live with.'

Serena jabbed a finger in Regan's face. Her patience with the nurse was gone. 'Don't pretend you're doing anything noble. You have no proof about Marcus. You simply want to sabotage their marriage.'

'I'm being honest,' Regan replied. 'You're the one who's filling Valerie's head with false hope. Desperate mothers will believe anything you tell them. If their child is at stake, they'll believe a lie even when the truth is staring them in the face. You tell Valerie that Callie will be coming home, but in your heart of hearts, you don't believe that. You think exactly what I do. So does your partner. So does Blair Rowe. The only difference is, I've got the guts to say it to Valerie's face.'

'Stay away from her,' Serena snapped. 'You're hindering a police investigation.'

'Investigation? It looks to me like you're at a dead end.'

'I think you're hiding something,' Serena told her. 'When I first talked to you, you were pushing me to look at Micki Vega. Do you know something about her and Marcus? Do you think she was involved in Callie's disappearance?'

Regan shook her head. 'I have no idea, but I imagine Micki would do anything that Marcus told her to do. She was obviously in love with him.'

'Why did Micki lose her baby?'

'Women miscarry. Bad things happen. There was nothing unusual about it.'

'How did she react?' Serena asked.

'How would you expect her to react? She was hysterical.'

'It must have been hard for her to lose a baby and then turn around and take care of Callie.'

'I'm sure it was,' Regan said. 'What are you suggesting? That Micki stole Callie Glenn to replace the baby she lost?'

'Is that possible?' Serena asked.

'Anything's possible. I already told you, mothers can be desperate creatures.'

'Desperate people can be manipulated.'

'By me? You think I persuaded Micki to steal Callie?'

'Did you?'

'Of course not.'

'You have a history of twisting people around your finger and getting them to do what you want,' Serena persisted.

'I haven't talked to Micki in months. If anyone manipulated her, it's Marcus. Who knows what ideas he put into Micki's lovesick head?'

'Why would Marcus want Micki to harm his child? Or take her away?'

'If you can figure out why,' Regan said, her voice dropping into a whisper, 'then I guess you'll know everything.'

'I'm asking you.'

Regan stood up. 'Sorry. I don't want to hinder your *investigation*.'

Serena stood up too and got in Regan's face. 'Were you involved in Callie's disappearance?'

'You know I wasn't. I was here at the hospital that night.'

'Do you know what happened to her?'

'We both know, but you don't want to face reality. You want to take something simple and make it complex. Marcus was obviously involved. Maybe Micki, too.'

'Who was in your house the night I talked to you?' Serena asked.

'Excuse me?'

'There was an old Escort in your driveway when I arrived. When I left, it wasn't there any more. Someone sneaked out while I was with you. Who was it?'

'I'm a medical professional. It's none of your business who I talk to.'

'So it was a patient?'

'I think we're done,' Regan said. 'If you want to talk about my nursing, you can get a judge to give you a warrant. And good luck with that.'

'This isn't over. You'll see me again.'

'I'm sure I will,' Regan told her. 'You're obviously obsessed with me, Ms Dial. But I wish you'd give it up and do something useful. Like catching the killer in my neighborhood.'

'The Duluth Police will get him.'

'Really? Is that supposed to be a comfort?'

'The police are doing everything they can.'

'Tell that to the four women who are dead,' Regan said. 'Me, I'll keep sleeping with my shotgun.'

Twenty-eight

Stride parked on the steep west-side slope of Lake Avenue in the area of downtown Duluth known as the Central Hillside. It was the seamy section of town, prone to vagrants and hookers during the warmer months. Winter sent most of the itinerant population south like migrating birds, but a few hearty souls always hung around to keep the cops and the social service agencies busy. As he parked, he saw a cluster of youths in heavy coats eyeing his car suspiciously from the corner of 4th Street.

Maggie sat next to him with her chin on her fist as she stared out the window. They hadn't spoken much since it happened.

'Is this Nick Garaldo's place?' Stride asked, nodding his head at the four-story brick apartment building with the broken windows.

Maggie nodded. 'Yeah, this is it.'

He knew he should be the one to go first. It was his fault. For more than ten years, he had tiptoed around Maggie, aware of her feelings for him and careful not to lead her on. Now he had put both of them in an impossible situation.

He stared at her on the other side of the car. The fire-engine red hair – that was so Maggie. Wild and hip. Doing whatever she wanted. Same with the diamond in her nose. He had always been closed-off and serious, and she was funny and on the fringe, but they had clicked. Yin and yang. He couldn't imagine the idea of her not being in his life. That was one of the reasons he had always kept a safe distance between them, even in those moments when she had made it clear he could cross the line. Now the safe space was gone.

Mistake. He had to say it. Mistake. She was waiting for him to break the silence and give them both a chance to pretend it had never happened.

Except he didn't feel that way. Something was different. He felt alive again. He realized that the coffer dam of dead logs and debris inside his head had finally broken free, but the flood that came with it was out of control. Emotions ricocheted around his soul, threatening to do serious damage. As if he hadn't done enough damage to his life already.

Serena.

He felt a stabbing wave of guilt. Serena. She had been the center of his life for the past three years, and he had turned his back on her and cheated on her. Serena was no fool. She had always known how Maggie felt about him. If there was one thing she had feared in their relationship, it was that he would sleep with Maggie one day.

And now he had.

'Mags,' he said.

She swiveled her head to stare at him. He watched her face, which was patient and expectant. She assumed he was about to run like hell. She was waiting for him to say it. Mistake.

When he didn't say anything, Maggie rode to his rescue again.

'Look, do we have to make a big deal out of this?' she asked. 'You feel guilty as hell, but you shouldn't. I don't. We needed each other, and something happened. Serena never needs to know. You can go back to the way things were.'

'What about us?' he said.

She turned away without replying. He knew why. Even if he entertained the fiction that he and Serena could go on as they had before, he was certain that his relationship with Maggie had changed forever. They couldn't pretend otherwise.

'Let's go check out the apartment, OK?' she said, ducking his question. 'That's probably the manager over there.'

They climbed out of his truck and approached a short black man who paced in front of the apartment building. He greeted them with a firm handshake and introduced himself as Rufus Durand. Durand had steel-gray hair and was in his late fifties. He used his key to let them inside the street door.

'Mr Garaldo's apartment is on the top floor,' he said, handing them a master key with an old wooden spoon tied to the chain with a rubber band. 'It's number four hundred and five. I guess you guys want to do this by yourself, huh?'

Durand's tone made it clear he didn't want to go upstairs with them. If there was a body inside, he didn't want to see it. It probably wouldn't be the first time one of his tenants had gone out feet first.

'We'll bring the key back,' Maggie said.

'Yeah, take your time, I'll sit down here and do the cross-word.' He withdrew a newspaper from under his arm and sat down in a card table chair on the wall opposite the elevator.

Stride and Maggie took the elevator upward. It was old and slow. Maggie shoved her hands in her jeans and danced impatiently on the balls of her feet.

'When was this guy last seen?' Stride asked.

'Saturday.'

'And nothing since then?'

'Nope. No calls on his cell, and he didn't show up at work. I called his parents in Des Moines. They haven't heard from him.'

They found Nick Garaldo's apartment and knocked. No one answered. Maggie twirled the key on the spoon and pushed it into the lock and let them inside. Garaldo's apartment had a single bedroom, an open space that doubled as living room and dining room, and a kitchenette. The furniture was sparse and had an estate sale smell. Stride headed for the bedroom, and he heard Maggie opening drawers in the kitchen. He found a twin bed, unmade. Garaldo had a nightstand next to the bed with a lamp and alarm clock and a dog-eared paperback book. It was a Minnesota private eye novel by David Housewright.

Stride snapped on gloves and opened the nightstand drawer. Garaldo hadn't accumulated much junk. The drawer included a half-empty box of condoms, Old Spice cologne, several other paperback mysteries, and debris ranging from paper clips to potato chip crumbs. He closed the drawer and got down on his knees to look under the bed, where he found several dusty pairs of athletic shoes. Next to one of the shoes he saw a black disk no bigger than a postage stamp, which he removed and held between his fingers. It was an XD picture card for a digital camera. He bagged it.

He checked the attached bathroom and found nothing unusual. No illegal drugs in the medicine cabinet. A prescription for allergy medication. Soap-crusted bottles of shampoo. He returned to the living room.

'Anything?' he asked Maggie.

She shook her head. 'He likes red pistachios. Big honking jar in the kitchen. Otherwise, nothing.'

He handed her the photo card. 'He's been taking pictures.'

'Did you find his camera?'

Stride shook his head. 'No.'

'That's interesting,' Maggie said.

A phone sat on an end table near the television, and they noticed the red light flashing to indicate that Garaldo had messages. She pushed the button to play them. There were seven messages in all, three from his girlfriend, two from his boss in the harbor, and two from his parents, who mentioned that the police were asking about him. They sounded concerned.

'I don't see a calendar or PDA,' Stride said. 'How about his mail?'

'Bills. He does a lot of shopping at REI. Must be a back-packer or camper.'

'So maybe he went hiking and had an accident,' he suggested.

'Maybe. I'll put out an alert with the park service.'

Stride surveyed the room again. Garaldo owned a television set propped on laminate shelves on one wall. There was a pair of iPod speakers on the shelf above the TV, but the iPod dock itself was empty. Beyond the shelves, he saw an oak desk with a Dell computer monitor.

'Did you find hiking boots in the closet or under the bed?' Maggie asked.

Stride shook his head.

'No way this guy doesn't own boots,' Maggie said.

'What about his car?'

'He's got a Chevy Malibu registered in his name. I've got an ATL out on it. Nothing yet.'

'Let's check out his computer,' Stride said.

The green power light glowed on the monitor on the oak desk. Stride pulled out the keyboard drawer and moved the mouse around. Nothing happened. He swung open the panel on the desk. Inside, he found a surge protector and a slot for a CPU tower.

The computer CPU was gone. Cables from the keyboard, monitor, and Ethernet connection hung uselessly inside. Beside him, Maggie whistled.

'Somebody took it,' she concluded. 'I'm starting to get a bad feeling, boss.'

He noticed the way she dropped into her old habit, calling him 'boss' the way she usually did.

'It could be a simple break-in,' he said, 'or maybe we're not talking about a hiking accident after all.'

'I'll get a forensics team out here.'

He heard Maggie's cell phone ringing. When she dug it out of her pocket, she shot him an uncomfortable look. 'It's Serena,' she said.

Stride's gut turned over.

'Hey,' Maggie said, answering the call with a casualness that sounded false to Stride. She listened and then said, 'Yeah, sure, fine. Yeah, he's with me, I'll tell him. We'll see you in a few hours.'

She hung up. Stride raised his eyebrows.

'Serena's in Duluth,' Maggie told him. 'She wants to grab a pizza at Sammy's later.'

Stride closed his eyes. 'Shit.'

'I'll bring Kasey along,' Maggie suggested. 'That might make things a little less awkward.'

Stride nodded.

'I'm not going to say anything,' she added. When he was silent, she tried to read his face. 'I'm giving you an out, you know that, right? A free pass. Just say it was a mistake.'

That was the easy thing to do. For both of them. Add it to the list of secret regrets you keep in your life.

'I can't say that,' he told her. 'I don't know if it was a mistake.'

Twenty-nine

Serena staked out a booth at Sammy's Pizza on Tuesday evening. She had her head down, reviewing emails about Callie, when Stride and Maggie arrived. She looked up as Maggie slid into the booth across from her, and when she saw Maggie's hair, she dropped her BlackBerry into the basket of garlic toast.

'Holy shit.'

Maggie winked. 'What, is something different?'

'Wow.'

'Good wow or bad wow?'

'Sexy wow,' Serena said.

Serena knew that Maggie was one of those women who bad-mouthed her own looks with sarcastic put-downs. But not tonight. Her streaky crimson hair made her look like a New York model. On any other day, Serena would have been happy for her, but she found herself resenting Maggie's transformation. She wasn't feeling particularly attractive herself, and the change in Maggie made her feel worse.

Stride sat next to Serena and kissed her cheek. She saw Maggie's eyes flick between the two of them, watching the obvious tension.

'Hi.'

A young police officer with hair as shock red as Maggie's stood awkwardly beside the table.

'Serena, this is Kasey,' Maggie said.

'Yeah, I heard about you,' Serena told her. 'You showed some real guts out there.'

Kasey's face cracked into an uneasy smile. She sat stiffly next to Maggie, as if she was at attention.

'You doing OK?' Maggie asked her.

'I'm freaked out,' Kasey admitted.

'Do you want me to get someone to stay with you tonight? You guys might feel better if you weren't alone.'

Kasey shook her head. 'We'll be fine. Bruce has got the house locked up like a prison.'

The waitress laid a steaming, sixteen-inch pizza on an aluminum tray between them. Sausage meatballs and red discs of pepperoni dotted the pie in neat rows. Silently, they nudged apart several squares and pulled them on to each of their plates.

'Is there anything new on Callie?' Maggie asked, pursing her lips and blowing on a piece of pizza to cool it.

'I think that Regan Conrad knows more than she's telling me,' Serena said.

'I'm sorry, who?' Kasey asked.

'Regan's a nurse who was having an affair with Marcus Glenn,' Serena explained. 'She had a key to their house, and she knows the layout. She also has a prior relationship with Migdalia Vega, who was *in* the house when Callie disappeared. That's a lot of connections.'

'So what do you want to do?' Stride asked.

'Get a search warrant.'

'I'm not sure we've got probable cause,' he said.

'She *told* Valerie Glenn she knew what happened to Callie,' Serena insisted. 'Plus, I heard a baby when I was at her house on Saturday.'

'You really think Callie is there with Regan?' Maggie asked dubiously.

'If I said yes, I think a judge might give me a warrant.'

Stride frowned. 'Maybe.'

Serena popped a piece of pizza in her mouth. She tried to decipher the odd dynamic among the three of them. She and Stride were already acting like strangers, but even Stride and Maggie seemed to be avoiding each other. She told herself that it was a virus, starting in Stride's head, spreading to herself, and now infecting Maggie, too. Kasey looked uncomfortable being with them. The young cop pushed around the pizza on her plate and barely ate a thing. She had nervous, darting eyes, like a sparrow hopping on the lawn, aware that a cat might be ready to pounce.

Beside her, Stride checked his watch. 'The news is on.'

He slid out of the booth. A television was suspended on a stand in the corner of the restaurant twenty feet away. He turned it on and flipped through the channels until he found a summary of current news. They didn't have to wait long for the hot story of the week. When the network cut away to a live feed of Blair Rowe in front of the county office building in Grand Rapids, Stride turned up the volume. Serena could hear it from the table.

'. . . *a new twist in the disappearance of Callie Glenn,*' Blair reported with high-pitched excitement, adjusting her black glasses on her nose. '*As you know, we've learned disturbing facts about Callie's father, Marcus Glenn, in the days since this little girl vanished. However, tonight the buzz in Grand Rapids is not about Marcus Glenn, but about Callie's mother, Valerie. She's been the beautiful, tragic figure in this story, pleading for the return of her daughter and insisting that her husband is innocent. The police have pointedly raised no suspicions in this case about Valerie herself, perhaps in part because her sister is a senior member of the Sheriff's Department. When we come back, however, I'll take a closer look at Valerie Glenn and her history of mental illness. I'll also share startling new information that may well prove to be the missing motive that police have needed in their investigation of Marcus Glenn.'*

The station went to commercial.

'Valerie's history of mental illness?' Serena exclaimed. 'What is this bitch trying to do to her?'

Stride returned to the table. 'Did Valerie give you any hints about this so-called secret?'

Serena shook her head. 'She didn't say a thing.' But she thought about Regan: *If you know why, you'll know everything.*

Stride's phone rang. He took it out and checked the caller ID. 'Good news travels fast,' he said. 'It's Denise. I better take this.'

He headed for the door, leaving the three women alone.

Serena kept an eye on the television. With Stride gone, Maggie fidgeted. It was as if the virus had spread between the two of them, too. Their friendship felt strained.

'I should go,' Kasey announced during the lull in the conversation. 'I don't want Bruce to worry.'

'You sure you don't want a cop in the house tonight?' Maggie asked. 'I can have somebody there in an hour.'

'No, thanks.'

'OK, I'll see you tomorrow.'

Kasey hesitated and looked down. 'I, uh, I don't know about tomorrow.'

'If you need a day, take a day,' Maggie said.

'Yeah, well, here's the thing. I'm going to quit.'

'You mean quit the force?'

Kasey nodded. 'After what happened last night, Bruce and I think that would be best. You know, get away, start over. Go someplace where this guy won't find me.'

'I don't want to lose you, Kasey,' Maggie replied, 'but I wouldn't blame you if you decided to go.'

'It would be different if it was just me, but I have to think about my family.'

'Of course.'

'Anyway, I'll call you tomorrow.'

'Sure.'

Kasey stood up. Serena watched her red curls bounce as she left the restaurant using quick, determined steps. The young cop pushed through the door, turned right on First Street, and disappeared.

'What would you do in her shoes?' Serena asked.

'I'd probably run like hell, too.'

Maggie still didn't look at Serena.

'What's going on with you?' Serena asked. 'Is something wrong?'

'Nah, just the usual,' Maggie replied.

'Did Jonny tell you anything today?'

'Like what?'

'Like what's bothering him.'

'No, he clammed up,' she said.

Serena studied Maggie's face and realized to her dismay that she didn't believe her. 'He said nothing?' she asked.

'No, sorry.'

Serena leaned across the table. 'I could really use your help. I need to know what the hell is going on with him.'

'I shouldn't get in the middle of this,' Maggie told her.

'I think you already are.'

'What do you want from me, Serena?'

'The truth.'

'You can't handle the truth,' she said in a Jack Nicholson voice.

'Don't joke,' Serena said.

'I'm sure he'll tell you when he's ready.'

'Tell me what?'

'Whatever's bothering him.'

'You sound like you already know what that is,' Serena said.

'Oh, fuck, can't you leave me out of this?' Maggie snapped, startling her. 'He's your lover. I'm just the third wheel since you two shacked up. Talk to him, not me, will you?'

Serena stood up. She found herself blinking back tears. 'Fine.'

'I'm sorry,' Maggie said.

Serena said nothing.

'Panic attacks, OK?' Maggie said.

Serena looked down at her. 'What?'

'Ever since the fall, Stride's been having panic attacks. Flashbacks.'

'He *told* you that?' she asked.

Maggie nodded. 'I think it's PTSD. He needs help.'

Serena wondered why she hadn't recognized it herself. It made sense to her now, hearing Maggie describe it.

'I didn't say anything to you about this,' Maggie said. 'All right?'

She nodded. 'Yeah.'

Serena thought about Jonny watching his life come apart at the seams, and she felt guilty that she'd been unable to help him through it. Because he hadn't said a word to her about his pain. Instead, he had bared his soul to Maggie.

She'd thought that knowing the truth would make her feel better, but it didn't. Maggie and Jack Nicholson were both right. She couldn't handle it.

'Denise,' Stride said into the phone outside the restaurant.

'Are you watching the news?' she asked.

'Yeah.'

'Blair fucking Rowe,' Denise said.

'It looks like she has her sights set on Valerie now.'

'Yeah, my angel of a sister.'

'Do you know what this big secret is?' Stride asked.

Denise's voice was flat. Her emotions had drained out of her like oil from her car. 'Yeah. I know.'

'So what is it? Does it affect the case?'

'I have no idea. As far as I'm concerned, I don't care what happens to my sister anymore.'

'What's going on, Denise? What did Blair find out about Valerie?'

'Keep watching, and you'll see. Enjoy the show like everybody else. Blair's going to tell the whole world that Valerie was having an affair.'

Stride had a bad feeling. 'An affair? With whom?'

'With Tom,' Denise replied. 'Apparently it's not enough for Valerie to have the looks and the money in the family. She had to have my husband, too.'

Thirty

Regan Conrad climbed down from her Hummer in the driveway outside her house and thumped the door shut. Behind her, the porch light threw her shadow down across the dormant fields like a giant. She walked a few steps into the open land where the fields began. There, she cocked her head and listened. In the trees, the wind sounded like the roar of a river. Miles away, a train rattled and rumbled south from the Iron Range. She heard a truck's air horn bellowing on the highway. That was all. Nothing else moved or stared back at her. Instead, the wind blew stronger, and the fat, drooping arms of the spruces shook with laughter.

Under her scrub top, however, bumps of gooseflesh rose on her arms. It wasn't just the cold night. She also had a sensation of eyes in the darkness.

You're paranoid, she told herself.

Regan let herself inside her house and turned on the lights. She lingered in the foyer, noticing the closed doors on both levels. Most nights, she didn't give it a thought. It was odd how you could let your mind carry you away, and when you did, every door and dark space felt like a threat. You didn't have to be a child to worry about monsters in the closet.

She wandered into the kitchen and poured herself a shot glass of Scotch. Before she sat down, she saw the flashing light on her answering machine. Two messages. She punched the play button and downed the shot as she listened.

The first message was from Marcus Glenn. Poor Marcus. He was upset.

'Regan, damn it, what are you trying to do to me? What did you tell Valerie? My nurse told me she found you in my office over the weekend. I want to know what you were doing there. We need to talk right now, you crazy bitch. I need to see you. I want to know *what in the hell you did*.'

He hung up.

Her lips curled into a smile. She wondered if he suspected what she had stolen from his files. What a fool he was, cuckolded by that blonde bitch. How could he tolerate that woman in his bed? A woman who barely moved as he made love to her and then had the nerve to give her body to someone else.

He could have had her, Regan. They could have been together. It was his mistake to choose so badly.

'How does it feel?' she growled at the machine. 'How do you like having the whole world turn against you? Even your pretty little wife.'

The second message was time-stamped an hour ago, but the message was blank. Empty. It went on for a full minute with nothing but silence on the machine. Her face twisted with concern as she listened. The longer the dead air stretched out, the more threatening it became.

She got up and checked the log of callers on the phone. The last call was labeled PRIVATE.

Regan replayed the message and leaned close to the machine. This time, she realized that she could hear someone breathing in the background. Whoever it was let the call drag out without saying anything, but he or she breathed near the phone, loud enough for Regan to hear it.

She deleted both messages. Maybe it was Marcus again,

playing with her head. She wouldn't give him the satisfaction of being afraid.

Regan poured another shot and finished it in one swallow and then went upstairs. She thought about leaving the downstairs lights on, but she told herself that she was overreacting. The house was empty. The doors and windows were locked and secure. In her bedroom, she removed her scrubs and dropped them down the laundry chute to the basement. She brushed her teeth and took a shower and then slid into bed with her body warm and damp.

She reached out with her right hand. Next to the bed, propped against the wall, was a shotgun. Two cartridges loaded. Pick it up, point, and shoot. She stroked the glossy wooden shaft with her fingers, and she felt better. She reached for the lamp on her nightstand and turned it off, throwing the room into complete darkness. Only the green glow of the clock gave any light.

She closed her eyes. Moments later, she was dreaming.

Regan had no idea how much time had passed when she started awake.

Her eyes flew open. She glanced at the clock, but the face was dark, and the absolute silence of the house told her that the power was out. With the furnace shut down, the bedroom had already grown cold. Her bare arms and shoulders lay above the blanket, chilled. Her dream faded as her mind wrapped itself around the real world again. She stared blindly at the ceiling.

Regan shivered. Something was wrong.

The sensation of eyes in the darkness was back, but it was inside now, with her, in the room. She lay frozen, not wanting to draw attention to herself. She thought about closing her eyes again and pretending that everything was fine. Go back to sleep. Dream. It was nothing but her imagination.

Maybe she was dreaming right now. But she knew she wasn't.

He's here, she thought.

Her right hand came alive. Inch by inch, her fingers crept along the edge of the blanket, moving invisibly in the black bedroom. No one could see. Her hand nudged over the side of the bed, and she reached out, hunting for the barrel of the shotgun, ready to yank the gun into her arms. She knew exactly where it was, had measured the distance in the darkness count- less times in the last month, had practiced and rehearsed in case this moment ever came.

The gun was gone. It wasn't there.

Her heart jumped with panic. She bolted up in bed, not pretending any more. The blanket slipped down. She took open-mouthed breaths, and her chest heaved in fear. She leaned down and felt desperately along the ground with her hands, thinking the gun had slipped to the floor.

But no. She heard a noise. Someone was in the room, across from her, settled into the armchair, watching her. She eased against the headboard and tried to see. Her eyes grasped for a beam of light, but everything was dark.

A voice came from across the room. Bitter and intense.

'Why couldn't you keep your mouth shut?'

She understood. Everything made sense now.

'You're making a mistake,' Regan said in her calmest voice. 'You don't have to do this.'

They were sweet, persuasive words, but they didn't work this time. The voice split the silence again.

'You lied to me.'

Regan wondered if she had any hope of escape. She had gone to sleep with the bedroom door open, but now, staring at the dark wall, she knew the door was closed. In less than five seconds, she could be out of bed and in the hallway, and from there, she had a chance. She searched for the right moment to run.

There was no time.

Regan heard the noise of someone shifting in the chair. Getting up. The wood and metal of the gun moved.

She threw back the cover and sprinted for the door, but she wasn't fast enough. On the third step, in the middle of the plush carpet, the shotgun spat lead and flame and lit up the darkness. She howled as the shell ravaged the flesh and bone of her hip and spun her around. Her legs stopped working; she sank to the ground. She dragged herself toward the door, but the six feet between her and the hallway was infinite.

Warm liquid ran on her skin. She grimaced as pain radiated outward from its hot core at her middle. There was blood in her mouth where she had bitten her tongue. She smelled burnt powder hanging like a cloud in the room.

She heard someone coming closer. Standing over her. As she writhed, the cold metal of the barrel sank into the skin of her forehead. The dead weight sat there, pressed against her skull, as the person holding the gun hesitated.

Regan found herself laughing. Blood bubbled out between her lips. All she could think about was that damn song by Duffy, as if she could hear its beat thumping along with her heart, spilling blood on the floor. It occurred to her to beg for mercy, but that was pointless. It was too late for that. She didn't expect it, and she didn't get it.

A flash of flame erupted again.

At the speed of light, the brightness reached her eyes a millisecond before the shell detonated inside her brain.

No mercy.

PART THREE

SILENT SCREAM

Thirty-one

Valerie opened her front door on Wednesday morning and found her sister Denise standing on the porch. She cringed, watching the stony expression on Denise's face that covered up wounds of betrayal and humiliation. Valerie would have felt better if Denise had screamed at her, but instead, her sister marched past her into the house without a word.

'Where's Marcus?' she asked after Valerie closed the door.

'In Duluth. He had surgery this morning.'

Denise worked her jaw uncomfortably as if she had something caught in a tooth.

'Do you want some coffee?' Valerie asked.

'Yeah. Fine.'

They walked silently down the white hallway. Valerie retrieved a heavy mug and filled it with coffee and pushed it across the kitchen island to Denise. She sat on a bar stool and waited, but her sister didn't sit down immediately. Valerie could see Denise's eyes comparing the granite countertops and stainless appliances to her own shoebox kitchen. It was the same routine every time Denise set foot inside their house. Valerie knew the bitter envy Denise felt over the money she had. She felt guilty with every withering look.

'Look, Denise,' she began, but her sister held up a hand to stop her.

'Don't say you're sorry. I don't want to hear that.'

'Then what can I say?' Valerie asked.

'Right now, don't say anything.'

Denise stared down the vast, sloping backyard toward the lake. She pushed her hair back behind her ears and drank her coffee in silence. She wore no make-up. Valerie knew that Denise deliberately avoided looking feminine, and for years she'd assumed it was because of her job. Cops weren't girls. They had to be tough. Now she wondered if the real reason was to avoid comparisons with herself. To pretend that there was no competition between them.

'You've been selfish your entire life,' Denise announced in a harsh, angry voice. 'Everything came easy to you. You've never cared what I had to go through. I worked my ass off to get a tenth of what you've got, and you never worked for a damn thing, did you?'

Valerie said nothing to deny it or to protest. Denise believed it, and she deserved a chance to lay blame.

'I always wondered if you gave a thought to me and my life,' Denise continued, turning back from the window. 'I guess now I know, don't I? If there's something you want, you take it, and to hell with everyone else. Do you even have *a clue* what it's like to raise four kids and be on call every hour of the night and day and wonder if you're going to scrape up enough money to make this month's mortgage payment?'

'No. I don't know. You're right.'

'Well, maybe once in a while you could try to put yourself in someone else's shoes. That would be nice. Do you think I don't know that Tom and I have drifted apart? I've watched it happening for years. But guess what, sometimes life just grinds the love out of you. It sucks, but that's the way it is. I may have a crappy marriage, but it's *my* marriage. Not yours.

Or at least it was until Tom decided that he preferred a fantasy with you to real life with me.'

'Don't blame Tom, please,' Valerie told her. 'This was my fault.'

'Do you think I need you to defend my husband? I know Tom. He wants to be the strong shoulder. And here you come all beautiful and weepy and lonely, and gosh, one thing led to another. Right? Is that what you were going to explain to me? Well, don't bother. Tom had a choice, and he made the wrong one. It doesn't matter whether either one of you intended it to happen.'

'You won't let me tell you I'm sorry. You won't let me explain. I'm not sure what you want me to say.'

'Oh, am I making this hard on you, Valerie?' Denise snapped. 'Isn't that thoughtless of me. I should be more concerned with how *you* feel.'

Valerie didn't want to cry, because she didn't want her sister to believe it was another play for sympathy. But she cried anyway and wiped her eyes. 'I know you won't believe this, Denise, but I've always been jealous of you.'

'Oh, right.'

'It's true,' Valerie insisted. 'You've got these great kids. You're married to your high school sweetheart. You have this amazing job.'

'Don't patronize me.'

'I'm not. I just admire how strong you are. I'm not like that. I've been fragile my whole life, and here my sister is this cop, wife, and mother who can handle anything. Just once in my life, I'd like to have the courage to do the right thing and stand up for myself. To be strong like you.'

Denise shook her head. Her eyes were tired and hard. 'How could you, Valerie? How could you sleep with my husband?'

'It wasn't about sex,' Valerie told her. 'I don't care about sex. I never have. I just – I just needed to be close to someone.

There's no explanation. There's no excuse. It may not matter to you that we never intended it to become physical, but we didn't.'

'I don't care.'

Valerie nodded and spoke softly. 'It didn't last long. A couple times, that's all. We both knew it was wrong. But you have to understand that Tom rescued me. I'm not sure I'd be alive right now without him. I was thinking of suicide again back then.'

Denise slammed her mug down, making a loud crack of stone against stone. Coffee spilled on the granite countertop. 'You are such a narcissistic little bitch. What do you want me to say? I'm so happy my husband saved my sister's life by fucking her brains out? You want to know what I really think, Val? I wish you'd gotten the balls and done it right. Tom's not your husband. If you needed to be rescued, you should have found somebody else to do it, or you should have taken a bottle of pills and gotten it over with.'

Valerie paled, and she looked away, not wanting her sister to see the body blow she had landed. She separated a few paper towels from the roll on the counter and wiped up the spilled coffee. As she did, Denise reached out and put her hands over Valerie's.

'I'm sorry,' she said.

'You don't have anything to apologize for,' Valerie replied. 'You're right. I was suffering, and I wound up hurting my own sister. I'm selfish, and I'm a coward.'

'Don't start with the self-pity.'

'What else do I have? The only thing I did right in my life was have Callie, and I couldn't even protect her.'

Denise pulled away in frustration. 'This always happens. In the end, it's always about you. And I buy into it. It's been that way all our lives.'

Valerie didn't know what to say. She rubbed the counter until it was dry, making sure the coffee didn't leave a stain.

'I have to ask you something,' Denise told her. 'As a cop and as a wife. I have to know.'

'What?'

'Is Tom the father?'

Valerie's eyes widened in shock.

'Don't play games, Val,' Denise continued. 'I need to know. Is Callie Tom's baby?'

'No.'

'Are you sure?'

'Of course I am.'

'Tom's not sure,' Denise said. 'He told me so last night.'

'He's not Callie's father.'

'How do you know?'

'I just know. I can see Marcus in her.'

'Did you have her tested?'

'Of course not. I couldn't do that.'

'So you're just guessing,' Denise said. 'I asked Tom. He said the two of you had sex not long before you got pregnant.'

Valerie shook her head. 'Marcus and I had sex, too. He was the last one.'

'That doesn't make any difference.'

'My husband is the father of my daughter,' Valerie insisted.

'Do you believe that, or are you just trying to convince yourself?'

'It's true.'

'You tried for three years, and you didn't get pregnant. Then you started sleeping with Tom. Wake up, Valerie. Believe me, I know exactly how fertile Tom's swimmers are.'

'Callie is Marcus's baby. I know it.'

'What about Marcus? Does he know it?'

Valerie's eyes narrowed. 'What do you mean?'

'I mean, did Marcus know you were having an affair?'

Valerie heard Marcus shouting at her from the landing. *You're not exactly innocent, are you?*

'He didn't know,' she murmured.

'Are you sure? Grand Rapids is a small town. It's hard to keep secrets. Obviously someone saw the two of you together. Blair Rowe found out, so why couldn't Marcus?'

'There's no way he could have known,' Valerie repeated.

Denise shook her head. 'You know what it means if Marcus knew about your affair, don't you? He may have suspected that Callie wasn't his child. Didn't you ever wonder why he was so cold with her? What would he have done if he realized the little girl who was screwing up his perfect life wasn't really his?'

'I don't want to hear this.' Valerie put her hands over her ears, but Denise reached across the island and yanked her arms away.

'You can't run away from this. It gives him a motive. *Did he know?*'

In her head, Valerie heard Regan Conrad taunting her outside the church after midnight. *I don't have to tell you why, do I?* She thought about the hospital envelope, hidden unopened in her dresser upstairs. The envelope that Regan had given her.

I can't believe you didn't know.

'No,' Valerie told her sister. 'Marcus didn't know about the affair. He never had any reason to think Callie wasn't his. And she is. She's his daughter. He loves her.'

Thirty-two

Maggie watched the contents of the photo disk that Stride had found in Nick Garaldo's apartment sprinkle in thumbnails across her computer monitor. She leaned closer and chewed on her lower lip. The photos were dark and difficult to distinguish. She clicked on one of the thumbnails and enlarged the image on her screen. The photo showed an industrial locale, with a concrete floor and dusty pipes suspended from a bare ceiling. When she clicked on the next image, she saw a pair of giant boilers caked over with rust in front of a windowless wall. As she scrolled through the photographs, she found more images from the same underground site.

One thumbnail – but only one – showed a picture of a person. Maggie saw a short, wiry man wearing jeans, rubber boots, a navy neoprene jacket, and a black wool cap. When she compared the picture to the driver's license photo in her file, she recognized Nick Garaldo.

'Where the hell are you, Nick?' she murmured.

Guppo poked his head around the corner of the office. He stood under a hot air vent, which fluttered his comb-over like a runaway hose. 'We're getting some network interference out here,' he told her.

Maggie twisted around in her chair. 'Oh?'

'Yeah, we think it's your hair.'

He chuckled, and Maggie growled at him. 'Don't poke the bear, Max. I'm not in the mood. Come check this out.'

'Whatcha got?'

He joined her behind the desk and squinted at the monitor. He breathed heavily, and his forehead was dewy with sweat.

'Stride found this photo card in Nick Garaldo's apartment,' Maggie told him. 'It looks like this guy was inside some kind of factory.'

'It doesn't look operational. The place is a mess.' He worked her mouse with a beefy hand. 'That looks like some kind of coal burner. He must be in a sub-basement somewhere.'

'But why?'

Guppo straightened up with a groan. 'Maybe this guy is one of those nutjobs who break into old buildings.'

Maggie probed her memory. 'Didn't we have an intruder report at the old Armory a couple of months ago?'

Guppo nodded. 'Yeah, somebody triggered the interior alarms. We sent a car over there, but we didn't find anyone.'

'Pull the report for me, will you?'

'Sure.'

Guppo waddled out of the office. Maggie set the images into a slide show and leaned dangerously far back in her chair with her boots propped on Stride's desk. After the first few pictures, she drifted off, staring through the window at the mottled gray sky. She became aware of a hollow, guilty pit in her stomach as she thought about her and Stride together. It was one thing to wish for something for ten years of your life and something else altogether to have it happen when you least expected it.

She didn't think he'd meant what he said. In the end, he'd want to go back to the way things were. When he woke up – in a day, a week, or a month – he would curse himself for letting his relationship with Serena slip through his fingers.

The only question was whether he would be alone in bed when it happened, or whether Maggie would be with him. If that was how it was going to end, she didn't want to be there.

She also knew that her friendship with Serena was doomed. Stride would tell Serena the truth. She didn't know if Serena would forgive Stride, but she would never forgive her. That was fair. Their relationship had always been a high-wire act. Behind every barb, Serena had sent Maggie a message loud and clear. *Hands off – he's with me, not you.* And every time Maggie talked about the past, she sent a reply. *I knew him first.*

Sooner or later, one of them was bound to fall.

'You OK?'

She looked up. Guppo was back.

'Yeah, I'm fine,' she replied. 'Did you get the report on the Armory?'

'I did.'

'Let me have it.'

He placed it in her hands, and she flipped through the handful of pages. He lingered, waiting for her to say something, but she waved her hand toward the door without another word. He left and closed the door behind him. She knew he was annoyed. She wasn't normally gruff with Guppo, and he didn't deserve it, but she didn't care. Let him tell the others that she was on the rag.

The officers who responded to the call at the Duluth Armory had taken interior photos near the downstairs access doors, and it was obvious to Maggie that the photos matched the images on Nick Garaldo's disk. If that wasn't sufficient confirmation, she also spotted a notation in the police report that they had found red pistachio shells scattered throughout the Armory rooms. She remembered the mason jar of pistachios in Garaldo's apartment. He had been inside the old building.

She had no idea why Garaldo would invade the abandoned Armory – which contained nothing worth stealing, only detritus from years of disuse – but she knew that urban explorers were like Scuba divers or mountain climbers. They did it because it was there. She also thought it was a safe guess that Garaldo had been engaged in another break-in when he disappeared on Saturday. But where? Urban ruins were unstable and dangerous, and if something had happened to Garaldo, it might be years before they found him. If ever.

Maggie studied the photos that looped across her monitor and spotted a single image of a different structure, outside, under the sunshine. She broke out of the slide show and scrolled down to the corresponding thumbnail, which was the last picture on the card. When she enlarged it, she saw an old-fashioned school building set in the middle of an overgrown grassy field. The windows sported gaping, jagged holes that resembled bats. The walls were eroded and crumbling. A sink-hole sat where part of the school had collapsed and been hauled away, leaving only the foundation.

Seeing it, Maggie recognized the locale. It was the old Buckthorn School. The ruins had been a headache for the police and the township for years. Teenagers were always getting inside and getting hurt, and just a few weeks ago, the city had scraped together the budget money to have the place boarded up and secured. Since then, she didn't think there had been any calls to the site.

Looking at the photo, she realized that the school ruins would be an irresistible lure for someone like Nick Garaldo.

Maggie pulled out her city directory and found the number for the administrator for the township of Buckthorn. She dialed, and Matt Clayton answered on the first ring. He had a big, exuberant voice.

'Matt, it's Maggie Bei in the Duluth Police,' she said. 'Remember me?'

'Hey, sure, Sergeant. Good to talk to you. What's up?'

'It's that damned school again,' Maggie told him.

Clayton groaned. 'Oh, shit, what now? We had that place locked up like Fort Knox.'

'I don't know what's going on. Maybe nothing. We haven't had any reports at our office, but I was wondering if you'd heard anything from neighbors on the farms up there. Complaints, nuisances, stuff that might not get to us.'

'Nothing,' Clayton replied. 'I thought we were finally done with that place. We had a contractor seal off the building, and we hired a local security guy to come by every couple of days and keep an eye on it. You know, walk around, tug on the locks, that kind of thing. He hasn't reported anything unusual.'

'What's his name?'

'Uh, hang on, let me check. Here we go. It's Nieman. Jim Nieman. You want his number?'

Maggie grabbed a pen. 'Yeah, and could you get hold of him and give him my number, too? I'd like him to go over and do a look-see on the place inside and out. Tell him to give me a call and let me know what he finds.'

'No problem. What's going on?'

'There's a guy missing,' Maggie told him. 'A twenty-something kid named Nick Garaldo. Nobody's seen him since Saturday. I think he may be one of these urban explorers who like to break into abandoned properties just so they can say they've been there.'

'You think he was at the school?' Clayton asked.

'Could be. I found a picture of the school on a photo card in his apartment. It was taken before you guys secured the property. He might have been scouting it for a raid.'

'Damn, can't these guys just go bungee jumping or something?'

'Tell me about it. Anyway, it may be a wild goose chase. For all I know, Garaldo was there and gone weeks ago, but it's worth checking out.'

'I'll call Nieman and ask him to get out there today. I hope that kid's not inside. There's a lot of dangerous debris in that place. Not to mention rats.'

'I'm not a big fan of rats,' Maggie said.

'You and me both.'

Maggie took another look at the police report from the Armory break-in. 'Hey, tell Nieman to keep his eyes open for something else, too.'

'What?'

'Red pistachio shells.'

Thirty-three

Stride and Serena spent the morning in silence.

They sat on opposite sides of the desk in the war room in Grand Rapids, with a pretense of paperwork between them. Her perfume drifted across the short space and smelled sweet and familiar. The heat in the building had been cranked until it was uncomfortably warm in the tiny office. When her head was down, with her dark hair tumbling across her face, Stride found himself staring at her. She was one of the most beautiful women he had ever met. Complex, wounded, attractive. Three years ago, she had seemed like the perfect fit for him, as if two broken souls could come together and make a whole.

Serena looked up and met his eyes. They didn't need to speak to send a message between them. She felt angry and rejected. It had been bad enough before, but it was worse now, and he realized that they were spiraling out of control. She knew it, too. She waited for him to talk to her, and when he didn't, she got out of her chair and closed the office door. She leaned against it and folded her arms.

'You told her,' Serena said, her voice fierce.

Stride didn't understand. 'What do you mean?'

'Not me. You told *her*.'

'Maggie,' he said.

'Yeah. Maggie. She told me what's been going on.' Serena cupped her long fingers in front of her chin. 'I want you to understand something, Jonny. I'm hurting for you. I knew you were pushing me away, but I didn't know why. Now I do. I get it. And I'm sorry.'

'So am I.'

'But I'm having a lot of trouble with this,' she continued. 'You were going through hell, and rather than talk to me about it, you let it sabotage our whole relationship. And when you finally opened up about what was going on, it wasn't to me. Do you have any idea what it felt like to hear about this from her?'

'You're right. I should have told you myself.'

'But you didn't. You couldn't open up to me. I was hoping you and I were past that, but obviously we aren't.'

'I guess not.'

'But you *were* able to talk to Maggie.'

'Sometimes it's easier to talk to someone who's not in the middle of it,' he said.

'Yes, but she is in the middle of it, isn't she? She always has been.'

Stride ran his hand back through his messy hair. He normally had a good poker face, but not now. He shook his head in frustration. 'It's always been complicated between me and Maggie. You know that.'

'It's not so complicated. She loves you.'

'That was years ago,' he protested.

'It's not like a disease, and you wake up and you're cured. The only one in denial here is you. And I think it's because you have feelings for her, too.'

'We're friends. We've been friends forever. Sometimes it's hard to know where the line is.'

Serena sat down across from him again. 'I was getting a strange vibe at dinner last night,' she said.

He didn't reply.

'I thought about it all last night, trying to figure out what it was,' she continued.

'Serena,' he murmured.

She knew without asking, but she asked it anyway. 'Something happened between the two of you, didn't it?'

He didn't even think about denying it. He met her eyes and nodded.

Serena slashed her arm across the desk, tumbling stacks of paper to the floor. 'So with me you have nothing to give, but with *her*?' she asked bitterly.

'I'm really sorry.'

She stood up. 'I think we're done here.'

'Let's talk about this,' he said.

'Now you want to talk? Isn't it a little late for that? You've had weeks to talk to me, and you didn't. But in one day with Maggie, you managed to jump into bed and tell her everything that was going on in your head.'

'It's not that simple.'

'Maybe it is, Jonny. Maybe it is.' She grabbed her coat from the hook. As she twisted the doorknob, she stopped and closed her eyes. 'Look, I know I'm not being fair with you. I haven't opened up to you, either.'

'I'm not looking for excuses,' Stride told her. 'This is my fault. Not yours. Not Maggie's.'

Serena shook her head. 'Let's not talk about Maggie. She knew exactly what she was doing. Don't tell me she didn't.'

'It wasn't like that.'

'Not to you, maybe. She saw her opportunity, and she took it. End of story.' She added in a quiet voice, 'Are you in love with her?'

'I have no idea. I know I love you.'

'But that's not enough for us, is it? Can you tell me right now that you're choosing me? That you can reject whatever feelings you have for Maggie? That's what I need to hear. If you can do that, then maybe we can try again.'

'I want to say yes,' he told her.

'But you can't.'

'It's too soon. I don't want to tell you what you want to hear and wind up lying to you. For weeks, until yesterday, I didn't feel a thing. Not for you. Not for Maggie. Not for myself. Nothing. Now everything is flooding back, and I haven't had a chance to work through any of it. You can't ask me to sort this out in a few hours.'

Serena nodded. 'You're right. That's not fair. We both need to think about what we're going to do.'

She walked over to him and kissed him with her soft lips. He didn't need a reminder of how good it felt. Then she turned and left the office and closed the door behind her.

Serena drove to Duluth on Wednesday afternoon and found a bar and grill north of the airport. She pulled into the parking lot and stared at the entrance door. Inside was vodka. Glass after glass of it. She could taste it and imagine it dulling her into unconsciousness. She hadn't fallen off the wagon in fifteen years, but now seemed like a good time. It was as if no time had passed at all since her last drink. She could still remember it on her lips.

She hadn't anticipated this crossroads. She had been slowly getting her mind around the idea of staying in Duluth forever. Of staying with Jonny forever. Those weren't decisions she made lightly, not given her past, but she had begun to believe it. She should have listened to the warning signs and realized that nothing lasts forever. She loved Jonny. He loved her. That didn't mean they could make it work. They both had too many walls and sharp edges.

She had no idea what she would do next. Stay. Go. Try again. Give up. It wasn't the first time in her life she had considered starting over, and it probably wouldn't be the last. Her instinct was to forgive Jonny, but she couldn't do it alone, and she couldn't do it without his whole heart in it. It killed her to think of walking away, but she wasn't going to sit in the background while Stride and Maggie worked side by side every day. The threesome was over.

She stared at the door of the bar. The lure of vodka was so vivid and clear that she could hear it calling to her. She could see the liquid in the bottle. Watch it splash into her glass and swirl around the ice. One drink after another after another. Until she was in the same state of mind that Jonny had been, feeling nothing.

Serena opened the car door.

As she did, her phone rang again. It was Denise Sheridan. She answered the phone and felt as if she had been given a temporary rescue, dragging her back from a cliff's edge.

'What's up, Denise?'

'I heard from the team we had following Marcus,' she reported. 'He was in Duluth this morning in surgery.'

'So?'

'So he left the hospital to go back to Grand Rapids, and they lost him.'

'How?'

'He knew they were back there. He deliberately ran a light and got them off his trail. It may not mean anything, but I wanted you to know.'

'Where was he when he skipped?' Serena asked.

'Rice Lake Road near Martin. They thought he was heading back home, but we staked out Highway 2 and he never showed.'

'What's he driving?'

'A burgundy Lexus.'

Serena thought about Marcus Glenn speeding into the north farmlands. She was in the same area herself, and she was pretty sure she could read the surgeon's mind. 'I know where he's going,' she said.

Thirty-four

Kasey, Kasey, Kasey. You're running, aren't you?

Her face came into focus through the binoculars. She stopped in the front door of her farmhouse, as if she knew she was being watched. Her nervous eyes flicked to the woods behind their garage, then to the open fields and down the dirt driveway to the highway, where a police car was parked on the shoulder. A bored policeman eyed the traffic in both directions.

Kasey balanced two boxes in her arms. She carried them to a rental truck parked next to the garage and disappeared up the ramp into the rear of the truck. A minute later, she returned to the house with empty arms for another load. He had been watching the back-and-forth from his vantage in the trees for nearly an hour. Kasey's husband had arrived with the truck around noon, and since then, the two of them had led a steady parade as they packed the truck with their belongings.

You can't run, Kasey. It doesn't work that way. We're not done.

Bruce Kennedy opened the front door with his boot and trudged down the steps. He watched him. Kasey's husband was a big man, with fair blond hair and a bushy beard. He wore jeans and an untucked flannel shirt. He had the look of a plodder, a follower who did what he was told. No doubt

Kasey could lead him around by the nose, but she deserved better. It made him angry, looking at Bruce Kennedy through the binoculars and imagining this clumsy man with no idea what a special prize he had. When he lost her, he wouldn't even have a clue what he'd possessed. The fool.

His phone vibrated in his pocket. He was secluded in the woods, invisible and out of earshot, but he looked around cautiously before answering.

'Yes?'

'Nieman, it's Matt Clayton in Buckthorn.'

'What can I do for you?'

'Have you been out to the school lately?' Clayton asked.

Nieman hesitated. 'Yeah, I make the rounds out there every few days to make sure the site is secure.'

'Do you think anyone could have gotten inside?'

'Not likely. It's locked up tight. Why, is there a problem?'

'I don't know. I got a call from Maggie Bei in the Duluth Police. She's trying to track down a missing person who may have had his eyes on the school.'

'I haven't seen anything wrong out there,' he said.

'When were you last inside?'

'Sunday.'

'Well, this kid supposedly disappeared on Saturday, so if you've been in there since then, there's probably nothing to worry about. Even so, I'd appreciate it if you could go over there today and do a walk-through, OK?'

'Sure.'

'The last thing we need is another insurance claim at that place.'

'I understand.'

'When you're done, call Sergeant Bei and give her a report.' Clayton rattled off a phone number. 'Oh, and keep an eye out for pistachio shells, too, all right? I guess this kid drops them wherever he goes.'

'Yeah, no problem,' he said. He added, 'Why do the cops think this guy was at the school? Did somebody see him out there?'

'No, nothing like that. He was taking pictures of the place. Like I said, it's probably nothing.'

'I'll check it out.'

'Thanks, Nieman. You're a good man.'

He hung up and shoved his phone back in his pocket. He was annoyed at his bad luck. There was no way the cops should have been able to tie Nick Garaldo to the school so quickly. He had found the kid's digital camera in his back-pack, and he had gone to his apartment and taken out his computer and anything else that might have tipped them off that Garaldo was an urban explorer. But obviously he had missed something, which was the kind of mistake he didn't usually make.

He knew he could report back to Clayton and the cops that he had found nothing amiss at the school. The stall would buy him a few days, but the clock was ticking. Sooner or later, they would circle back to the school and check it out them-selves. It was only a matter of time before they broke inside and found his collection. He needed to disappear long before they made their discovery. Move on to a new city, somewhere in the south this time, where the winter was warm. Shed his skin, as he had done many times before. Start over.

When he lifted his binoculars, he saw Kasey again. The wind blew her red hair across her face. Her jaw was clenched. She looked desperate and fierce, like a wounded animal that fights even harder when it knows it's about to die. He admired her courage. That was why he had something special planned for her.

As he thought about it, he realized that the timing was perfect. Tonight was the night to wrap up his stay in Duluth. The hunt for Nick Garaldo might even work to his advantage. If he didn't act, Kasey would be gone in the morning, and he didn't want to risk losing her. He could chase her across the country if necessary, but it was much better to do it now. They had a date at the school, like a spotlight dance at the prom, while the others watched them.

He smiled as he stood in the shadows of the spruce trees. He would wait until dark, and then he would bring the game to an end.

Thirty-five

Serena turned off the highway into the driveway at Regan Conrad's house. She saw the nurse's black Hummer near the garage and, beside it, a wine-colored Lexus with a custom license plate that read KNEEDOC.

It was Marcus Glenn's car.

She parked behind both vehicles, blocking them in. She didn't want a repeat of her night-time visit to Regan's house, when the old Escort had slipped away while she was inside. She climbed out of her Mustang and kept an eye on the living-room window as she walked up the front steps. No one watched her.

Before she rang the bell, she realized that the door was ajar. She put her ear to the inch-wide gap and listened for voices. When she heard nothing, she pushed the door open with her shoulder and crept into the foyer. The house was dark and frigid. She waited in the cold and listened again. A cop's instinct whispered to her that something was wrong. The house was too cold. Too dark. Too quiet.

Serena looked down and spied a smear on the light oak near the door. The stain was dried and red. She knelt and caught a mineral smell that was unmistakable.

Blood.

She reached inside her jacket and withdrew her gun. Overhead, she heard the noise of footsteps. She kicked off her shoes rather than let her heels click on the wooden floor. As she made her way to the stairs, she watched the balcony above her. The lights were off, and the doors to the second-floor rooms were closed. She tested her weight on the first step, but the stairs didn't give off a sound. Slowly, she climbed to the upper floor.

She studied the doors stretching down the hallway. One door, at the very end of the hall, was half-open. She heard the slamming of a drawer, followed by the rustle of paper. With her gun leading the way ahead of her, she moved toward the room. Through the crack in the doorway, she saw a metal file cabinet with its middle drawer open. File folders were littered across the floor. She heard frantic, agitated breathing.

Serena held her gun high as she peered around the door frame. She saw Marcus Glenn with his back to her, on hands and knees in the middle of the office floor. He pawed through a foot-high stack of files, tossing each one aside as he reviewed it.

'Don't move,' Serena called.

Glenn spun round in shock, his eyes wide. He clutched one of the files as papers spilled to the floor.

'Put your hands in the air,' she told him.

He saw her gun pointed at his chest, and he spread his fingers wide and jerked his hands over his head. The folder fell to the ground beside him.

'What the hell's going on?' she asked.

Glenn stammered. The normally unflappable surgeon was terrified. His skin was drained of color. 'I was looking for something.'

'What?'

'I wanted – I thought she might have—' he began, then stopped himself. 'I don't think I should say anything.'

'Where's Regan?'

'She's not here.'

'How did you get in?' Serena asked.

'The door was open.'

She pushed apart the file folders with her foot and realized that Glenn was reviewing medical records. Baby records. 'You want to try again, Dr Glenn? Exactly what were you looking for?'

He hesitated, and she thought he needed time to come up with a convincing lie. 'I began to think you were right. I wondered if Regan could have found someone to steal Callie or to – to harm her. I thought maybe I would find something in her files. Something to tell me who.'

'Did you find anything?'

'No.'

'Did you search any of the other rooms?' Serena asked.

'No. I knew she kept her files here.'

She looked at him. 'There's blood near the door.'

'Blood? I didn't notice.'

There was a false lilt in the way he said it. The panic in his face wasn't just about being caught in the middle of a break-in. Something else was going on.

'Where's Regan?' she repeated.

'I told you, I don't know. The house was empty when I arrived.'

'Exactly what did you do?'

He stammered again. 'The door was open, and I came inside. I called for Regan, but she didn't answer. When I realized she wasn't here, I came upstairs to see what I could find in her files.'

'Whatever you're hiding, I'm going to find out. You might as well tell me.'

'I'm not hiding anything.'

Serena frowned. 'Lace your fingers together on top of your head.'

'What?'

'You heard me.'

Glenn complied.

'Now stay on your knees,' she told him. 'Crawl toward me. Slowly.'

Serena backed a few steps into the hallway. The tall surgeon came forward on his knees, watching her gun.

'Could you please put that thing down?' he asked.

'Shut up.' When Glenn was in the doorway of the office, she told him, 'Stop right there. Now get down on all fours.'

He went to his hands and knees on the carpet.

'This is crazy,' he said. 'I haven't done anything.'

'Put your hands on the carpet and lie with your face down and your hands and legs far apart. Keep your fingers spread.'

'Look, I already told you—'

'*Do it.*'

Glenn heard the ice in her voice. He slid on to the ground until his body made an extended X on the carpet.

'Stay that way,' Serena snapped. 'Don't move. Don't look up.'

She backed up to the first closed door on her right. She turned the knob with two fingers and pushed the door open, revealing an empty spare bedroom. Nothing was amiss. Keeping her gun trained on Glenn, she backed up to the next door and found an elegant bathroom with rose décor and a double shower.

'Where's Regan's bedroom?' she asked Glenn.

'At the other end of the hallway.'

'Stay where you are.'

She walked past the stairs to the closed door leading to the master suite. On the carpet, she spotted another wet stain extending from inside the bedroom under the crack of the door. She inhaled and didn't like what she smelled. When she glanced at Glenn, she saw him with his head up, watching her.

'What am I going to find in there?' she asked.

'I have no idea.'

He was lying.

'If you went in there, we'll find your prints,' she told him. Glenn's face twisted in dismay. 'I didn't do it,' he said.

'Do what?' Serena asked, but she could guess what was waiting for her.

'It's not good,' he told her.

Serena dug in her pocket for gloves. She snapped one on to her right hand and twisted the knob with a light touch, then eased the door open with her foot. The bedroom was shadowy, its curtains closed. Light from the skylight in the hallway cascaded through the open door in a stream and illuminated the wall.

Her breath caught in her chest.

She took two steps into the room, far enough to see the king-sized bed, with its turquoise blue sheets in disarray; the shotgun lying on the carpet, emanating a smell of burnt powder; and the blood. Halfway between the bed and the door was a massive pool of blood spread out like the spidery fingers of a lake, and behind it, on the wall, she saw gruesome splatters of brain, tissue, and bone.

There was no body. But whoever had lain in that pool wasn't alive.

'Son of a bitch,' Serena murmured.

She stared at the wall and realized that someone had dipped into the blood like red paint and written a message. Each letter was six inches tall, printed awkwardly, the way a child would write. Streaks dripped from the words and made parallel lines down the wall. The message read:

HI, KASEY.

Thirty-six

Maggie carried a chair into Regan Conrad's living room under one arm and set it down with the back facing the sofa and the bay window. She straddled the seat and leaned her forearms on top of the chair. Her heels sank into the plush carpet. She eyed the glass artwork in the room with casual curiosity and then focused on Marcus Glenn, who sat on the sofa with his hands in his lap.

'When can I go home?' Glenn asked.

Maggie shrugged. 'What's the rush, Doc?'

'I have surgeries scheduled in the morning. I can't just walk into the hospital and cut someone open. I have to prepare.'

'Yeah, those knee jobs, ka-ching, right?' she said. 'I saw your Lexus outside. KNEEDOC, that's pretty cute. But right now I'm not too worried about some CEO who needs help with his golf game, OK? We found you at a crime scene, Dr Glenn, so whether you make it home today really depends on the conversation we're having right now.'

The surgeon settled back into the sofa with an exaggerated sigh. 'I told Ms Dial, and I'm telling you, I had nothing to do with whatever happened here.'

'So you were just in the wrong place at the wrong time. Again. This is becoming sort of a habit for you, isn't it? You were in the house when your daughter disappeared, but you had nothing to do with it. You were in the house where a murder appears to have taken place, but you had nothing to do with it.'

'That's right.'

Maggie had dealt with doctors before, and she knew they were tough to rattle, but Glenn's eyes were nervous underneath his annoyed façade. He had been caught with his hand in the cookie jar, and he knew it. When Maggie didn't say anything more, Glenn added, 'Look, if someone killed Regan, it happened hours before I arrived.'

'Really? How do you know that?'

'I'm a doctor. I see a lot of blood.'

'But you're not a pathologist, are you?'

'I'm also not a magician. I can't make a dead body disappear. The one good thing about being under surveillance is that the police always know where I am. Ms Dial knows perfectly well that I was here for less than an hour before she arrived.'

'Yeah, let's talk about that,' Maggie said. 'Why exactly were you here?'

Glenn shrugged. 'I thought that Regan may have had something to do with Callie's disappearance.'

'Why is that?'

'We were having an affair. The break-up was extremely bitter.'

'So what were you planning to do? Ask her if she was involved in stealing your daughter? Did you think she'd break down and confess?'

'You didn't know Regan. If she did something, she was the kind of person who would throw it in my face.'

'But she wasn't home when you arrived?' Maggie asked.

'Obviously.'

'Did you break in or was the door open?'

'The door was open.'

Maggie nodded. 'Do you have a key?'

'I didn't need a key. I told you, the door was open.'

'Let's try answering the questions I ask. Do you have a key to Regan's house?'

'Yes, I do,' Glenn admitted. 'Regan gave me a key while we were involved.'

'Do you have it with you?'

'I imagine it's still on my key chain. I haven't thought about it in months.'

Maggie smiled. 'Sure. You came here with Regan's house key, but you didn't even think about breaking in. So why *did* you go inside?'

'I was concerned when I saw the door was open,' Glenn said. 'I shouted, but there was no answer. I began to look around the house, and that was when I saw that something terrible had happened.'

'Why didn't you call the police?'

'I was about to call them.'

'Really? Ms Dial said you were too busy ransacking Regan's medical files.'

'I thought Regan might have kept something that would tell me if she was involved in what happened to Callie.'

'Did you think you were likely to find something that the police would miss? Or were you planning to make sure we *didn't* find whatever you were looking for?'

Glenn didn't reply.

'When was the last time you spoke to Regan?' Maggie asked.

'It was months ago.'

'Have you called her recently?'

'No.'

'You're sure?'

Glenn backpedaled as he read Maggie's face. 'Actually, I left her a message last night. I told her I wanted to talk. But I didn't actually speak to her.'

Maggie nodded. 'People think they can delete answering machine messages, but they're among the easiest things to recover. We pulled up your message to her. You said something about Regan being in your office over the weekend.'

Glenn didn't look happy. 'Yes, my nurse told me she was there.'

'Why would Regan be in your office?'

'I don't know. That's what I wanted to find out.'

'Would you like to make a guess?'

'I have no idea,' Glenn told her.

'Were you concerned that she stole something?'

He blinked uncomfortably. 'I told you, I don't know,' he repeated.

'Regan told your wife that she thought you were responsible for your daughter's disappearance,' she said.

'That's completely untrue.'

'It makes me wonder if your story is a little backwards, Dr Glenn.'

'What do you mean?'

Maggie leaned forward. 'I mean, are you sure you weren't going through Regan's files to find out if she had any evidence that *you* were involved in Callie's disappearance? Evidence she may have taken from your office?'

'Of course not.'

'It's quite a coincidence, you showing up at Regan's house after someone else killed her.'

'I had nothing to do with it.'

'Did you know she was dead? Did you come here to erase evidence before the crime was discovered?'

Glenn shook his head. 'I didn't know anything had happened to Regan until I got here.'

'Who do you think killed her?' Maggie asked.

He shrugged. 'She lives in the north farmlands. There have been some terrible crimes here recently.'

'So you think the same person who killed the other women also killed Regan?'

'I have no idea, but doesn't that seem likely? The women in the hospital are all afraid of this man, whoever he is. Regan bragged about sleeping with a shotgun by her bed.'

Maggie raised her eyebrows. 'You knew she had a shotgun?'

'A lot of people did,' Glenn replied defensively. 'Regan didn't make it a secret. She was scared of this maniac like everyone else.'

'Not everyone is scared when a serial killer comes to town,' she told him.

'What the hell does that mean?'

Maggie pushed her red hair out of her eyes and frowned. 'Every now and then, Doctor, someone sees it as an opportunity.'

Serena sat in her Mustang in Regan's driveway, staring through the open window at the snow-covered fields. It was almost dusk, but she wore sunglasses, and Maggie suspected she had been crying. She didn't say a word as Maggie opened the passenger door and sat beside her. They didn't look at each other. Maggie left the door open and kicked at the dirt outside with her boot. When she took a sideways glance at Serena, she could see that her face was rigid with fury.

She didn't blame her for being angry, and she had no idea what to say. There was no way to make it better.

'Glenn didn't do it,' Maggie announced after an uncomfortable stretch of silence. 'Or at least, he didn't pull the trigger. That doesn't mean he's not involved.'

Serena didn't say anything. Maggie glanced at the highway and saw media vans parked on the shoulder. 'The press already has the story,' she continued. 'Blair Rowe was on CNN half an hour ago speculating about a link between the murder here and Callie's disappearance.'

Serena shrugged. 'Blair Rowe knows everyone in the Grand Rapids Police. Someone leaked.'

'What do you think? Is there a link between the two cases?'

'I think Marcus is lying about why he was here,' Serena said. 'I'd like to know what he was really looking for in those files.'

'Yeah.'

'What does Guppo say about the crime scene?' Serena asked. 'Is it the farmlands killer?'

'The MO is similar,' Maggie said. 'The right locale, the missing body. I'm not sure about the shotgun, though. This guy likes to use his hands.'

'Maybe Regan surprised him, and he grabbed the gun.'

'Maybe, but that's not how it looks. Guppo thinks he had the gun the whole time. There was no struggle. That's not how this guy operates.'

'Except there's the message on the wall,' Serena said.

Maggie nodded. 'Yeah. The message feels authentic. This guy is playing with Kasey. But I still don't buy the coincidence that he went after Regan Conrad just for the hell of it. There's a connection to Callie in all of this.'

'Have you told Kasey about the message on the wall?'

'Not yet. I asked her to come over here. She's not far away.'

'I talked to Stride,' Serena said. 'He's going to talk to Micki Vega. She's the one link we know about between Marcus and Regan.'

'Yeah, I talked to him too.'

Serena shook her head and laughed bitterly. 'Of course you did. What was I thinking?'

'Look, Serena,' Maggie said.

Serena held up a hand, stopping her. 'I don't think we should do this now. Do you? We're professionals. That's all.'

Maggie heard the message loud and clear. We're professionals. Not friends. Not anymore.

'I know it doesn't mean shit, but I'm sorry,' she said.

Serena stripped off her sunglasses in a fierce gesture. Her eyes were red and angry. 'You want to talk about this now? Fine. Don't bullshit me or give me fake stories about being sorry. This was no accident. You knew that Jonny and I were having problems, because I was stupid enough to tell you. You sabotaged our relationship to get what you've always wanted. Well, bravo. I never thought you were that ruthless. I was naïve enough to think you were my friend. So now I pay the price for trusting you.'

Her words hit Maggie like a frigid breeze stinging her face. In the aftermath, she heard Serena breathing loudly.

'You can believe it or not, but it was *not* like that,' Maggie told her softly. 'Stride had an attack. I found him like that. Serena, he needed someone. It just happened.'

Serena rolled her eyes. 'It just happened? Is that the best you can do? Sure, you didn't plan anything. Oh, and by the way, *nice hair*, Maggie.'

She knew her excuse was lame. 'I just wanted something different.'

'Well, you got it. Now get the fuck out of my car.'

Maggie climbed out and closed the passenger door behind her. She leaned back in the window. 'I never meant to come between the two of you,' she said. 'I still don't. I'm out. It was one time. It was an accident. He loves you, and I'm not going to mess that up.'

Serena put on her sunglasses again. 'Too late.'

Maggie opened her mouth to say something more, but she had nothing to say. She took a step backward and then walked away in quick, angry steps toward Regan's house. She could see strands of her red hair dangling in front of her eyes, and suddenly she hated herself and her damn strawberry hair and what she had done to Stride. Serena was right. She could tell herself that she had never meant for anything to happen, that she had never meant to stumble into the middle of their relationship, but on some level, she knew she was lying. Consciously or not, she had known all along what she was doing. She had gone into Stride's house with her eyes wide open.

Thirty-seven

It was already night by the time Stride arrived at the base of the sloping hillside of the Sago Cemetery. He got out of his truck and felt the craving for a cigarette. There was something about cold, sweet air that made him want to smoke. He leaned against his truck and studied the tall pine trees standing guard around the perimeter of the graveyard, protecting the dead. As the wind blew, they shrugged their tufted black shoulders at him.

He hiked up the slope through the thin coating of snow, navigating around the dark outlines of the marble stones. The metal flagpole banged incessantly, like a child demanding attention. At the top of the hill, he crept along the ragged edge of the woods, looking for the path that led to the trailer where Micki Vega lived. When he found it, he plunged into darkness between the columns of tree trunks. He took careful steps, avoiding noise, as if he were intruding on something sacred. He remembered what Micki had told him: this was a place where people buried things they didn't want found.

Ahead of him, fifty yards away, he saw the squares of light from a mobile home in the clearing. It was an isolated place to live, hidden from view. As he got closer, he heard the canned noise of a television, sounding odd and artificial in the forest. When he knocked, he heard a female voice speaking loud, rapid Spanish, and then the television went silent.

Micki Vega opened the door. She scowled when she saw him. 'You again. What do you want?'

'Can I come in?'

'What if I say no? You going to bust down my door?'

'No.'

Micki shrugged. 'Yeah, what do I care, come in. See how I'm taking bread out of the mouths of American workers.'

He climbed three steps into the trailer, which sagged under his weight. It felt claustrophobic with its low metal ceiling and narrow walls. The furniture smelled musty, like a wet dog, and the tiny space was messy, with magazines on the floor and dead plants on the window ledges and empty beer cans stacked on card tables. The room was uncomfortably warm, and Stride began to sweat.

Micki wasn't alone. On the far side of the trailer, near the half-open curtain that led to the bedroom, a heavyset woman with long black hair lay in a recliner in front of a small television. She was in her early fifties and wore a plastic mask across her nose and mouth that was connected to an oxygen tank on the floor. He could hear her lungs wheeze with each breath. On the television, with muted sound, he saw a word puzzle on the *Wheel of Fortune* game show.

'That's my mama,' Micki said. 'I told you she was sick.'

Stride nodded politely at the woman, but she didn't react, other than to watch him with open suspicion in her dark eyes.

'You can see we're rich,' Micki said. 'What were you expecting to find anyway? Did you think I had Callie Glenn hidden in here? You think I'd take a baby out of that beautiful mansion and bring her to this place?'

'That's not why I'm here,' Stride said.

'Yeah, well, what is it now? It's time for dinner.' Micki

stirred yellow rice and ground beef in a frying pan on the small stove near the door. She took a swig from an open can of beer. She wore a roomy white T-shirt from the Minnesota State Fair and a pair of jeans that hugged her fleshy thighs. Her feet were bare.

'We think Regan Conrad is dead,' Stride told her.

Micki wiped foam from her lips. 'Really? How?'

'It looks like someone murdered her.'

Micki crossed herself and murmured under her breath. 'Sweet Mary. That's a terrible thing. Murdered?'

'Yes.'

'How?'

'Someone shot her in the head.'

'My God.'

'We found Marcus Glenn in her house,' Stride added. 'He was searching her medical files.'

Micki's mouth fell open. 'Dr Glenn? You think Dr Glenn killed her?'

'We want to know what he was doing there,' Stride said.

'You won't be happy until you bring him down, will you? Dr Glenn would never do something like that. He couldn't.'

'He's acting like he has something to hide. I think you know what it is.'

'Me? How would I know?'

'You know Dr Glenn. You knew Regan Conrad. You were in the house when Callie disappeared.'

'So what? I hadn't talked to Nurse Regan in months. I've told you all that before. Why can't you leave me alone?' Micki went back to stirring the rice with angry swirls of a wooden spoon.

'If you know anything about Dr Glenn and Regan Conrad, you really need to tell me,' Stride said. 'I understand you feel gratitude for what he did to help you, but if he was involved in these crimes—'

'He wasn't,' she snapped.

'Regan Conrad thought he was.'

Micki looked up from the stove. The steam from the pan raised a moist glow on her forehead, and she wiped herself with a towel. 'Why do you think that?'

'Regan contacted Valerie Glenn. She told her that Dr Glenn was involved in Callie's disappearance.'

'How would she know?' Micki asked.

'I don't know, but now Regan is dead, so she'll never have a chance to tell us.'

'She was wrong.'

'How can you be sure?'

'I know Dr Glenn,' she insisted. 'He would never have deliberately harmed his child. Never. Whatever happened, it was something else.'

'Deliberately?' Stride asked. 'Do you think it was an accident?'

'You're twisting my words. I'm telling you, he's innocent.'

'Migdalia,' a raspy voice called from the other side of the trailer.

Stride saw Micki's mother pointing an index finger at her daughter. The oxygen mask that had been draped across her face was clenched tightly in her fist. She inhaled and coughed raggedly and then, dragging in another breath, she spat out words in Spanish. 'Migdalia, dígale.'

Micki slapped the spoon down and shoved the frying pan off the heat. 'Mamá, cállate. No te metas.'

'Si no le dices, le estas dando tu espalda a Jesus.'

Her mother blinked and put the mask back over her face. Her chest heaved as she sucked in air.

'No lo voy a traicionar,' Micki retorted, stamping her foot on the metal floor.

Her mother waved a hand at Micki insistently, and her face paled with the effort. She spoke again behind the mask with strained, muffled words. 'Dígale.'

Micki folded her hands over her chest. She kicked a beer can on the floor of the trailer and muttered under her breath.

'What did she say?' Stride asked.

'She said I should stay out of this,' Micki retorted loudly, eyeing her mother. 'She said nothing good ever comes from talking to the police.'

'Maybe I should ask her myself,' Stride said.

'Leave my mama alone! You see how she is. She has no strength. I don't want you putting her in the middle of this.'

'Is she involved?'

'Of course not,' Micki snapped. She pushed past Stride and sat down in a metal folding chair. She laced her hands tightly together and stared at her feet. Her left leg twitched. 'Why don't you just go?' she told him.

Stride squatted beside her. 'Think about Callie. You felt something for that little girl, didn't you? You took care of her.'

'She was an angel,' Micki said with a little smile.

Stride nodded. 'Imagine if your own baby had disappeared and you never knew what happened to her. Imagine how desperate you would feel. If you know something, Micki, you simply can't remain silent. Callie deserves better than that.'

'Dr Glenn didn't harm her,' Micki repeated.

'Then what is he hiding? Why was he in Regan Conrad's house?'

Micki shrugged. She got out of the chair and turned her back on Stride. She walked to the recliner in front of the television and used the remote control to shut it off. She stroked her mother's hair. The two women didn't speak to each other, but as Stride watched, Micki's mother reached out and clutched her daughter's wrist in her thick fingers. Micki's lower lip bulged as if she was about to cry. She separated herself gently from her mother's grip and bent down behind the recliner. Her mother watched her. When Micki stood up, she held a cardboard shoe box in her hands.

Stride waited, saying nothing.

Micki sat down again with the box in her lap. She covered the lid with her forearms and stared at the trailer door.

'I was late coming home that night,' she said. 'Mama was worried.'

'The night Callie disappeared?'

Micki nodded. 'She kept looking out the window for me.'

'What did she see?' Stride asked.

'A light,' Micki said. 'She saw a light in the woods near the cemetery. Someone was out there.'

'When was this?'

'Somewhere around midnight. She told me about it on Saturday, and all I could think about was how people bury things out there. And I thought, you know, that Dr Glenn's family is buried here. He comes to see his mama a lot. So I went to look.'

'What did you find?' Stride asked.

Micki hugged the box in her lap and didn't say anything.

'Please,' Stride urged her. 'What did you find?'

She peeled the lid off the box. Inside, Stride saw an odd mix of memorabilia crammed together. Dirty plastic flowers. Dog collars with rhinestones. Wrinkled, faded photographs.

'This is my collection,' Micki said. 'People leave things behind at the graves. And in the woods, too. I keep them. I like to think I can feel a little of the love, you know? It's silly, but I can spend hours this way.'

'Did you find something in the woods?' Stride asked. 'Near where your mother saw the light that night?'

Micki reached into the box and pulled out a small toy, a rolled-up paper horn with a plastic mouthpiece. Stride recognized it. It was the kind of blow horn that revelers used on New Year's Eve. 'I found this in a little clearing,' she said.

'Do you realize what this means?' Stride asked. 'Callie was a New Year's baby.'

'Yeah, I know.'

'Did you find anything else?'

Micki nodded. 'Someone tried to cover it up, but I could tell from the ground when I kicked the leaves away. Something was buried there.'

Thirty-eight

Maggie saw Kasey's eyes dart with fear as the young cop got out of her car. Her body was caught in the cross-section of headlights from the squad cars parked in the fields around Regan's house. Kasey squinted and held up her hand with her fingers spread as she passed through the gauntlet of lights.

'What's going on?' she asked. 'What do you want?'

'He struck again,' Maggie told her.

Kasey shivered and pulled her coat tighter around her body. 'Who is it?'

'The house belongs to a nurse named Regan Conrad.'

'A nurse? Isn't she the one Serena was talking about at dinner yesterday? The one connected to the baby case in Grand Rapids?'

Maggie nodded.

'So why'd you want me here?'

Maggie frowned. 'I have to show you something. It ain't pretty, Kasey.'

Kasey put her hands in her pockets. 'I know I'm a cop, but I'm not awfully good with dead bodies, you know? It doesn't come up a lot on my beat.'

'There's no body.'

Kasey cocked her head. 'What?'

'No body, just a lot of blood. He took the body with him the way he did with the other women.'

'No body?' she repeated. 'How do you know it's Regan? How do you know she's dead?'

'We won't know for certain until we run tests, but no one has seen her today. As for being dead, you don't lose that much blood and tissue and stay alive. Looks like she took a shotgun shell to the head.'

Kasey looked flustered. 'What do you need to show me?'

Maggie jerked her head toward the front of the house. 'Come on.'

As they walked, Kasey said, 'I don't know if it makes a difference right now, but I handed in my resignation today. Bruce and I talked about it, and we both think this is the way to go. I know I was supposed to call you, but it's been busy with us packing up the truck and all. We're going to leave first thing in the morning.'

'I understand.'

'I feel like I'm bailing on you.'

'You're not bailing on me. If it were me, I might be doing the same thing.'

'Do you think I'm being paranoid?'

Maggie shook her head. 'No, I don't.' At the front door, she added, 'Take your shoes off, and put on some plastic booties. Don't touch anything, OK?'

'Sure.'

The interior of the house smelled like glue from the fume boxes used by the evidence technicians to raise fingerprints. The carpet had been freshly vacuumed to gather trace materials. Maggie led Kasey up the stairs. At the open door of Regan's bedroom, she turned and stopped her with a hand on her chest. 'I'm not trying to be cruel, Kasey. If you don't want to go inside, just tell me, but I think this is something you need to see for yourself. It'll probably make you feel better about getting into your truck tomorrow morning.'

'What's in there?' Kasey asked.

'He left you a message.'

Maggie let Kasey go first. The young cop crossed the threshold, and her eyes flitted around the room. The massive bloodstain attracted her attention, and she inched closer and squatted down, where the smell was strongest. Maggie thought Kasey was about to touch the stain itself, and she prepared to call out a warning, but Kasey pulled her hand back. Then her head twisted, and she saw the writing on the wall.

Two words. A ghastly greeting.

Kasey's hands flew to her mouth.

'I'm sorry,' Maggie said. 'It's not the same to hear about it on the phone. I thought you should know exactly how dangerous this situation has become for you.'

Kasey stumbled to her feet and collided against the wall of the bedroom. Maggie heard the lurching noise of Kasey's stomach turning upside down. Kasey ran for the toilet, but she only made it to the bathroom doorway before sinking to her knees. Vomit spewed through her clenched fingers and splattered on the tile. She fell forward on to all fours, head down, red hair tumbling over her face. Her body shook with dry heaves.

Maggie stood over her and put a hand softly on her back. 'Are you all right?'

Kasey took deep, ragged breaths without speaking. She eased upward on to her heels, and her head fell back. She blinked as she stared at the ceiling.

'Shit, I'm sorry,' she murmured.

'Don't worry about it.'

'How did it come to this?' Kasey asked. 'How did this become my life?'

'It's not your fault.'

'I need to go,' Kasey said. She staggered to her feet and swayed. Maggie put an arm around her waist to steady her. She helped Kasey toward the bedroom door, steering her around the pool of black dried blood.

'I don't want to scare you,' Maggie said, 'but running away may not be enough. For some reason, this guy has become fixated on you. You're special to him. He may not give up just because you leave the area. Wherever you go, watch your back.'

In the door frame, Kasey stopped and stood on her own. She took a few steps closer to the wall, where the message taunted her.

'You're right.'

Maggie saw something unexpected in Kasey's eyes. The fear was gone, as if she had hit bottom and realized there was nowhere else to fall. She looked older, not like an immature kid any more. Her face held a fury so deep that Maggie found it unsettling.

'It's him or me,' Kasey added. 'That's the way it is. Only one of us is coming out of this thing alive.'

Stride recognized the Ford Taurus parked at the end of the road leading to the Glenn house. When he got out of his truck, he found Blair Rowe sitting on top of the white picket fence that bordered the driveway. She kicked her heels back and forth against the wooden beams like a tap dancer. A cigarette hung from her lips. She jumped down when she saw him and bounded across the grass.

'Lieutenant!' Blair sang out.

He shoved his hands in the pockets of his leather coat. The tiny reporter stopped uncomfortably close to him.

'Hey,' she said breathlessly. 'I figured you'd be coming here.'

'Why is that?' Stride asked.

'Oh, I've got an ear to the ground.' She took the cigarette

out of her mouth and played with it between her fingers. Ash sprinkled to the street. 'So how's it going?'

'I didn't figure you for a smoker, Blair,' Stride told her.

'It's not just adrenaline that keeps me skinny,' she said, grinning. 'Besides, I'm a reporter. We have to smoke. It's required. That's the first thing they teach you in journalism school.' She tapped the square outline of a cigarette pack in the shoulder pocket of her jacket. 'You want one?'

He did, but he shook his head.

'What about a toasted pecan?' she asked, digging in her side pocket and popping a nut into her mouth. 'My mom makes them. They've got a cinnamon glaze. Really good.'

'Your mom's quite the cook.'

'Well, she's home with my kid a lot, so she has to keep busy when he's sleeping. She's a stick like me, but we both love to eat.'

'What do you want, Blair?' Stride asked.

She dropped her cigarette on the ground and shoved her glasses up her face with her finger. 'I heard about Regan Conrad. Is it true that Marcus Glenn is under arrest for the murder?'

'No.'

'Really? Word is you caught him red-handed. Someone told me he set up the crime scene to make it look like that serial killer popped Regan.'

'I'm not in charge of the murder investigation, Blair,' Stride said.

'Yeah, sure, except I can connect the dots. Regan's dead, and you found Marcus pawing through her files. Sounds like she had dirt on him and Callie.'

'We're done here, Blair.'

He walked past her down the circular driveway that led to the Glenns' house. Blair spun and struggled to keep pace with him, her short legs moving quickly. Puffs of steam came out of her mouth and blew away in the wind.

'You're here to see Valerie, huh?' Blair asked, panting. 'You should be thanking me, you know. I'm the one who broke the news about Valerie's affair. You guys didn't know about that, did you?'

'It's not relevant,' Stride snapped.

Blair's glasses slipped again, resting on the tip of her nose so she had to tilt her head back to see him. 'Are you kidding? Come on, it gives Marcus a motive. We both know that. His pretty little wife is banging her brother-in-law? That's not going to sit well with King Marcus. And you know what I think? I think Marcus had Regan run a paternity test that *proved* he wasn't Callie's father. That's what he was looking for in her medical records. He wouldn't want it coming out that he knew the truth about Callie.'

Stride stopped and looked at her. 'Do you have any evidence of that?'

'Not yet, but I'm looking.'

'Then you have nothing but speculation.'

He continued walking, but Blair tugged on his arm. 'So what's the deal, Lieutenant? When do you start the search out at the cemetery?'

'What did you say?'

Stride was shocked. He had left Micki's trailer less than an hour earlier, and the only person he had called was Denise Sheridan.

Blair smirked, as if she could read his mind. 'Are you going to run the search at night or are you waiting until morning? Snow's coming soon, so that's going to make it harder. My bet is you'll bring in the Klieg lights and go at it tonight.'

'No comment.'

'Hey, the news is coming out, like it or not. You may as well make sure I've got the story right. You're searching in the cemetery where half the Glenn family is buried and Micki Vega is the caretaker. So what did Micki tell you? I said from the beginning that she and Marcus were probably in on this together.'

'I'm not confirming a search at the cemetery,' Stride told her.

'Right, you have to talk to Valerie first and give her the bad news. I get it. But I'm going on the air about the search.'

'I told you, I'm not confirming that any search is planned.'

'You say no, but Craig Hickey says yes, and my money's on Craig.'

'Who the hell is he?' Stride asked.

Blair shrugged. 'You'll find out soon enough, so what the hell. Craig has a spread near Cohasset, and I dated his son Terry for a couple years in high school. I still bum around with Terry sometimes. Remember, Lieutenant, this is my town. I know everybody.'

'So?'

'So Denise Sheridan called Craig, and Craig called Terry, and Terry called me. That's just the way things work around here. You see, Craig is the go-to guy on the Range when the police need dogs. Rescue dogs. Bomb-sniffing dogs. Drug-sniffing dogs.' She got on tiptoes and whispered, 'Or cadaver dogs.'

Thirty-nine

Stride hadn't spent much time with Valerie Glenn, but he knew that she was the kind of woman that men wanted to rescue. He talked to Valerie in her kitchen, where she used a gleaming chef's knife to dice a yellow onion on a cutting board. Her eyes were hooded as she looked down, following her work, but every so often she froze and glanced through the window at the pitch-black night. Then, with nothing more than a flick of her blue eyes, she would let her gaze fall on Stride as if to say: it's dark out. There are monsters. Protect me.

The onion brought tears to his eyes, but Valerie seemed unaffected. She cut it with precision, as if one cube larger than another would destroy the orderliness of what she was doing. He thought he understood her. She was a woman of walls, like Serena, but unlike Serena, she was desperate for someone to break them down.

'You're not saying much, Lieutenant,' Valerie told him. 'When people avoid telling me things, I'm afraid it's because they have bad news to share.' She stopped what she was doing, and her broken eyes pierced him again. 'Is it bad news?'

'It's too early to tell,' he said, stalling.

He gave bad news all the time, but he was reluctant to destroy this woman, and that was what he had to do. The toy horn was in his pocket. He had to show it to her, and he knew what it would mean when he did. Her hope would be shredded. Her prayers would have been met with silence. For all her calm, she was balanced on a precipice.

'I already know about what happened to Regan Conrad,' she said. 'I won't pretend I'm upset.'

'I understand.'

'Where is Marcus?' she asked.

'We're still questioning him.'

She performed another even stroke with the blade. 'He was in her house?'

'Yes, he was going through her medical files,' Stride said.

'But Denise says you don't believe he killed her.'

'Whatever happened in Regan's bedroom took place overnight. Was Marcus here?'

'Yes.'

'Then he didn't kill her.' Stride added, 'I was wondering if you had any idea what your husband was looking for in Regan's files.'

He watched her hand stutter, and the point of the knife stabbed her finger and drew a drop of blood. She winced and put the tip of the finger in her mouth and sucked on it. When she took it out, a red trail of blood reappeared.

'Are you all right?' he asked.

'I'm fine. I'm not normally careless.' She ran cold water over her finger in the sink and then unwrapped a small bandage from the cabinet.

'You didn't answer my question,' he said.

'I'm sorry. No. I can't imagine what Marcus would have been looking for.'

She was a bad liar. She knew what Marcus was looking for, but she wasn't going to admit what it was. Stride looked at her in a way that said they both knew she was lying, but she simply picked up the knife and resumed her work. This time, a single tear dripped from her eye, and he didn't know if it was the onion or her sense of impending grief.

'I have to show you something,' he told her.

'Oh?' Her demeanor had cracks, as if she were about to split apart.

He reached into the inner pocket of his coat and withdrew a plastic bag, where he had preserved the powder-blue toy that Micki had found in the forest. He dangled the bag in his hand, close enough for Valerie to see. 'Do you recognize this?'

She leaned forward, confused. 'What's that?'

Then she saw. She understood. The warm blush on her face turned white. She reached out to take the bag, but Stride pulled it away. 'I'm sorry.'

'Where did you get that?' she asked.

'Do you recognize it?'

One tear became many. 'They had those toys at the hospital that night.'

'When Callie was born?'

Valerie didn't reply. She walked away in a daze and ran the water again, letting it flow over the knife blade to clean it. She used a new sponge to rub the shiny surface and then wiped it dry with a towel. She laid the knife next to the wooden block, leaving the single slot empty. The onion sat on the cutting board in a mountain of perfect, tiny cubes. She walked away from the kitchen island and sat down in a chair beside the elegant glass dinette table.

'Mrs Glenn?' he persisted in a quiet voice.

'I told Serena that I was tired and in pain for much of the night,' she said. 'I didn't have any sense of time. I was alone a lot, waiting. I remember the noise of the horns waking me up. It was midnight. People were in the hall, and everyone was laughing, and they were kissing each other. A nurse came in to wish me happy New Year, and she put one of the toy horns on the tray near my bed.'

'The horn she gave you, was it blue like this one?'

'I don't remember. I think so. Where did you find it?'

'Micki Vega says she found it in the woods near the Sago Cemetery. On the night Callie disappeared, her mother saw someone in the forest.'

Valerie wrapped her hands around herself and rocked in the chair. 'Oh my God.'

'I'm afraid we have to search the cemetery.'

'Search?' she asked, dazed.

'We have to see if someone buried something in the woods where the toy horn was found.'

'*Callie,*' Valerie moaned.

'Please don't assume the worst. It may mean nothing at all.'

She covered her mouth with her hands and didn't say anything. The pull of her despair made him want to go to her and wrap her up in his arms. Stiffly, like a soldier, he stayed where he was, letting her suffer alone.

'I have to ask you a few more questions,' he said.

Valerie's empty stare didn't change. She didn't react.

'Did you bring a toy like this home with you from the hospital?'

She spoke through her hands. 'I wanted to.' She wiped her eyes and slowly put her hands in her lap. 'I thought we should keep it. Save it. It was like a symbol of what that night meant to me. A new year. A new baby. A new lease on life. But it wasn't with the things we brought home from the hospital.'

'What happened to it?'

'I gave it to Marcus. I asked him to make sure we didn't lose it.'

'Did you ask him about it?'

'Yes. It was weeks later. There was so much to do with Callie being home, and she needed so much, and I was always so tired. I didn't have a chance to catch my breath for the first month. Then I started gathering up the keepsakes from her birth, and that was when I realized the little toy was missing.'

'What did Marcus say?'

Valerie shook her head. 'He told me he threw it away.'

Forty

'I threw it away,' Marcus Glenn told Serena.

They sat in the front seat of his Lexus on the dirt road near the Sago Cemetery. The night was ablaze with light – rotating red lights on the tops of the squad cars, flashlight beams intersecting the woods, and Klieg lights on tall tripods reflecting off the snow. Behind them, the road was blocked, keeping the media at bay. The windows of the luxury car were closed, leaving the interior oddly silent, despite the frenzied activity around them.

'When was that?' Serena asked.

'I don't remember.'

'Did you bring it home with you from the hospital? Did you leave it in your office? Or did you never take it with you at all?'

Glenn shrugged. 'I have no idea. It was a stupid ten-cent toy.'

'What color was it?' Serena asked.

'Do you think I paid any attention? It could have been purple, pink, red, blue, who knows.'

Glenn's patience was wearing thin after hours with the police. They had spent the afternoon and early evening at Regan Conrad's house in the north farmlands. Just as Serena had been about to cut Glenn loose, she'd received the call from Stride about Micki Vega's discovery and the impending search in Sago. So they had driven here, accompanied by a Duluth Police car on the lonely stretch of Highway 2. Glenn didn't like it.

'I don't know why you've brought me here,' he added. 'There's nothing I can tell you.'

'I'm trying to figure out how this toy made its way from your wife's hospital room to the woods outside your family cemetery,' Serena said.

'Oh, please. How many millions of those toys pour out of Chinese factories every year? You can't possibly believe that there's any connection at all between something that Micki allegedly found in the woods and a keepsake my wife had when she gave birth to Callie.'

'Did your wife blow into the horn?' Serena asked.

'What?'

'Did she use it at the hospital that night?'

'I don't remember. Everyone was using the annoying things.'

'Then she may have left DNA inside the plastic mouthpiece. We'll test it.'

'Wonderful. You do that. If you find any DNA, I'm sure it will belong to someone else.'

'Why are you so sure about that?' Serena asked.

Glenn thumped the dashboard in exasperation. 'Because I threw it away! Do you think someone went burrowing through my trash in order to plant that ridiculous thing in the woods eleven months later?'

Serena watched the surgeon fidget. His long legs were uncomfortable in the sedan, even with the seat pushed back. 'Coincidences keep piling up around you, Dr Glenn,' she told him.

'What do you mean?'

'Well, say you're right. This isn't the toy that Valerie had in the hospital. Doesn't it seem strange that Micki Vega would find a toy just like that next to the cemetery you visit every month? That she'd find it two days after your daughter disappeared? That she'd find it in the exact place where her mother saw someone in the woods on the very night your daughter disappeared? That the toy left there would be exactly like the one Valerie asked you to keep as a memory of your daughter's birth?'

Glenn stared through the windshield at the police officers gathered in clusters around the grassy field. His long, graceful fingers curled tightly around the steering wheel as if he were steering a race car.

'I agree with you,' he said. His voice was calm and scientific.

'You do?'

'Yes, you're right. It doesn't sound like a coincidence.'

'Then how do you explain it?' Serena asked.

Glenn twisted to face her. 'I can think of three explanations. First, it really is a coincidence, and that's just my bad luck. Strange things like that do happen.'

'And the others?'

'The second possibility is that Micki is lying. She may not have found the toy in the woods, or she may not have found it when she said she did. But personally, I think Micki is telling the truth.'

'You do?'

Glenn nodded. 'I don't believe she would deliberately try to do me harm.'

'Except if you were sleeping with her, if you fathered her baby and her baby died, it can play with a girl's head.'

'I never slept with Micki,' Glenn insisted. 'I wasn't the father of her child. If you want to dig up her baby to prove it, you can get a court order and do so. But you'll just look like heartless fools. Ms Dial, I freely confess to being a hard case in every aspect of my life *except* my medical profession. I helped Micki because I'm a physician and she needed someone. That's all.'

'You said you could think of three explanations,' Serena said. 'What's the third?'

'The third is that someone is deliberately trying to make it appear as if I was involved in Callie's disappearance. Which I wasn't.'

'You mean someone planted the toy?'

'Yes.'

Serena knew the next obvious question, but she wasn't ready to go there yet. It hung unasked between them. She wondered if Glenn wanted to hear her say it. *What are we going to find in the woods?* Instead, she went another way.

'How did you feel about your wife cheating on you?' she asked.

'I haven't been a model of fidelity myself, so I can't really complain.'

'Maybe so, but most men have a double standard. It's OK for me to cheat, because it's just about sex. But my wife? She better not look at another man.'

Glenn shrugged. 'I'm not saying I feel good about it.'

'When did you find out that she was sleeping with Tom?' Serena asked.

He took a long time to answer. 'I found out the same time that you did,' he told her finally. 'When Blair Rowe blabbed the news to the world.'

'And not before?'

'No.'

'You took your time deciding what to say. Were you trying to figure out if there's any way we could prove that you knew about Valerie's affair?'

Glenn didn't reply.

'I hope you didn't tell anyone,' Serena continued, 'or hire an investigator to follow her. It'll come out if you did.'

'I trusted my wife,' he replied.

'Did you have any reason to doubt that Callie was your baby?'

'Of course not.'

'What about now?'

'Now I can't help but wonder,' he admitted.

'Didn't you wonder before? It was three years. You must have thought it was odd that Valerie couldn't get pregnant for so long, and then she suddenly did.'

'It's not odd at all. I'm a doctor. People think conception is predictable, but it's not. It can happen with one sexual encounter, or it can take six months or six years, or it can never happen at all, even when both partners are perfectly healthy. Don't try to outguess God, Ms Dial.'

'I thought most surgeons believed *they* were God.'

'Confidence and ego make you a better doctor, but you also have to be smart enough to know when you don't have all the answers.'

'You certainly seem like you have all the answers,' Serena told him.

'I wish I did.'

'Tell me something. Why did *you* cheat on Valerie? She's beautiful. She's smart. She loves you. Wasn't that enough?'

'It has nothing to do with Valerie,' he said. 'It doesn't mean I don't love her.'

'She nearly killed herself because of your neglect.'

She regretted saying it, but he didn't react with anger. Instead, there was resignation in his voice. 'Do you really believe that her suicide attempt was my fault? Valerie has suffered from depression for most of her life. It's a medical condition.'

'Are you saying you bear no responsibility for her state of mind?'

'I'm saying I didn't make her who she is. I may not wear my heart on my sleeve, but Valerie knew that from the beginning. I keep her clothed and fed and give her all the money she could ever use. A lot of women would welcome a marriage like that.'

She didn't want to debate him. His warped view of love

and marriage didn't matter. It was time to get back to what she really needed to say.

'What are we going to find in the woods?' she asked.

He didn't answer.

'Did you hear me? They're starting the search. What are we going to find?'

'I have no idea.'

Serena pointed through the window. Across the dirt road, away from the cemetery, a short, balding man held tight to a beagle that strained at its leash. Its ears flapped, and its nose was buried in the long grass. The dog was hungry to run. Smell. Hunt.

'See that dog?' she said. 'It's trained to recognize the gases of decomposing human flesh.'

Glenn stared at the beagle. 'It's an awful skill to give an animal, isn't it?'

'What is she going to find?'

'I can only speculate. I don't know.'

'So take a guess.'

Glenn's face was oddly passive, as if he were detached from everything that was happening around them. 'I guess you're going to find Callie.'

Serena felt her heart race. 'You think Callie is buried there?'

'Don't you? Isn't that why we're here?'

'Did you put her there?' she asked.

'No,' Glenn told her with a raspy sigh. 'But if someone is framing me, if someone left the toy there for you to find, well, I can't escape the obvious conclusion.'

'You think your daughter is dead.'

'I'm afraid so. We'll find out soon enough.'

'That's all you can say?' Serena asked.

'What else is there?'

What else but grief, Serena thought. What else but tears and desperation. What else but a horrible, irreparable sense of loss.

'Who could have done this?' She didn't add: *if not you*.

'It must have been Regan.'

'She had an alibi,' Serena reminded him.

'So maybe she was working with someone.'

Serena tried to read the surgeon's face, but there was nothing in his expression. 'You probably won't believe this, Dr Glenn, but I've been the one defending you. I'm the only one who hasn't been convinced from the beginning that you were guilty of murdering your daughter.'

'And what do you think now?' he asked.

'I think you may be the coldest man I've ever met,' Serena said. 'Cold men have no conscience. No empathy. They can do terrible things.'

'Or they can save lives on an operating table,' Glenn replied with a shrug.

Outside the car, the beagle unleashed a fury of impatient barking. Serena saw Stride approach the man with the dog and point to a spot on the north side of the trees. When he turned toward the Lexus, Stride caught Serena's eye and looked away.

Micki Vega was by his side. She saw the Lexus too, and Serena watched her eyes widen in dismay as she stared at Marcus Glenn. Her mouth fell open, and she took a step toward the car as if she would run to him. Serena thought she might cry. Micki said out loud, in a voice that barely carried through the glass, 'I'm sorry.'

Beside her, Serena watched Marcus Glenn offer Micki a small smile. He mouthed two words to her: 'It's OK.'

Micki turned away, bowing her head.

'Am I under arrest?' Glenn asked Serena.

'No.'

'Then I'm going home.'

Forty-one

Valerie sat on the floor. Her fingers kneaded the white carpet. Ten feet away, a fire burned in the middle of the stone fireplace that dominated the wall. It was a gas fireplace, with fake logs that burned forever and didn't crackle or pop like real wood. The circle of heat from the artificial flames barely reached across the drafty room to warm her shoulder. She was cold.

She thought about the fire pit behind Denise and Tom's house by the river. Every year, on Christmas Eve, Tom stoked a bonfire that roared for hours, and the kids squealed and played games, and the adults drank beer and wine. Before she had married Marcus, she had joined them for their holiday tradition. She would sit silently in the shelter of the fire and envy her sister for everything she had. Husband. Kids. Responsibilities. Joy. Every year, she had felt like an outsider at someone else's feast, but even so, she missed being part of it. She missed simplicity. Christmas with Marcus was lavish but sterile. One year, they had gone to Italy. The next year, they had cruised in the Caribbean. Another time, they had catered a party for hospital staff with roast turkey, elaborate canapés, and expensive California wines. Even in her own home, she had felt as if she were on the outside, looking in.

This year, she had thought that it would all be different, because this year, she would have Callie in her arms. They could build traditions of their own. But it wasn't going to happen now. It wasn't going to be like that at all. She would be as alone as an island in the middle of the lake.

Valerie knew they were searching. They were in the woods, with lights and dogs and cameras. They weren't going to bring Callie back to her, pink and happy, giggling as her mother laughed and cried. They were going to call her with other news. The phone would ring in the middle of the night, shattering the silence. It would be Denise or Serena or Stride. Their voices would have the low, ominous bass of tragedy, and they would tell her how sorry they were. Marcus would put an arm around her, and his comfort would be as false as the logs in the fire that refused to burn.

Marcus.

I was wondering if you had any idea what your husband may have been looking for in Regan's files.

Valerie stared at the hospital envelope. She had unearthed it from the drawer of lingerie in her dresser and brought it with her, unopened, to the living room. A gleaming pair of oversized silver scissors sat next to her. She could snip off the end of the envelope and extract what was inside, or she could cut it into miniature pieces and add them to the fire, where they would dissolve into the only real ash ever to burn there. She could know the truth, or she could cover it up.

She thought: this is what you were looking for at Regan's house, isn't it? Tell me, Marcus. This is what you so desperately wanted to find. What could be worth so much? What do you not want me to know? Regan laughed at the idea that I didn't know already. She thought I was a fool. And maybe I am.

Did you kill Regan, Marcus? Is the secret so terrible that you had to silence her? But you're too late.

All she had to do was pick up the envelope, but she couldn't bring herself to touch it. Instead, she picked up the scissors. They were hefty and sharp. She nestled them in her hand and spread the blades wide. They formed her initial, V, in a mirror finish. The blades reminded her of other things, too. They were the mouth of a fish, gasping for air on the floor of a boat. They were legs opening wide, inviting a man to make love to her.

She took the edges of the envelope with her other hand and lifted it in the air. Held it. Felt its weight. She couldn't imagine how a single sheet of paper could change a life, or be worth the price of a life. Some sins, some secrets, are not worth knowing. She wanted to cut it up, put it in the fire, pretend, forget, grieve, move on.

But no. She had to know.

Valerie wielded the scissors and in a single motion slit the side of the envelope open. She made an oval of the envelope and let the paper inside fall out into her hand. It was folded. The truth was inside. She separated the folds, turned it over, and tried to make sense of what she was holding.

It was a dirty Xerox copy, hard to read. A medical form, heavy with codes and scribbled over in a doctor's unintelligible writing. The first thing she saw that she understood was a date stamped in the corner from nearly five years earlier. The paper was old. How could something so old have any relevance to her today? Five years was a lifetime ago. Five years was the time when she had sat in this very room at two in the morning, with the fake fire glowing and her husband asleep upstairs, and she had poured the tablets of aspirin into her palm.

It was that same month, she realized. The month of her despair and rebirth.

The form was dated two weeks after she had tried to kill herself.

She studied the codes, the handwriting, the notes in the

margin, and tried to interpret it, as if it were a foreign language. And then one word jumped out at her. It was a medical term she didn't really understand, but it didn't matter, because she knew. Other words began to make sense. The timing, the implications, everything was clear.

She knew how a single sheet of paper could rewrite history.

It hit her like a rogue wave. Her mouth fell open in a silent scream, so deep and anguished that no real sound could emerge. The form dropped from her hand. She toppled slowly, sideways, sinking like a fallen statue into the carpet. Her knees drew up to her chest, and she wrapped her arms around them. The outside world escaped. The wailing pierced her ears, but only inside her head. Her tears flowed, but they stayed inside her eyes. Like a child, she rocked back and forth, willing away the knowledge and drowning in her grief.

The snow began to fall.

The flakes navigated the web of branches like silver balls in a Pachinko game, ultimately landing and melting on Stride's skin. The white bed on the forest ground was thin now, and bare in patches, but as the night stretched on, the blanket would deepen. After decades in Minnesota, he was still amazed that snow could be so insubstantial and yet gather into drifts that brought the entire world to a halt. The calendar said autumn, but November here meant winter.

The three of them stopped in the woods. They were only thirty yards from the slope of the cemetery, and he could see the lights of the police cars revolving on the dirt road beyond the graves. Stride shone his flashlight beam ahead of him and watched Migdalia Vega, who looked uneasy as her eyes studied the trees. The beam illuminated streams of snow. He directed the cone of light at the ground and swept it back and forth.

'Are we close?' he asked Micki.

'Everything looks alike,' she said.

'Five minutes ago, you said we were almost there.'

'I'm not sure now.'

Stride frowned. He thought she was stalling.

Beside them, Craig Hickey restrained his beagle, whose tongue lolled out of its mouth as it bit at the snowflakes. The squat handler wore heavy gloves and a red wool cap yanked down over his ears. The frigid wind raised a rosy glow on his face.

'Bitch of a night,' Hickey said, stamping his feet in the pine needles littering the ground. 'Don't know why we can't wait until daylight to do this.'

'It won't be any warmer in the morning,' Stride replied, 'and there'll be a foot of snow covering up everything.'

Hickey shivered. He chewed gum and worked his jaw like a teeter-totter. 'My Cujo don't care about snow. She'll sniff through it.'

Stride didn't ask why anyone would name a cadaver dog Cujo. He wanted to move the search forward quickly. Part of it was practical; he didn't want to be shoveling into a crime scene through deep snow. Part of it was human; he knew this was going to be the longest night of Valerie Glenn's life.

'Maybe he's right,' Micki said. 'It looks different in the dark. Maybe we should try again tomorrow.'

'The snow will erase all the landmarks by then.'

'Well, I don't know if I can find it again.'

Stride noticed the stubborn bulge of her lower lip as she pouted. He nodded his head at Craig Hickey. 'Give us a minute, OK?'

'Yeah, whatever.'

Hickey dragged Cujo back through the tangle of brush growing between the birch trees, leaving Stride and Micki alone.

'What's going on?' Stride asked her.

Micki kicked at the ground. 'Nothing. You try finding anything in these woods at night. I'm lost. I got turned around.'

'You saw Marcus Glenn back there,' Stride said. 'I think you're having second thoughts about helping us.'

She rubbed her runny nose with the back of her glove. 'I know how it works. You find something, you're going to arrest him.'

'Not necessarily.'

'Yeah, like I can trust anything you say. I'm fucking cold. Let's get out of here and try again in the morning. I don't know where I am.'

Stride shook his head. Snow sprayed off his damp hair. 'I saw your face a couple minutes ago, Micki. You know exactly where you are. You know every inch of these woods by heart. Are we close? Is that it?'

'I thought so, but now I'm not sure.'

He switched off his flashlight, and they stood in darkness. Over his shoulder, he could make out the lights of Micki's trailer not far away. 'You knew the significance of that toy horn as soon as you found it, didn't you? You knew what it meant. I think you studied the landmarks in the forest. Maybe you even left yourself a clue to find the place again. You knew we'd be here sooner or later.'

She said nothing.

'Tell me something,' Stride continued. 'Do you visit your own child?'

'Yes. Sure I do. All the time.'

'It's nice that you know where to find him,' he said, turning on his flashlight again and directing it ahead of them. 'Imagine not knowing.'

Micki cursed under her breath. 'If I tell you, then I go, OK?'

'OK.'

Micki's eyes followed the light, and she pointed into the trees. 'There's a cluster of four birches there. Twenty feet north, there's an old pine by itself with a thick trunk. I carved a cross in the trunk. I thought she deserved that, you know.'

'Where did you find the toy?'

'The pine's on the edge of a clearing. Not big. I found it right in the middle. Like someone put it there special, not by accident.'

Stride whistled for Craig Hickey, who returned with Cujo on the leash. 'Follow me,' he said.

He led the way forward with Hickey following in his footsteps. Micki stayed where she was, letting them go. The four birch trees ahead of them grew from a single trunk, bending in different directions, and he knew that north lay straight ahead, based on the location of the cemetery. He went slowly. With each step, he swept the ground with the flashlight. The soft pine bed didn't keep footprints. He saw a black pile of animal scat, dried pine cones, and a rusted coffee can.

The tree was exactly where Migdalia had said, standing lonely where it had grown for years. Thick, spiny bushes hugged the pine and made a wall. As he came closer, he squatted and studied the trunk and found a tiny cross, three inches by three inches, carved into the bark with a pocket knife.

'There,' he said, pointing into the brush.

Hickey let Cujo go. The dog shot into the bushes and disappeared. Stride heard the noise of its frantic paws.

'How will we know?' he asked.

'You'll know,' Hickey said.

Stride stood next to the pine, where he could see over the crown of the brush into a small, open patch of flat land. His light captured Cujo, nose to the ground, snuffling through the litter of pine needles. The dog looked busy and excited. It ran back and forth around the clearing in a blur of brown and white fur, always making its way back to the very center and pawing at the earth. Whatever smell was coming from under the soil, the dog buried its face down to get more of it.

'Wait for it,' Hickey said.

Cujo stopped all of his movements abruptly. He sat on his haunches in the middle of the clearing and sneezed. His snout pointed toward the sky. Then, as mournfully as a wolf baying for a lost pack, the dog began to howl.

Forty-two

Kasey packed a box in the basement, where the air was damp. She wore wool socks, but she could feel the chill of the concrete floor under her feet. As she pulled books off the metal shelves, she eyed a patch of black mold that had grown into the shape of a spider on the wall. She hadn't noticed it before, and she wondered in horror if spores had been floating through the ductwork all year, infesting their lungs. She stared at the giant patch as if she expected it to mutate in front of her eyes.

When her phone vibrated in her pocket, she jumped in surprise. She answered but heard only a long stretch of silence. Then, finally, a voice whispered to her.

'Hello, Kasey.'

Her hands tightened into fists. She knew the voice. It was him.

'Did you get my message?' he said.

Instinctively, her eyes darted around the basement, but she was alone. The only movement she saw was a mouse that scampered along the ledge of the foundation and vanished into a burrow-hole in the pink insulation. She shivered.

'What do you want?' she said.

He took a long time to reply. 'You're leaving.'

'That's right.'

'But our game isn't over, Kasey.'

'Yes, it is. I'm ending it. I'm not playing any more.'

The silence stretched out. She stared at the rust stains under the wash basin and prayed he had hung up.

'It's over when I say it's over, Kasey.'

'Fuck you,' she hissed, slapping the phone shut. She knew her bravery was hollow. Seconds later, the phone buzzed again in her palm, like the whine of an insect. She wanted to let it ring, but she couldn't.

'Leave me alone,' she insisted.

'We're way beyond that. You know it. I know it. This is about you now, not me.'

'What do you want?' she repeated.

'I want you to meet me.'

'You're crazy.'

'You're talking like you have a choice, Kasey. But you don't. We both know you don't.'

She squeezed her eyes shut. Tears pushed their way under her eyelids. 'We're leaving. Tonight. We're driving away. You'll never find us.'

'I *will* find you. I'll find your husband, too. And your child.'

'*Leave them alone!*' Her voice was a strangled scream, choked and heavy.

'I'd like to. This is between you and me. But if you leave, then I have no choice. I'll have to make sure you pay, and then your family pays, until there's nothing left. You don't want that.'

'Oh, my God, why are you doing this?'

'You're the one who put yourself in the middle of my game.'

'It was an accident. I never meant for it to happen like this. I never wanted anything to do with you.' Her cheeks flushed red as she cried. '*Please.*'

'You're going to meet me. Now. Fifteen minutes.'

'I won't do it.'

'Yes, you will. You'll do anything to save your family. I know you.'

Kasey said nothing. Her brain raced, and she looked for a way out, and she saw nothing but the walls.

'Fifteen minutes,' he repeated. 'Meet me where it started between us. Alone.'

'No.'

'If you're not there, I'll kill them, Kasey. In awful ways. You know I'll do it. If you're late, or I smell a cop, you can expect to come back home and find them both gone. You better hurry.'

He hung up.

Kasey put her hand flat on her chest as she hyperventilated. She saw a rusted hunter's knife on the shelf and thought about killing herself, cutting open her wrists and bleeding to death on the concrete floor. But it wouldn't save them. If she was gone, he'd still come after them. She knew it. She knew his game. Instead, she grabbed the knife and shoved it in her back pocket.

Fifteen minutes. She didn't have much time. She wiped her face and steeled her nerves. If he wanted a fight, she would give him a fight. Only one of them would end up alive, and it would be her, not him. He was right about one thing. She would do anything to save her family.

Kasey climbed the stairs out of the basement. Bruce was in the kitchen, watching her strangely.

'Did I hear you talking?' he asked.

'It was Guppo. He needs me at the crime scene out at the old dairy.'

'Why?'

She shrugged. 'He can't figure something out, and he needs my help. He knows we're leaving in the morning.'

'You don't have to go. This is their problem now, not yours.'

'As long as that guy is out there, it's my problem,' Kasey blurted out, her voice growing shrill with anger and frustration. 'It's our problem.'

Bruce stared at her. 'What's wrong?'

'Nothing. Nothing's wrong. I have to go. I won't be long.'

Her coat was draped over the back of the couch. She put it on and zipped it up to her neck. Bruce watched her, and she hoped he couldn't read her mind. He always told her he didn't trust anyone in the entire world except her, but there were days when that felt like a burden she couldn't handle. He was her opposite in so many ways. That was one reason they were good together. She would never have survived this past year without him.

'It'll be better when we're in the desert,' he told her. 'You'll see.'

Kasey nodded as she put on her gloves and tried not to cry. The desert felt like a dream. She wondered if she would ever see it. She opened the front door, where the wind gusted into the foyer, bringing a cloud of snow. Before she left, she turned back and put a gloved hand on Bruce's bushy beard.

'I'm sorry,' she said.

'For what?'

'For putting us in the middle of this.'

'It's not your fault,' he told her. 'You can't blame yourself.'

'I do anyway.'

She kissed him and closed the door before her emotions betrayed her. As she tramped across the dirt toward the garage, she cringed in the cold air. The fierce wind bit at her exposed skin, and the wet snowflakes clumped on her eyelids, making her blink. Her eyes moved constantly, studying every corner and shadow. She wondered where he was. When she yanked open the garage door, she made sure the space was empty before hurrying to their car and climbing inside. She locked the doors and didn't let the engine warm up before backing through the drifts and speeding toward the highway.

Kasey was alone on the road. Snow poured across the headlights and made it difficult to see. She remembered the same lonely drive a week earlier, lost in the fog, but she knew where she was going this time. She remembered how the gun on the seat beside her had comforted her that night, but she had already surrendered her gun. She put the knife there now instead and eyed its dull blade, but no sense of security came with it.

It took her less than ten minutes to criss-cross along Highway 43 and retrace her steps to the abandoned dairy on Strand Avenue. She came from the northeast, past the house of the woman who had died in the field, across the bridge over the rapids of the Lester River. Her body felt the icy grip of the water again, the way it had knocked her off her feet. She remembered the screams and the sounds of the shots coming from her gun. She remembered standing over the woman's body after the man had escaped.

She turned into the driveway near the white dairy building. No other cars were parked there. She saw no one waiting for her. She grabbed the knife and secreted it in her pocket as she got out of the car. The wind howled. She swayed on her feet as images of that deadly encounter a week earlier hammered her brain. She had spent the days since then trying to forget, and now she was back here, the last place on earth she wanted to be.

Kasey shoved her hands in her pockets. She squinted against the snow. When she wandered toward the dairy, she saw water stains on the cinder blocks and broken frosted windows. If she looked closely, she expected to see her own footsteps, coming up from the river, winding between the pines and stealthily hugging the rear of the building. As she came around the corner of the dairy into the open stretch of grass, now white with snow, she had a vision of the woman still lying there, her body in the field. Susan Krauss. Kasey could run and run and never escape her.

But it wasn't a vision. It was real.

Kasey peered through the snow that blew sideways across the grass, and right where the woman had been, right where she had died, was another body.

'Oh, no.'

She ran, slipping, toward this new victim, who lay face down and half buried by the driving snow. The body was a woman. She was naked, her skin oddly bloodless and blue, as if she had lain there for hours. Her head was turned to the side, but where her face should have been, there was mostly a pulpy mess of bone and brain.

Kasey lurched back in revulsion. It was Regan Conrad.

She spun around, but he was already behind her, near the wall of the dairy ten feet away, smiling.

'I knew you'd come.'

His voice was husky and unafraid. He wore no mask this time, and she could see his face. His right cheek was pockmarked with acne scars. His black hair was short and wiry. His dark eyes were reptilian as they focused on her, seeing her for what she was: prey. She had no illusions about why he hadn't bothered to hide his face. This was the end.

Kasey screamed for help, but it sounded like a whisper above the hiss of the storm.

'No one will hear you,' he said. 'It's the just the two of us out here.'

'You sick son of a bitch,' she blustered, covering her terror.

'This doesn't have to end badly, Kasey. You belong with a man like me, not that beer-bellied husband of yours. Come with me.'

'Go to hell.'

'Think about it. Running won't get you where you want to go. But I can protect you.'

She felt humiliated and furious. She wanted to cry and, just as badly, she wanted to destroy him. This was the man who stood between her and the rest of her life. Between her and all her plans.

'I love watching your mind work, Kasey,' he told her. 'I told you. I know exactly who you are.'

'What if I kill you right now?' she demanded.

He smiled, taking a step, and his long gait brought him inches closer to her than he had been before. 'Then you'd be free, wouldn't you?'

'Come any closer, and I'll blow your head off,' she warned him.

'If you had a gun, I'd already be dead.'

She took a step backward, and he took another step toward her, and again the distance between them shrank. But he was still beyond her reach. She was conscious of his size and strength. His eyes never left her. His gloved hands dangled at his sides. She kept the knife hidden in her pocket, but her fist was curled round the hilt.

'What do you want with me? Do you want to kill me like the others?'

'The others meant nothing to me,' he told her. 'This is something else, Kasey. I have special plans for you.'

'What plans?'

'You'll find out soon enough.'

She stared into his black eyes, and her heart filled with bloodlust. There was only one thing to do. Fight. Attack. Murder.

'Why are you doing this?' she asked. 'Who are you?'

'My life story doesn't matter. It only matters that I am who I am, and you are who you are.'

She took another slow step backward, but this time she let her weight settle on to her right leg. She readied herself to charge.

'I don't deserve to die. Not now. Not like this.'

'Neither did Susan Krauss. Neither did any of the others. But our paths crossed. Life is random like that.' He added, 'Or maybe God sent you to me. Did you think about that?'

'There's no God,' Kasey told him.

She pushed off with a scream, springing across the short space. She whisked the knife through the air in front of her and imagined it slicing across his skin. Felt it burying deep through skin and bone and organs. She was so close.

But it was futile. He was waiting for her, as if he was inside her mind and could see her thoughts. As she reached him, his hand twisted, revealing a black device barely larger than a cell phone. She was barely conscious of it, barely knew what it was, before she heard the sizzle of electricity. The knife spilled from her limp fingers. In the next millisecond, pain exploded throughout her body, savaging her nerve ends and cascading her off her feet. Her blood became fire. She twitched in the snow, in agony, her brain scrambled into floating fragments.

He loomed above her, out of focus, doing cartwheels in her eyes. She wanted to resist, but she felt like a helpless rag doll, with useless arms and legs stuffed with sawdust. She was his toy. He owned her now. He had owned her since that night in the fog.

She was aware of being turned over. Felt snow and dirt pushing into her mouth. Felt her hands being taped. Felt him stroke her hair and whisper in her ear: 'Bad girl.'

He stood up, lifted her limp body into his arms, and carried her across the snowy ground.

PART FOUR

IN RUINS

Forty-three

Valerie heard the front door open. She hadn't moved from where she sat near the fire. Her tears had dried on her cheeks. She heard the footsteps of her husband on the floor of the foyer, and the pounding of his leather heels felt like nails driven into her palms. He didn't call her name. He walked around the house the way a ghost would, ominous and unseen. She dreaded seeing him in the flesh. It was as if, all these years, he had hidden behind a disguise, and now she had finally seen his real face.

The footsteps stopped. When she looked up, she flinched, watching his tall frame fill the doorway. He brought a smell of cold and sweat. His suit was wrinkled, his tie loose. His angular jaw was dark with a long day's growth of beard.

'I need a drink,' he said.

He went to the wet bar and dropped ice into a lowball glass. He poured an inch of whiskey, drank it down in a single swallow, and gritted his teeth as the burn hit his chest. He poured more, draining the rest of the bottle.

'You heard?' he asked. When she didn't answer, he added, 'I'm sorry.'

He made no move to come to her or comfort her. Thank God. She couldn't bear for him to touch her. He sipped his drink and ignored the hostile silence. Her head swirled with words to say, but none of them felt right. It was like being caught outside in the rain, only to realize it was really the deluge.

'Is that all you have to say?' she murmured. 'You're sorry?'

'What else do you want from me? I don't have anything to give you right now.'

That was true. He had never had anything to give. Not from the very beginning.

'I want you to tell me what you did,' she said. 'I want to hear it from your mouth.'

He put down his drink and shook his head. 'Ah, fuck, not you, too.'

Valerie pushed herself off the floor. 'I always wondered how a father could hate his daughter,' she told him. 'Secretly. Deep in my heart. I never admitted it to anyone, even when I saw how you were with her. Denise used to tell me that she was scared, that I shouldn't leave Callie alone with you. I told her she was crazy, but somewhere inside, I wondered.'

'This is crap. I never felt that way. You've been brainwashed.'

'You're right, I have. By you. I've worn blinders for years. I wouldn't allow the thought into my brain. I willed it away. Even when Callie disappeared, I convinced myself that the rest of the world was wrong about you. Blair Rowe was wrong. Your lovers were wrong. You didn't really say what you said to them, about wishing Callie had never been born. Not you. You couldn't think that. No man could think that.'

'Valerie, I didn't mean it like that.'

'How did you mean it?'

'I was angry. I was blowing off steam. That's all it was.'

'Angry? At a little baby girl?'

'Angry at you.'

She tensed. 'OK. I deserve that. I cheated on you.'

'Oh, Christ, it's not that. I'm no saint, and I never pretended to be. Hell, if Tom Sheridan could make you happy, good luck to him, because I sure as hell could never figure out how to do it. I gave you all the money you could ever want. You had a life that every woman in this town envied. But that wasn't enough. You walked around this house like you were an empty shell. Once a week, you spread your legs and let me inside like you were doing me some kind of favor. Get it over with, Marcus, so I can get back to feeling sorry for myself. Yeah, I was angry. I'm still angry.'

'You could have divorced me,' she said. 'You could have found someone else. Why did you have to take your anger out on Callie?'

'I did *not* do that. And I don't want a divorce.'

'Were you waiting for me to go away?' she asked. 'Did you need a night when I wasn't in the house?'

'You're out of control. Let me get you a sedative.'

'Absolutely. Drug me up. That's the answer.'

He didn't reply.

'At least tell me it was an accident,' she whispered. 'Tell me you're not really that cold-blooded.'

'I'm tired of accusations,' he told her bitterly as he turned for the door. 'I'm going to bed.'

'*You stand there and listen to me!*' Valerie screamed.

He froze and slowly turned back. Valerie stalked across the room. Her face was twisted in fury.

'Did you ever love me, Marcus? God, look who I'm asking. You can't love anyone but yourself. I knew you were selfish, but I had no idea how far you'd go to keep me focused solely on you. Was that the problem? Were you jealous that Callie made me happy and you didn't?'

'Yes, a little,' he admitted. 'But that doesn't mean anything.'

'Poor Marcus. His beautiful wife wasn't paying enough attention to him. She was too busy with another man's child.'

He opened his mouth to say something and then shut it.

He rubbed his chin with the tips of his fingers. When he spoke, his voice was quiet. 'Are you telling me Callie's not mine?'

'Don't you lie to me and pretend you didn't know,' Valerie hissed. 'Don't you even dare.'

He shrugged. 'Having doubts isn't the same as knowing. It was three years, Valerie. You were having an affair. You must have wondered too.'

Three years.

Valerie heard the words and felt them cut her open. He was so casual about it. Three years. As if it were a moment in time, not the hell she had suffered month by month, falling into the blackness of a hole that never ended. The hole he had dug for her. Knowingly. Deliberately. With malice aforethought.

'Three years,' she told him, her voice raspy with grief. 'Three years, Marcus. You saw what I went through.'

It was in his eyes. They became nervous and feral. For the first time, the thought must have entered his brain that she *knew*.

'You agreed to have a child to make me happy,' she continued. 'To shut me up. To throw a bone to your poor, suffering, suicidal wife.'

'I told you from the beginning that I didn't want children,' he said. 'You said you were OK with that.'

Valerie shook her head. 'I really believed it back then. That was when I thought I would have a husband to live with, not a robot. But you. You sat there and agreed that we could have a baby. Did you see what it did to me? Did you see I was happy for the first time in my entire life? Was it really asking so much to make that a part of our lives?'

'I said yes,' he told her without conviction.

'Stop it! Stop! My God, how could you? How could you do that to me? How could you let me spend three years looking at myself like a broken machine? The one thing I had finally found to do with my life, and I thought I couldn't have it. I thought God was *punishing* me, Marcus. But it was you.'

'Valerie, don't.'

'Don't? Don't what? Don't say the word?'

She turned on her heel and grabbed the medical form where it lay on the carpet. The form Regan had given her. 'I want to make sure I use the right word,' she told him. 'Doctors have their own words for everything. Deferentectomy. Is that it? Is that what I should call it?'

He closed his eyes. 'Yes, that's it.'

'See, I would have just called it a vasectomy, Marcus, but I'm not a doctor like you.' She waved the paper in his face. 'This is what you were looking for in Regan's files, isn't it? This is what you were so desperate for no one to find. Two weeks after I nearly died, Marcus. Two weeks after you said we could have a baby, you went and got a vasectomy. To make sure it didn't happen. And then you let me lie there for the next three years, hoping and praying and blaming myself and blaming God when I didn't get pregnant.'

Her husband shook his head. 'Shit,' he murmured. He looked up at the ceiling and added, 'Regan, you fucking bitch.'

'Did you kill her? Is that how badly you wanted to keep the secret?'

'No.'

'Did she know all along? Did you tell her the truth about Callie?'

'She knew,' he acknowledged.

'God, you both must have laughed at me. Or was Regan laughing at you? You had the perfect plan, and then another man went and got me pregnant. And you couldn't say anything. You know what's ironic? I never doubted it was your baby. It didn't matter that I was sleeping with Tom. I always believed Callie was yours. I thought we would finally have something we made together.'

'I could have divorced you then,' he said, 'but I didn't. I let you bring her into our lives. I accepted her as our own.'

305

'Don't make it sound like you made the slightest effort, Marcus. Don't pretend you invested an ounce of compassion in my baby. I wish you'd told me the truth and chucked us out on the street. Instead, you took her away from me. The one thing in my life that I loved. You took her away.'

'We're done here,' he told her, walking out of the room. 'This is over.'

Valerie watched him go and knew he was right. It was over. The long fall ended here. There was nothing to do but wait in silence and guilt. Wait for the searchers to do their work and the forest to give up its secrets. Wait for the night to grow long.

Wait for the phone to ring.

Forty-four

Kasey awoke with the stench of death in her nose, like a fetid pool in which she was drowning. Dead flesh rotted somewhere close by, emanating a cloud of decay that hung in the air as thick as fog. She tried to breathe through her mouth, but the smell climbed into her nose and festered there. Her throat gagged. She coughed up a harsh mouthful of acid, and sour chunks bubbled out of her lips.

When she opened her eyes, she saw nothing. No light at all, just black darkness. She listened and heard a steady rain of water dripping and splashing into puddles from the ceiling. Animals scurried on the floor below her, their nails scratching on metal and stone. Rats. She had no idea how many.

It was bitterly cold. There was no wind, but the freezing air pricked at her skin and made her numb. Deep inside, pain lingered in her muscles from the impact of the stun gun. Kasey tried to move and found she couldn't. Her arms were overhead, fastened with handcuffs to some kind of pipe. Where her bare wrists brushed the metal, the frost was almost hot. Her ankles were taped together, and she stood on top of a wooden platform that swayed unsteadily when she moved.

'Where am I?' she said aloud. Her voice had a strange echoing quality in her ears. No one answered.

She turned her head. Something heavy and rough, a length of rope, was wound around her neck. The tightness constricted her breathing, almost choking her. She struggled at the bonds that confined her, and as she did, she felt the platform under her feet rocking on uneven legs.

His voice came out of the darkness. Shockingly loud and close.

'Careful, Kasey.'

She bit her lip and shut up. Fear mingled with the pain and cold. She thought about praying, but prayer was worthless.

'Where am I?' she repeated.

'This is my school,' he told her, still invisible, but no more than a foot away. 'It's where people come to learn the sad truth about life.'

A light flashed in her eyes, blinding her. She squinted and closed her eyes, seeing hot orange circles in her brain. The brightness dimmed. When she opened her eyes again, the flashlight was pointed at the ceiling. She could see bits and pieces of the room around her. It was some kind of ruin, littered with rusted machinery and debris. Gaping, crumbling holes were punched in the walls. Water fell everywhere, as if the ceiling was a sieve.

'What the hell kind of place is this?'

'A long time ago, it was a classroom. You see what happens when nature and vandals have a few decades to reclaim a building.'

Kasey tried to look up, but the rope around her neck constrained her. She couldn't see her hands. Below her, she was barely able to see her feet, which were tied with gray tape. He had taken off her shoes and socks. She stood precariously on a five-foot circular table, and her bare, cold toes poked over the round edge of the surface.

He waited as she assessed her condition. He stood on top of a long oak desk, pacing slowly from one end to the other and avoiding the holes where the wood had rotted away. She tried to quash the terror in her face and focus on him with anger and contempt. When he stopped in front of her and leaned close to her face, she sucked in her breath and spat at him.

'You're a sick fuck.' Her voice was raspy. The rope squeezing her throat made it difficult to talk.

He wiped his cheek. 'You could teach other women something about courage, Kasey. That's why I put you behind the teacher's desk, so your students can look up to you.' With a flick of his wrist, he turned the flashlight behind him and toward the floor.

Kasey moaned. The beam of light illuminated four bodies – three women, one man – tied into schoolroom chairs. The women were naked. They had been dead for days, and the remnants of skin had caved in on their skeletons, leaving them sunken and hideously white. Their eyes were open, staring with empty horror. Two dozen black rats, caught as they gnawed on protruding bone and decomposed flesh, scattered in fear as the light struck them.

Kasey squirmed instinctively to escape. The table swayed underneath her.

'That's not a good idea, Kasey.'

He came up to her and stroked her face with the back of his hand. She cringed and tried to pull away.

'You're handcuffed to one of the old water pipes,' he told her. 'It's corroded. Not very sturdy.' He fingered the rope on her neck. 'The noose, though, that's tied to one of the joists in the ceiling.'

'You bastard. What do you want?'

'I told you I have special plans for you.'

'What plans?'

'This is school, Kasey,' he said. 'You have to pass a test.'

'Let me go. Don't do this to me. Don't kill me.'

He fingered the buttons on her shirt and idly popped the first three and spread the fabric apart. His hand pressed on her chest and felt it rise and fall. 'Maybe I won't need to kill you. Maybe we can leave together. Both of us. Would you go with me?'

She grimaced. 'Go where?'

'Away.'

'What if I did?'

'Are you saying you'd stay with me?'

'To save my life?' she stammered. 'Yes.'

Slowly, he undid the rest of her shirt and let it hang open. 'You forget, you can't lie to me. I'm just like you.'

'Why ask if you won't believe me?'

'Because I like to hear you say yes. I like it when you're scheming and ruthless. What would you do if we went away? Would you plot to kill me? Would you spend every minute looking for your chance?'

'You know I would,' she snapped. There was no point in a charade. She wasn't going to change the outcome.

'You may be the most exciting woman I've ever met,' he said with admiration.

He laid the flashlight at his feet. From inside his pocket, he pulled out Kasey's knife. She sucked in her breath. He extended the thin strip of elastic at the base of her bra. Dragging the rusted point of the knife against her skin, he sliced through the elastic and nudged the cups of the bra apart, baring her breasts. In the cold, her rose nipples puckered into rocks. He bent down and covered each nipple with his mouth in turn and sucked on it. She felt her breasts releasing milk.

He licked his lips, tasting her. 'I hear breast-feeding gets a woman horny. Is that true?' He straightened up, stroking the globes of her breasts with his hands.

'Don't touch me.'

'I can't stop,' he said.

He reached down to the button at the waist of her jeans and undid it. Her jaw hardened with fury as he slid the zipper down. She shunted her knees tightly together and made it hard for him to strip her. He paid attention to her clothes, not to her, and when she saw her chance, she took it. She jacked her knees into the air, dangling from the pipe above her, which groaned and sank two inches, pulling slack from the noose and nearly strangling her. Her knees caught her tormentor solidly under the jaw and snapped him backward, where he tumbled off the long desk and landed in a crash on the floor. The flashlight rolled away and went black. She hunted for the swaying table with her feet and caught it before it wobbled out of her reach. With a gasp, she eased on to the table and let go of the pipe. The rope remained taut, and she struggled to inhale.

Below her, she heard him moving slowly and painfully. Getting up. Limping. Hunting through debris for the light.

'That was a mistake, Kasey,' he growled from the darkness. The teasing in his voice was gone. Only the cruelty remained. She didn't care.

The light went on again, but it was dimmer. He climbed back on to the desk, and she could see his face. Blood trickled from his mouth. His eyes had narrowed into dots of fury and coldness. He reared back and drove his right fist under-handed into her abdomen. Her body doubled over with pain, and the rope grew more constricted, and air flooded from her lungs. Each breath felt labored as she tried to suck in oxygen. She thought she would gag and choke on her vomit.

'I was going to leave you like this to wait for me,' he told her. 'But not now. The test just got much harder.'

He drew out a key from his pocket and reached up and undid the handcuffs from each of her wrists and let them clang to the floor. Kasey dropped her arms back down to her sides. She didn't know what he was doing. Why he was freeing her.

Then he got down from the desk and dragged it away from her, and she understood his plan. She stood on the table with only its shaky base propping her up. The noose dragged on her neck, pushing her head forward. If the table fell, she would hang herself.

He breathed heavily and tended to the blood on his face. 'How long can you hold on to the pipe, Kasey? Five minutes? Fifteen?'

She didn't talk.

'I have to leave, but I'll be back soon. Can you hang on until then? Or will you just give up and die? I'm giving you a choice, Kasey, but remember, if you fail the test, your family dies. It's not pretty, but those are the stakes. Understand?'

She didn't say anything.

'*Do you understand?*' he repeated.

'Yes,' she gasped.

'Good. That's good. Now hold on tight.'

Kasey knew what was coming. She watched him closely, but she didn't put her hands up immediately. She wanted blood flowing into her arms as long as possible to give her strength. Only when she saw him moving closer, his face dark and menacing, did she finally reach up and take hold of the pipe again. The freezing metal was like a flame. Touching it burned her, and she could barely hold on. But she had to hold on.

He swept the table from under her feet. Her legs dangled in mid-air. Only her grip on the pipe kept her suspended.

'If you survive the next few minutes, the rest will be easy for you,' he said, stroking the bare skin of her stomach as she twitched over the floor. 'I want you to prepare yourself while I'm gone, because your family is counting on you. You see, I'm going to bring someone here for you, Kasey. A new student for our classroom. And all you have to do to pass the test . . . is kill them for me.'

Forty-five

Serena slid inside the patrol car next to Denise Sheridan, who propped a cigarette outside the driver's window and tapped ash on the ground. When Denise wasn't smoking, she jammed the fingers of her other hand between her teeth and chewed on her nails. They sat in silence on the dirt road near the cemetery. Fifty yards away, bright lights beamed like white sunshine through the trees. Silhouettes of evidence technicians came and went, carrying plastic bags. They'd been searching and digging in the forest for an hour, making their way through frost-hardened soil toward whatever was buried below.

'I'm sorry it's come to this,' Serena told Denise.

Valerie's sister sighed. Her face was tight with anger and resignation. 'I knew we'd end up in a place like this sooner or later.'

A place like this. A place to dig up the dead.

Serena was just as happy not to be in the woods. She wasn't sure she could handle it when the searchers found what they were looking for. This was a case where she couldn't switch off her emotions. She had sacrificed her objectivity by getting too close to Valerie and too close to Callie.

'It's better than not knowing,' Serena said.

Denise shrugged. 'If you don't know, you can still hope.'

Snow gathered in a wet film on the windshield as they waited. When it became hard to see, Denise flipped the windshield wipers, pushing the slush aside and clearing an arc on the glass. Inside, heat blasted from the vents, keeping the car warm.

'How are you?' Serena asked.

Denise said nothing. She chewed her nails harder.

'Sorry,' Serena said. 'Bad subject.'

'Yeah.'

'Do you want to talk about it?'

Denise looked at Serena as if she was crazy. Then she shrugged, as if anything was better than sitting in silence as the shovels carved up the ground.

'I wasn't expecting a bomb to go off under my life,' Denise replied.

'What happens next?'

Denise took a pack of cigarettes out of her pocket and then scowled and put it back. 'When you've been married as long as Tom and I have, it's not like divorce is easy. There's a lot of practical shit standing in the way. Starting with the kids. Then again, I'm not going to do nothing. Some women can put on blinders and live with a crappy marriage, but not me.'

'What about Valerie?' Serena asked. 'If it's Callie out there in the woods, she's going to need your help.'

'Let her get help from someone else, not me.'

Serena hesitated. 'She's going to be alone.'

'Are you *lecturing* me?' Denise asked in annoyance.

'No, but Callie's her whole world.'

Denise took a photograph out of her pocket. Serena could see it was the picture of Callie that had been broadcast all over the country. 'What is it about wives married to shitholes? They always think having a kid will make it better. Like it's some kind of miracle cure. Valerie should have gotten a divorce, not gotten pregnant.'

Serena didn't reply.

'Don't get me wrong,' Denise added. 'I'm sick about Callie.'

'I know that. You don't hide it as well as you think.'

Denise frowned and put the photograph away. 'As long as you're prying into *my* secrets, what about you? What's up with you and Stride?'

Serena was caught off guard. 'What do you mean?'

'Oh, don't play dumb. I can see you two are having problems.'

Serena thought about making an excuse, but she realized that she needed to say it out loud. 'He slept with Maggie.'

Denise didn't look surprised. 'Well, they've been dancing around it for years. So what are you going to do?'

'Same as you,' Serena said. 'I don't have a clue. But we don't have kids to worry about. I guess that makes it easier for me to walk away.'

'You think it would have been different between you if you had a baby? It wouldn't.'

'Maybe I wonder if *I* would have been different.'

Denise twisted toward Serena and pointed a finger at her. 'It's not a magic bullet, Serena. You'll never feel more vulnerable than when you have a kid. If you let it, the responsibility will kill you. If something happens, it can drive you insane.' She turned back and looked through the steamy windshield of the patrol car. 'Oh, shit.'

Serena looked too. Through the snow, she saw Stride coming toward them, his face weary and grave. Even in the cold, he had his sleeves rolled up, showing bare arms, tracked with dirt. He stopped in the glow of the headlights.

They both climbed out and met him. Serena saw Denise's jaw trembling. She was a sister and an aunt now, not a cop, and she didn't want to hear the news. Neither did Serena. She had known from the beginning that the odds were against a happy ending. That wasn't how child disappearances played out. You hoped for a miracle, but you steeled yourself for the harsh reality. Most kids didn't come home. Most kids didn't stay alive.

Stride's face was bathed in sweat. He wiped his forehead, leaving a trail of mud. His thick hair was wet and flat. He didn't make them wait.

'We found the body of a child,' he said.

Denise spun around and lashed out at the tire of her car with her boot and pounded both fists on the hood. '*Goddamn it!*'

'Hang on, Denise,' Stride said, but Denise didn't hear him. She hit the car until Serena was afraid she would break the bones in her hands. Tears streamed out of her eyes and ran in glistening streaks down her face.

It didn't matter if you knew it was coming. It was one thing to expect the truth and another to hear it. It was one thing to be furious with Valerie and another to hear that her daughter was dead.

'Denise, wait,' Stride called.

Serena watched his face. Behind his sorrow, something was different. Whatever had happened was not what they had all expected. Something else was going on.

'Listen to me, *it's not Callie*,' he said.

Denise's head snapped around. 'What?'

'It's not Callie in the woods.'

Her hands flew to her mouth. 'Oh, my God, are you sure? How can you be sure?'

'It's not a girl,' Stride told her. 'The body that was buried there, it's a boy.'

Forty-six

Valerie stood in the doorway of their bedroom. The hallway light cast a rectangular glow from behind her. Marcus lay in bed, asleep on his back. His breathing came easily and steadily. She stared at her husband and wondered how he could sleep so calmly when men were hunting for Callie in the ground, when her precious baby was cold and alone.

She knew the answer. Callie had never been his daughter. She was a stranger who had lived in his house. Someone else's child. The offspring of his wife's affair. He had known the truth from the very beginning.

'Do you really wish she'd never been born?' she asked.

He slept without answering.

She approached the bed and stood over him. He was a handsome man. Fit, strong, attractive. She wondered if he was really asleep or just pretending. Part of her wanted to scream and make noise, to force him to acknowledge her, but she didn't. They were beyond that. Beyond rescue.

Valerie undressed and went into the master bathroom and closed the door behind her. The marble tile was cold under her bare feet. She turned on the shower and waited as the water grew hot. She studied the reflection of her naked body in the full-length mirror. People told her she was beautiful, but they didn't understand how she could hate her body. They never saw that one brown nipple was slightly larger than the other. That her knees were ugly. That her stomach was a constellation of pale freckles.

She got under the water, which poured from the shower like rainfall, straight down over her head. It flowed through her blonde hair and over her shoulders and breasts and between her legs and over her feet and then swirled into the drain. She didn't move or wash her body with soap or knead shampoo into her hair. Instead, she stood straight, with her eyes closed and her arms at her sides and her face tilted into the spray. Her skin became clean and pink. She stood, not moving, until she had been there for so long that the hot water drizzled away and became cold.

Outside the shower, she shivered on the bath mat. She toweled herself dry but left her hair wet. She returned to the bedroom and stared at Marcus and felt nothing. She dressed again, not for sleep, but for the day ahead. A day when she would finally be free.

She was hungry, so she went downstairs. It felt odd to think about food now, but she hadn't eaten in hours. She turned on the lights in the kitchen and took a small bowl from one of the cabinets. Inside the refrigerator, she found a stalk of celery, a cluster of green grapes, an avocado, a Granny Smith apple, a lemon, and a cup of yogurt. She put the ingredients on the counter.

'This is called a Waldorf salad,' she said to her daughter.

It didn't matter that Callie wasn't really there. In her imagination, she saw her little girl in the high chair beside the kitchen island, smiling back at her.

'I use yogurt instead of mayo, because who needs all the fat and calories? And I add in half an avocado, because I like avocados.'

She separated a piece of celery, sliced off its frilly head, and carefully cut the stalk into half-inch segments, which she dumped in the bowl. She ran the grapes under the faucet, pulled off a dozen, and cut each one in half. She added them to the bowl.

'It's supposed to include walnuts, but I don't have any walnuts. Apples are crunchy enough, so I won't miss them.'

Valerie sliced the apple down the middle and cut away slices from the core. She tasted one and made a face. It was tart. Like an angel, Callie giggled at her mother and slapped the tray in front of her with tiny hands. Her blonde curls danced on her forehead. Valerie winked and diced the apple slices and mixed them in with the celery and grapes.

'Now for my top-secret ingredient,' she said.

Valerie ran the knife all the way around the black avocado and twisted the two halves apart. As she buried the blade in the avocado seed to remove it, her phone rang on the kitchen counter. She froze, her lower lip quivering. The noise went on, musical and insistent. When she glanced at the phone, she saw her sister's name in the Caller ID box.

'That's Aunt Denise,' she said with a strange lilt in her voice. 'I don't think we need to talk to her right now, do we? Not when we're busy making a salad.'

The phone went silent. Her smile cracked as she stared at Callie.

'There's plenty of time to call her back. We can call her when we're done here. OK? Now where was I? I think we're almost ready.'

She scooped half of the avocado out of its husk and cut it lengthwise into strips, which she dropped one at a time into the salad. She pried the lid off the yogurt and spooned it into the bowl. She cut the lemon in half and squeezed juice over the salad. With a fork and spoon, she mixed everything together.

'Doesn't that look delicious?' she said. She took a forkful and tasted it. 'That's good.'

She sat down at the island and ate each bite of the salad slowly, staring at Callie as she did. Her daughter's eyes followed her. Callie made noises; she'd be talking soon, saying words. She memorized her little girl's face, her two new white teeth, her dimpled smile. She savored these quiet moments when it was just the two of them.

When her bowl was nearly empty, her phone rang again. She stopped with the fork halfway to her mouth. The horror of anticipation bled across her face.

The caller ID this time said Blair Rowe.

Valerie's eyes went blank. The phone rang and rang, and then the music ended. She snapped out of her trance.

'Isn't it amazing how everyone always calls when you're in the middle of a meal?' she asked her daughter. 'I think we'll just turn off that silly phone now. There really isn't anyone I want to talk to tonight. Other than you, of course.'

She switched off the power on her phone. When she bent over the salad bowl again, something dropped from her face and splattered on the counter. Tears. She touched her cheek in surprise. 'Look at that, I'm crying. Isn't that strange?'

Callie cocked her head with a serious expression on her face. It always looked to Valerie as if she was thinking about something very important.

'You're getting so big,' Valerie told her. 'And so beautiful. When you grow up, you're going to be a gorgeous young woman.'

She took her empty salad bowl to the sink and washed it and put it away. She returned the avocado half, the lemon half, and the celery and grapes to the refrigerator. Opening the chrome garbage pail with her foot, she slid the remnants into the trash and then used a paper towel to wipe the counter. She ran the knife under the water and rubbed it with a sponge until it was spotless.

When she was done, she opened a spice cabinet and slowly

spun the lazy susan inside until she found what she wanted. It was a bottle she had purchased a year ago, before she got pregnant. A bottle she had never opened. A bottle filled to its narrow neck with tablets of aspirin.

She turned back and looked at the high chair. Callie was gone. Valerie's smile slowly dissolved, and the light went out of her eyes.

'From now on, I'll never leave you alone,' Valerie promised her. 'Never ever. I'll always be with you.'

Kasey had no idea how long she had been clinging to the frigid metal pipe. It could have been seconds. It could have been an hour. Time had no meaning in the darkness. Her arms grew thick and heavy, and the cold burned her skin, and all she wanted to do was let go. But she didn't. She couldn't.

He was gone. For now. She had watched him take the flashlight and pick his way through the debris, and then the light had vanished behind a fragmented wall. Somewhere on the far side of the building, she'd heard a steel door opening and closing. Since then, she had heard only the other noises of the ruins: the water torture dripping from overhead and the morbid squeal of the rats.

She held out little hope of rescue. She screamed – *'Help me! Help!'* – but her voice bounced around the decimated building, and in the aftermath, she heard nothing at all. No one came running. No one shouted back. Wherever she was, she was on her own.

In the early minutes, she didn't dare move for fear of dislodging the pipe or slipping and losing her hold on the metal itself. Eventually, as her strength waned, she decided she had to try. If she made a mistake, she died, but if she did nothing, she died anyway. She had to stay alive. She had to escape.

Carefully, she eased one hand off the pipe and examined the rope with her fingers, looking for a way to undo the knot and slip the noose from around her neck. She pried at the twine, but the knot was tight and unyielding. With two hands, she might have been able to dislodge it, but not with one. She worked at it until her other arm groaned in protest, and when she felt her grip slipping, she brought her hand back to the pipe.

She thought about shimmying up the rope itself to where it connected to the ceiling joist, but she didn't think she had enough strength in her arms to make the climb. She also thought about bringing up her legs like a gymnast and slinging them over the pipe, but she worried that the fragile metal would buckle under the pressure.

Kasey decided to see where the pipe itself went. Prying her fingers off the metal, she slowly moved her left hand three inches. She repeated the process with her right hand. The metal was cold and wet, and her fingers nearly gave way. She moved again, another three inches. And then again. The progress was excruciatingly slow. The pain and cold thumped in her brain and made her dizzy. Her eyes saw strange things in the darkness. She tried to move again and couldn't. When she screamed at her muscles, they refused to take orders. Instead, she hung there, paralyzed, feeling the pipe grow loose and slippery under her fingers.

It would be easy to let go. Easy to give up. Let the metal slip away, and let the rope take over.

No.

It was a test. She couldn't fail. Calm descended over her like a wave, and she sloughed her body along the stretch of pipe. She shunted her bound legs and slowly swept the space to her left with her feet extended. At the very edge of her toes, she brushed something hard. Concrete. A wall. She peeled away her fingers and moved again, three more inches, and when she extended her legs, she could brace the bottom of her feet against the side of the wall. Flakes of paint scraped away under her skin. If she could find a toehold, she could reposition herself and use both hands to attack the rope around her neck.

Kasey tried to slide another few inches, but her head snapped to her right, choking her against the coil of rope. She had extended all the play left in the rope where it connected to the ceiling. It wouldn't go any farther. She was trapped.

She reached out again with her legs, but this time, she moved too quickly, and her left hand lost its grip and fell. Her right hand clenched the freezing pipe and hung on, but the rope cut into her neck and choked off her breathing. She gasped and spat, dangling by one hand. Frantically, she grabbed for the pipe with her other hand, and as she did, her fingers brushed a scrap of metal hanging just above her. She grasped it, dropped it, and tried for the pipe again, and finally she curled her fingers around the thick length of pipe and pulled herself back up. The pressure on her neck eased enough for her to breathe.

Kasey gave herself a few seconds to recover, but she was running out of time. Running out of strength.

She groaned and reached up with her left hand. Her fingers bumped against something square and sharp, dangling on a thin strand of plastic wire. She yanked on it and felt it give way, but before she could grab it, her right hand slipped, and she had to stop and hold on to avoid falling. She took a few long breaths. Sweat gathered on her palms, making both hands slippery.

She tried again. This time, the metal plate and the thin wire came away. Dust settled over her face. She coughed and nearly lost her grip again, but she held the plate in her hand. Her right arm howled in pain as the fingers of her left hand traced the outline and found a metal corner that was bent and sharp, where it had obviously torn away from a larger frame.

Kasey knew she had only one hope. Cut the rope.

She found a reservoir of strength and bent her elbows to do

a chin-up. Her body climbed, slow inch by slow inch. The pipe wobbled. Her fingers twisted and slipped as blood and sweat gathered under her skin. When she felt her chin touch the metal, she nudged her right arm over the pipe and then let go with her left arm, hanging by her crook of her elbow.

The pipe made an ominous lurch downward. The rope yanked her chin back and tilted her head up. Kasey sawed the edge of the metal plate against the rope around her neck. She felt the cord fraying, threads splitting and cutting loose.

The pipe shifted downward again. The rope choked her. She couldn't breathe, and she felt her cheeks puffing out and leaching the rest of her air. Her face was wet with tears. Her right arm grew numb and lifeless.

She sawed frantically. The rope thinned but refused to yield. Her body twitched as she jerked the jagged metal up and down, and the repeated pounding added to the stress on the pipe.

It was all too much. She had no air. She had no strength. Her left arm collapsed, and the metal plate dropped from her hand and fell to the ground below her with a clang. Unconsciousness began creeping in.

Oh, God, no.

Then, from the wall beside her, came the groan and squeal of metal tearing.

The pipe separated and gave way. Kasey felt her body falling, with the rope still clutching her windpipe like powerful hands.

Forty-seven

Troy Grange opened the door of his house with a bottle of beer in one hand. Over his shoulder, Maggie saw a basketball game on the wide-screen television in his living room. He wore an untucked flannel shirt and jeans. His eyes were rimmed in red, and his skin was pasty.

'Sorry to stop by so late,' she told him.

'It's OK. Come on in.' He led her into the main room and muted the sound on the television. 'You want a beer or something?'

'No thanks.'

'So did you lose a bet?' Troy asked.

'What?'

'The hair.'

'Oh. Yeah, funny. It was just a stupid whim.'

'Uh huh.' He added after a long pause, 'I saw the news.'

'Yeah.'

'Same guy, huh?'

'Looks that way.'

Troy swore. He finished his beer and wiped his mouth. 'Are you any closer to catching him?'

'I'd like to say yes, but so far, he's one step ahead of us. We're pursuing a lead down in Colorado, but it's too early to tell whether that will pan out. The car he was using was stolen in Colorado Springs, so we're checking on pattern crimes in the area.'

'You think he's been at this for a while?'

'I don't know, but these guys don't usually quit until they're caught.'

Troy shook his head. 'It's a fucked-up world.'

'How has it been for you at work?' Maggie asked.

'Oh, it's crazy, which is a good thing. I get into the office, and the first crisis hits about two minutes later, and the shit keeps up until it's dark and I'm driving home. I don't have time to think about anything until then.'

'Is the baby still with Trisha's parents?'

Troy nodded. 'I'll probably go get her this weekend. Debbie misses her. So do I.'

'The offer still stands, Troy. Anything I can do to help.'

'I know. I appreciate it.' He added, 'What about the kid? Do you have anything on Nick Garaldo?'

'We think he's one of these guys who likes to break in where he doesn't belong,' Maggie told him. 'Urban ruins.'

'Really?'

'We found a photo card in his apartment. He was inside the Duluth Armory a few months ago.'

Troy rubbed his chin. 'We've had break-ins at a few of the unused areas of the port over the past couple years. I wonder if Nick was involved.'

'Half the fun for these guys is staying ahead of people like you and me,' Maggie said

'So you think he had an accident somewhere?'

Maggie nodded. 'That's our best guess right now. Nick may have been casing an abandoned school in Buckthorn. I've got a guy from a local security agency taking a look at the site. I haven't heard from him yet.'

'Well, keep me posted. Nick's girlfriend is worried sick.'

'I will.'

'You look tired, Maggie. Is the investigation wearing you down?'

'Yeah, a little,' she admitted.

'Stride's back on the job next week, right? That should help.'

She grunted affirmatively, but Troy picked up on her mixed emotions.

'You don't sound thrilled to have him back,' Troy said. 'Do you not want to give up the big chair?'

'He can have it.'

'So what's the problem?'

Maggie shrugged. 'It's complicated. I'm not going to bother you with my troubles.'

'Right now, it's easier to worry about someone else's problems,' he told her. 'We're friends. If you want to talk, talk.'

Maggie sighed. She was tired of keeping it a secret from everyone. 'It's me and Stride. Something happened.'

'Something?' Troy asked. Then he read her face. 'Oh, that kind of something. Yeah, well, that is complicated.'

'Tell me about it.'

'Isn't he involved with someone else?'

'Yeah.'

'So now what?'

'Now I tell myself what an idiot I am.'

Troy chuckled. 'Sorry. Wish I could help. Romantic advice isn't really my thing.'

'Me neither. Listen, keep this to yourself, OK? Nobody knows.'

'My lips are sealed.'

Maggie heard her cell phone ringing. She dug it out of her pocket and checked the caller ID, but the source of the call was blocked. 'This is Maggie Bei,' she answered.

'Ms Bei, my name is Jim Nieman.'

Maggie didn't recognize the name or the voice. 'What can I do for you, Mr Nieman?'

'I got a call from Matt Clayton in Buckthorn today. He said you were making inquiries about that falling-down school they've got out there. I handle security on the place for the township.'

She remembered the name now. 'Did you have a chance to check it out today?'

'I did. As a matter of fact, I'm over there right now. I was hoping to get out here earlier in the day, but I got pulled into some home security jobs.'

'What did you find?' she asked.

'Matt said something about looking for red pistachio shells. Is that right? What's that all about?'

'Did you find any?' she replied without explaining.

'Actually, I did.'

Maggie covered the speaker with her hand and said to Troy, 'This is the security guy for the Buckthorn School. I think Nick Garaldo was out there.' She spoke into the phone again. 'Did you check inside the school?'

'I was going to do that, but I thought I'd call you first. Since I found those shells, I didn't know if you wanted me to hold off on searching the interior. I didn't want to screw up any evidence if you think we've got a crime scene there.'

'When were you last inside?' she asked.

'A couple days ago, I guess.'

'Have you been inside since Saturday night?'

'Yeah, I think it was Sunday,' Nieman told her.

'Did you find anything out of the ordinary?'

He laughed. 'Well, the whole thing is pretty creepy, if you ask me.'

'Was there any evidence that someone had broken in recently? Could someone have been inside and you didn't realize it?'

She heard him pause. 'Anything's possible, I guess. There are a lot of nooks and crannies in the place. I didn't see evidence of a break-in, but that doesn't necessarily mean anything.'

'OK.'

'You want me to go inside?' Nieman asked. 'Like I said, I'm outside the place right now.'

'Yeah, I do. Check it out carefully. We've got a missing person, and I think he's been at the school recently. It's possible he broke in, or tried to break in, and got hurt. Call me back when you've checked it out, OK?'

'Will do.'

Maggie heard him hesitate. 'Is something wrong?'

'Oh, no, I'm happy to do it. Anything for the boys and girls in blue, you know. I just thought, if something did happen to this guy inside, you might want to have a cop with me when I search the place. I know it's late, but I thought maybe you could get someone to join me here.'

Maggie thought about it. 'Sure, that's a good idea.'

'I'd leave it in your hands entirely, but I'm the guy with the keys,' he added.

'Understood.'

'I'll wait for the cavalry before I open the doors. Do you think it will be long?'

Maggie checked her watch. 'Tell you what, Mr Nieman. I'm just five minutes away from the school right now. I'll drive over there myself.'

Forty-eight

Denise Sheridan slapped her phone shut. 'Still no answer,' she said.

'Are you going to drive over there?' Serena asked.

Denise shook her head. 'It's late. If Valerie's in bed, let her sleep.'

Serena didn't think Valerie was sleeping. If she was in bed, she was staring at the ceiling. If her phone was off, it was because she didn't want to hear the news about Callie.

The two women rejoined Stride among the scattered head-stones of the cemetery. Behind him, one of the light towers set up by the crime scene technicians cast his shadow across the grass into the trees. He stopped in front of a line of graves that all bore the name GLENN.

Serena watched him. His arms were folded over his chest, and his face was dark and thoughtful. Snow flew sideways through the light, landing on him and turning him into a white statue. He wore the leather jacket he had owned for years. His hair looked as if he had just rolled out of bed. In his eyes, she saw the intensity of a man who never let go. She couldn't help herself, she was still in love with him. She couldn't imagine turning her back on what she felt, not when they had spent three years together. The easy thing for her was to whisper,

I'm not going anywhere. See what he did. See how he reacted. See if he still felt the same things for her.

But she didn't do that. She said nothing at all.

'So what the hell does this mean, Stride?' Denise demanded. 'Who's the boy in the ground?'

Stride stared at the graves. 'I don't know yet.'

'What's the medical team saying?' Serena asked. 'How did the baby die?'

'There's no sign of foul play,' he replied. 'There's no trauma, no obvious evidence of injury or abuse, but we won't know until the autopsy is completed.'

'Recent death?' Denise asked.

'Based on the condition of the body, yes. We're talking days, not weeks.'

'But nothing to help with identification?'

'No.'

Serena took a long look at the cemetery and at the surrounding forest. She put herself in the shoes of someone who would carry a baby to the woods and dig its grave. There were so many places you could lay a body where it would never be found. Why so close to the cemetery?

'How was the body placed in the ground?' she asked Stride.

She wanted a sense of the kind of burial that had happened here, whether it was something sacred or profane. Their eyes met, and she knew he had been thinking the same thing. That was another part of their relationship she couldn't escape – their minds were connected.

'He was wrapped in a white sheet.'

'Carefully?'

Stride nodded. 'Someone took time to do it right. It was almost tender.'

'This doesn't make sense,' Denise protested. 'Who takes the care to wrap up a dead child and then buries it in the woods like garbage?'

'Not like garbage,' Serena said, shaking her head. 'Whoever did this couldn't bury the baby in a cemetery where he might be discovered. But the baby was close to the cemetery. I think that's significant.'

'I agree,' Stride said. 'It feels ritualistic. Almost religious.'

'But what does it have to do with Callie and Marcus?' Denise asked.

'I don't know. Maybe nothing at all. Maybe we stumbled on to something unrelated to Callie's case.'

'Or maybe Micki's lying,' Denise suggested.

They heard a harsh, tired voice cut through the wind. 'I'm not lying.'

When they turned, they saw Migdalia Vega on the slope of the cemetery behind them. Her round face glistened with melting snow. Her feet were planted in the ground, and she had her hands on her hips. 'You hear me?' she continued. 'I'm not lying. I did what you asked. I showed you where I found the toy. Where Mama saw the light.'

'You knew we'd find a body,' Denise snapped, 'but we only have your word that you found the toy there at all. Who's the kid, Micki? Who did we find buried there?'

'I don't know. And I found the horn in the woods, just like I said.'

Stride put a hand gently on Denise's arm. He stepped closer to Micki, his voice calm. 'We don't think you're lying,' he told her.

'Tell that to her!' she retorted.

'We're all tired, Micki. It's been a long night. You've helped us a lot, and I appreciate it, OK? But I need to know if you have any idea who that little boy could be.'

'I already told you, I don't know. But it's not Callie, and that's good, right? I knew Dr Glenn wasn't involved. He couldn't do something like that to his daughter.'

'What if Callie wasn't his daughter?' Denise interjected.

Stride shot her a warning glare. He turned back to Micki. 'You told me that you lost your own son early in your pregnancy,' he said softly. 'I'm sorry, but I have to ask. Was that really true?'

'Yes! You know what happened to my baby!'

'OK. I know. And the light your mother saw in the woods, you're certain this was on the night that Callie disappeared?'

'Yes, she told me about it on Saturday, and that's when I went to search. That's when I found the toy.'

Stride nodded. 'OK, Micki. That's all for now. You can go home.'

The girl stamped past them up the slope. Serena watched her disappear between the trees as she headed for the lights of the mobile home. 'Where does that leave us?' she asked.

'Nowhere,' Stride said.

Denise reached for a cigarette and put it in her mouth without lighting it. 'Look, the toy horn was obviously intended to make us think there was a connection to Callie. Right?'

Stride thought about it but shook his head. 'No, that doesn't make sense. As soon as we put a shovel in the ground, we were going to find out that it wasn't Callie buried there.'

Serena thought again about someone bringing a child's body to the woods in the darkness and how much the burial felt like a religious ceremony. Something private and painful. 'What if the toy is exactly what it looks like?' she suggested. 'A memorial.'

'What do you mean?' Stride asked.

'I mean that no one ever expected us to *find* that toy. It was put there the way you'd put flowers on a grave.'

'But whose grave?' Denise asked.

Serena retraced her conversations with Valerie. She realized that when Stride had told her about Micki's discovery of the toy horn, it had felt *familiar* to her. It had already been part of her consciousness about the case, because she had heard about it before. Valerie had told her about her night at the hospital on New Year's Eve, about the staff blowing toy horns when the clock turned to midnight.

She could almost picture the scene in her mind. See it. Hear it. Valerie drowsy with pain and drugs. The noise and excitement of the New Year in the maternity ward. The horns squealing. Lullabies playing on the hospital speakers with each new baby born.

'Another baby,' Serena said.

Denise looked at her. The unlit cigarette drooped in her mouth. 'What are you talking about?'

'There must have been other babies born in the hospital that night. New Year's night.'

'So what?' Denise asked.

'So I'd like to find out who they were. And whether Regan Conrad was the nurse for any of the mothers.'

'Yes, but if it was a stranger's child, why bury him here?' Denise asked. 'What does this have to do with Callie?'

'I don't know,' Serena admitted.

Even so, her instincts told her that the body in the ground was inextricably linked to Callie's disappearance. Somehow, she knew that this child, whoever he was, was the key to everything.

Stride was already on the phone. Serena watched him dial.

'Guppo, it's Stride,' she heard him say. 'I need some information. I'm looking for a list of babies born on January first, preferably those at St Mary's. See if you can find birth announcements on the *News-Tribune* website, OK? Boys only, don't worry about the girls. I'll hold.'

He waited. He stared at Serena, and she stared back at him. She realized that more than anything else right now, she wanted to kiss him.

'I'm here,' he said into the phone. 'That was fast. Give me the names and addresses of the parents, OK?' Then he said, 'Hang on, repeat that. Are you serious?'

Stride hung up the phone.

'We have to get back to Duluth *right now*.'

Troy Grange activated the security system on the downstairs level of his house before he went upstairs to bed. It was a useless gesture. He had purchased the system to protect Trisha and the kids, and the killer had gotten inside anyway and taken away his beautiful wife. He wanted to rip the panel off the wall and throw it in the fields.

Troy cried. He didn't let himself cry often, never in public, and never in front of his children. He needed to be strong for them. He couldn't bring back their mother, so the only thing he could do was go on with life. Keep them safe. Try to keep them happy. But when he was alone, in his private moments, he cried. He remembered Trisha's face as vividly as if she were still there beside him. Her touch. Her laugh. How her skin felt when they were in bed. He pounded the wall as he realized that those sensations would begin to dim now, and eventually they would slip out of his memory altogether.

Safety. Security. There was no such thing. You could live in a fortress and still not keep out the monsters. The sensors, the alarms, the locks, the bars were mostly an illusion. If someone wanted to come in, they could. People like Nick Garaldo would always figure out a way. Sometimes their motive was no more than mischief, to say they went where no one else wanted them to go.

Sometimes their motive was to kill.

Troy thought about Nick Garaldo. And Maggie. And the ruined school. He wondered if they would find Nick inside, trapped, suffocated, neck broken, or blood drained from his body. There were so many ways to die in ruins.

That was when the thought, the memory, poked into Troy's head. He stared at the security panel on the wall and remembered the man who had installed it a few weeks earlier. A tall man with

335

scarred skin and eyes like a dead fish. The kind of man who smiled in a way that made you think he wasn't smiling at all. Troy hadn't liked him.

He didn't know why his mind had dragged up a memory of the security man's face, and then he remembered that he had been thinking about Maggie's phone call. A security guard had called her about Nick and the pistachio shells. A security guard out at the old school.

Jim Nieman. That was the name. He was almost sure of it. Nieman was the same man who had been inside his house.

Forty-nine

The rope snapped Kasey's chin back as she fell, and a shiver of pain coursed through her spine. She felt a crushing weight on her throat as her body dragged the thick cord into a vise around her neck. Her legs danced spastically. She clawed at the cord with her fingers, but the knots held, and all she felt was blood oozing from her abraded skin. She reached above her head to pull herself up and relieve the pressure, but she had no strength to lift her body.

Her mind grew cloudy. She knew she was dying.

Then the frayed section of rope where she had sawed with the metal plate split and gave way. The rope broke, and she fell in darkness and landed with an agonizing, bone-deep blow as her calves slammed the cement floor below her. A loose nail drove into the meat of her leg, and she had to bite her tongue to keep from wailing in pain.

But she could breathe. Sweet air flooded her lungs. She collapsed on to her hands and knees and air swelled her chest.

Something scurried across her fingers, and she reared back. It was a rat, and it wasn't alone. The squeals of the animals were excited and close. She clawed the tape from her ankles and lurched to her feet. The blackness made her dizzy, and she waited for her head to clear. She listened for the noises of her captor, but for the time being, she was alone. Alone with no light. No weapon. No phone. She may as well have been lost in the fog again.

She started to walk with her hands and arms outstretched in front of her. Almost immediately, she tripped and fell. When she squatted and ran her fingers along the floor, she found a jagged block of concrete, three feet by four feet. She traced its edges and then stepped around it. As she inched forward, her numb feet crushed against pebbles of glass with each step and bled. Water dripped on her face. She kicked a piece of scrap metal that clanged on the cement and hissed in pain. She bent down and picked up an L-shaped joist, heavy and rusted. She nestled it in her fist and felt better that she had something she could use in self-defense.

Her hands touched a smooth wall ahead of her. She explored it with her fingers and felt lines of grout between square tiles. With her palms flat, she followed the wall, letting it lead her steps. She found the opening of a door frame where the wall ended, but the doorway itself was blocked with a sodden, rotting stack of wooden planks at least three feet high. She stopped, squinting, trying to see if there was an escape route on the other side of the doorway, but the interior was black.

Beyond the doorway, the wall continued, and she followed it until her fingers bumped into a new wall, made of plywood, not tile. She had walked herself into a corner. She turned, making her way along the perpendicular wall, moving more quickly than before. Her hands missed a wooden beam propped against the wall at waist level, and before she could stop it, the beam toppled noisily to the floor. She froze, expecting him to come for her, anticipating a cone of light stabbing through the darkness.

Nothing happened. Only the rats continued to stalk her.

Kasey grew bolder as she wondered if he had left her entirely on her own. She decided that time, not noise, was her biggest enemy now, and she stumbled quickly along the wall. Water dripped louder and faster, and her fingers banged into cold pipes hanging from the ceiling like spider webs. She collided with a concrete I-beam and weaved around it. The wall ended, and she took two steps into open space, in the middle of a dark nowhere.

She heard something close by. Soft, like a distant hiss. Wind.

The outside world wasn't far away. She steered for the sound and realized she was near a boarded-up window, and on the other side of it was freedom. Her fingers frantically examined the frame, looking for a spongy weakness where the water had softened the wood. Snow pecked against the window an inch away from her. She could feel the cold.

'Let me out,' she whispered.

Before she could punch through the heavy plywood with the metal joist in her hand, she ran out of time. She heard voices. His voice.

Down the long, black tunnel, she saw light streaming through the cracks.

Maggie climbed out of her yellow Avalanche outside the Buckthorn School. The moon, which was no more than a haloed glow behind the gray clouds, illuminated the desolate ruins. Snow drifted against the tan brick walls and weighed on the flat roof. The school, or what was left of it, was sheltered by two giant oaks with spindly branches that looked like witches' fingers. Every window was shuttered with heavy plywood. Every metal door was looped with chain and locked shut.

She imagined the school as it had been after the war, beside a dusty dirt road, surrounded by corn fields, with farm boys dropped off at its doors in shirts and ties. That was long ago. Now it was forgotten, falling down, eroding a little more with each bitter winter. After thirty years of abandonment, the animals and the weather owned it. That was what attracted explorers like Nick Garaldo.

Maggie saw a tall, athletic man in his early thirties approaching her truck. He wore a black fleece jacket, and he shoved his hands in his pockets and gave her a cocky smile. He had a back-pack over one shoulder.

'Nieman?' she asked.

'That's me.'

'Thanks for sticking around,' she told him.

'No problem.' He gestured at the school with a flick of his head. 'You want to go inside?'

'Let's take a walk around the perimeter first.'

'Sure thing.'

He led her across the field, which crackled with snow, oak branches, and dead leaves. The ground sloped sharply down-ward as they hiked around the western wall. She shuffled down the hill in her boots past a cluster of towering spruce trees. Where the ground flattened, they were at the rear of the school. The lower level was open to the elements. She poked her head past the exposed concrete pillars and studied the mess of bricks and pipes.

Nieman turned on a flashlight and pointed it at the ground. 'Those are the pistachio shells,' he said. 'That means some-thing to you, huh?'

'It does. Keep that light on them, will you?'

Maggie bent down. The ground was littered with shells, and she noticed that they weren't covered with dust and that their color was still bright red. Nick Garaldo had been here recently. She stood up and asked, 'Have you noticed any evidence of intruders recently? Anyone prying back the window coverings or tampering with the locks?'

'No, nothing like that. The place is sealed up pretty tight.'

Maggie nodded. The wind shifted, swirling snow down from the roof of the school and into the debris of the lower level. She smelled the sweet, cold air, but somewhere in the eddy of the breeze, something else came and went. It was so fleeting she wasn't sure if it had really been there, or if her senses had imagined it.

She backed up into the field behind the school and looked at the upper level, which was boarded shut with a wall of plywood covering the rear windows. Nieman eyed her curiously.

'Something wrong?' he asked.

'I'm not sure. Did you smell something?'

He shrugged. 'Lots of dead animals inside. Raccoons. Dogs. Squirrels. Rats. They don't pay me to play animal control officer.'

'Yeah.'

The stench that had flitted through her nostrils was vile and fresh. She stood in the field as the choppy currents of the storm fought with each other, and when the air blew directly toward her across the roof of the school, the smell hit her again. This time, it lingered, and even in the crisp night, it made her pinch her nose shut.

This was no dead squirrel. This was a corpse smell, the kind of revolting gas that a body gives off when it's shut inside with the dead air.

'What the fuck is that?' Maggie asked.

Nieman sniffed the air. 'Shit, you're right. That's new. It wasn't like that over the weekend.'

'Let's go. Somebody's dead in there.'

She led the way this time, back up the hill and around the corner to the front of the school. Four concrete steps led up to a series of steel doors. Here, where the wind didn't reach them, she didn't notice the smell. She felt an urge to hurry, but she knew the urge was irrational. If Nick Garaldo was inside, he wasn't alive.

'Open this up, will you?' she asked.

Nieman hunted for the key to undo the lock that held the chain together on the doors. When he found it, he unlocked the padlock and slid it in his pocket. He let the chain fall on the steps. Maggie pushed past him, swung open the door, and bolted inside. Nieman followed, letting the door swing shut behind him.

She stopped, because she couldn't see. The world turned black.

The smell suffocated her. Locked inside the ruins, the stench multiplied like a runaway strain of bacteria, turning the air rank. It was so sudden and overwhelming that she could barely breathe, and she wanted to bend over and vomit. She clapped her hand over her entire face, trying to keep out the smell, but it wormed inside her anyway.

'Oh my God,' she screamed. 'Turn on your flashlight!'

Nieman didn't answer. Maggie reached out in the dark to make sure he was there, and as she did, she heard her phone ringing in her pocket. She pulled it out and saw on the caller ID that it was Troy Grange.

'Troy—' she began, but then someone slapped the phone from her hand, and she heard it shatter on the concrete floor.

When she tried to shout, the words died in her throat as a steel wire encircled her neck.

Fifty

Stride and Serena barely spoke on the drive across the empty night highways. He drove fast. They both felt the urgency of time and of not knowing what they would find when they arrived. He concentrated on the road, which was slick with snow, but every now and then he stole a glance across the front seat at Serena. He knew she felt his eyes, but she never looked back. Her face was in dark profile beside him.

'Watch out for deer,' she warned when they entered a long stretch of highway bordered on both sides by thick forest. 'They come out when you least expect it.'

'I know.'

He thought about the advice that Minnesota drivers learned in school. Don't steer for deer. Drive right over them. Kill them. Better them than you, because you're more likely to kill yourself trying to avoid them. He'd hit deer a few times over the years. Each time, he told himself it would be different if he slowed down, if he kept his eyes on the road, if he used his high beams. But it didn't matter. You couldn't stop deer from running, and if they crossed the road at the moment you were there, you were going to have a collision. The best thing to do was come out of it alive.

They come out when you least expect it.

Serena wasn't talking about deer. She was talking about the two of them. Or maybe the three of them. Their collision.

He knew that, at the end of the day, she didn't care about Maggie. Serena had known all along about Maggie's feelings for him, and she had dealt with them for better or worse. What mattered was whether he could walk away from the accident alive. Whether he could walk away and leave Maggie behind. That was what she was waiting for him to say. He didn't know if she could live with the idea of him working side by side with Maggie every day, but the first step was his. He had to tell her. *I love you more. I want you to stay.*

He thought about Maggie. He could still feel her in his arms. After all their years together, it had been strangely easy to glide across a line from friends to lovers. His feelings for her had become entangled with their history. That was why he couldn't say what Serena wanted. He couldn't lie to her when he didn't know what he felt. By not saying anything, he knew he had told her something she didn't want to hear.

They didn't speak for the rest of the trip. They crossed back into Duluth, and then into the north farmlands, in silence.

Stride parked on the shoulder of the highway, and they both got out of the car. Guppo was parked in a pickup truck on the other side of the road, and he squeezed out of his truck when he saw them. The highway was deserted. Snow whisked across the pavement.

'Do you have the warrant?' Stride asked.

Guppo yanked a folded white paper out of his back pocket. 'Judge Kassel isn't too happy with you. I interrupted her beauty sleep.'

'She's never very happy with me,' Stride said. He looked at the two Duluth patrol cars parked behind Guppo's pickup. 'These guys didn't use sirens on the way in, right?'

'Silent running,' Guppo said.

Stride saw Serena staring at the farmhouse. She was unusually tense, and he didn't know if it was caused by the stress between the two of them or her anxiety over the investigation. He knew without her saying a word that she had become emotionally engaged with Valerie and Callie. It was one more thing they hadn't talked about.

Serena turned to Guppo and asked, 'Have you been up to the house yet?'

'No, I was waiting for the two of you.' He shoved his hands in his pockets and added, 'So how do you guys want to play it?'

'I'm hoping we can do this the easy way,' Stride said. 'Whatever the hell is going on, I don't think anybody wants to get hurt. The biggest risk is someone bolting. Have one of the squad cars block the driveway, and keep your motors running.'

'You want me to go with you?' Guppo asked.

'We'll call you up when we're ready to do the search. But Serena and I want to go first and have a chat. I don't want anyone getting spooked, OK? The key is to do this calm and steady.'

'You got it.'

Guppo sloughed his body toward the patrol cars to give them instructions. Stride and Serena continued across the highway and stood at the base of the driveway. The farmhouse was fifty yards away, sheltered by trees. They could see lights inside.

'Did you call Valerie?' Stride asked.

Serena shook her head. 'We don't know what we're going to find up there. We could be wrong about this.'

'I said we want to do this the easy way, but do you have your gun with you?' he asked.

She looked at him. 'I have it, but do you really think that's necessary?'

'I don't know. I hope not, but they could be desperate.' He added, 'I didn't want to say anything, not until we knew, but this whole thing raises a lot of questions.'

'You mean Regan,' Serena said.

'Not just her.'

Serena thought about it and cursed under her breath. 'My God. Do you really think that's possible?'

'Right now, anything's possible,' Stride said. He heard his phone ringing, and he pulled it out of his pocket. He held it closely against his ear to hear the call over the roaring of the wind. 'This is Stride.'

'Lieutenant, it's Troy Grange calling.'

Stride was surprised. 'Troy, what's going on?'

'I'm sorry to call you so late, but this has been bothering me, and I couldn't sleep.'

'What is it?'

'Maggie stopped by my house earlier this evening. While she was here, she got a call from a security guard who keeps an eye on the Buckthorn School property. You know, it's that ruined building out on Township Road.'

'I know it,' Stride said. 'Was this about Nick Garaldo?'

'Yeah, exactly. The guard told Maggie he found something out there, and he wanted a police escort before he went inside the school. The old building's not too far from me, so Maggie told him she'd meet him there herself.'

'OK.'

'The thing is, I thought about it afterward, and I realized that the guard at the school was the same guy who did the security installation on my house. That was right after the killings began up here.'

'Is that a problem?'

Troy hesitated. 'Oh, hell, I don't know. I just don't like co-incidences, you know. And to tell you the truth, I didn't really like the guy. So I called Matt Clayton, the township administrator.

He and I play tennis a couple of times a year. I asked Matt what he knew about this security guy, Jim Nieman.'

'What did he say?' Stride asked.

'He said he's never had any complaints. But here's the thing. When I asked if he'd checked references on Nieman, he said he had. Nieman gave him the name of a guy who owns a strip mall in Pueblo.'

'I'm still not following you, Troy.'

'Pueblo's half an hour from Colorado Springs. Maggie told me that the van the killer was using was stolen in Colorado Springs.'

Stride gripped the phone tighter.

'I called Maggie to tell her about it,' Troy continued, 'but just as she answered, the phone cut out. I've tried her several times since then, and there's no answer.'

'I'll check it out, Troy,' Stride told him. 'You did the right thing by calling.'

'Let me know when you talk to her, OK?'

'I will.'

Stride hung up. Serena studied him with her eyebrows arched in a question, but he didn't answer right away. Instead, he dialed Maggie's cell phone and listened. The call went directly into her voicemail.

'Is something wrong?' Serena asked.

He told himself that nothing was wrong, but his gut told him otherwise. Everything was wrong. The cold air wrapped fingers around his neck. His stomach knotted in fear. He didn't hesitate.

'I have to go,' he told her. 'Maggie's in trouble.'

Fifty-one

Kasey huddled in the darkness. She lay on her stomach, freezing and wet, hidden behind a stack of rotting wooden beams. Her hair fell in limp curls across her face, and she clenched her fists to keep her body from shivering. Cold water dripped from overhead, landing on her back and legs. She could barely feel her feet. She wasn't sure how long she had been hiding, but she knew he was looking for her, and sooner or later he would find her.

The flashlight beam searched the room like a laser. He shot it into corners and crevices, hoping to surprise her. The light lingered over the wall just above her head, and she flattened herself further against the concrete floor and held her breath. Where the beam illuminated the wall, she could see orange rust stains, graffiti spray-painted by vandals, and pockmarks where someone had used the stone for target practice. Five seconds later, the light disappeared, and she was blind again.

He spoke to her out of the darkness. He couldn't have been more than twenty feet away.

'I know you're here, Kasey.'

She waited with a growing desperation for him to search elsewhere in the school, but after a long minute of silence, he switched on the light again. It lit up the floor inches in front of her face, and she shrunk backwards. The concrete was littered with nails and bricks. A foot-long rat froze, staring at her with pink eyes. The animal was inches from her face. Caught in the light, it charged directly at her, and she had to cover her mouth not to scream as its furry body scratched across the skin of her back.

'You can't hide forever, Kasey.' He added, 'Someone's waiting for you.'

Kasey tensed and inched forward. She heard a violent clap and a wince of pain. *'Talk,'* he barked.

She heard a new voice.

'Forget about me, Kasey. Save yourself.'

Maggie. It was Maggie's voice. Kasey wanted to pound her fists on the floor. She pushed part of her face past the pile of wooden beams, far enough to see as he shone the light on Maggie's body. She was tied to a chair with her hands behind her back. Her neck was ringed in blood, and Kasey had a flashback of that night in the fog and of Susan Krauss appearing out of nowhere at her car window. Looking just like that, with her throat half cut. Behind Maggie, in the dim glow of the flashlight, she saw the other bodies, posed as if they were decomposing dolls.

She was angry. Angry that God had dropped her in the middle of this, when she wasn't prepared. Angry that God had abandoned her. But maybe this was His revenge. Over the past year, she had stopped believing in God and found herself believing only in despair and betrayal. She had grown bitter at the world. She had simply never imagined that the awful road would lead her here.

'You can't run, Kasey,' he taunted her. 'What do you do now?'

She bit her lip, listening to his slow footsteps as he walked away. The beam of the flashlight shifted, streaming through a gaping hole in the far wall. His back was to her. This was her chance, and she didn't dare wait any longer.

I kill you, she vowed to herself. *That's what I do now.*

She scrambled to her feet and picked up the heavy metal joist. She held it like a club as she edged around the stack of wooden pilings. She put a foot ahead of her, tested the ground, and laid her heel down without a sound. She kept an eye on the flashlight beam in the corridor as she inched across the floor, but as she watched, it went dark. She froze where she was, feeling exposed. She thought about retreating to her hiding place, but she knew she was close to Maggie. In a voice that was barely audible, she murmured, *'I'm here.'*

She heard noises of struggle. The chair to which Maggie was tied rocked loudly on the floor, and she heard Maggie grunting with effort as she strained against her bonds. Trying to free herself.

She took another step and spoke again in a soft hiss. *'Maggie.'*

This time, Maggie whispered back immediately. *'Get out of here, Kasey.'*

It was too late to run. Light flooded the room and pinned Kasey like a convict in a searchlight. She still had the metal joist poised over her head, but he was in the doorway, twenty feet away, too far for her to charge him. Behind the light, he was in silhouette, but she could see that he held Maggie's gun, pointed at her chest. He walked closer, stepping over dirty glass, and stopped six feet away from her. The gun was outstretched in his left hand.

Kasey's back stiffened in defiance. 'You better shoot. That's the only way you're getting close to me again.'

'That's not how this goes down, Kasey,' he said. 'You know what I want you to do.'

'Fuck you, you sick bastard.'

'I want to see you kill her,' he said.

'You're crazy.'

'Take the joist, and crush her skull.'

'I won't do it.'

'Yes, you will. You'll do whatever it takes to save yourself.'

'You don't know me.'

'I know you better than anyone,' he said. 'You're just like me.'

'I'm *not* like you,' Kasey snapped, breathing harder, watching him.

'We both know you are. *Kill her.*'

'I'll kill you instead,' Kasey swore, raising the joist higher over her head and clutching it tightly with her hand.

'Don't be stupid.'

'I don't care what happens to me any more.'

'Yes, you do. You know the stakes, Kasey. You know what happens if you fail the test.'

'Leave my family alone. They're not part of this.'

'You weren't a part of my game, but you put yourself in the middle of it. You can't stop playing now.'

'You are *done*,' she shouted, taking a step toward him. 'You are *dead*.'

He read the violence in her face. 'It's a powerful feeling, isn't it? To hate so much you want to kill. That's when you know you're really alive.'

'This ends right now,' she said.

'I'll sweeten the deal for you, Kasey. Kill her, and I'll let you go.'

'What?'

'I'll let you go,' he told her. 'Game over.'

'You're a fucking liar.'

'I'm not lying.'

The joist felt slippery in Kasey's hand. 'You'll never let me go. I've seen you.'

'But you're not going to turn me in, are you? You wouldn't take that chance. Come on, Kasey, what's another death on your conscience? I'm giving you a chance to walk away.'

'*Kasey.*' It was Maggie's voice, interrupting him sharply. 'Kasey, *look at me*. Don't listen to him. Don't believe him.'

Maggie's eyes were calm and focused, as if she were talking Kasey down off a high ledge.

'This guy is pathetic,' Maggie went on, her voice growing loud and sarcastic. 'He's a joke. Look at him. Acne Face here probably had dates laughing at him in high school, and now he's taking it out on women everywhere. Or maybe Mommy liked to dress him up in her lingerie. Which was it, Nie-Man? Nie-Man, isn't that like German for "not a man"? Wow, the shrinks'll have a field day with that one.'

'Maggie,' Kasey murmured.

Nieman didn't move or say a word, but Kasey saw his muscles quiver as his body knotted up in rage. His smile froze on his face and turned ugly.

'So what's your story, Nie-Man?' Maggie asked. 'What turned you into such a miserable excuse for a human life, huh? Did Aunt Penny like to take you into the closet when you were a boy and play with your little wee-wee? Did you grow up on a farm and spend too much time fucking the pigs and goats?'

Nieman's eyes never left Kasey's face. 'Kill her, Kasey,' he said calmly. 'Kill her right now, and *you are free.*'

'The whole school thing, what's that about?' Maggie persisted, buzzing around his brain like a mosquito. 'Was it a teacher? Did one of your teachers introduce your ass to the end of a broom handle? Or was it the other kids? Did they make the girls watch? Did they laugh at you? Poor, pitiful little Nie-Man.'

'Kill her, Kasey,' he growled. 'Do it right now, or I'll torture both of you in ways you can't even imagine. *Do you hear me? Do you think I won't do it?*'

Kasey recoiled as he shouted at her, but she understood. Maggie was trying to give her a split second to get to him. One moment of distraction. One chance to attack. And it was working.

'So what's the deal? Are you just an impotent piece of shit,

Nie-Man? Can't get your tiny noodle off your balls? You blame women because all you've got is a floppy inch of licorice between your legs? Maybe next time you should pick a name like Harry No-Dick, huh? That's a good name for you.'

Kasey could see it in his eyes. So could Maggie. She had scored a direct hit. Nieman blinked faster, and his blood rage bubbled toward a boil.

'Drop your pants, No-Dick. Go on, do it. Give us a last laugh.'

'*Shut the fuck up! Shut up! Shut up!*'

Nieman stormed toward Maggie with his right hand clenched into a fist and his arm cocked for a back-handed blow across her face. The barrel of the gun followed his body. His head turned. *One split second.*

Kasey leaped. He wrenched back and fired as he saw her coming, but he wasn't fast enough. The gun went off with a flash and roar, burning past her ear, and before he could fire again, she hurtled the joist down on to his wrist. The heft of the metal snapped the joint with a loud crack. He howled in agony, and the gun tumbled to the floor.

Kasey reared back to swing again, aiming at his head this time, but he grabbed her shoulders and toppled them both off their feet. They landed hard amid the glass and debris. The flashlight spun away but stayed lit, casting a tunnel of light across their bodies. Before she could twist free, she felt him on top of her, leaning into her throat with his thick forearm. He loomed above her, his eyes black and intense. Seeing his eyes, she took her index finger and jabbed a sharp nail directly into the moist center of his pupil. He screamed, loosening his grip and covering his face with his hand. She hammered a fist into the center of his throat, and then again, slamming the side of his head and rolling him off her.

In the triangle of light, she saw the gun among the rubble on the floor and threw herself toward it. He kicked as he felt her move, and his boot connected with her skull, dizzying her and spinning her on to her back. He jumped and landed on her chest and drove the side of her head into the floor, where the broken glass sliced her cheek and lips. Before he could grab her skull again, she clutched his other hand and twisted his broken wrist. He let go with a screech of pain, and she wriggled backwards.

Her hands scrabbled on the floor for the gun but couldn't find it. He crawled toward her, and she skittered away from him, bumping against something cold and wet. She wrapped her hand around it, and her fingers sank into dead, decaying flesh. She was among the bodies, drowning in the smell. She kept backing up, using the row of corpses to block him from her, but he came forward, climbing from his knees, towering above her. His right eye was squeezed shut. His left hand dangled at an odd angle. But he was standing, and she was on her back.

Kasey reached the wall and couldn't go any further. He threw aside the chairs, grotesquely tumbling two bodies to the ground and scattering rats. Their eyes met. He smiled and came for her. As he landed, his body crushed her with his weight, forcing the air from her chest in a rush. His good hand locked around her throat like the jaws of a dog and choked off her windpipe. Kasey clawed at his fingers and pummeled his head and body with her fists, but he hung on.

Blood pounded in her ears. Her open mouth sucked for air and found none. She pawed the ground, hunting for a weapon. When she found a shard of glass, she scored his skin in streaks, but the blood and pain didn't dislodge him. His hand was a clamp, crushing the cartilage of her neck.

'You lose, Kasey,' he hissed.

Maggie screamed at her. 'On your left! Kasey, on your left!'

Her left arm swept the floor in a twitching, up-and-down motion. Blood vessels popped like firecrackers on her face.

'Higher!'

Kasey reached backward until her shoulder almost separated. That was when she felt it. Her fingers closed over a jagged block of heavy concrete. She clutched the stone like a baseball and hefted it off the floor. Her arms swayed with the weight, and she nearly lost her grip.

'Yes! Do it! Hit him!'

She took an unwieldy swing and missed. Her fingers grew numb. The brick tottered in her hand. Drunkenly, she swung again, down into the back of his head, and this time she heard the block land with a fierce, satisfying crack as it broke bone.

His hand loosened from her throat. She felt him crumple and become dead weight, unconscious as he lay on her body. Lines of blood trickled through his hair and on to her face. With a heavy thrust, she flipped his body over and staggered to her feet. The world spun. She coughed, gasping for air.

'Kasey!' Maggie shouted. 'Are you OK?'

Kasey stumbled toward the flashlight. She bent down and picked it up, and the beam of light danced crazily in her hand as she steadied herself. She scanned the floor and located Maggie's gun, and she retrieved it and held it tightly in her other hand. She took a tentative step toward the wall and cast the light down on his body.

'Is he dead?' Maggie asked.

Kasey watched Nieman in the light. A dark pool grew under his skull, but she could see his chest rise and fall. She hadn't hit him hard enough to kill him. The nightmare wasn't over yet. He groaned, and his limbs moved. Blood bubbled from his mouth. His eyes fluttered as he began to wake up.

'Quick, help me get free,' Maggie urged her.

Kasey stood frozen. She couldn't move. She stared at him as he slowly regained consciousness. Her own blood ran in streams down her neck. Beside him, sprawled on the floor, she saw the blue skin of one of the women he had killed, and something wriggled in the wound on her neck. Maggots.

'*Kasey*,' Maggie said, her voice a warning.

His eyes opened. That was what she was waiting for. They opened just enough for him to see her standing over him. For him to realize she was there and for her face to penetrate his mind.

He saw the gun in her hand. He knew what she was going to do. And why.

'You're a killer, Kasey,' he breathed, his lips folding into a broken smile. 'Just like me.'

She nodded. 'You're right.'

Kasey lifted the gun and fired a single shot into his brain.

Fifty-two

Serena left tracks in the snow with her boots as she marched up the driveway. The farmhouse was ablaze with light, and through the windows, she saw the shadow of someone moving on the second floor. As she got closer, she found the front door wide open. A moving truck was parked outside, its engine running. Behind the truck, hooked for towing, she saw an old Ford Escort.

It was the car she had seen at Regan Conrad's house, the car that had vanished while she was inside.

Everything made sense, but she wished it didn't.

Serena was conscious of her gun hidden in her shoulder holster under her jacket, but she left it where it was. At the threshold, she hesitated. The house was mostly stripped, but she saw an old television in the family room, tuned to the local network. She heard the breathless voice of Blair Rowe and saw the crawl for breaking news scroll across the bottom of the screen.

POLICE RECOVER CHILD'S BODY NEAR CEMETERY.

The news explained the frantic rush to escape. They knew about the search. They knew what the police were going to find in the woods. After that, it wouldn't be long before someone wound up at their doorstep.

Serena walked silently into the house. The main floor was

empty, but upstairs she heard heavy, panicked footsteps in the hallway. As she watched, a burly, bearded man thundered down the stairs and froze in horrified surprise when he saw Serena.

Her heart lurched. The man carried a baby wrapped in a blanket in his arms. She couldn't see the baby's face, which was covered by a hood, but she knew who it was. She had suspected all along what she would find inside the house, even though she hadn't allowed herself to believe it could end this way. The baby's hand reached up out of the folds of the blanket and tugged at the man's beard. The hood slipped off her head, and Serena saw her blonde curls. Her beautiful face with its wide eyes and toothy grin. Valerie's child.

It was Callie Glenn. Alive. Safe.

Serena put up her hands to steady him. 'Stay right there, OK? Let's be calm about this. No one wants anyone getting hurt.'

He didn't move. He didn't say anything.

'Where's Kasey?' Serena asked Bruce Kennedy.

Bruce wilted on to the steps. His head burrowed into his thick neck. 'She's out.'

'Did you two really think you could get away with this?'

Bruce put out a thick finger, and Callie grabbed it and put it in her mouth. His eyes welled with tears. 'I don't know what I was thinking. You have to believe me, I never thought any of it would go this far. But when I saw the news, I knew you'd be coming for us. I knew you'd want to take her back.'

Serena gestured toward the sofa. 'Why don't you come downstairs, Bruce? Tell me about it. Tell me why you and Kasey did this.'

Bruce held Callie like a treasure as he came downstairs. She was a tiny bundle in his huge arms. His eyes shot to the open door behind Serena, and she shook her head.

'Please don't try that,' she told him. 'There are police outside. All you would do by running is put her in danger.'

'I'd never do that.'

He sat on a corner of the sofa, and Serena sat opposite him. She couldn't take her eyes off Callie. The little girl was even more beautiful than she had dreamed. All she had seen until now was a photograph, and for days she had steeled herself to the eventual reality of finding her dead. Or never finding her at all. And here she was, perfect and gorgeous. She wanted to take her in her arms and never let go. She was so happy that she thought her heart would break, and she realized that she was crying herself. The reality of seeing Callie hit her harder than she could ever have imagined.

'Isn't she wonderful?' Bruce said.

Serena nodded mutely. She couldn't speak.

'You can't take her away from us,' he said.

'Tell me what happened,' Serena told him, her voice cracking. 'For God's sake, why would you two do something like this?'

Bruce sank back into the sofa with Callie on his chest. 'Our own little boy never had a chance.'

'Your son? He was the baby we found in the woods?'

'Yes.'

'What was wrong?'

'Jack's lungs didn't develop properly.' Bruce shook his head. 'That poor little boy, he would turn blue fighting for breath. As he grew, he struggled more and more.'

'Did you take him to the doctor?' Serena asked.

'Of course we did. They ran tests and scans and put him through hell and all they could say was the defects were too severe. Surgery would have killed him, and he was going to die without it. It was just a matter of time. We didn't want him to die in a hospital. We wanted him home with us. At least we could make him comfortable as long as we could.'

'I'm sorry.'

'Kasey was so depressed. She never slept. She would have killed herself to make that baby healthy, and she thought it was her fault that we were losing him.'

'You're talking about severe congenital defects. It's nobody's fault.'

'I know, but Kasey thought God had abandoned us. She was desperate.'

Serena watched the frantic longing in Bruce's face. She could imagine their minds fraying after months of their child slowly getting worse. 'What about Callie?' she asked.

Bruce stared at the girl in his arms. 'Regan put the idea in Kasey's head. She was our nurse at the hospital. She helped us all year. She came by our house every day. I don't think Kasey would have survived without her.'

'What did she tell you?'

'Jack was dying,' he said with a sigh. 'There was nothing we could do. Regan told us how unfair it was and how we'd been cheated. She said we deserved to have a baby. She told us about Marcus Glenn and how he didn't love Callie because she wasn't his, and how he and his wife were both cheating on each other, and how awful it would be for a baby to grow up in that household. She said it was like God had made a mistake that night and switched the babies. That's what it was – a mistake. They had a wonderful, healthy little girl, and we were forced to live through the agony of watching our sweet little boy fighting and fighting and not making it. Don't you see? It wasn't supposed to be that way.'

Serena grew angry, imagining Regan preying on their vulnerable souls, using them as pawns in her own game of revenge against Marcus and Valerie Glenn. 'What happened?' she asked.

'Jack finally passed away last week,' Bruce said. 'We lost him.'

'What did you do?'

'I thought, if it really was God's mistake, I could put it right, you know? So I had the idea that I should bury him with the Glenn family. I wanted him to be protected. Taken care of. I took him with me that night and I buried him near the cemetery. He was finally at peace. He was where he was meant to be all along.'

Serena closed her eyes. 'What about Kasey?'

'Kasey went to get Callie,' Bruce said. 'Regan told us it was the only way. She offered to help us – she had a key to the doctor's house. She said we had to go rescue her.'

Serena stared at Callie in Bruce's arms. The little girl knew none of the heartache around her. None of the sorrow and desperation that had become focused on her.

'Bruce, may I hold her?'

She waited, holding her breath, to see what he would do. To see if he could give her up and let her out of his hands. Somewhere in his mind, he had to know that he would never get her back. She would never be in his arms again. She was someone else's child. Their child was in the ground.

Bruce sobbed. He laid a soft hand on the girl's curls. 'I can't lose another baby,' he murmured.

'I understand. Just let me hold her for a while.'

Give her to me. Let her go back home to her real parents. Grieve for your son.

Bruce held up Callie in his outstretched arms. She giggled as he held her. His mouth contorted in an awful, wounded frown, even as he tried to smile for the girl's benefit. Serena got up and reached out her hands. Her fingers touched the child's blanket, and her hands took hold of her soft sides. For an instant, Bruce didn't let go. He clung to Callie, as if the moment of parting were too painful to bear. Then, with gentle pressure, Serena took the girl into her own arms and folded her up against her chest.

Bruce watched the two of them sit down and then buried his face in his hands. He was grieving for both babies now. One dead, one alive, but both of them out of his life. Serena knew he loved Callie, even if she wasn't his own.

'Tell me what happened that night, Bruce. What did Kasey do?'

'She drove to Grand Rapids. She went inside the doctor's house. She got Callie.'

'And then?'

'And then she got lost in the fog.'

Fifty-three

'*Are you crazy?*' Maggie screamed. 'Kasey, what did you do?'

The gun smoked in Kasey's hand. The burnt powder briefly rose above the stench of the dead. She watched him lying there with the gray tissue of his brain blown against the wall behind him. Bloody, dazed, she found a concrete pillar and slid down to the floor, laying the gun beside her. She turned the flashlight toward Maggie's face.

'He knew,' she told Maggie.

'What are you talking about?'

'He knew about Callie.'

Maggie stared at her, and her mouth fell open. The confusion in her eyes became something else. Recognition. Horror. Anger. Kasey felt Maggie judging her, and she hated it, because she liked Maggie. She had never wanted it to end this way. All she had wanted to do was drive away to the desert with her husband and her daughter.

'Why?' Maggie asked.

Kasey shrugged. 'God took away my son for no good reason. He just let him die. I didn't deserve to lose my baby like that. There was no reason I got a sick baby, and Valerie Glenn got a beautiful, healthy baby. I decided that I wasn't going to live with it.'

It was a relief to say it out loud. To tell someone the truth. She had accepted what she was doing, accepted who she was. She had made up her mind that she would do whatever it took to erase the previous year and all the hell and suffering she had gone through. She had faced the truth about herself that night in the fog, and once you choose to cross the line, you can't go back.

Maggie understood. She was smart. 'Susan Krauss,' she said quietly. 'What really happened?'

'Callie was in the back seat of my car that night,' Kasey explained. 'I was almost home. Can you believe it? I was a mile from home when I got lost. And suddenly there I was in the woods, and Susan Krauss was bleeding outside my car. She *saw* Callie. It's not like I could let her go. I had to go after her. And after him, too.'

'Nieman didn't kill her.'

Kasey shook her head. 'No, she was still alive when he ran for the highway. He dropped the garrote. She was barely breathing. I went over to her, and I thought, I can save her. That's what I should do. But then she would see the pictures of Callie on TV, and she'd know what I'd done. After all that sacrifice, I couldn't let that happen. I figured that this woman was almost dead anyway, and he'd be blamed for it. So I took the garrote, and I finished the job.'

Maggie struggled against the bonds that held her to the wooden chair. 'My God, Kasey.'

'I know. I've disappointed you. I'm sorry.'

'Nieman knew you'd killed that woman, not him. That's why he was hunting you.'

'Yeah. He knew I was a bad girl. What can I say?'

The light on the flashlight dimmed. Kasey jiggled it, and the brightness came back. Her head snapped round as she heard a noise beyond the crumbling walls of the classroom. She waited, but nothing moved.

Except the ghosts. There were plenty of ghosts here to haunt her.

Kasey stared at the bodies near the wall and their lifeless eyes. Every night, Susan Krauss had visited her in her dreams with those same dead eyes. She had stood over her in the field behind the dairy, and her eyes had pleaded for help. For rescue. She had looked at her as if Kasey had brought her salvation. And then the look had turned to panic and disbelief as Kasey tightened the wire around her neck.

Once you cross the line, you can't go back.

'What about Regan Conrad?' Maggie asked.

Kasey's face flushed with anger. 'Regan and I planned the whole thing, but she couldn't keep her mouth shut. I realized she had lied to me all along. This wasn't about me and my baby. It was about her hating the Glenns. She started taunting Valerie, and I knew she would ruin everything. Serena told us that night at dinner that she was getting a search warrant. If she did, she'd find records about me and Regan and our son. So I had to take care of Regan first. I pulled my file so no one would find it. I assumed Nieman would get the blame for that murder, too, but I never thought he'd be watching me. He must have seen me go in, and then he stole the body. To drive me crazy.'

Maggie stared at her as if she were seeing her for the first time. 'Kasey, what happened to you?'

Kasey eyed her with regret. Her heart hardened, the way it had time after time in the past year. 'Just imagine watching your little boy slowly waste away. Day after day, night after night, and all he does is get worse, and there's nothing you can do. You just have to watch him die. And you're alone. No God. No mercy. All you can do is blame yourself and tell yourself what a worthless excuse for a mother you are. You try living through eleven months of hell . . .' she began to shout, '*and then you tell me why Valerie Glenn should have Callie, and I should have fucking nothing nothing nothing.*'

She slammed her fist repeatedly on the concrete. The rats scampered in fear. She breathed hard in the aftermath, and the room was silent except for the sound of her breath and the ceaseless dripping of water overhead.

Then, in another room, she thought she heard a noise again. Her eyes narrowed. Her imagination ran wild.

'I'm sorry,' Maggie murmured.

Kasey shrugged. She was anxious to get away from this place. 'Don't patronize me.'

'What happens now?'

'You know what I have to do. I wish there was another way. I've gone too far to go back now.'

'You can't expect to escape. They'll figure it out. They'll find out about Callie and about everything else.'

'It's too late now,' Kasey told her. 'Believe me, I never wanted you in the middle of this. It was between me and him. But now I have no choice.'

'Kasey, you're not like him. If you kill me, you're no better than he was.'

'You're right. I'm not.'

Kasey picked up the gun, which was still warm. Tiredly, she pushed herself to her feet against the concrete pillar. She jiggled the flashlight again and watched the beam flicker. She went over to Nieman's body and dug a hand in his pocket and found his keys. Her escape route. When she turned back to Maggie, her hand trembled. She knew what she had to do, but she didn't want to do it. She was in a corner with nowhere to go. In the last week, she had killed three times. This was just one more murder. The last. And then she was finally free.

Six feet away, Maggie struggled, squirming to get free. 'Don't do this,' she told her. 'Kasey, I know you, this is not who you are. Don't do this.'

Kasey realized that no one knew who she really was. Not Bruce. Not Regan. Not Maggie. The man on the floor, the man who had chased her, the man she had killed, had boasted that he understood her. He had claimed to be able to see into her head. Claimed that they were kindred spirits. The terrible irony was that he was right. In the end, he had known her better than anyone.

'I'm sorry,' she said.

She raised the gun and pointed it at Maggie's head. She took a step closer.

Then she froze. The noise was real and unmistakable this time, not the product of her wild fear. She heard the echo of footsteps on glass, getting closer. Someone else was in the building.

'*Stop*,' said a voice from the darkness across the ruined space.

Fifty-four

Serena's Mustang was a cocoon of perfect silence. Just her and Callie. In the mirror, she could see the little girl sleeping in the car seat she had taken from Bruce Kennedy's Escort. She slept the way an angel sleeps, in peace and innocence, unaware of anything that had happened to her. That was the bliss of being so young. She would never remember Kasey lifting her out of her crib or getting lost in the fog, never remember being left alone in the back of the car as Kasey chased Susan Krauss through the woods. She would never remember the days spent in a strange house. In her sleep, she had probably already forgotten and was dreaming of being back home in Valerie's arms.

That was the sad part of being so young. She wouldn't remember her mother's tears of joy at their reunion. The cry of relief and exultation. The never-ending embrace. She would never know that she had once been gone, and now she was back.

Serena drove slowly. She told herself that the roads were lonely and dark in the middle of the night, and she didn't want to take any risk in the snow. It was too easy to hit a deer. Too easy to skid off the road. The reality was that she didn't want the drive to end. For one hour, Callie was totally within her care, almost as if she were her own, and she realized that Valerie had been right all along. Without kids, Serena couldn't understand the desperation of loss or the depth of responsibility. Now, for a brief moment, she did understand. She would have thrown herself in front of a bullet for Callie.

She wished she could hold this moment in a kind of suspended animation, until she passed the responsibility for the little girl back to Valerie. Tomorrow would be different, when the press surrounded the house, and photographers shot pictures for magazine covers, and champagne flowed in the war room in Grand Rapids. Tomorrow would be filled with noise and elation.

Tomorrow would be her first day to confront the new world. Her own new world. Alone.

Tonight was for her and Callie.

'You can read all about it when you're older,' she told Callie, who slept calmly and didn't hear a word.

She wondered at what age a girl would want to learn more about being kidnapped as a child. Fifteen? Eighteen? Maybe never. Maybe Valerie would try to keep it a secret, but Serena knew there were no secrets about that kind of experience. It would seep into Callie's consciousness as she grew older, something people talked about but that she didn't understand, something that made her different. Someday she'd want to know more.

It wouldn't be easy. It wouldn't be happy. The ending was happy, but everything else about the time in between would have been better kept as secrets. When do you choose to read that the father you lived with was the principal suspect in your disappearance, a man that everyone in the world assumed had murdered you and buried your body? When do you want to read about him wishing you had never been born?

When does your mother tell you that this man was not your father at all? When do you begin to think you're alive not because of love, but because your mother was so lonely she turned to comfort with another man? When do you realize that no one is innocent and understand what betrayal is all about?

Not now. Not for a long time.

'I hope you never blame yourself,' Serena told Callie in the back seat. 'I know it's easy to do. The mind is a funny thing. Something happens and you have no control over it all, and somehow you still think it's your fault.' She smiled as she looked in the mirror and added, 'If you ever feel that way, call me, OK? I'll come back and talk to you. I'll tell you how you rescued your mother long before she ever rescued you.'

She passed the turn-off that led through the dirt roads to the Sago Cemetery, and she shivered. That was how fate worked. Two children were born on the same night; one lived, one died. It wasn't fair.

'You're almost home, Callie,' she said.

The last miles melted away, disappearing with the hypnotic throb of the engine. The forest thinned, and she drove closer to civilization again. Buildings appeared. Dark houses hugged the highway. It was two in the morning as she wound through the downtown streets, which were as vacant and artificial as a movie set. The silence followed her across the last bridge over the water.

Then, behind her, the noisy whine of a police siren shattered the peace. Red lights swirled and grew large in her mirror, and a Sheriff's vehicle sped past her. The car turned where she was about to turn, on the road that led to Valerie's house.

Serena didn't need to be told. She realized with despair where it was going.

'Oh, no,' she said.

Stride watched Kasey's flashlight swivel in his direction and capture him where he stood amid the rubble and hanging wires of a jagged gap in the wall. He held his gun with both hands. Kasey's head turned, and she saw him, but she didn't lower her gun. She aimed it at Maggie at point-blank range.

'It's over,' he warned her.

Her face was covered with blood and dirt. Her ripped shirt hung open, exposing the swell of her breasts. Her red hair was matted down. The gun quivered in her outstretched arms. He held her stare and didn't like what he saw in her eyes. Behind the exhaustion and panic, she was obsessed. Desperate to escape.

'Put the gun down right now,' he said.

Kasey's lower lip trembled. Her chest heaved as she hyper-ventilated. The cage she had built began to close in around her.

'Kasey, I'm not alone. Do you understand me? Cops are coming. There is no way out. Are you listening? No way out. Just put the gun down, so no one else gets hurt.'

His eyes flicked to Maggie. She was pale, and her neck was bleeding. She showed no fear with the barrel of a gun inches from her face. Instead, when she saw him watching her, she mouthed two words back to him.

I'm OK.

But she wasn't. Kasey's finger was still curled round the trigger.

'We know about Callie,' Stride said. 'Listen to me, Kasey, it's over. The police are at your house right now. Callie's going home to her parents. Nothing you do here is going to change that.'

'You're taking Callie?' Kasey murmured. Her voice sounded like a lost little girl.

'I'm sorry.'

'You *can't* take her away from me.'

'The secret is out, Kasey. Everyone knows the truth. It's time to get help.'

Hopelessness and horror washed across Kasey's face. 'My God, it was all for nothing.'

He watched the gun. He watched her finger. Neither moved. 'I need you to put the gun down *now*.'

'Nothing,' she repeated. 'It was all for nothing.'

'Kasey, do what he says,' Maggie instructed her sternly. 'Put the gun down.'

Kasey's wide eyes turned toward Maggie again. 'I'm sorry. I can't. I need to get out of here.'

Maggie's voice softened. 'Listen to me, Kasey. I understand. I've had miscarriages, and I blamed myself. I went crazy. I did things I'll always regret. I know how it must have been for you. You loved your boy, and there was nothing you could do for him. That's the worst pain a woman can endure. It's worse than dying yourself. But this isn't the answer. You know that.'

Kasey's elbow sagged downward. The barrel of the gun tilted toward the blasted foam tiles in the ceiling. Her whole body caved in on itself. Stride took a step closer, with both hands still tightly wrapped around the butt of his gun.

'That's good, Kasey, now bend down and lay it on the floor, and put your hands on the top of your head.'

Kasey stared at him with those same wounded eyes, putting him off guard. She knelt to the floor. He began to relax, but then he realized that her hand was still locked fiercely around the gun. Her grip hadn't changed. She hadn't taken her finger off the trigger. He looked into her eyes and realized that her submissiveness was a ruse.

She wasn't giving up.

Maggie saw it too. '*Stride,*' she warned him, her voice urgent, but he reacted too slowly.

Kasey's finger moved, not on her gun hand, but on her other hand. She switched off her flashlight, throwing the ruins into blackness again. Stride knew what was coming next. He threw himself sideways as fire flashed from Kasey's gun. Something hot burned through the skin of his neck, and he felt warm blood running on his skin and soaking into his shirt. He hit the ground and spun, rolling through sharp glass and a mountain of fallen stone.

More bullets exploded, pounding the floor and walls around him, ricocheting madly. Dust and flakes of concrete fell in a cloud over his face. He kept rolling until his body collided with a concrete pillar, and then he slid behind it and pushed himself up into a crouch. He peered around the beam, but he couldn't see or hear anything in a room filled with blackness and silence. The air around him was choked with smoke.

Twenty feet away, Kasey's flashlight flicked on again, but before he could aim and fire, the light switched off. He heard her footsteps in the aftermath, running, getting further away. The light went on and off again in a split second in a room beyond the far wall, as she used it to guide her.

'Mags,' Stride hissed.

'Over here.'

He followed the sound of her voice, leading the way with his hands. He kicked through a jumble of metal spikes and ducked as the noise clanged through the open space, but no one fired at him. He could still hear Kasey stumbling through another room, looking for a way out.

'Stride,' Maggie whispered. He felt along the chair to find where she was tied.

'Are you OK?' he asked.

'I'm alive.'

He clawed at the tape with his fingers but couldn't unwrap it. He felt on the floor and found a sharp piece of glass and used it to tear a cut in the tape that he peeled open, ripping it quickly off her skin. Maggie gave a strangled cry. He used the glass to free her other hand and then her feet.

'Don't stand up too fast,' he whispered, but she didn't listen. She bolted off the chair, then wobbled and fell backward.

She toppled against him, and he caught her in his arms. The chair overturned. Her hands wrapped around his neck and got lost in the blood flowing from the open wound.

'Fuck, you're hurt,' she said.

'It seared me. It burns like hell, but I'm OK.'

A cone of light stabbed through the corridor opposite them, throwing shadows past the concrete towers. For the first time, Stride caught a glimpse of the bodies hidden in the school, and he swore. Maggie gestured at the nearest body on the floor – a large man with a bullet hole in the center of his forehead.

'That's our guy. The farmland killer. Kasey shot him.'

Stride nodded. In a distant corner of the school, at the source of the light, they heard Kasey hammering against the plywood boards nailed over the windows. Explosions rattled between the walls as she fired twice more. Wood splintered and broke. They saw smoke in the beam of light. After a pause, they heard the impact as Kasey threw her entire body against the wooden barrier.

The plywood tore away with a scream. They felt the air pressure change as a gap opened in the school wall. The light vanished.

'She's out,' Maggie said.

Stride put an arm around her waist to steady her. 'We have to get out of here,' he said. 'The first thing she'll do is go after Callie.'

Fifty-five

'Valerie's disappeared,' Denise told Serena.

'Disappeared? What happened?'

Serena didn't get an answer. Denise looked over her shoulder to where Callie slept in the back seat. The mask of the tough cop on Denise's face melted away. Serena heard Denise catch her breath and watched her cover her face with cupped hands as if she was praying. Denise opened the back door and gently undid the straps of the car seat. She lifted Callie like fragile china into her arms. The little girl didn't wake up.

'Oh, my God,' Denise murmured. 'Oh, baby, I never thought I'd see you again.'

She wrapped her niece in a bear hug and buried her face in the girl's mop of curly hair. For a moment, nothing else mattered. There was no infidelity. No anger. No complicated life. There was only jubilation.

'I didn't have any hope,' she said. 'We always tell the families not to give up, but I didn't believe it. I thought she was gone. God forgive me, I should have had faith.'

Serena got out of the car. 'Denise, what about Valerie?'

'She left a note,' Denise said. The relief on her face disappeared, and her eyes turned grim with worry. 'Marcus found it and called the police.'

'A note?'

Denise nodded. 'It's pretty clear what she was going to do.'

'Oh, damn it, no, not now!' Serena exclaimed. 'When was this?'

'The cop on the street saw her leave about two hours ago.'

'He didn't report it?'

'We were watching Marcus, not Valerie. We haven't been following her. When Marcus called, I scrambled units all over town to look for her car. Nobody's spotted her yet.' She added, 'Come on, let's get Callie out of the cold.'

Denise carried the girl up the driveway. A police officer at the front door let them inside. They followed the hallway to the kitchen at the rear of the house, where they found Marcus sitting at the island with a mug of coffee. He wore a chocolate-brown silk bathrobe and slippers and had half-glasses pushed down his nose. He was reading an online medical journal on a laptop in front of him.

Marcus saw Callie in Denise's arms. He'd known for an hour that she was coming home, but it was one thing to know it and another to see her alive. Serena watched him and tried to decipher the changing emotions on his face. He stripped off his glasses. His mouth tightened, and he blinked faster. A smile flickered on his lips, like a flame that couldn't quite catch.

Denise made no effort to hand Callie to Marcus or to hide her hostility. She stared at her brother-in-law, her eyes fierce.

'May I hold her?' he asked finally.

Denise clung to Callie and didn't move. 'She's not yours, is she?'

'Do you think that matters right now? Do you think I care about that?'

'I think the only person you care about is yourself.'

'You're wrong. You've always been wrong about me.'

Serena murmured under her breath, 'Come on, Denise.'

With her jaw clenched, Denise took a step closer and eased

the girl away from her shoulder. Marcus put his coffee down and climbed out of his chair. He reached out his arms, and Denise passed Callie to him with obvious reluctance. The girl stirred and made a noise but didn't wake up.

Marcus held Callie against his chest. She looked small in his big hands. He sat down again.

'Well?' he said to Denise.

'Well what?'

'Don't you have something to say to me?'

'You don't want to hear what I have to say, Marcus.'

'I was expecting an apology,' he told her.

'Excuse me?'

'An apology,' he repeated, his voice hushed, but his tone harsh and bitter. 'For the last week, I've seen my name trampled through the mud and rumors flung around town about me. People calling me a murderer. Friends not returning my calls. Patients dropping my services. My marriage in ruins, my private life put on display for the world. I know where it all started, Denise. It started with you. Well, guess what, the truth is exactly what I said it was all along. I had nothing to do with any of this. And I think the least you can do is have the decency to tell me you're sorry.'

'Sorry?' Denise put her hands on her hips. 'Sorry? *You* caused this, Marcus. You let it happen. You and your little psycho bedmate, Regan Conrad. Yeah, I'm sorry. Sorry Valerie ever laid eyes on you. Sorry you're such an arrogant bastard. Maybe instead of feeling pity for yourself you could thank God for the people who brought this little girl back home safely. And maybe you could shed a tear and pretend to show an ounce of concern as we try to find your wife.'

She stalked from the room with heavy footsteps. The noise made Callie stir, and her eyes blinked open before shutting again. Marcus scowled as his eyes followed Denise, but then he scrubbed the anger from his face and nodded at Serena.

'I am grateful for everything you did,' he told her. 'Don't misunderstand. I'm just furious at how I've been treated.'

'I do know how you feel,' Serena replied. 'Innocent people often wind up destroyed by these crimes. I won't pretend it's fair.' She added, 'Do you have Valerie's note? May I see it?'

He gestured at a three-by-five card on the kitchen counter. 'It was taped to the mirror in our bathroom. I saw it when I got up overnight.'

Serena read the note, which said: *Now we're both free.* She tried to reconstruct Valerie's fragile state of mind, and the implications scared her.

'Did anything happen between the two of you this evening?' she asked.

'A fight.'

'About Callie?'

'Yes.'

'Do you think she would harm herself?'

'I don't know,' Marcus said. 'She was poisoned by all the rumors against me. She was in despair of ever seeing Callie again. I think she was capable of anything.'

'If she turns on her phone, or turns on the radio, she'll know Callie is safe.'

'Yes, if it's not too late,' he said. He glanced down at the sleeping child and added, 'I should put Callie to bed now.'

'Did Denise tell you about the woman who took her?' Serena asked. 'Kasey Kennedy?'

'I hear she's still at large.'

'That's right, and we don't know what she's going to do. With your permission, we'll keep police officers around the house. I'd also like to have a policewoman stay inside in the nursery with Callie.'

'Fine, but you don't really think this woman is foolish enough to try this again, do you?'

'She's desperate and unstable. Until we find her, I think we need to take every precaution. It might be better for you to take Callie somewhere else for a few days, with police protection. Your house is an obvious target.'

He shook his head. 'I won't be driven out of my home.'

'I understand.'

They both looked up as Denise Sheridan reappeared in the doorway of the kitchen. Her face was stricken, and her voice caught in her throat.

'Someone spotted Valerie's car by the river near the radio station,' she said. 'It's empty.'

Valerie sat on the wet ground with her arms wrapped around her knees. In front of her, the dark water of the Mississippi was crusted with ice. It was the kind of brittle sheen that would crack like glass and open up a hole for her as she walked from the shore. She wondered if that was the easier way to do what she had to do. Walk on the ice. Let herself be swallowed up by the grip of the frigid water.

She was numb with cold. Tears had frozen into pearls on her face. She couldn't feel her fingers, and her feet tingled as if they had been stung by bees. She had been sitting here, alone with the chill and the water, for an hour, and still she couldn't bring herself to do it. She had taken the bottle of aspirin from her pocket a dozen times, and each time, she had put it back without opening it. She hoped if she simply sat here a little while longer, the cold would do its work for her, taking away her sensations until she felt nothing at all.

Nearby, she heard voices floating in the wind like the whispers of ghosts. People were above her, on the crest of the river bank at Canal Street. Shouting. Insistent. On the bridge of Highway 169 upriver, she saw the speeding lights of cars. She ignored them all.

She withdrew the bottle again. Her raw fingers felt clumsy as she handled it. She stared at the tablets and imagined washing them down her throat with melted snow. Last time, she had used a bottle that wasn't full. That had been her mistake. That was why she had awakened in the hospital. This time, the bottle brimmed with hundreds of pills. She could swallow them all before they dulled her system and lulled her to sleep.

She fingered the plastic wrapper around the neck of the bottle. With the edge of her nail, she tried to cut it away, but her hands felt thick. She put the cap in her mouth and scraped the wrapper with her teeth. A little piece of it tore. She tugged at the flap and finally pulled it free, unwinding it like a ribbon. That small success felt like a huge victory.

Valerie squinted to line up the arrows on the cap in the darkness. She tried to pry off the cap with her thumb, but her skin was damp, and her fingers slipped on the ridged plastic. Finally, attacking it with both thumbs, she popped the cap off the bottle, and it flipped like a coin into the air. She punched through the foil seal, and the bottle squirmed in her numb fingers. A dozen tablets spilled on to the ground around her legs. She didn't care about losing them. They weren't enough to make a difference.

She put out her left palm. Her arm trembled. The bottle shook as she overturned it, tumbling a pyramid of white pills into her hand. She balanced the open bottle in her lap and stared at the tablets. It wasn't hard. Put them in your mouth. Grab a handful of fresh snow. Do it over and over until the bottle was empty.

But she couldn't. She wanted to, and she couldn't.

'Oh, Callie, I'm sorry,' she said.

She was angry with herself for hesitating. Her baby needed her. Her daughter was alone. All it would take to rescue her was one small, meaningless step; all she needed was to do the right thing, and they would be together. Even so, she couldn't bring herself to die like this. Giving up felt like a selfish and faithless act for which she would never be forgiven. It was as if she could hear a lonely voice talking to her grave and shaming her: *How could you give up on me?*

Valerie listened to the voice and spread her fingers wide. The aspirins fell and bounced and made dimples in the snow. The wetness began to dissolve them into paste. She got up, limping as the blood made its way back into her legs. She wandered until she was nearly in the water. Ice crept from the shore like a foggy window. She put one foot down in the water, cracking the ice with the heel of her boot, and then again, making jagged holes in the surface. She turned the bottle upside down and let the tablets cascade through the ice and disappear into the river. Finally, when it was empty, she flicked the bottle end over end beyond the ice. It floated for a while, and then, as water leached through the neck, it turned over and sank.

She knew she should feel like a failure, but she felt a rush of adrenaline instead. A new sensation washed over her, coming from nowhere, making her feel restless. Somewhere, somehow, something had changed, like a shifting in the earth under her feet. She felt drawn away from here. When she touched her face, she found warm tears streaming down her cold face again. Pouring. A waterfall. A deluge. It didn't matter why. She only knew she had to go. Go now. Go fast.

Valerie walked, and then she stumbled, and then she ran. She clawed her way up the slope away from the river. Her breath hammered in her chest. She couldn't go fast enough to satisfy the impatient urge that had taken hold of her brain. She heard them again, louder and closer as she neared the street: people calling for her, shouting her name.

She burst from the low brush near the parking lot where police had surrounded her car. Red and blue lights lit up the street like fireworks. She saw Denise. She saw Serena. Everyone looked everywhere in the empty town, except at her. She was invisible. She stayed where she was, catching her breath, unable to move or to shout, 'I'm here.'

Then Serena turned. Their eyes locked on each other, thirty yards apart. Valerie watched Serena's face erupt into a smile and heard her yelling excitedly, the same words over and over. The wind drowned her voice, but it didn't matter, because she already knew what Serena was saying. She knew the impulse that had drawn her away from the river and back to her life.

She knew who had saved her. She knew.

'We have her,' Serena repeated, running toward her. 'We have her, we have her, we have her.'

Valerie crumbled to her knees and wept for joy.

Fifty-six

Kasey still had the key.

The key that Regan had given her. The key that had let her inside the Glenn house. She had used it once, and she would use it again tonight, and then she and Callie would drive west and disappear. They would lose themselves in the small towns of the desert, where they would both be safe.

She still had the gun, too. Maggie's gun. It was shoved in the waist of her jeans, and she felt the hard metal when she breathed.

She had avoided Highway 2 and used the twisting back roads on the drive from Duluth. She had stopped only once at a roadside convenience store, where she'd broken into the dark shop and cleaned up and bandaged her wounds. The bleeding had quit for now, but she was exhausted and weak.

Her mind and body were both fraying. But she couldn't give up.

Nieman's car was parked in the trees on the shoulder of County Road 76, out of view from the highway. From there, she had plunged into the woods and hiked half a mile to her hiding place fifty yards from the Glenn house, on the shore of Pokegama Lake. She hunkered down near the water and studied the activity around the house.

Police officers patrolled the backyard, and she knew they were hunting for her. She didn't care. Her goal was the side door leading into the garage, where the yard was unlit. No one would see her breaking from the woods, and she only needed a few seconds to get inside. Then she could wait for the right moment to move deeper into the house.

With the snow silencing her footsteps, she zigzagged to the edge of the forest bordering the rear lawn of the mansion. Despite her care, she flushed a rabbit that shot noisily from the brush and made tracks across the open snow. She froze, sheltered behind the bushy arms of a spruce. A policewoman near the corner of the house spied the rabbit and scanned the forest where it had emerged. She studied the darkness, staring right at Kasey. Her hand rested on the butt of her gun.

The policewoman wandered closer and stopped twenty feet away. Kasey tensed. In her head, her breathing sounded loud. The cold made her shiver, and the branches swayed where her body touched them. Water dripped from her red hair. Behind the policewoman, she could see the dark recess of the doorway leading inside the garage. It was only a few steps away across a trail of flagstones.

The policewoman lost interest in the rabbit. She dug in her pocket and pulled out a handkerchief, then blew her nose loudly and unleashed a hacking cough. She took a last look at the woods before turning on her heel and disappearing around the front of the house.

Kasey waited to make sure the cop didn't return. The strip of ground between the woods and the garage was dark and empty. The lake wind had blown the snow into drifts by the side of the house, leaving most of the stonework clear. Taking a breath, she bolted from the trees and across the flagstones and ducked inside the doorway. When she looked back, she saw that she had left two footprints near the edge of the forest. They were barely visible, but if she looked closely, she could see them in the snow near where the policewoman had stood. Two boot marks four feet apart.

She couldn't worry about them now.

Kasey slid the key from her pocket. It was warm in her hand. With a cautious glance in both directions, she pushed the key into the deadbolt on the side door and turned. The key didn't budge. She jiggled it and tried again, twisting furiously, but the key didn't fit. She yanked it out and squeezed it in her fist and shut her eyes. In frustration, she threw her shoulder against the door, but it was locked and solid.

She cursed silently and spun round. She had to retreat to the woods, but she ran out of time before she could move. As she stood in the doorway, paralyzed, she heard the scrape of footsteps on rock. The policewoman was back.

Kasey squeezed her body hard against the door, but she couldn't hide. As soon as the cop glanced in her direction, she would see her, no more than six feet away. She watched the woman get closer, and she slid the gun out of her belt and nestled it in her sweaty hand. The policewoman's eyes were focused on the forest. If she looked closely at the snow, she would see the footprints emerging from the woods. And then she would turn around and spot Kasey in the doorway.

Kasey held her breath. Her mouth was open. Her eyes were scared and wide. The cop's body swung toward her, and Kasey coiled like a spring, ready to pounce. She had to be on top of her before she could shout.

Then, in the moment before their eyes met, the cop stopped and sprinted back toward the front of the house.

Kasey knew why. In the driveway around the corner from where she was, a woman was screaming.

'*Where is she?*'

Valerie didn't wait for the car to stop. The wheels rolled as she scrambled out of Serena's Mustang. She screamed Callie's name and ran for the door and pounded until a police officer let her inside. Serena got out of her car and held up both hands to calm a policewoman who appeared from the side of the house at a run, her hand on her gun. 'It's OK,' she told her. 'Everybody's fine. Don't worry, this is a good thing.'

She followed Valerie into the house. Upstairs, through the open door of Callie's bedroom, she heard wrenching sobs of relief. Serena made no move to join her. It was a private moment for mother and child. It was also one of those rare moments in her life when she believed that there really was some justice in the world.

Marcus Glenn, still dressed in his bathrobe, joined her in the foyer. He heard the noise of his wife upstairs and glanced at the bedroom door. 'So she didn't go through with it,' he said.

'You must be relieved.'

'Yes, of course.'

Serena didn't hear relief or joy in his voice. He frowned, as if he could read her mind. 'I'm trained to consider what might go wrong,' he told her. 'I didn't think this situation would end happily for any of us.'

'But it did,' Serena said. She wanted to add: *No thanks to you.*

She stared at the surgeon as he waited by the banister at the stairs and realized that the naked outpouring of emotion they could hear above them was painful for him. He preferred an environment that was as sterile as his operating room. Clinical. Passionless. That was what made him so easy to dislike. That was why he was capable of doing so much damage.

More quickly than Serena expected, Valerie reappeared in the hallway. Callie was in her arms, wrapped in a heavy coat, her small hands in mittens and pink boots on her feet. Valerie carried Callie with an easy grace, as if she were floating. She never took her eyes off her daughter's face, and the girl, who was wide awake now, stared back at her mother with delight.

Valerie took each step slowly and carefully until she was at the bottom of the stairs. She carried a duffel bag over one shoulder, which she laid at her feet. She handed Callie to Serena long enough to grab a winter coat from the hall closet and slip her arms into the sleeves.

'Where are you going?' Marcus asked. He looked genuinely surprised.

Valerie ignored him and looked at Serena. She took back Callie and picked up her bag. 'I know it's late, but can you drive us to a hotel?'

'It would be safer if you stayed with me,' Serena told her. 'We can keep police around the house. Will that be OK?'

'Yes, that's fine. Let's go.'

'Valerie,' Marcus interrupted them. He reached for Valerie's shoulder, but she shrugged away his touch. 'What do you think you're doing? Don't be rash about this.'

Valerie hugged Callie to her chest and marched through the open door leading out of the house. She didn't look back. She deposited her bag in the back seat of Serena's Mustang and fitted Callie into the car seat with tender hands. The police on the lawn watched her, and no one moved or spoke.

Marcus followed her as far as the porch and called after her. He folded his arms over his chest in anger and annoyance.

'Do you want me to say I'm sorry?' he said. 'All right then, I'm sorry. But remember, I was innocent in all this.'

Valerie stiffened. Her back was to him. She turned around slowly, and her eyes were like stone. 'Innocent?'

'You know what I mean.'

Valerie didn't say anything more. She waited in silence. Her breath came and went in clouds of steam that dissipated into the cold air.

'Oh, for God's sake, come inside,' Marcus told her. 'What do you want from me?'

Valerie shook her head. 'I don't want anything from you,' she replied. 'I'll have someone come by to get my things.'

'You're not in any shape to be making decisions,' Marcus insisted. 'Take a few days with Callie. It's been a difficult week for all of us, and you need some time. When you come back home, we'll talk.'

Serena joined Valerie outside and climbed into the driver's side of her car and started the engine. Valerie stood by the open passenger door.

'I'm not coming back,' Valerie said as she got into the car and reached for the door. 'Goodbye, Marcus.'

Fifty-seven

The two of them drove in silence as the town gave way to the empty lands and the bright lights gave way to darkness. The highway felt familiar to Serena now, as if she had gone back and forth so many times that the distance to the city had grown smaller. It was still hours from dawn.

'Are you OK?' she asked finally.

Valerie twisted round and stared at Callie, who had drifted back to sleep with the motion of the car. She reached out a hand to touch the girl and then pulled it back so she didn't disturb her. 'I'm perfect,' she replied.

'Did you mean what you said?' Serena asked.

'About not going back? Yes. I'm done. I'm free.'

'Good for you.'

Valerie reached out and put a hand over Serena's on the steering wheel. 'I owe you my whole life.'

'You don't owe me anything,' Serena said. 'I should thank you. Seeing the two of you together restores a little of my faith.'

Valerie smiled. 'I used to think about all the terrible mistakes I've made in my life. Now I realize, without them, Callie wouldn't be here. We wouldn't be together. That can't just be an accident, can it?'

'Maybe you're right.'

'At least I won't wish I could go back and change them. Not anymore.' She added, 'I appreciate your doing this for me. Will Stride mind my staying with you?'

'It's fine,' Serena said. 'We'll both feel better knowing you and Callie are safe.'

She didn't say anything more. Instead, she thought about Stride and wondered where she would sleep herself tonight. It wouldn't be in their bed. It wouldn't be beside the man she'd loved for the past three years. They had both made their share of mistakes, and now she wondered where their mistakes would lead them and whether, like Valerie, she would be able to live with her regrets.

'Tell me something,' Valerie said. 'The woman who took Callie, this young cop, did you know her?'

'I met her this week, but I didn't really know her.'

'She escaped?'

'Yes, but don't worry, we'll find her. We won't let her get near you.'

'What was she like?' Valerie asked.

Serena glanced across the seat. 'What do you mean?'

'I mean, what was going through her head? How could she do this? I just want to understand.'

'It doesn't really matter, Valerie.'

'I know, but I don't want to hate her.'

'She put you through hell,' Serena said. 'You can hate her if you want to.'

Valerie shook her head. 'That wouldn't accomplish anything.'

'All I know right now is that her own baby died,' Serena said. 'She couldn't deal with it. She became obsessed with Callie.'

Valerie was quiet. 'So she was desperate,' she said finally. 'I know what that's like.'

'Don't put yourself in her shoes,' Serena told her. 'She crossed lines you can't cross. It doesn't matter how many bad things happen to someone. You don't do what she did.'

'I know, but I've been at the end of my rope, too.'

'That's the past,' Serena said.

She watched Valerie's face and saw exhaustion and emotion catching up with her. The roller coaster of the night was taking its toll. 'Why don't you get some sleep?' she suggested. 'We won't get to Duluth for another hour.'

'I'm not sure I want to sleep,' Valerie admitted. 'I want to be sure this is really happening. I'm afraid I'll wake up and it'll be a dream, you know?'

'It's not. You're both safe.'

'I'll sleep when we get there,' she said, but she leaned against the window anyway, and her eyes blinked shut. When Serena looked over again, Valerie was sleeping peacefully.

Serena was tired herself, and the dark highway was hypnotic, but she had plenty of adrenaline to keep her awake. Part of it was the knowledge that, like Valerie, she was about to be free, even though it wasn't a freedom she had sought or expected. Part of it was the knowledge that Kasey Kennedy was out there somewhere, and she didn't know how far Kasey would go or what she would do next.

I know what it's like to be desperate.

She followed her high beams down the lonely road and thought about Kasey on this highway as the fog gathered in a cloud around her. A young cop who was blind and reckless, toppling a set of dominoes that would leave so many people in ruins. She would have been alone on the road then as Serena was alone now, alone with the deer, lakes, and trees of the northland.

Except as Serena drove, she realized she wasn't alone.

As the road flattened into a long straightaway between the swamplands of the Indian reservation, she glanced into her mirror, and there they were again, a mile behind her. She had first spotted them five miles outside Grand Rapids, coming and going behind the shelter of the curves.

Headlights.

Kasey leaned against the wall of the old house, almost too tired to stand. She knew she had to keep going, but she didn't know how. She was bleeding again under all the bandages. When she touched a finger to her neck, it came away sticky and red. Her head throbbed. She was dizzy. She could barely hold the gun in her hand.

All she wanted to do was lay down. Lay down and sleep. Lay down and die.

She waited in the frigid night for her last chance. The harbor water lapped at the shore behind her, and she could hear the louder rumbling of Lake Superior on the other side of the street. Behind the dune. Behind Stride's house.

When she looked up and down the Point, she didn't see cops waiting for her. There were no squad cars, no flashing lights, no one patrolling in the shadows. There was only Serena and Valerie, at home where she had followed them along the deserted highway. She could see them in the front bedroom that looked out on the street. Bright lights were on, shining through the clean glass of the window. Valerie held Callie in her arms.

Kasey's heart broke, seeing Callie. Her anger came back, the same anger that had propelled her for the past week. Fury that her child was dead. Fury at God's mistake. Desperation to hold a child again. Crying, breathing raggedly, she coughed and tasted something wet in her mouth and realized it was blood. She staggered and propped herself up with a hand on the wall. The gun slipped from her fingers and hit the pavement with a clatter. She bent down and picked it up.

She checked the street again. Empty.

In the bedroom, behind the window, Valerie hugged Serena as they separated for the night. Kasey saw Serena return to the great space behind the front door, and she ducked as Serena peered through the sheer curtains out to the street. Serena opened the door and stepped out on to the wooden porch, where she carefully studied the house and shadows around her. Kasey huddled behind a trash bin, hiding. When she peered past the bin, she saw Serena go back inside and heard the sharp click of the deadbolt. Inside the house, the lights of the living room went black.

A moment later, in the other room, she saw Valerie reach for the light too. The entire house was dark. Valerie and Callie were alone.

Kasey let fifteen minutes pass before she pushed herself off the wall and weaved across the narrow street. She eyed the parked cars as she passed quickly in and out of the glow of a street light. Flurries blew down in a cold rain and bit at her skin. The roar of the lake got louder, as if it were a large animal out of sight on the other side of the sand.

She avoided the front door. On the west side of the house, she spotted a twisting wrought-iron staircase that led to the upper floor. She limped toward it, not caring about the tracks she left in the snow. When she tried to climb, she found the metal steps slippery with ice. She put a hand on the railing and dragged herself up step by step. The effort exhausted her, and the openness of the iron frame made her light-headed when she looked down. By the time she reached the top, she had to stop to let her vertigo subside.

She looked down at her feet. Drops of blood dotted the snow like cherries.

Kasey tugged the sleeve of her coat over her hand and punched the small chambered window near the doorknob. The window shattered with a low, musical crash. Glass sprayed on to the floor. She bent down to the broken window and listened for noise from the floor below. When she heard nothing, she reached through the hole for the doorknob, undid the lock, and let herself inside the house.

The attic level was dark and cold. Nails hung down like teeth from the wooden beams in the ceiling. The unfinished floor was littered with boxes and equipment. Through the shadows, she spied a staircase leading to the ground floor, and she stepped carefully over broken glass to reach it. The stairs were pitch black, and she felt for a handrail and didn't find one. She held her breath and put her foot blindly on the first step. Then the next. She swayed and thought she would fall. Her eyes adjusted and she could see the outline of a dozen steps below her, but she froze with every footfall as the wood squealed in protest. She didn't know if the noise would carry through the closed door below her. To her, it sounded loud.

Kasey reached the bottom step and waited. She felt warm air on the other side of the door. Silently, she turned the handle and pulled the door open. She could make out the shapes of leather furniture in the great space. Another handful of wooden steps led to the carpet. She heard wind sucking air up the chimney with a rush. The front door and the wall of windows leading to the porch were on her right. So was the bedroom where Valerie and Callie were sleeping.

She made wet tracks to the door. She undid the lock and opened it, giving herself an easy escape to the street, and she thought about going through that door and walking away. Go back to the car. Drive. Start a new life. But it was too late for that. She had already lost Jack. And Bruce. She wouldn't lose Callie, too.

Kasey stared at the closed door of the bedroom. No light shot under the crack between the door and the carpet. She listened for breathing inside and heard nothing at all. The gun was heavy in her hand. She wondered if she would have to kill again and hoped it didn't come to that. She was tired of death. Tired of killing. Nothing had gone as she'd planned and dreamed.

She reached for the knob and opened the door silently, pushing it inward. On the wall to her right, in the gloom, she saw a twin bed and the humped outline of a body. She took two tentative steps until she was fully inside the room. She lifted the gun and crept toward the bed.

With blinding brightness, the overhead lights burst on and turned night to day.

Kasey squinted involuntarily and thrust her arm in front of her eyes. When she lowered her hand, she realized that the bed was empty. The outline of a body was just pillows lumped under a blanket. When she looked at the opposite wall, she saw someone sitting in an easy chair by the window, staring at her, a gun in her hand, pointed at Kasey's chest.

It was Maggie.

'Put the gun down right now, Kasey,' she said.

Kasey backed away toward the bedroom door, but as she did, she felt another gun, this one in the back of her skull.

'She said put it down,' Stride said. 'It's over.'

Kasey heard the thunder of boots everywhere around the house. On the porch. In the yard. In the great space. There were police at all of the windows. Faces. Guns. She stood, paralyzed and trapped, and felt Stride reach round and peel the gun away from her fingers.

'Serena saw you coming, Kasey,' Maggie told her, getting up from the chair. Her voice was hard and sad. 'She called ahead to arrange a welcoming party.'

'Oh, my God,' Kasey murmured. 'Oh, God, no.'

Stride yanked her hands behind her, and she felt him clamp cuffs tightly round her wrists. He pulled her on her heels out of the bedroom. She let him drag her, and then she couldn't feel her legs anymore or support her weight. She toppled backward into Stride's chest. Her body collapsed in on itself. She felt him holding her under her shoulders and easing her on to the floor, and when she stared at the ceiling, she saw all of their faces going in and out of focus as they looked down at her. Stride. Maggie. Police in uniform.

Somewhere in her head, she heard Stride say, 'She's lost a lot of blood. Get an ambulance down here.'

She tried to get up, and hands gently pushed her down. The room spun and floated lazily away from her, carrying her down a river. She watched bodies come and go in a blur of motion, and among all the people crowding around her, she saw a new face. Valerie Glenn. Serena was behind her in the brightly lit living room, holding Callie. Kasey saw Valerie staring at her the way a mourner stares at a grave, and she wanted to say something, wanted to explain, wanted to scream, but she was lost in the fog.

Valerie said aloud, 'Does anyone know what her child's name was?'

Jack, Kasey wanted to say. It was Jack. He was my baby, and God took him away from me. Don't you understand? Doesn't anyone hear me?

'Jack,' Maggie answered for her. 'It was Jack.'

Valerie nodded. Kasey saw her squat down beside her. Her face was inches away, and her skin emanated the fresh smell of a mother holding a child. She put a hand on Kasey's cheek and caressed it, feeling the dampness of her blood and sweat. Valerie was crying. Kasey realized she was crying too.

'I'm sorry for what happened to Jack,' Valerie murmured in her ear.

Kasey tried to speak again but heard only the wheeze of her own breath. The metal of the cuffs gnawed at the small of her back. She closed her eyes, but she could still feel the touch of Valerie's hand, and she felt it there, soft and warm, until the sirens drew near.

Fifty-eight

First day. Last day.

Stride sat in a folding chair in the long grass behind his cottage on the Point, watching the angry lake waters in the early morning. Red clouds on the horizon marked the glow of dawn, but it was still more night than day. His leather jacket was zipped to his neck, providing meager protection against the cold and wind. His hands were in his pockets.

He waited for Serena. He didn't want to be inside as she packed the last of her things and loaded them in her Mustang. It was one thing to know she was leaving, another thing to watch her go. Sooner or later, he would have to go back home, after she was gone, and face the emptiness she had left behind. That could wait until later. He would be working until midnight, catching up on everything that had gathered in his absence, postponing the moment when he returned to a house where the only thing that lingered was her scent.

He didn't look when he heard her footsteps in the snow behind him. She sat down in the chair next to him and didn't say anything. The two of them spent a minute of silence, putting off the inevitable.

'You're ready?' Stride asked finally, when he couldn't stand the tension anymore.

Serena nodded without looking at him. 'Yeah.'

'You don't have to go,' he told her. 'You can stay in a separate bedroom for a few weeks if you like.'

'We've talked about this, Jonny.'

'I know.'

That was the reality staring him in the face. It was done between them. Over. At least for now. At least for a while. 'You know I love you,' he told her.

'I love you too, but you need time, and I need time. I don't know whether it was just the heat of the moment, but you're more comfortable with Maggie than you are with me. You opened up to her, and you shut me out. That doesn't work for me.'

'I'm sorry.'

'So am I. I'm not blaming you, Jonny. It's my problem, too.'

'What's next?' Stride asked.

Serena shook her head. 'I don't know yet.'

'Are you going back to Las Vegas?'

'No,' she told him. 'Not now, anyway. I could go back there and get a job, but it's not really home anymore. I'm not sure where home is to me. I'm not like you. I don't have roots.'

'So what will you do?'

Serena shrugged her shoulders, as if the future were a small thing compared to the present. 'Denise asked me to stay on with the Sheriff's office in Grand Rapids. I may do that for a while. Valerie's getting settled on her own with Callie, and I'd like to help her. She's renting a house and said I could use one of the spare bedrooms.'

'I like the idea of you staying close by,' Stride said.

It was an olive branch, but she left it where it was. He watched the sadness in her face and wished he could wipe it away. He knew there had always been something missing in Serena, some part of her unfulfilled. Maybe she just needed to be on her own. The prospect didn't seem to scare her as much as it scared him.

'I have to go,' she told him, standing up. She cast her eyes out toward the lake and then at the cold sand of the beach. Three years ago, on a hot summer night, they had made love out there for the first time.

'If you need anything at all, call me,' Stride said. 'Any time, day or night. You know that, right?'

'You're always trying to protect the women in your life, Jonny,' she murmured. 'We don't all need protection.'

'I'm just saying.'

'I know. If I do need someone, you're my first call.'

'I may show up on your doorstep someday,' he said.

She gave him a weak smile. 'You never know, I may show up on yours first.'

Serena put a hand on his shoulder as she turned away to walk over the snowy slope toward the cottage. He didn't watch her go. The lake was loud, and he couldn't hear the sound of her car engine on the street as she drove off. He waited on the beach, not moving, getting colder and feeling numbness on his face. Time passed, and by the time he got up, the sun had climbed over the edge of the water.

The Detective Bureau in City Hall was mostly empty. No one was there to greet him. He had been gone, and now he was back. He went inside his office the way he had done thousands of times over the years and hung up his coat. The room still held a trace of Maggie's perfume about it. Otherwise, nothing had changed. Time had stood still while he was away.

Stride didn't sit down immediately. He ran his fingers over the framed photos on his credenza and picked up the one of himself and Serena, taken atop the Stratosphere tower in Las Vegas. He remembered thinking back then that he had borrowed time with her and that one day someone would ask for it back. Suddenly, unexpectedly, that time was now. He put the picture back down where it had always been, so he could still see her face.

Leaning against the window frame, he looked out at the traffic on First Street and at the lake beyond the city buildings. Duluth was a city of struggle, of faded glory, of the new always colored by the old. It was small enough that you could wrap your arms around it and big enough that you could never quite hold it in your grasp. It was bitter cold, primitive, and intimidating, like an outpost on the border of the frontier.

He realized he had an advantage that Serena didn't. He knew where his home was. Home was here. Home was Duluth.

Stride sat down in his chair. He hadn't replaced it in years. It molded to his body the way old jeans did, moving when he moved. The three months he had spent away from this place felt like the longest, ugliest detour of his life. It had been a mistake to take refuge in a cabin in the woods; he should have followed his instincts and come back early. This was where he belonged.

'Welcome back, boss.'

He looked up and saw Maggie in his doorway. Her neck was bandaged, and she grimaced in pain as she came into his office, but she slid sideways into the chair in front of his desk the way she always did. It had been the same for more than a decade.

Boss, she said.

Was that how it was going to be? Partners, not lovers? He wondered if they could really stay that way. Or if either of them wanted it that way.

He pointed at the bandage. 'Shouldn't you be flat on your back right now?'

'Is that the way you want me?' she asked with a wink. She was serious but not serious. Joking but not joking. Things were already complicated.

'You're such a pain in the ass,' he said.

'Actually, that's the one place where I don't have any pain.'

He shook his head and looked away. Maggie read the soberness in his face and followed his eyes, which had wandered to the photograph of Serena.

'So?' she asked.

'She's gone.'

Maggie swore softly. 'I'm really, really sorry.'

'It's not your fault.'

'Yeah? Then why do I feel like it is?'

'Don't go there, Mags. It won't change anything.' After a moment, he added, 'Maybe things happen the way they do for a reason.'

'Or maybe things just suck on a completely random basis,' she replied. 'Did you think about that?'

'I'm trying not to think about it at all right now.'

She nodded. 'Understood.'

He dragged his eyes away from the photograph and changed the subject. 'Did you see the news? Kasey's lawyer is going to use an insanity defense. He claims the death of her child and the manipulation by Regan Conrad left her incapable of distinguishing right from wrong.'

'A jury just might buy it,' Maggie said.

'Do you think she was insane?'

'Don't you think so?'

'I think she kidnapped a baby and killed three people,' he said.

'Yeah, but she was also a mother who had to watch her child die.' Maggie added pointedly, 'We all have our breaking points.'

He didn't reply, but he thought to himself, *yes, we do.*

'What about Nieman?' he asked. 'What have you found out about him?'

'Nieman's a ghost,' she said. 'We're going to be unraveling his secrets for months. So far, we've linked him to murders in Colorado, Iowa, and New Mexico, but we still don't know exactly who he is or where he came from. The FBI is helping us put the pieces together.'

'Kasey's lawyer will claim that killing him was a public service,' he said.

'It was.' Maggie stared at Stride with her hair falling across her face. 'What now? Do you and I plead temporary insanity too?'

'Minus the temporary part,' he said.

'So do you want to get to work right away or do you want to do it on the desk first?' she asked.

Stride couldn't do anything but laugh. 'You're going to make sure this isn't easy for me, aren't you?'

'Damn right.'

'Are you done?'

'For now.'

'Then let's get to work,' he said.

Maggie pointed at a file folder on his desk. 'Remember that teenage boy who washed up from the lake last year? We called it suicide, and the parents said it was murder. We got some new evidence, and it looks like they might be right.'

'OK, I'll catch up with the file,' he said. 'We can go talk to them this morning.'

'You got it.' Maggie climbed out of the chair and headed for the door. He realized that nothing had changed, and nothing was the same.

'Hey,' he called after her.

She turned and looked back at him.

'I like your hair,' he told her.

Maggie grinned, pushed the blood-red bangs out of her eyes, and left.

Stride stared at the dusty oak surface and everything that crowded his desk. The silver letter opener, shaped like a knife. The stacks of yellow pads scribbled with notes. The clock ticking away the seconds, minutes, hours, and days. The crime files. His whole life.

He grabbed the case folder and pulled it toward him. As he did, his hand bumped against the silver letter opener and sent it tumbling to the floor. His eyes followed it. He tensed, waiting for the flashback to wash over him. His heart rate accelerated. He felt sweat on the back of his neck as he wondered how bad this one would be and how long he would be gone. But the attack never came. He didn't fall through the black night air toward the unforgiving water. The bridge was somewhere else, out on the lake, and he was still in his office.

Stride reached down and retrieved the letter opener and put it in his drawer. Then he put his feet on his desk and began to read.

Acknowledgments

Many people were helpful to me in writing this book. My thanks go first to Gail Foster, who has been my advance reader for several years and gave me her typically helpful and insightful comments on the early drafts of the manuscript.

In Duluth, Kim Homick helped me locate the ruined school that plays such an important role in the novel. Yes, there really is such a place, although I have 'sealed it off' for dramatic purposes. I've also changed the name and location so that the ruins aren't overrun with visitors. It really is a dangerous place. Don't go there. Also in Duluth, Pat and Bill Burns have been our hosts for several years at the Cottage on the Point (www.cottageonthepoint.com), where Stride lives in the books. We are very much indebted to them for their hospitality and friendship. In Grand Rapids, Randy McCarty helped me identify key locations for scenes in the book and was kind enough to take me and Marcia for a tour of Pokegama Lake.

One of my long-time readers, Migdalia (Micki) Colon, was kind enough to share her knowledge of Spanish for translating several lines. She also allowed me to borrow her lovely name for one of the characters.

Matt Davis and Paula Tjornhom Davis offered their advice on the manuscript, as did my wife of twenty-five years, Marcia.

I'm always grateful for their objective and critical counsel (even if I occasionally grit my teeth at it).

Very special thanks also go to my agents, Ali Gunn, Deborah Schneider, and Diana Mackay, and my editors, Marion Donaldson and Jennifer Weis, as well as to the international editors, agents, and booksellers who are so wonderful in helping bring my books to readers in countries around the world.

Finally, I have to add my personal thanks to the people who add such joy to my life: my parents; my brother and his family; dear friends such as Barb and Jerry, Matt and Paula, and Keith and Katie; and my wife Marcia, who has been my partner, best friend, and biggest supporter for most of my life.

How to Contact Me.

You can send me email at brian@bfreemanbooks.com or join the mailing list at www.bfreemanbooks.com. Or you can find me on Facebook by clicking the Facebook link on my website. I write back to every reader and would love to hear from you.

Now you can buy any of these other bestselling
Headline books from your bookshop
or *direct from the publisher.*

FREE P&P AND UK DELIVERY
(Overseas and Ireland £3.50 per book)

Immoral	Brian Freeman	£6.99
Stripped	Brian Freeman	£6.99
Stalked	Brian Freeman	£6.99
The Watcher	Brian Freeman	£6.99
Smoked	Patrick Quinlan	£6.99
The Takedown	Patrick Quinlan	£6.99
The Hit	Patrick Quinlan	£7.99
Bones	Jonathan Kellerman	£6.99
Evidence	Jonathan Kellerman	£6.99
Count to Ten	Karen Rose	£6.99
Nothing to Fear	Karen Rose	£6.99
Don't Tell	Karen Rose	£6.99
Don't Look Back	Scott Frost	£6.99
Point of No Return	Scott Frost	£6.99

TO ORDER SIMPLY CALL THIS NUMBER

01235 400 414

or visit our website: www.headline.co.uk

Prices and availability subject to change without notice.